TIME GOD
WARLOCK

SHAMI STOVALL

Published by
CS BOOKS, LLC

This is a work of fiction. Names, characters, places, and incidents either are the product of author imagination or are used fictitiously, and any resemblance to actual persons, living or dead, business establishments, events, or locales, is entirely fictional.

Time God Warlock
Copyright © 2025 Capital Station Books
All rights reserved.
https://sastovallauthor.com/

Cover Design: Chris McGrath
Editors: Nia Quinn, Celestian Rince

IF YOU WANT TO BE NOTIFIED WHEN SHAMI STOVALL'S NEXT BOOK RELEASES, PLEASE VISIT HER WEBSITE OR CONTACT HER DIRECTLY AT
s.adelle.s@gmail.com

To John IV, my son.

CONTENTS

BOOK 3 RECAP

Adair Finch—warlock, time manipulator, and professional magnet for trouble—had a plan. After years off the grid, he was back in business, running *24-Hour Investigations* out of a sleek new office in Stockton, California. Sure, he didn't have any clients. Or much cash flow. Or sanity. But he had a desk, a team, and the illusion of progress. And that was a good start.

His team consisted of: Enzo, a werewolf ex-cop, who was trying to stay on the straight and narrow despite his occasional tendency to turn into an eight-foot-tall murder machine. Liam Blackstone, a timid craftsman warlock, who would serve Finch as researcher and worrywart. And lastly there was Liam's twelve-year-old daughter, Bree—Finch's self-appointed apprentice, warlock-in-training, and full-time source of chaos.

But one morning, two things of interest happened.

First, brownies showed up. Not the chocolate kind—the fae kind. Tiny, squeaky, German-speaking goblins. Liam had hired them to clean messes and gather rare materials.

Secondly, Finch got a call from a name he hadn't heard in

ten years: *Jessica Finch*, his late brother's widow. She wanted to meet in person. Said she needed his help. Finch didn't hesitate. Not this time.

When Jessie arrived, she wasn't the same shy, rule-following half-elf he remembered. She was leather and gasoline and covered in scars. Whatever innocence she'd once had was long gone. She told Finch she was being hunted by *Alonso del Maldonado XIV*, a sadistic Mexican wizard infamous for binding demons and liquefying magical creatures. Jessie had once made a deal with him for information about the coven of witches who had killed Finch's brother, Carter. Now, that deal had come due.

Before Finch could pry for details, the office exploded into violence. A shadow imp—a literal demon made of darkness—burst into the room and wrapped its claws around Liam's chest. Enzo transformed, Bree screamed, and Jessie revealed she wasn't as helpless as she looked. With a single word, she summoned hellfire chains that ripped the imp into a black pit of nothingness.

That was when Finch realized the truth: Jessie wasn't just running from Maldonado. She had bound herself to one of his demons and fused it into her very soul. The only way for Maldonado to reclaim his lost pet was to kill her.

Finch didn't like that option.

After Carter's death, Jessie had been consumed by grief. She wanted revenge against the full moon witches who had destroyed her family. Maldonado offered her the one thing she craved: their names, locations, and magical patterns. All she had to do in return was kill a few SHADOW agents—government operatives who policed supernatural crimes. Jessie had refused, but by the time she changed her mind, it was too late. She had already taken one of Maldonado's demons.

Jessie needed Finch's help to take down the powerful

Maldonado, but a normal person would've balked. It was basically a suicide mission.

Finch, being Finch, didn't see that as a reason to turn her away. He saw it as a challenge.

He started by investigating Maldonado's network in Stockton. With Enzo's nose, Bree's enthusiasm, and far too many near-death experiences, Finch tracked down all Maldonado's weaknesses.

At the same time, Bree's coming-of-age magic was becoming a ticking time bomb. She had one year from her first period (or, as she called it, "shark week") to complete her ritual and become a full-fledged witch—or lose that chance forever. Liam begged Finch to convince her to take the safer witch route, but Bree was determined to be a warlock like her mentor.

Things got worse when Finch discovered Maldonado wasn't the only one after Jessie. The SHADOW organization wanted her arrested for the attempted murder of an agent. They sent a half-angel by the name of Steele to bring her in, which meant Finch had to deal with him, too.

And since so many guns were involved, Finch needed to make a new pact. He found Heslop, the King of the Simonside Dwarves, in the fae realm and promised to bring the man a gun in exchange for his metal-altering powers. The king agreed, and his magic was bound to Finch's eyes core.

Along the way, Finch rescued a goblin from a cage, returned an endangered elf to the fae realm, busted a meth lab (macing addicts and serving them papers in the process), and saved a half-buried cat named Methusepaws from a litter-box nightmare.

Then, after defeating Agent Steele, and then gathering all Maldonado's weaknesses, Finch engaged in a *spellrift*—a type of duel where the participants gambled their souls. If Maldonado won, he would take Finch's, and if Finch won…

Well, this is a recap, so spoilers don't matter.

Finch won, and he gained Maldonado's soul (and all his soul-binding contracts) in one fell swoop. Jessie was no longer in danger, nor was she wanted by SHADOW.

And before the day was over, Finch helped Bree find her own path in life. She decided to become a full moon witch, and for one of her cores, she turned it into a *warlock core*, so she could continue to study under Finch and be his apprentice.

It was a touching moment, but it didn't last long.

Chronos came calling.

The mighty Titan of Time spoke to Finch and presented him with an egg. His pact with Chronos involved protecting the egg until it hatched, especially from the likes of rival time gods, like Aeon, the Father of the Zodiac.

Finch took the egg and returned to his apartment to find Kull.

As a social media influencer, she was rarely around, but when she did arrive, it was always with a bombshell, and this time was no different. Kull had gone on tons of terrible dates, and now she wanted Finch's help experiencing something special. She wanted to go on a date with him.

Kull had also brought a pair of magical guns as a gift. Starfall and Agony. So, Finch didn't really have a choice. He had to go on a date.

Now on to "Time God Warlock," the fourth book in the series…

CHAPTER
ONE

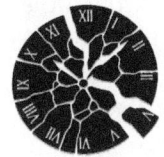

I t had been over ten years since Adair Finch had been on a date.

The last one had been memorable for all the wrong reasons. He had taken a girl, Hannah, to a nightclub. Nice place. It had throbbing bass, overpriced drinks. And also sweaty, sexy people rubbing themselves all over everyone. Finch hadn't expected a hag to ruin the entire evening, but in hindsight, he really should have. The hag had been following him for days, hell-bent on murdering him. As hags tended to do.

Unfortunately, hags also tended to carry noxious, fast-acting magical diseases. One whiff of her death-stench and the whole nightclub had turned into a vomitorium. People had collapsed, clutching their stomachs. Finch had never seen so much puke in his life.

Hannah, to no one's surprise, never returned any of his phone calls.

The date before that? Finch hadn't even realized it was a date until halfway through. A man named Joseph had stopped him at a used bookstore and asked, somewhat accusingly, why Finch was buying five books on the occult and one on goat anatomy. One thing led to another, and an hour later they were drinking overpriced espresso at a local coffeehouse during open-mic poetry night.

Finch had been enjoying himself... right up until a red-eyed werewolf crashed through the front window and tried to host a lycanthropy giveaway. Everyone in the café could have a free bite.

Joseph, convinced beyond reason that Finch was to blame, had become a nightmare. Apparently, Joseph moonlighted as a bounty hunter for a local witch coven, and after the werewolf incident, he had decided Finch was overdue for execution.

Which, frankly, was just Finch's luck. Somehow, a pleasant evening had spiraled into a bounty on his head and a bizarrely personal vendetta from a man who thought they had been something more than just random acquaintances.

Those ancient memories felt like they belonged to another person entirely, though. He had been so cocky and confident—Finch had assumed *everyone* wanted to be with him.

He didn't feel like that anymore.

So when Finch parked his car in front of the Hilton and sent Kull a text that he had arrived, his stomach knotted. This wasn't really how he wanted to spend his Friday evening.

But this wasn't a *real* date. No. Finch never would've agreed to that. Instead, this was a *practice* date, one to show Kull what it was like to go out with a normal and stable individual. Apparently, all Kull's efforts to find love had been disasters in their own right, and she was starting to feel disheartened.

Since Kull had originally been Kullthantarrick the Sneak, a mischief spirit, and had only recently inhabited the body of a human woman, she wasn't well versed on how people handled their personal affairs.

To make matters worse, she had taken the body of a social media star named *Fox-Pistol*, recognizable by most of her fans. That made most outings awkward at best and painful at worst. She was also drop-dead gorgeous, so even if people weren't fans already, they quickly became one while staring for uncomfortable amounts of time.

That kind of beauty always attracted the craziest types of people.

"This is going to be a long night," Finch said with a sigh.

"Adair! There you are!"

Kull's voice cut through the quiet evening as she stepped up to the side of Finch's Toyota.

Her outfit was clearly chosen to obliterate common decency. She wore a shimmering black halter dress that twinkled in the moonlight. It was tight enough to count her ribs, but loose enough around the waist to swirl when she walked, and had a slit so high up the side it probably violated at least three of the Ten Commandments.

Kull's heels were red and pointed enough to be weaponized. Around her neck hung a delicate chain bearing a pendant in the shape of a fox. Her lips were crimson to match her stilettos, her blue-gray eyes were sparkling, and her vibrant red hair was pinned up with silver chopsticks, exposing her long and slender neck.

When Kull leaned down to peer through the passenger-side window, Finch almost rolled it up out of sheer instinct. Women this beautiful were always trouble.

"Do I look good enough for our date?" she asked, smiling wide as she did a little twirl.

Normally, Finch would have a quip for this, but he found himself at a loss for words. She was *way* overdressed for any restaurant in Stockton, California. It was one of the most dangerous cities in the state—and tenth most dangerous in the nation—and *definitely* didn't have any locations worthy of red-carpet-level dresses.

"Well?" Kull stopped twirling, her brow furrowed.

"You look like a million dollars." Finch motioned to the passenger seat with a tilt of his head. "Now get in before you attract a mugger."

Kull's jovial demeanor returned. She giggled as she walked around the car and then slid into the passenger seat. The scent of lavender and mischief filled the vehicle.

Finch exhaled through his nose and turned the key in the ignition. "This is still a practice date."

"Yes, of course," Kull said matter-of-factly. "This is purely for educational purposes." She gave him the once-over. "So... when I date someone, they should just basically wear what they already wear? Men don't have to dress up?"

Finch glanced down at himself. He wore a white button-up shirt, tucked into the fanciest pair of jeans he owned. He also had a black belt and black dress shoes, but that was about it.

He was at least three tiers underdressed compared to Kull.

"This *was* me dressing up," Finch sardonically replied.

"Oh."

"If I had known you were going to dress as fancy as you did, I would've rented a tux."

Kull bit her lip and frowned. "So... you're disappointed? I already messed this up? I *shouldn't* dress like this?"

"N-No, that's not what I'm saying." Finch leaned back until he was staring at the roof of his car. "I'm saying that, on dates, people should be on the same page about... their clothing. And where they're going. And how fancy it should be. If anyone messed up, it was me."

Kull let out a long sigh, but her smile returned halfway

through. "Humans are *sooo* complicated." She playfully smacked his arm. "And you definitely didn't mess up. You never mess up anything!"

Finch gave serious thought to rewinding time to correct his choice of outfit. He had marked the time an hour before leaving his apartment, just for mistakes like this.

As if she could read his mind, Kull held up a hand. "Hey, don't go rewinding time or anything, okay? The date has to feel natural and fun. I don't want you acting all... stiff and perfectionist on me, okay?"

"I'm not a stiff perfectionist," Finch said as he gripped the steering wheel with both hands.

"You are after you've rewound time like thirty-seven times and you're tired of having the same conversation over and over again." Kull poked him in his bicep. "I've seen you. I know the expressions you make. So don't repeat this date, okay? I'll know if you do!"

"Fine."

Kull buckled herself in and half squealed in delight. "Really? You won't?"

"No," Finch said with a groan. "I won't."

"Oh, this is going to be so fun! I can't wait to see where we're going."

Finch pulled away from the hotel, desperately trying to think of someplace fancy to bring Kull. He had originally intended to just take her to the local Olive Garden. That was the most *standard* and *ordinary* place he thought of when trying to imagine the most average of dates.

But he couldn't take Kull to an Olive Garden, not when she was dressed like the girlfriend of a successful rockstar.

Where else could he go? It had been ten years since Finch did anything like this, and for some reason, a weird sort of teenage anxiety filled him. Were those butterflies in his stomach?

No. Definitely not.

He would just take Kull someplace nice, eat some food, answer her questions about dating, and then take her back to her hotel. Nothing was happening. This wasn't a real date.

It was a practice date. There was nothing to be nervous about.

And absolutely nothing crazy was going to interrupt them this time, because that was preposterous. Finch was long done with hags and random werewolves.

CHAPTER
TWO

Finch parked his Toyota in the parking lot of the fanciest Chinese restaurant in all of Stockton. Dave Wong's.

There it stood, the bright backlit letters DAVE WONG'S buzzing, casting a heavenly glow across the windshield. The building itself looked like a Cantonese casino. Lights everywhere, Chinese words hung on the outside walls, and a large entranceway for guests to wait.

It was absolute chaos. Family after family waited in line, some inside, and some out. They each spoke over each other, creating a din of innocuous conversation.

Finch stepped out of his vehicle, walked around to the other side, and then opened Kull's door. She leapt out, smiling like a lunatic.

"I've never been here before," Kull said with an energetic laugh. "It looks so popular!"

"It's a shining glass bottle in a landfill full of rusted cans." Finch closed the door. "Let's hope we can get a table."

As they walked to the front door, Kull slipped both her arms around one of Finch's, holding him close. He fought off the urge to rip out of her grip and then sighed. He supposed, on a good and normal date, this would be acceptable behavior.

Once inside, Finch took a deep breath. The air was a perfect storm of Szechuan pepper, duck fat, and perfume. Waiters wove through the chaos, carrying trays piled high with sizzling beef and pots of green tea, all while dodging handbags and small children with the grace of seasoned stuntmen.

Finch exhaled as he made his way to the hostess. She frantically wrote and scribbled out names on a long piece of paper, so distracted that she didn't even realize Finch had arrived until after he cleared his throat.

"Oh, welcome to Dave Wong's," she said, never glancing up. "How many?"

"Two."

"It'll be an hour wait. Name?"

Finch pulled out his wallet and then slowly slid three hundred dollars over the waiting list. The hostess, finally glancing up, gave him a thousand-yard stare only restaurant workers and war veterans could achieve. Then she took the money.

"Let me seat you right now." The woman grabbed two menus and gestured for them to follow.

She eventually pointed them toward a booth sandwiched between a family of eight and what appeared to be an influencer couple livestreaming their dumpling experience.

"Here you are."

It was a C-shaped booth, and Finch waited for Kull to scoot in first before he sat down. The hostess smiled as she left. It almost seemed genuine.

Tucked away in the booth, the chaos of the restaurant seemed distant. Finch was pleased with the acoustics, though he wasn't entirely sure what to talk about. Struggling to come up with a topic of conversation, he grabbed the menu and half-heartedly glanced through the options.

Kull didn't even reach for her menu. She nervously chuckled and scooted closer to Finch. "So, this is the part of dates I hate the most. *What do I talk about*? You know? Uh, what do you think is best, Adair?"

He set his menu down. When he turned to her, he steeled himself to discussing romance, but he was determined to do it in a clinical fashion. "The first thing you should do is compliment them about something you genuinely find appealing. Maybe even the first thing that really drew you to them."

Kull's eyes widened. "Oh! That's a great idea." She poked Finch in the shoulder as she continued, "When you summoned me, you had this aura about you. It was, like, harsh, but kind. And the way you looked after Bree... I could tell you were gentler than you wanted to let the world see. It made me think you were a trustworthy human. Honest. *Good*. Beautiful in a way you can't see with your eyes."

Finch's face heated. He hadn't known Kull felt that way. "Well, thank you... but that's not quite... what I meant."

"It's not?"

"Since you probably don't know much about your date, I meant you should compliment them on something physical you appreciate. That lets them know you're attracted to them."

With an ever-widening smile, Kull nodded. "Oh! I get it now. Okay, well, I love the bulge in your pants, Adair. You must be hung like a horse."

Finch grabbed the nearest napkin and pressed it against his crimson face.

Maybe he could suffocate himself with it? At least then he could exit this conversation in an ambulance. Unfortunately, the napkin was too thin. Instead, he used it to shield his face so everyone in the restaurant wouldn't see his tomato-red embarrassment.

"Are you okay?" Kull whispered as she leaned in closer. "Because I've watched a *ton* of romantic comedies. I know men are, like, worried about their length, and people calling them small, so I figured I'd give you a compliment that also boosted your self-esteem!"

"How… thoughtful," Finch said directly into the napkin.

"Right? It's the perfect compliment."

"I meant you should compliment someone on their face, or hair, or clothing. Something not so… forward." He lowered the cloth, his face still scarlet. "Subtlety goes a long way. You want them to know you're interested, but not *that* interested, or else they'll start thinking about you like a hamburger."

This was an inside joke the two of them shared. Whenever someone lusted after Kull, they referred to it as "treating her like a hamburger"—something to consume and then forget. It was also a general term for any sort of sex-first mentality, and Finch hoped he could steer Kull away from turning all her dates into *hamburger events*.

Finch's phone buzzed in his pocket. He ignored it.

Then the waiter came by. Finch ordered the Mongolian beef and fried prawns. Kull ordered the egg drop soup. Then the waiter was off, rushing to another table that looked like they were having a chopstick emergency.

Finch's phone buzzed a second time. Probably voicemail.

"You know, speaking of auras, and weird feelings…" Kull lifted an eyebrow. "You seem different, Adair. Magically. Have you made any new pacts lately?"

He shook his head. "No. I only have the three. Chronos, the Titan of Time; Ke-Koh, the Ifrit of Rebellion; and Heslop, King of the Simonside Dwarves."

He had two cores left. He *could* make two more pacts, and

develop more magics, but he currently didn't have the need. Additionally, Chronos was bound to the crown core, Ke-Koh to his heart, and Heslop to his eyes. That meant only his spirit and loins were left, and both were complicated cores that required a little more focus than Finch was willing to give at the moment.

Kull sniffed deep, practically huffing Finch's shoulder. "You seem… *extra* Chronos this evening…"

Finch nervously chuckled. "You're imagining things."

"Hmm. Nope. I know you too well." Kull sat straight and playfully waggled her finger. "You're hiding something from me. That's okay, I'll forgive you since we're on a date."

"*Practice* date."

His phone buzzed a third time. He wasn't sure who it was, but they were persistent. And annoying.

"The last date I went on, the guy wanted to make a viral YouTube video." Kull's shoulders slumped, and she frowned. "He wanted to do *spank wars*. It made me feel really icky."

"I'm going to regret this," Finch said with a groan, "but what is *spank wars?*"

"He said it's when we should take turns spanking each other until one person gives up because it is too painful." Kull huffed out a sigh. "When I said no, he just kept pressuring me to do it. What would you do in that situation? Maybe say no in a different way?"

"I'd break his fucking nose and throw him out of the place," Finch stated matter-of-factly.

"Huh. I hadn't thought of that. Maybe I'll try it next time."

"*Next time?* How do you keep finding yourself on terrible dates in the first place?"

Kull shrugged. "I don't know. I live in LA, and I go to lots of parties, looking for people, but I just keep finding the same types? If that makes sense. I really want to find love, but it seems, uh, everyone else *doesn't.*"

"It can happen sometimes. Maybe you should find a good dating site where people state they're looking for a long-term relationship."

"Well, I really keep hoping I'll just meet someone like you, Adair."

The statement caused him to tense a bit. Surely, she hadn't meant that. He was a wreck. There were plenty of other good men out there—she just needed to meet them.

For a fourth time, Finch's phone buzzed. He wanted to be polite. He didn't want to look at it. But the temptation was becoming almost unbearable.

"Which reminds me." Kull brightened again as she tilted her head to the side. "Can we practice kissing? I gave a man a kiss and he said, *That's it*? All grumpy, too. I think I messed it up."

"No. I'm not doing that."

"But I think I need a little bit of instruction. Just a little."

"*No*," Finch drawled.

Kull held up her fingers, nearly pinching them together. "Just a tiny practice session."

The waiter returned with plates full of food, as well as two glasses of water. His presence didn't deter Kull from her mission, though.

"I really want to practice kissing with you," she said, scooting closer. Her hip was pressed against his.

This was the strangest conversation since Finch *last* spoke with Kull. She always managed to one-up herself. "This is a bad idea."

"I read a romance book where a woman ran a kissing booth, and she became really good at making out because of all the practice, and I really want that! C'mon, Adair. Help me master kissing with my tongue."

The waiter, transfixed, almost dropped a plate onto the floor. His face grew redder than Adair's. He caught himself at the last second and managed to drop off everything before leaving without uttering a single word.

Finch dragged his hand down his face. "Kull. Please."

"You're not going to break my nose and throw me out of here because I was pressuring you, right? I hope not." Kull grabbed her soup and pulled it close. "Because I also wanted to try kissing people to see if there was a spark or something. A *lot* of romance novels have this sort of description about how someone made them tingle. Will we feel that? We don't know until we try!"

Finch pulled his Mongolian beef over, a small portion of his thoughts focused on Kull's physical contact. He hadn't really felt like this in some time. Years, really.

He took a bite of his beef and savored the flavor. Then he glanced over at Kull and held up a piece on the end of his fork. "Would you like a taste?"

She smiled wider than before. "*Really?*"

"It's... romantic... to share food on a date."

"Oh, heck yeah. I love food so much!" Kull leaned over and gingerly took the beef right off the fork without even touching the utensil. She chewed it, looking thoughtful, and then swallowed. "It was tasty—ten out of ten—but I don't feel *romance.*"

"Hmm."

Finch tapped his fingers along his fork. Compliments about physical appearance and feeding each other food were some of the only things Finch could think of. When he glanced back over at Kull, she was pulling her soup closer, obviously forcing a smile. When she noticed him staring, her smile became more genuine, but just barely.

Kull was clearly waiting for him to do something.

"Uh, I like your *hair*," Finch said.

He had never felt more inadequate at a task in his life.

Kull touched the bun on her head, her red hair lush and

shiny. "I miss the ability to change my shape, but this hair is nice." Then she rolled her eyes. "But I have to clean and style it *so much* that I almost wish it would fall off."

"Right…"

"You know what I just thought?" Kull giggled and then shrugged. "We're a reverse vampire couple."

It took Finch a good thirty seconds to mull over that bizarre statement. "*What?*" he finally asked, incredulous.

"You know. In movies and books, the vampire is always a man, and he's *super old*. Thousands of years old, sometimes! And the lady is like eighteen or nineteen." She leaned in closer to Finch and whispered, "But in this relationship, I'm the lady, and I'm four hundred years old. You're only thirty-nine, so I'm ten times older than you. That's funny, right?"

"I…" Finch gritted his teeth. "First, this isn't a relationship. Second, you haven't been a human for four hundred years, so I don't think it's the same."

"Shh!" Kull pressed her finger against his lips. "You don't want anyone to hear! Human women are supposed to hide their age at all costs."

Finch sighed. He had thought she was keeping their magical nature hidden from non-magical humans, but it seemed he was incorrect. She was hiding her age. Because that was what humans did.

Finch was about to try a different topic of conversation when the front doors of Dave Wong's slammed open with the force of a drugged-up meth head.

"*Where is it?*" a man roared. His ragged voice sounded as though he had gargled gravel. "Where's the egg?"

Every head turned. Chopsticks held mid-bite. A spring roll hit the floor with a tragic *plop*.

Egg?

Finch's chest tightened.

Framed in the entrance stood a man straight out of a

supernatural fever dream. His long duster coat flapping in a wind no one else could feel, the man had a scarred face that looked like it had lost a fistfight with a wood chipper and come back for round two. In one hand, he held a large black duffle bag. In the other, a crossbow.

"This cannot be happening," Finch said under his breath.

His phone buzzed again. This time Finch glanced at it.

Enzo had been calling him from the office. Over and over and over again. Finch answered the call and brought the phone to his ear.

"Adair?" Enzo asked on the other end. "Are you there? Because some lunatic broke into the office!"

"Let me guess—a man in a duster?" Finch whispered.

"That's right. And he's carrying a crossbow, and he's screaming something insane. He tore through your office, shouting about an egg. *A damn egg.*"

The man in the duster stomped forward, his boots ringing against the tile. "I know the egg is here in the city! You can't hide it forever! The temporal distortion is too noticeable!"

Kull sipped her soup. "Wait a minute. Is he talking about you, Adair?" She took another sip. "That's crazy. Do you know him?"

"I doubt it," Finch muttered. Then he addressed the phone. "Thank you, Enzo. I'll be at the office shortly."

Enzo snorted. "Okay. But watch out. I think that psycho is coming for you."

"Oh, he found me," Finch quipped.

CHAPTER
THREE

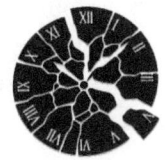

"**S**ir, *sir,*" the hostess shouted. "Weapons are not allowed in the restaurant." She pointed to a sign behind the front desk. Sure enough, it read: NO WEAPONS ALLOWED. A classic Stockton staple.

The deranged stranger wasn't deterred. He shoved the crossbow into his duffle bag and then tossed it to a man waiting in line. The man, unprepared, stumbled backward upon catching the bag, a grunt escaping him. It was obviously heavy, and he almost dropped it while trying to regain his balance.

"Hold that," the duster-wearing lunatic said, gruff and unapologetic.

Then he stomped into the dining room, his eyes frantically scanning the tables and booths, his nostrils flaring. The man's brown hair was peppered white at the temples, and his striking blue eyes were bloodshot and freakish. Was he high on drugs? Or was he always this ugly? Finch didn't know.

"I know the egg is here," the man announced, manic laughter in his words. "*I can smell it.*" He slammed his fist down on a nearby table, and all the plates leapt an inch upward, some spilling chow mein onto the pristine white tablecloths. "There's no use hiding from me! I'm *Jack Holt*, the best goddamn bounty hunter this side of the Rockies!"

"*Wow*," Kull muttered between sips of soup. "I wonder how many bounty hunters are on this side of the Rockies to begin with..."

She was literally the only patron still consuming food, so unbothered by the bizarre scene unfolding in front of everyone.

Finch had heard of a bounty hunter who called himself *Holt*. He specialized in ending monsters and demons, and minored in avoiding apocalypses. From what Finch could recall, the man had prevented a vampire attack in the early nineties that threatened to turn all Californians into the undead. Holt had been a legend after that.

He was pushing fifty now, though. While he was still tall and muscled, he strode forward with a slight limp, his left leg not as strong as his right. Logic said it was probably time for him to retire, but the wild look in his eyes told Finch that Holt would rather impale himself with his own crossbow bolt than ever stop hunting supernatural threats.

Finch didn't want to fight the man. Holt worked for the side of justice and virtue—just not so much common sense.

A waiter cautiously approached Holt from the side, his arms up and his movements tense, like he was approaching a wild animal. "Sir? Can I help you with—"

"*Stay out of my way,*" Holt roared. "There's a highly dangerous individual here who'll likely kill us all if I don't find him!"

It only took a second for that information to sink in. People screamed, and then the whole restaurant exploded in a flurry of movement. Families rushed out the front, side, and emergency exit doors, causing an alarm to sound.

People leapt over one another in their rush to leave the restaurant.

Holt was unfazed. He stormed ahead, sniffing deeply, and even flipped a table standing in his way, sending all the plates, food, and silverware crashing to the floor.

He was heading for Finch.

"Time for us to go," Finch said, pushing Kull to the edge of the booth.

She resisted his efforts, frowning. "What? But why? We're not done with the date."

"*Are you not paying attention?*" Finch hissed under his breath. The blaring alarm hurt his ears.

"That bounty hunter doesn't seem *too* scary. You could easily take him."

"I could just rewind time," Finch sardonically stated. "But you asked me not to. Are you saying I can now that there's a problem?" He already knew the answer, but he asked regardless.

Kull shook her head. "Do you have to? He hasn't hurt anyone yet."

"Then. We. Have. *To leave.*"

Kull protested, but Finch didn't stop shoving her until they were both out of the booth. Then, as a family of five went running by, Finch pulled Kull along and pretended to be part of the fleeing group.

Holt knew about Chronos's egg. Clearly. But it quickly became apparent he didn't know *Finch* had the egg. As Finch ran by the madman, Holt got a good look at him, but there was no recognition in his bloodshot eyes. He was squinting— looking for *something*—and hoping he would spot it in the dozens of people fleeing.

He was following a scent, and he didn't know where it led.

Finch thanked the good stars he had *some* luck, though he

noted this was the third date in a row interrupted by something insane. He was cursed. It was the only explanation.

Once outside, Finch immediately headed for his vehicle. Kull stumbled behind him, her tall heels giving her problems.

"Wait, Adair," she said, trying to fix her footwear.

Finch simply scooped her up in his arms, carrying her bride-style over to his vehicle. He *really* didn't want to brawl with a bounty hunter. They didn't typically have personal magic, but they always had tools to make up for that fact. Sometimes really *annoying* tools. And if this crusty douche-canoe knew the egg had temporal abilities, he might have brought tools to somehow deal with that specifically.

Which was just rude.

Dozens of people fled to their vehicles, then all attempted to pull out at the same time. But this was California. Every parking lot was half the size it needed to be, and everyone began playing bumper cars in their frantic need to flee the scene.

Finch had to dodge and weave between SUVs, all while holding Kull close.

Kull giggled as she wrapped her arms around his neck. "Oh, my hero. Whisking me off my feet, I see."

"I'm not *whisking* you," Finch said through clenched teeth. "This is a normal rescue. I'm just protecting you. Nothing romantic about it."

"Isn't this the exact definition of whisking?" She playfully kicked her legs as she leaned into his chest. "You can't deny it's romantic. I would say this has been a *good* date so far."

"*No.* It's not."

"But I think it is," Kull replied with a singsong tone.

Finch reached his Toyota and groaned. "Our restaurant was wrecked by a loon before we managed to eat half our meal. I submit to you that we didn't have a *good date*." He set

Kull down and then opened the passenger-side door. "I would, however, say we made a good escape."

"That's a win!"

Just as he said that, the *plink plink plink* of bullets hitting the side of a car filled the parking lot. Several holes appeared on the side of the Toyota, mere inches from Finch. He visualized metal being repelled from him—the magic Heslop provided, which made him immune to bullets—but it didn't make Kull immune.

When Finch whirled on his heel, he spotted Holt holding a 9mm handgun, pointed straight at the area just next to him. Had the man figured out who Finch was? Already?

And the bullets weren't random. They were precise.

Holt was sending a message. He wasn't aiming to kill. Yet.

"You're not getting away," Holt shouted. He held his duffle bag in his left hand, his grip freakishly tight. "Do you even know what you're doing? What kind of carnage and destruction you're incubating?"

Finch cursed under his breath. Why did things like this always happen to him? He stared down Holt, wondering how the man had even come to know about Chronos's egg in the first place.

"*You're* the one opening fire in the middle of a crowded parking lot," Finch yelled back at the man. "And you want to lecture *me* about carnage and destruction?"

A truck pulled out, tires screeching, and it came between Finch and Holt, blocking line of sight. Finch wasn't about to miss his opportunity to leave. He ducked into his car and started the engine.

Through it all, Kull was reclining in her seat and casually fixing her heels, humming a little tune.

Finch squealed out of the parking lot, keeping his eyes on the area behind his Toyota. He came within half an inch of hitting another car, but then he quickly turned, drove over a decorative grass hill, and then slammed across a sidewalk before skidding out onto a main street. Someone honked as they swerved around him.

"*Watch it, asshole!*" a man shouted from the vehicle.

"Wow, this evening is so exciting," Kull said as Finch sped down the road, putting as much distance between them and the restaurant as possible.

"I wish my dates were less exciting," Finch murmured.

"Really? Because this is kinda similar to my favorite movie ever! It's about a lady who is the target of an assassination attempt, and the man is a CIA agent sent to protect her. They fell *so* in love. It's such a great movie. We should watch it together sometime! It's called *Bullets and Butterflies!*"

Kull giggled for a moment, but then she abruptly stopped, her eyes wide. She turned to Finch. He frowned, wondering if something terribly wrong had happened and he just couldn't see.

"Kull? Are you okay?"

"I just realized… *You're* the girl who's being chased by an assassin, which means *I'm* the CIA agent."

"No." Finch shook his head. "Please, for the love of all that is holy, stop this line of logic."

"But… I should be protecting you, Adair!" She pointed to the steering wheel. "Turn around. Let me deal with the bounty hunter. I'll handle this."

Finch turned down another major road, heading straight for his office. He wanted Enzo with him, and he definitely wanted tools of his own. He would need to subdue Holt; there was no way around that.

"C'mon," Kull said. "Don't you like roleplaying? I heard that *really* strengthens relationships. And apparently, it brings spice back into the bedroom, which is, like, what *every* couple wants."

Finch didn't dignify any of those statements or questions with an answer. He wasn't entertaining Kull's fantasies, not when they were running from a gunman.

"Aren't you a little worried about the threat chasing us?" he sardonically asked.

"No. Definitely not." Kull huffed a laugh and rolled her eyes. "Did you see that man? He's nothing compared to you. We're fine."

"Anything could happen."

"I think you don't give yourself enough credit. I feel like…" She tapped her lips with one finger. "I'm hanging out with Superman. Would Superman's girlfriend be afraid if a normal human busted into a restaurant? I don't think so."

Her utter, unmitigated confidence chilled some of Finch's irritation. He slowed the car and took the next turn like an average civilian, his grip on the steering wheel loosening. Kull was right. Even if the man had tools—even if he knew about Chronos—he didn't have the power to stop time.

"Well, I wish you'd take the situation a little more seriously," Finch stated.

Kull nodded once. "Okay. Thank you. I appreciate you being honest. I'll take it more seriously." She held out her arm and poked the smooth skin on her wrist. "Draw me a Mark of Chronos."

"*What?*"

"If we're going to actually deal with this guy, I need to make sure I can remember everything. Draw me the mark, and let's do this for real."

Finch could rewind time, but in doing so, everyone forgot all previous events. Except, of course, for those who carried the Mark of Chronos. If Finch drew the mark on people, they would remember the events from the previous cycle, though he usually ended up having to draw the mark over and over again because he drew it *after* he marked the time.

Finch parked his vehicle in front of his PI office. Then he glanced at his phone.

8:31 p.m.

He reached over to the glove compartment, tore it open, and took the first pen within reach. In just four strokes, he drew the Mark of Chronos on Kull's forearm.

Then he marked the time.

Now he wouldn't have to draw it over and over again. She would have it until the ink faded from her flesh.

"Okay, I'm ready now," Kull stated. "Uh. So what should we do first? Call the police?"

Finch shook his head. "No. We should probably subdue the man and hand him over to the FBOI."

"Oh! Excellent plan. And then, afterward, we can finish our date, okay? We only did half of one, really, and I want the full experience."

Finch knew he would never escape this. He had said he would take her on a date, and Kull would get her date, even if it meant dragging him kicking and screaming. It was better to go along with it.

"Fine," he said. "Once we take down this muppet, we'll... go get some ice cream. Or something."

With a gleeful smile, Kull nodded. "It's a promise!"

CHAPTER
FOUR

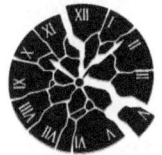

inch pulled up to his PI office and parked as close as possible to the door. The interior lights made it easy to see all the damage. The front of the office was a wall of floor-to-ceiling glass windows, and one of them was thoroughly shattered. Irritated, Finch unlocked the door and went inside.

"You could've gone through the window," Kull said as she followed behind.

"Ever since I watched *Die Hard*, I've avoided large piles of broken glass," Finch replied.

The front room was a modern, wide-open space with a reception area and several workspaces complete with computers, chairs, and desks. They were the fancy kind, made of metal, glass, and way too many pointed edges.

Nothing had been stolen, which was practically unheard of in Stockton. The computers sat just as everyone had left them. The reception desk still had tons of supplies, including its own high-tech computer with a widescreen monitor.

Unfortunately, the door to Finch's personal office was

wide open, practically torn off its hinges and squeaking as it swayed back and forth.

"Finally! I was waiting for you."

Finch turned toward the new voice.

Enzo. A man so burly, no one would be surprised if he sold his own line of protein powder. He strode over in a tank top and sweatpants, his muscles on full display, almost like he was showing off. But Finch knew better. Enzo was a werewolf and had to wear clothing that could stretch to fit his transformed body. Well, he didn't have to, but Enzo preferred to stay clothed, both during his "wolfing out" phase and afterward.

Enzo ran a hand over his perfectly bald head. "I told you. Some lunatic came screaming through here, shouting about an egg. He demolished your office."

"And he took nothing?" Finch asked.

"Not a *got damn* thing. I even checked our security cameras just to be certain."

Enzo's gaze was almost as dark as his complexion, but the moment he glanced over at Kull, his expression shifted to something curious.

"What's with the outfit?" Enzo asked, looking her up and down. "Were you at a movie premiere or something?"

"Adair and I were on a date," Kull said, smiling. She draped an arm over Finch's shoulder. "He took me to a fancy restaurant."

"It was a practice date," Finch quickly stated.

Enzo snorted back a laugh. "*Practice date*? What the hell are you practicing?"

"Well, Adair was showing me how a real date is supposed to go, and we were going to practice kissing, but then the man in the trench coat came busting into the restaurant!" Kull's voice grew more dramatic with each word she spoke until the end sounded like a grand finale.

"Really?" Enzo asked.

"No," Finch replied. "We were never going to practice *kissing*."

"Not that! The thing about the trench coat lunatic. He charged into the restaurant? Is that what was happening when I called you?"

"Oh, yes. That's true." Finch walked over to his shattered office door. Its sad squeak as it rocked back and forth made Finch frown. "His name is *Holt*. He's a local bounty hunter known for being a little overzealous."

"Feh. Seems we should be a bit more prepared."

Enzo went to the front windows and drew the large blinds, shutting them even over the front door, so no one on the sidewalk could see inside. An angry breeze blew through the broken window, rustling the blinds.

He turned his attention to the far bathroom. "You can come out now."

The door opened enough for a dime to squeeze through. Four tiny men came scurrying out, each wearing a peculiar hooded cloak styled to look like an animal's head. One wore a toad's head, another wore a hat that was a kitten's head, and the last two had squirrel heads.

They were the office brownies. They kept things neat and tidy and also helped retrieve valuable crafting materials.

Finch wasn't fond of fae-folk, but he had to admit the brownies were always helpful. They were each less than ten inches tall and wore 1800s German doll clothes, which was, in its own way, adorable.

The brownie with the toad's head ran straight to the broken window. He stopped at the edge of the broken glass, his eyes growing wider and wider with each passing moment. Then the tiny man fell to his knees and dramatically threw his head back to belt out an anguished cry. He sobbed as though he had just witnessed his best friend's murder.

The other three brownies quickly circled around the first and spoke in German, their tone soft and comforting. Finch had never learned German, and had no idea what was going on, so he ignored the scene to focus on his office.

"Do you think you can clean this up?" Enzo asked the brownies.

"Yeah," one replied with a thick German accent. "We will fix this up good."

"Great."

Finch stepped around the loose door and stared at his desk. It was in disarray, the drawers all open, papers scattered everywhere. The computer monitor was on its side, and the wall-mounted shelves had all been emptied, their contents on the floor.

As he had been told, nothing was stolen—it just looked like a tornado had ripped through the room and dissipated.

Kull walked in a moment later, her heels clicking with each step. She glanced around, both eyebrows heading for her hairline. "Oh my."

Then Enzo entered, his arms crossed. He didn't even bother looking. "I told you."

"I believed you," Finch muttered.

"Why is this Holt guy rummaging through your things, Adair?"

Finch hesitated for a moment. He hadn't wanted to tell anyone about his pact with Chronos, but he supposed now was the correct time to do so.

"I have an egg," Finch said.

Kull and Enzo remained quiet, their eyes glued to him, almost unblinking.

"Chronos gave it to me." Finch sighed. "As part of my pact to get his magic, I have to protect the egg until it hatches."

"What kind of egg?" Enzo asked. "A chicken egg? Duck egg? Ostrich? Tell me it's something normal. Please, for the love of god, don't tell me it's crazy and supernatural."

"It's crazy and supernatural," Finch quipped. "It's a new modern god. New pantheons are being born, and apparently, Chronos had to be part of the action."

"D'aww." Kull ran over and gave Finch a hug. It lasted longer than Finch would've cared for, and he awkwardly patted her back. When she finally broke away, she was smiling. "You're protecting a little baby god? That's so cute and wholesome and nice of you."

"I *have* to do it." Finch pinched the bridge of his nose. "I made a pact. Warlocks have to fulfill their pacts. If I don't…"

There was a long and awkward silence.

"You'll die," Enzo finally said, his tone grave.

Finch nodded. "That's right. So, under no circumstance can Holt have the egg. I have to keep it away from that madman until it hatches."

With squinted eyes, Kull glanced around again. She crept over to his desk and shifted some of the papers around. Then she opened and closed a few drawers. "Well? Where is it? It's not here, right?"

"I'm not telling you," Finch replied.

"*What?* Why not? We're good friends!"

"I'm not telling anyone."

With a shrug, Enzo chuckled. "Good move. The less people who know its whereabouts, the safer it is." He waggled a finger. "The only criminals who kept their stashes safe from the Oakland PD were the ones who never told anyone else where they were."

Kull stood straight and rubbed her chin. "Wait. How does Holt know about the egg? I mean, Chronos wouldn't tell him, right?" She lifted an eyebrow. "*Right?*"

"I doubt it." Finch shrugged. "But it seemed Holt had

some way to detect the egg? He knows it's in the city, and he seems to vaguely know it's in my care, but I'm not entirely sure how."

"Let me guess." Enzo frowned. "A *god egg* is valuable and plenty of people would kill to get their hands on one."

Finch nodded once. "It's probably one of the most valuable objects in the world. Exceedingly rare and filled with untapped magical potential. In the hands of the right witch or wizard, it could be used to create a brew or magical item with untold powers."

"Didn't one of the old gods get turned into a magical item that made a whole town vanish?"

"That's right. *Larkspur Hollow*, in the Ozarks. A town of 714 residents up and vanished in 1959, leaving no physical trace, all because some full moon witch had a grudge against the mayor. She used a piece of a dead god to *poof* them all out of existence."

Witches had the capability to use all sorts of magical objects in their brews, and sometimes to empower their very magic. In the case of Larkspur Hollow, the whole place was now a magical disaster. In the 80s, a brave reporter by the name of Diana Mulligan went to investigate the disappearance, but she ended up vanishing as well. The cruel magical spell lingered, continuing to harm any who entered the once peaceful township.

Which was why Finch couldn't allow anyone to get their hands on the egg. No doubt someone would use it as a magical nuke or some other weapon of mass destruction. It just couldn't be allowed.

Plus, Finch didn't feel like dying. At least, not anymore. He still had plenty of things to accomplish, and a brother to avenge. Under no circumstance could Holt or anyone else get the egg.

CHAPTER
FIVE

"So, what's the plan?" Enzo asked.

Without answering, Finch walked past both him and Kull, his thoughts on future events. He wanted to put distance between himself and Holt. There was no reason to actually fight the crazy bounty hunter... He just needed time for the egg to hatch.

On autopilot, Finch went to the receptionist desk and picked up the notes left for him from the previous day. Perhaps one of the jobs came from outside Stockton, and he could use it as an excuse to leave. Having a job would keep his mind occupied. A watched pot never boiled, after all. Or a watched egg never hatched, in this case.

Most of the messages were calls from various attorney offices asking for a PI to either question potential witnesses or serve subpoenas.

Two notes were requests for a PI to stalk a spouse to catch them cheating.

The last one was from a woman in Tahoe City... The note read:

Grace Stonewell – Tahoe City
Missing Son
Wants Best PI in Cali
Willing to pay any price

Tahoe City was up in the mountains, and a good three-hour drive from Stockton. And Finch never turned down cases for missing children. It was one of his personal rules—one his brother, Carter, had started.

"Well?" Enzo growled as he walked around the other side of the desk. "What's the plan, Adair? You must have one."

Kull strode over to Finch, smiling the whole way. She adjusted the chopsticks in her fiery hair as she said, "Are we going to beat up Holt? Because I'm thinking I can make *so* many viral videos if I just filmed him being a completely unhinged lunatic."

Finch tucked the note in his pocket. "No. We're going to leave town for a bit. Head to Lake Tahoe. Find someone's missing kid."

"*Leave?*" Kull's eyebrows shot for her hairline. "But… we're not done with our date! What about ice cream?"

After a short sigh, Finch turned to face her. "I think the best course of action is to lie low for a bit. If the egg hatches before Holt catches me, I'll have fulfilled my pact to Chronos, and we won't have to worry about anything else."

Enzo shrugged. "I liked Kull's idea of just whuppin' the guy's ass."

"*He's not—*" Finch pinched the bridge of his nose and calmed himself. "He's not a criminal. He's a bounty hunter who has helped a lot of people in the past. I don't want to jump the man because he might be trying to get the egg for the same reason I need to hide it."

"To keep it out of the hands of *actual* bad guys?" Kull asked, a smile blossoming across her face.

"Precisely."

"But... didn't he open fire on us in the middle of a parking lot?" Kull tapped her bottom lip with a finger. "He seems... unstable." She glanced at Enzo. "Is unstable the right word?"

"I would've used *psychotic lunatic*," Enzo quipped. "But *unstable* will work."

The mention of guns reminded Finch he had two new ones of his own. He turned on his heel and returned to his office. The box was locked up in his desk, and for a split second, he wondered if it would still be there. Enzo had said Holt stole nothing, but did Enzo even know about the guns?

Finch yanked open the drawer. No longer locked.

But the wooden box was still there. He lifted it, pleased to feel it weighed the same as always. Holt really hadn't stolen anything. And of course not. Holt probably felt he was working for the law, and had every right to search the office but not confiscate anything. The bounty hunter had a reputation for being cold, but just and honorable.

He snapped the box open like a man yanking the pin from a grenade.

And there they were. Nestled in dark velvet, lounging like royalty, lay two regal handguns.

The first... Well, the first looked like it wanted to kill something *right now*. Its obsidian metal drank in the light, giving it a darker than normal appearance. Silver filigree curled along the barrel, writhing like mist, or maybe smoke, or maybe the last breath of someone who never saw the shot coming.

The grip was made of bone. Real bone, if Finch had to guess. It was cold, smooth, and deeply unsettling. The barrel bore its name, etched clean and proud. *Starfall.*

The second handgun? It was just as impressive, but in a different way. If the first was *murder*, then the second gun was *torture*.

The second gun was heavier, broader in the barrel, every inch of it promising pain. The copper finish gleamed like old blood in firelight, edges darkened, scorched, battle worn. The grip was slick red and had a texture that turned Finch's stomach. It felt too much like skin. Like someone had loved this thing. Or hated it. Or both.

There wasn't any swirling elegance here. No beauty. Just scars. The name wasn't subtle. It was carved right into the grip. *Agony*.

Finch smirked to himself as he pulled the two weapons out of the box. "Time to make some memories with the two of you."

They were both gifts from Kull. One was meant to go to the dwarven king so Finch could complete his pact, and the other was simply a gift from her, for being so supportive. Finch dwelled on that thought as he got his shoulder holsters from another desk drawer. Once they were secured around his shoulders, he tucked the two handguns away and then pulled a jacket over them so they would remain concealed.

"Are we going to Tahoe right now?" Kull asked from the doorway. She leaned on the frame and then motioned to her gorgeous outfit. "Because I need to pack first. Apparently, people don't like it when I wear the same outfit in a stream multiple days in a row, and I don't want to go clothes shopping *again* when I just went on an epic spree last weekend."

"The height of first world problems," Enzo muttered from the lobby. "I'm glad growing up in poverty saved me from so much nonsense."

"That's fine." Finch walked by her and headed for the front door. "I'll call Jessie and Liam and let them know I'll be gone for a few days and that they should probably skip town as well. Then I'll rent us a car."

Kull thrust an arm in the air. "Oh, oh! Can *I* get us a vehicle? Pretty please? I know so many great people and places to get vehicles."

Fearing the worst, Finch hesitated. Finally, as he placed his hand on the front door, he said, "Fine. But we need to leave here as soon as possible, all right? I don't want Holt following us anywhere."

"You can count on me!"

After Kull left to gather clothes, Finch moved his vehicle down a couple blocks and parked it in a back alley. He was friends with the building owner and knew his car wouldn't get towed. Then he returned to the office to wait with Enzo.

The night was warm. They stood mostly in silence. Enzo had a pair of Crocs on, with his sweatpants and tank top, and he honestly had the appearance of a thug ready to rob someone. Except for the fact that he was holding a soft cat carrier. An elderly cat sat within, a feline at least twelve years of age and skeletal thin. He had dark stripes, patchy gray fur, and gigantic yellow eyes that were easy to get lost in.

"Why are you carrying Methusepaws?" Finch asked with a sigh.

"We can't leave him." Enzo cradled the carrier close. "The vet gave me medication that need to be administered every eight hours. Besides, Meth gets nervous when he's alone."

"You're really going to keep calling the cat *Meth*? I thought you had settled on *Paws* instead."

Enzo shrugged. "I was going to call him *Paws*, but *Meth* is the perfect name. We found him in a rundown meth lab.

Plus, the cat responds more to Meth than to Paws. He's probably used to it."

Finch couldn't argue with that logic. The cat's name was a combination of Methuselah, the first wizard, and *paws*, and it symbolized how they had met the cat while fighting Maldonado, the cartel wizard after Finch's sister-in-law.

And he had been found in a meth lab.

So *Meth* it was. Finch didn't say anything else on the matter, even though he wanted to argue that Paws was a much cuter name.

The street was quiet. Too quiet. One of those pregnant silences that felt like it was waiting to give birth to something awful.

Then came the music.

Bass first, so thick and heavy it rattled Finch's fillings. Then the synths—bright, neon, aggressively upbeat, like a sugar high with a criminal record. Lights flashed across the road, painting the inside of Finch's busted office in swirls of magenta and electric teal.

Finch sighed and rubbed his temples. He hoped to the good stars this vehicle wasn't for them, but he already knew better.

"What fresh hell is that?" Enzo growled, already tensing. Meth hissed inside his little carrier.

"It's... our ride," Finch replied with a groan.

A long, low honk blared throughout the street. The vehicle—the *bus*, really—that rolled up could only be described as a traveling nightclub built by engineers on Molly.

Their ride was a full-size, tricked-out party bus, dipped in matte black with streaks of shimmering red and gold glitter that sparkled under the streetlamps. A neon sign above the windshield flashed:

THE GRINDHOUSE RIDE: STREAMERS ONLY

Finch was tempted to just call himself a personal Uber and pay however many hundreds to get a ride up to Tahoe by himself.

"*Streamers only?*" Enzo muttered. "Kull, what in the ever-loving—"

The door hissed open like the entrance to a spaceship. Fog spilled out. A blast of artificial cherry-scented mist washed over them, followed by the unmistakable strobe-flicker of club lights and a high-pitched squeal of excitement from inside.

Kull leaned out of the bus, now wearing a neon pink hoodie, black leggings, and a smile that could light up a room like a firebomb. "*All aboard!*" Then she disappeared into the smoke, giggling the whole way.

"Do we have to get on?" Enzo sarcastically asked.

"I got us the Deluxe Dreamstreamer edition," Kull called out from inside. "Built-in green screens, ring lights for every seat, a smoothie bar that only serves drinks named after video game characters, and there's a hot tub in the back!"

"Jesus Christ," Finch whispered, shaking his head. "Not the hot tub…"

Enzo snorted back a laugh. "On a scale of one to ten, how conspicuous do you think this ride is?"

"I'm not in the mood for stupid questions."

"You said *lie low*. This isn't lying low. This is painting a neon target on our asses and putting on a synchronized dance routine."

"You want to tell her to pick another vehicle?" Finch asked. "Because you know she loves this one."

"C'mon, you two!" Kull called out again. "This trip will be so much fun!"

Enzo exhaled, the tension leaving his muscles. "Fine. Let's

get this over with." Even Meth seemed to calm down in his little carrier.

Finch glanced at his phone. The clock said 10:02 p.m., and he marked the time, just in case. Then he stepped forward, hands jammed in his coat pockets, guns comforting against his ribs. "Let's look on the bright side. Nobody expects a Twitch streamer bus to be smuggling a god egg."

Enzo snorted. "Nobody sane, anyway."

They both boarded.

Inside was a kaleidoscopic nightmare—mirrored panels on the ceiling, plush LED-lit seating, and three computer stations set up for streaming. A banner reading "#BusLife" floated above one of the stations.

Fortunately, Kull was the only one in the back. The driver, up front, was obscured by an opaque glass wall with a small door. That was it. Two people.

Kull was already curled up in a velvet booth, sipping something purple from a skull-shaped crystal cup. "Isn't this place amazing?" she asked, raising her drink.

Enzo grumbled as he glanced at the flashing lights, the rainbow mist, and the twelve mini-screens showing split-cam footage of the driver and various parts of the bus. "I don't usually feel old, but this bus makes me think I have one foot in the grave." He took a seat on a plush cushion and set the cat carrier gently on the seat next to him. "You like this? *All this?* It's so… noisy."

Finch took the final step aboard, the door hissing closed behind him. "Maybe if we turn the music down, we can nap on the way to Tahoe."

Pouting, Kull leaned back in her seat. "*Really?* You don't even want to see the setup for the hot tub?" She motioned to a door in the back. "It's pretty amazing!"

After glancing down at his button-up shirt and jeans,

Finch returned his sardonic gaze to her. "I'd rather gargle glass."

Kull rolled her eyes, stood, and then took the seat directly next to Finch. "You still have to show me a thing or two about *real* dating, but I think *I* need to show the *both of you* how amazing humans can get when they party." She elbowed Finch. "C'mon. You'll be feeling great in no time!"

The party bus revved its engine and pulled away from the curb, leaving the broken office behind. The brownies would fix the windows, likely before the sun rose, so Finch didn't mind leaving it in such a rundown state.

The bus sped off into the night, a disco-lit beast of steel and caffeine.

"Oh, and I hope you don't mind, but my streaming crew is going to meet us in Tahoe City," Kull casually added. "So, while we find this missing kid, I was also hoping we could film a couple fun viral videos. What do you two say?"

Both Finch and Enzo remained dead silent. Meth offered a weak meow.

CHAPTER
SIX

The trek to Tahoe City would take three hours, and Finch settled into his seat for the long ride. He sat with his arms crossed, glaring out the tinted window. Kull had provided him a pink smoothie she called *The Toadstool*, and Finch suspected it was a reference to something, he just didn't know what.

It tasted good, though.

Enzo shoved earplugs in so deeply they might've punctured brain matter. Meth had curled up in his carrier and adopted the hollow-eyed expression of a veteran recalling trench warfare.

Kull, however, was thriving.

She had discovered the built-in karaoke system and belted out a Taylor Swift song so passionately the tinted windows trembled in solidarity. Halfway through, she handed Finch a microphone.

"*No*," he said.

"C'mon, Adair. Couples who sing together stay together!"

"We're not a couple."

She leaned in close, the mic brushing his shoulder. "Yet."

Finch groaned but didn't respond.

"Wrong song choice, then. Don't worry, I'll pick one you know." She tapped at the control panel until the opening riff of Bohemian Rhapsody blasted through the bus. "Oooh! You two will like this, right? Adair? Enzo? *Hmm?*"

Although Finch would never admit it, Bohemian Rhapsody was his favorite song of all time. Did Kull somehow know? No. That was impossible. Wasn't it?

Enzo cracked one eyelid, muttered something about this being worse than silver bullets, and went back to pretending he was dead.

The bus barreled into the foothills, the driver having a party all his own in the front. Finch half-expected to see their obituary scroll across the LED news ticker on the dashboard:

LOCAL PI AND FRIENDS DIE IN STREAMER BUS CRASH. ONLY METH WAS FOUND.

That was the problem with the damn cat's name. No matter how it was used, it always sounded way worse than reality.

When it became obvious that no one would sing with her, Kull huffed, turned the music down to an ambient background volume, and then took her seat next to Finch. Despite everyone else's lack of interest, Kull's enthusiasm was ironclad.

She propped her chin in her hand, looking at Finch with a mischievous glint. "So... while we're heading to Tahoe, maybe you can tell me what kind of girls you like."

"No," Finch replied.

Kull poked his arm, ignoring his death glare. "Do you like mysterious loner girls? Or... fiery bombshells?" She struck a pose, one leg on the wall, nearly toppling her green smoothie. "Because, you know, I might fit one of those categories."

"We're heading to Tahoe to do a job—let's just focus on that." Finch leaned away from her, hoping some exaggerated irritation would deter her. Kull was quite beautiful, and he really didn't want to be distracted. Couldn't she just stop this weird game she was playing? It was cute, and perhaps if he wasn't so…

Finch shook his head. He just didn't want to risk a relationship. He couldn't. He needed to focus on other things. Maybe take a cold shower. That was all.

Kull pulled her leg back and then scooted even closer, her voice dropping into a playful whisper. "You know, Adair, if you weren't so allergic to fun, I'd think you were trying to flirt with me."

"This isn't me flirting."

"Exactly! The best kind of flirting is pretending you're not flirting. Mystery. Tension. *Boom!*" She clapped her hands once. "Instant romance."

"You've watched too many rom-coms," Finch said, pinching the bridge of his nose. "They're rotting your brain."

The party bus lurched around a mountain curve, lights flashing, smoothies sloshing. Finch grabbed the edge of the seat, bracing himself. He had fought vampires, sorcerers, and deranged lunatics, but this ride to Tahoe? This might actually kill him.

"Okay, if you don't want to talk about dating, why don't we talk about the egg." Kull frowned. "Like… where is it? Did you leave it back at the office? I don't remember you grabbing it. Do you have it on you?"

"I'm not telling anyone where it is."

"So it *is* back in Stockton?"

"It's hidden," Finch said. "That's all you need to know."

Despite Finch's attempts to rebuff her, Kull didn't change

a thing about her tone or attitude. She remained as close to Finch as ever. "But Holt could sense the magic of the egg, right? That was how he knew it was in Stockton in the first place? And how he found us at Dave Wong's? So... that means... you *have* to have it on you." She gave him a finger gun and winked. "And I bet it still is, isn't it?"

Finch remained quiet. Enzo, now interested in the topic of conversation removed his earbuds, and then turned to face them. "Wait, so we have the egg with us right now?"

"I never said that," Finch drawled.

"It's on him," Kull said in a comically loud whisper. "He won't admit it, but it is."

Enzo shot Finch a glower. "You're literally carrying around the most dangerous Fabergé egg in the world, and you won't tell us?"

Kull's eyes went wide, gleaming in the strobe glow. "Wait. Can you imagine if it was? Like, a glowing Fabergé egg, but it hatches into a god? Adair, you could make millions just streaming the unboxing. Do you know how many people watch toy unboxings? This would be like—" She snapped her fingers. "*Divine unboxing.* Hashtag GodHatch2025."

Finch exhaled. "You know we can't just expose mortals to magic. It would cause so much trouble, and I'm so tired of dealing with bullshit."

"Yeah, but it'd be bigger than Pokémon cards, I bet."

"I used to have Pokémon cards as a kid," Enzo muttered. "I traded my damn holographic Charizard for some Star Wars cards because I thought they'd be cooler and worth more." He snorted back a laugh. "Goes to show you I have no clue when it comes to pop culture."

The bus rattled, swerved and then *thumped.* Hard. Something solid had bounced beneath the wheels, jostling everyone in their seats. The LED ceiling lights flickered once, the neon signs cutting out before stuttering back to life. Meth hissed, his yellow eyes glowing inside his carrier like warning lights.

Enzo tensed, his nostrils flaring. *"Driver, pull over."*

"Y-Yes, sir," the driver called out from the cab.

The bus hissed to the shoulder, brakes squealing. The music cut off with a strangled gasp, leaving only the eerie hum of the engine and the whisper of wind through the mountain trees outside.

Kull glanced between them. "Sooo… we just hit… a deer, right? Or maybe a raccoon? Or a really unlucky mountain biker?"

"I didn't see anything!" the driver called out.

Enzo shook his head. He stood, looming, his voice grim. "Of course he saw nothing. This is Tahoe. And Tahoe's not normal."

Finch lifted an eyebrow. "Define *not normal.*"

"Lake Tahoe's a hotspot of supernatural activity."

"I consider the supernatural normal, actually."

Enzo frowned. "This isn't pleasant witches and vampire lawyers. I'm talkin' skinwalkers. Cult witches. Old-world spirits. Sometimes the things that live here don't hunt for food. They hunt for fun. Classic trick is to *accidentally* get hit by a vehicle. Driver steps out to check, then… *Bam.* You're never seen again."

Leaning in closer to Finch, Kull whispered, "You hear that? We're in a horror movie now. I love horror movies."

Finch shook his head. "You need to seriously get away from the TV every once in a while. This isn't a horror movie, and if something spooky-supernatural is outside, it messed with the wrong party bus."

Something scraped along the side of the vehicle, slow at first and then faster. Then the noise ended almost as quickly as it had started. Everyone exchanged glances.

"We're here looking for a missing kid, correct?" Enzo

asked. "We could go outside, see what the fuck is messing with us, and then ask it some questions. Maybe we can find the kid before we even get to town."

"Fine." Finch stood and headed for the door. "But let me draw the Mark of Chronos on you first. That way, I don't have to keep drawing it over and over if we need to redo this whole clusterfuck."

Enzo held out his arm. "Sounds good to me."

Using a pen near the coffee machine, Finch drew the mark in four easy swipes. Once he was finished, he turned to the door.

Kull held up a hand. "Wait!"

The two men turned to stare at her.

"Shouldn't you leave the egg on the bus? You don't want to take it outside, do you?"

With gritted teeth, Finch whirled back toward the door. "I already told you, *it's not on me*. Stop saying it is." He slammed out of the party bus and stepped into the quiet night air.

Tahoe smelled different than the rest of California. It was cleaner here. Fresher. The pine trees had a distinct scent that made this area something special.

Enzo came out a moment later, his Crocs squeaking as they scraped against the bus steps. He went to Finch's side and exhaled, his breath visible.

There was a moment of silence between them. Then Enzo lowered his voice and asked, "You really don't have it in your pocket or something?"

"No," Finch said. "It's not on me. Don't worry about the egg. It's safe. We just... have to make certain that Holt doesn't find us for a while. As soon as it hatches, this will all be over."

"And you think it'll hatch soon?"

Finch rubbed at his side. "Yes."

"All right. I'll trust you."

As they waited for Kull, Finch and Enzo glanced around,

and under, the bus. There were no logs, sticks, or other objects on the road. No body. No blood trail. But there were scratches along the side and across the front bumper. *Something* had been hit.

They continued to wait, the cold night air rushing over them. Finch pulled his coat closed as he scanned their surroundings. The old pine trees swayed at the tips, their needles falling in clumps.

The moon appeared to be a crooked smile in the sky, casting just enough silver light to make the shadows darker and deeper. Every rock and stump along the tree line looked suspiciously like something crouching and waiting.

Finch stuffed his hands into his coat pockets. "What's taking Kull so long?"

"I don't know." Enzo sniffed several times. He huffed and returned his attention to Finch. "What's with you two, by the way? Fake dating? What the hell is that?"

After a long exhale, Finch said, "I don't know. I think she's just messing with me at some level. You know how mischief spirits are."

"She seems pretty determined. And serious."

"Kull wants to fall in love with someone, and she wanted me to show her what that would look like, but… I don't think I have it in me right now. I told myself I wouldn't get involved with someone until I finished all this business with Carter's killer."

Enzo nodded along with Finch's words. "Would your brother want that?"

"*Don't,*" Finch snapped. "Carter isn't here. I need to make things right. Then I'll think about everything else."

"You're going to hurt her feelings if you keep rejecting her like you are."

The words settled over Finch like a wet blanket. He didn't want to upset her. Kull's love of life actually made him happier, even if he tried to hide the fact. She was warm, vivacious, and rivaled the sun in terms of intensity. Not many people could pull it all off, but Kull did. Somehow.

"I'll try to be less... severe," Finch muttered. "And maybe if I just take her on a pretend date or two, she'll be satisfied. Then she can move on to dating a TikToker or something."

Enzo snorted. "Good."

And...

Gixmoth had killed Carter. What if Finch found someone he couldn't live without, and then Gixmoth took that from him again? It was too much. Finch knew, in his heart of hearts, that if that happened there were only two options. He would give up on life entirely, or he would burn everything and everyone in his way of revenge. There would be no middle ground.

Kull finally stepped out of the bus, her neon hoodie making her glow like a radioactive firefly in the moonlight. She twirled once, shivering. "Wow. This is so atmospheric." She shoved her hands deep into her hoodie pockets. "So, what do we do first? Because in horror movies the first thing we'd do is split up to cover more ground."

"We're not doing that," Finch said, sardonic. "We stick together at all times, understand? No one wanders too far."

CHAPTER
SEVEN

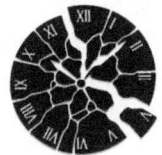

The bus door hissed open, and the driver stumbled out. He was a thin man in a gray suit, his brown hair slicked back, his eyes wide.

"I didn't see anything," he said. "Honest. There was nothin' on the road and then *bam*. The whole bus is rockin'. But there was nothin' there!"

"We believe you," Enzo said, holding up his hand. "Just get back in the bus. We'll look around."

"A-All right." The driver retreated back into the vehicle.

Before anything else happened, Finch glanced at the clock.

12:04 a.m.

He marked the time now that they were so close to Tahoe. He didn't want to have to relive the karaoke ride again.

Enzo motioned with a tilt of his head. When he strode forward, he did so with the confidence and authority of a cop. Some habits were difficult to break.

The pine trees loomed ahead of them as Enzo took point. Finch followed a step behind, coat pulled tight, his mind half on the egg and half on what his life would've looked like if he had just taken up bartending instead of becoming a PI...

Kull brought up the rear, bouncing on the balls of her neon sneakers.

The three of them slipped into the woods, leaving the road entirely. Pine needles muffled their steps, and the deeper they went, the darker the world became. Finch could barely make out the faint glow of the party bus anymore, a pulsing neon heartbeat in the distance. Out here, it was all shadows and silver light.

Kull sped up her pace and walked alongside Finch, wringing her hands the entire time. An owl hooted, and she jumped.

"What's wrong with you?" Finch asked, keeping his voice low.

"O-Oh. Nothing is wrong. I just... I don't know. This *does* remind me of a slasher flick and... well... I'm afraid of..." Kull glanced down at her unsteady hands. "I *just* became human. What if I die? I'll never get to do all the things I've longed for..."

"*You're not going to die,*" Finch snapped, then grabbed one of Kull's hands and held it tight. "Just hold on to me."

Kull gently squeezed his knuckles. "D'aww," she said with a smile. "Adair..."

"Listen—I'm just doing this to show you what a *good* significant other would do, okay? They'll be there for you when you're afraid. They'll help you feel confident. If you're dating someone and they don't do that, you have the wrong person."

"Right," Kull whispered, her gaze falling to their interlocked hands. "A good significant other will make me feel less afraid..."

Enzo lifted a hand, silencing them both. He lowered to a crouch, palm brushing the dirt. Finch stopped short, his pulse ticking faster despite himself. The forest was somehow alive with silence. There were no more animal sounds. No more rustling pine needles. Something was here, Finch knew. Whatever it was, it was just beyond his sight in the shadows. Lurking.

"We're close." Enzo's voice was a low growl, the kind of tone that made Finch's skin itch. "Tracks, fresh. Something crossed the road right before we hit it. Two feet, but small. Not human."

"It's a goblin," Kull said matter-of-factly.

Enzo glanced over his shoulder with a glare. "How do you know that? You're an expert tracker?"

She tapped the side of her nose. "I'm still part mischief spirit. I can smell magic. Can't you? Take a deep breath. It's definitely a goblin."

Finch inhaled and then exhaled. As a warlock, he had the ability to detect magic on the air. It was the same kind of faint scent that could be smelled after a gun was fired. Subtle. But the odor of the pine trees blocked everything else out. Finch couldn't smell a thing other than their lush environment.

"I'm not sure what kind of goblin, though," Kull muttered as she rubbed her chin with her free hand. "Something unusual, for sure."

Enzo stood, eyes gleaming in the moonlight. "All right. We're looking for a goblin. Keep your eyes low, people. And stay close."

The farther they went into the woods, the more Finch thought this was a terrible idea. He was prepared to rewind time at a moment's notice, but he knew if he didn't discover whatever was out here, he wouldn't be better prepared to deal with it on a second go.

Then the wind shifted. Something rustled ahead. Finch's

hand went instinctively to his coat, brushing the weight of Starfall.

Enzo froze again. He raised a single finger, pointing toward the darkness ahead. Finch squinted. Between the trees, half-veiled in shadow, something was crouched, its body hidden in the shrubs.

Without warning, Kull leapt forward and pointed. "Oh, look! It's a pukwudgie!"

A *pukwudgie* was a type of goblin that specialized in making others hallucinate. It ate meat, rarely associated with other types of goblins, and was generally seen as a nuisance, especially among the fae. Finch had seen one up close only once.

The small creature stepped out of the darkness.

The pukwudgie was no taller than a child, humanoid in shape, and had a tiny amount of white hair on the top of its round head. Its gray-green skin shimmered in the moonlight, its giant yellow eyes alight with intelligence as it straightened its posture to its full height.

The little goblin had clawed hands and feet and only wore an old pair of cargo shorts that were worn and torn in so many places, Finch assumed the pukwudgie had fished them out of a dumpster.

"Hello," Kull said, waving.

The pukwudgie bared its sharp, yellowed teeth and then hissed. When Enzo stepped forward, slight patches of black fur sprouting over his shoulders, Finch figured this wasn't going to end well for the goblin.

But then the pukwudgie's eyes slid over to Finch, and its whole demeanor changed. The goblin put away its sickly fangs and its giant eyes somehow went wider. With a shaky hand, the goblin pointed to its bare green chest, and then to Finch.

"Wait," Enzo whispered. "Is this the same pukwudgie you saved from Maldonado's mansion?"

Finch let go of Kull's hand and approached the pukwudgie. He knelt, and the goblin hesitantly smiled.

When Finch had first seen this particular pukwudgie, it had been trapped in a cage and awaiting a fate worse than death. Maldonado liked to liquefy mystical creatures into goo so he could make all sorts of exotic potions. Finch had pulled this one from a cage and set it free...

He had never thought he would actually see it again.

The pukwudgie visibly grew more excited, its mouth widening into a grin. Then it patted its chest.

"*Smudge*," it said in strained English.

"Ahh!" Kull jogged over and leaned in close. "That's his name! How adorable."

"Its name is *Smudge*?" Enzo sneered. "What an awful name."

Finch tilted his head, studying the goblin. Was this the creature who had stopped the bus? Had this pukwudgie intended to rob them? Or steal from the inside of the bus while they were wandering around the woods? Perhaps the pukwudgie was working with something else...

"Smudge," the pukwudgie said again. Then he pointed at Finch with the other hand. "Friend."

Enzo snorted. "Gross."

Smudge didn't so much as glance at Enzo. He shuffled closer to Finch, bare feet kicking up loose pine needles, and tugged at Finch's coat sleeve with surprising gentleness for something sporting claws sharp enough to fillet fish.

"Friend," he repeated.

Kull clapped. "Ohhh, he likes you! That's super rare. Most pukwudgies don't like *anyone*. They're, like... mean. And usually cause people all sorts of problems."

"This is a liability," Enzo growled. "Kull's right. That thing's dangerous. One wrong thought from him and you'll be seeing pink elephants until you run headfirst into a tree trunk."

Finch couldn't remember Smudge doing anything like that in Maldonado's mansion. As a matter of fact, Smudge had been trapped in a simple cage and nothing more. If he was really so dangerous, wouldn't Maldonado have kept him somewhere more secure?

Smudge patted his throat and then forced some more words out in English. "No hurt. No trick. Only... Finch."

"*D'aww!*" Kull said, ten times louder this time. "He really does like you, Adair. This is so precious." She stood straight and practically giggled. "Can we keep him?"

Enzo waved a hand. "Oh, hell no. We're not keeping him. We've got enough strays." He jerked his chin toward the bus, where Meth was no doubt meowing in loneliness. "One cat's already pushing it."

Finch sighed. He had saved Smudge once, but he hadn't thought about the pukwudgie since then. Now the little goblin was staring at him like he was the only star left in the sky.

With her hands on her hips, Kull moved over to Smudge. "Look at him. He needs us. And our bus can fit *way* more people."

Enzo rolled his eyes. "This is a circus show."

"Hey." Kull patted Smudge's scruffy head. "Every circus needs a mascot."

Finch held up a hand. "Smudge, do you live around Lake Tahoe? Do you know the area well?"

The little goblin nodded. Even if he couldn't speak much English, he seemed to understand it perfectly fine.

"We're here looking for a missing kid," Finch muttered. "Maybe you could—"

Then something rushed out of the darkness.

The trees shuddered as though hit by a storm, pine needles raining down in waves. Finch's hand was already in his coat, his fingers curling around Starfall, when Smudge screeched and hurled his small body at Finch's chest.

The impact wasn't much, but Finch was still kneeling, and he was toppled over by the little goblin. He hit a patch of damp pine needles, and a split second later, a blur of black fur and muscle streaked past, claws raking the air where Finch had just been.

Whatever monster this was, it was *fast*. Finch only caught a glimpse of red eyes as it went tearing back into the woods, diving into darkness.

"*Werewolf!*" Enzo shouted. His voice was already shifting, bones grinding, his body swelling with muscle and fur. "It's contagious! Stay back!"

The monster wheeled around, low and predatory, a growl reverberating from deep in its chest. The werewolf had to be over eight feet tall, with a well-muscled body and claws sharp enough to rend steel. Finch scrambled up, Starfall in his grip now, but he knew werewolves weren't really affected by bullets unless they were silver. His fire from Ke-Koh, the Ifrit of Rebellion, would probably be better suited for the task…

The red-eyed werewolf lunged again. Enzo met it head-on, half-shifted, his fist slamming into the enemy's jaw with a crack that echoed through the woods. The werewolf, barely fazed, turned its full hatred on Enzo. The two beasts collided, snarling, clawing, canine maws snapping inches from each other's throats.

Smudge darted in front of Finch, his tiny arms spread wide as if to shield him, hissing a sound that didn't belong in any human throat. His yellow eyes glowed like lanterns, fixed on the wolf. "No hurt Finch!"

CHAPTER
EIGHT

The werewolf tossed Enzo aside like he was nothing. Enzo slammed into a tree with a crack, shook it off, and then snarled. The red-eyed wolf turned back toward Finch, lips curling, drool falling in strands.

Smudge didn't back down. He hissed again.

When the enemy werewolf charged Finch, there was only a second's worth of reaction time. Finch held up a hand, and a burst of fire went over Smudge's head and filled the forest with bright white and orange light. The flames roared between the trees and washed over the werewolf, drowning it in deadly heat.

The beast howled as its fur and flesh charred away in a matter of moments.

Then Finch ended his fire and took a step back. Although Starfall didn't use silver bullets, it could still deal damage. He lifted his handgun and fired. The shots rang out as loud *bangs*, but also with a hint of a chime. It was unlike anything Finch had ever heard when unloading a firearm.

His three shots were true. Two tore through the wolf's chest, and one blew through its neck. The monster—still alive—staggered backward, blood gushing onto the charred and still flaming forest floor. Embers and ash swirled around them.

Kull pulled up her phone and obviously started filming.

Then Enzo tackled the beast. He was fully transformed, also around eight feet tall, and his claws were just as deadly. While on top of the werewolf, Enzo pummeled it with blow after unanswered blow. His claws tore through flesh and fur, which he tossed aside in sickening chunks.

The werewolf bucked hard as Enzo tore across its ribs. Blood sprayed, steaming against the fire-scorched earth, but the beast was not finished. Red-eyed werewolves were the most deadly and powerful of all, and Finch knew this wouldn't end quickly.

With a violent twist, the werewolf smashed a clawed hand into Enzo's chest and hurled him off in one brutal blow.

Enzo's body cracked through another tree trunk, splinters exploding outward. He landed hard, rolling, then staggered back to his feet, fur bristling, teeth bared in a feral snarl. "Don't let that bastard bite you!" he shouted.

The werewolf rose again, looming, its wounds already knitting together with unnatural speed. The charred flesh sizzled, then mended itself, bone pushing back into place. Finch cursed under his breath.

The real danger of a red-eyed werewolf was it could infect others with lycanthropy—the curse of the werewolf. Once cursed, there were no easy cures. It was a damage to the *heart and soul cores* of a person's being, forcing them to transform into a raging monster whenever they experienced powerful emotions.

Only red-eyed werewolves could pass the curse to others. They were a menace, and every magical society everywhere had a standing order to kill them on sight.

Curses were nothing to mess with.

And while Finch *could* rewind time, he knew certain things weren't undone by Chronos's magic. Like his memory. But that also meant some magics would linger with him... and one of those was curses. If Finch's heart or soul core was corrupted, he would take that with him when rewinding time. Just as his memory wasn't undone, neither would a time rewind undo damage to the deepest part of his core.

But he didn't want to escape the situation just yet. If they could handle this, perhaps this werewolf could be purged before it hurt anyone else.

The wolf's glowing eyes locked on Finch.

Smudge shrieked, leaping at the wolf's legs. The goblin clung with shocking strength, clawing and biting, distracting the monster for precious seconds.

Finch raised Starfall again, the grip of bone cold in his hand. He squeezed the trigger once more. The bullet ripped through the werewolf's shoulder, spinning it half around.

But the werewolf wasn't down for the count yet. Instead, with terrifying speed, it seized Smudge and flung him into the underbrush. The goblin wailed as he disappeared in the pine needles.

Enzo roared, shaking the trees. He charged again, and the two wolves collided in an explosion of claws and teeth. Finch took aim, desperate for a clean shot, but the two beasts were locked too tightly. He couldn't risk hitting Enzo.

With rage fueling his power, Enzo slammed the enemy wolf down and then sank his teeth into the beast's shoulder. The red-eyed monster clawed Enzo across the face, and blood splattered the nearby trees. They rolled, crashed, broke through another tree. The ground shook with their violence.

Then the werewolf raked Enzo across the ribs, and broke free.

It staggered backward, one leg torn and weeping blood. Still, its eyes burned like molten coals. Before Enzo could stand, the werewolf turned and ran into the darkness. It was gone from sight in less than a few seconds, seemingly slipping into the shadows.

Gone.

The woods fell silent, save for the crackle of smoldering pine and Enzo's ragged panting.

Kull lowered her phone, eyes wide, her neon hoodie glowing faintly in the moonlight. "Wow. That was epic. Enzo, you looked incredible! Adair, you weren't even injured. That's kind of impressive." She furrowed her brow and glanced around. "Wait, what happened to Smudge?"

The little goblin was nowhere to be found. Finch was certain he hadn't died, but he had no idea where he would be, either.

Finch holstered Starfall, scanning the tree line with hard eyes. The werewolf was still out there. Wounded, but alive.

Enzo, still in his werewolf form, stood to his full and impressive height. His clothing was torn in multiple places, his tank top barely a napkin's worth of fabric, and his sweatpants now a pair of shorts. His Crocs had been completely ruined by his clawed feet.

In this form, Enzo had a tail and tall, pointed ears. He was the spitting image of the classic werewolf, but at least he wasn't foaming at the mouth and out of control.

Enzo had been practicing for months to get his beast under control. And while he still panted and glared as though he was on the edge of killing, it was clear he wouldn't attack anyone randomly.

He shot a glower over at Kull. *"You couldn't smell there was a werewolf nearby?"*

"I thought I was smelling you," Kull said, indignant. "Why didn't *you* smell it?"

"I... don't know. Something isn't right with these woods. I

swear there's something lingering in the air that's making things difficult."

Finch went around and stomped on the still-burning embers. After a moment of silent contemplation, he pulled the note from the office out of his coat pocket. The client had a missing son...

"You don't think the werewolf is the reason this kid is missing, do you?" Finch asked.

Enzo shook his head. "I hope not." Then he flashed his fangs. "Most of those contagious wolves lose a lot of their mind. I suspect *your boi the goblin* was helping that monster. Smudge pretends to get hit by a vehicle, and then lures people into the woods so the wolf can eat them."

"Sounds like a Grimm fairy tale," Kull muttered.

Finch sighed. "Why would Smudge do that? What does the goblin get out of it?"

"Don't goblins like trinkets and treasure and all that bullshit?" Enzo growled. "He might've done it to pick the pockets of the corpses. Or maybe the wolf threatened his life, I don't know. Either way, he's an accomplice."

"Hmm." Finch gritted his teeth, hating the thought of leaving the woods in such a dangerous state. "We came here for a missing kid case..." Then again, the real reason they were here was to kill time until the egg hatched. What did it matter if they messed around and solved multiple problems while in Tahoe?

Contagious werewolves were a threat to everyone.

"We can't let that curse-carrying dog get away." Enzo's fur stood on end, and his ears lay flat against his skull. "Adair, we need to rewind time. Now. We have to kill that son of a bitch in these woods no matter what. He can't be allowed to escape."

His words were filled with conviction and rage, and Finch knew why. Enzo had once been a cop for the Oakland

PD, his real name *Elijiah Harris*, but an unfortunate run-in with a contagious werewolf had left Enzo cursed. The police chief hid Enzo's infection from his family and had instead claimed he had been killed on the job. That was when Enzo changed his name and career—and was forced to live away from his wife and daughter.

Finch was certain Enzo hated all red-eyed werewolves with a blazing passion.

"All right," Finch said. "I'll rewind time and we'll deal with the wolf here in the woods."

With a shaky hand, Kull touched Finch's shoulder. "Well, uh, do we really need to, though? I mean, every second counts in a missing kid case, right?"

While true, if the mother was calling a PI firm, Finch knew it meant the child had been missing for a while. Most individuals called the police first, and only once they got desperate—after several search attempts had failed and the police had no leads—did they start contacting everyone from *fortune tellers* to *private investigators in cities three hours away.*

"The mother probably isn't awake at midnight," Finch said. "We can handle this werewolf before moving on."

Kull tapped the tips of her fingers together, the corners of her mouth tilting down. She said nothing else.

Enzo patted Finch on the back. "Thank you. Let's do this."

Finch activated his magic. Everything froze. The remaining embers, the few pine needles falling to the ground, and even the wind. Then the color drained from the area. The blue and purple of the night sky, the green of the trees—everything became black and white, like an old movie from the 1940s.

And normally, everything would then melt until there was nothing left but a white void.

But that didn't happen this time.

Finch held his breath, confused when his magic didn't

immediately work like it always did. Enzo and Kull were frozen and colorless, like they had been ripped from a coloring book. They had the Mark of Chronos, but that didn't let them experience the temporal landscape between shifts. It just allowed them to remember what had happened after each loop.

So what was happening? Why had the time magic stopped?

"Hello, Adair Finch," someone said, their voice cool and confident.

Finch whirled on his heel, white embers flickering from his breath as his anxiety spiked. The only *thing* that had ever spoken to him in the empty timescape was Chronos himself, and this new voice was definitely not Chronos.

From between the blackened pines, a figure emerged.

He was tall, over six feet, and he wore a suit cut from something that wasn't cloth but more like the darkness between stars. It was a sharp three-piece ensemble that shimmered faintly with constellations whenever he shifted. The air bent around him, as if gravity itself bowed in deference.

His face was striking. He had a sharp jaw and a slight smirk. His hair was ink-black, swept back in a way that seemed both old-world regal and effortlessly modern. The man's eyes gave away his magical nature more than the outfit. One eye was a deep, human brown while the other glowed like an azure flame. Absolute blue.

Which made Finch realize this new person still had their color. He didn't. Finch was just as colorless as his surroundings, caught in the middle of time rewriting itself.

As the man walked forward, horns sprouted from his temples. They spiraled outward, seemingly made of silver, until they resembled the curled horns of a goat.

"Do you know who I am?" the man asked.

Finch took a few breaths to steady himself. "Judging by your fashion and the ego? Someone who wants me to think he's important."

The newcomer chuckled. "I didn't realize you'd be so... irreverent." He stopped short of Finch's reach. "I am Aeon. Father of the Zodiac. Keeper of the Thirteenth Sign."

That explained why he could appear within the timescape Finch had created. Aeon was another god of time, similar to Chronos and also his enemy. To make matters worse, Aeon was the one Chronos had said was hunting for the egg.

Aeon wanted it destroyed.

CHAPTER
NINE

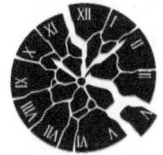

'**ve been looking for you,"** Aeon said. "Waiting until you activated Chronos's magic so I could finally spot your soul among the sea of billions."

"Why?" Finch asked, feigning ignorance.

Aeon narrowed his eyes, his smirk more realized now. "Don't be obtuse. You know why I'm here."

"All right. Fine. I don't have the egg on me."

It was *technically* the truth. Finch would never lie to a creature that considered itself a god, after all. There were too many problems that could arise from that. He wasn't being perfectly truthful, though...

Aeon laughed, his voice velvety, yet somehow as cold as iron. "Oh, I'm not *physically* here. This is my *Aspect*. Think of it as a projection of my mind come to speak with you."

In the realm of black and white, where time was frozen, Finch wasn't entirely certain what he could do to escape. If Aeon didn't release him, would he be stuck here for all eternity? He felt the presence of his guns, and wondered if this Aspect of Aeon would be susceptible to bullets or fire.

If Aeon was just a projection, Finch doubted it, but he needed to formulate a plan… just in case things went south.

"I've come to offer you a deal," Aeon continued.

"A deal?" Finch sneered. "Go fuck yourself."

"My, how gauche humanity has become. Back when the world was still new, beings knew how to treat divine beings."

Finch hated dealing with gods of any kind. They were all the same. They wanted people to grovel at their feet, but Finch had never been the simpering type. It made all conversations a tad tense. And awkward.

Aeon lifted the brow over his glowing blue eye. "Listen, mortal. Chronos is a primordial monster. There's a reason he was locked away in Tartarus, the Gods' Prison. He tried to eat his first set of children. Or haven't you heard?"

"I know," Finch stated.

Chronos, a model of fatherhood, had heard a prophecy that one of his children would overthrow him. His brilliant solution to the problem was to eat all his children. However, he only managed to eat five—Hestia, Demeter, Hera, Hades, and Poseidon. Zeus, the youngest, was hidden by his mother, Rhea. She gave Chronos a rock swaddled in blankets instead, and Chronos fell for it.

Or so the legends go.

Finch wasn't entirely sure they were accurate. He figured Chronos had attempted to kill his children, but Zeus eventually had overthrown him and locked him away.

But now that Chronos was free of Tartarus, did that mean he would continue to be a monster who went after his own children? It seemed Chronos had had a change of heart. His newest child seemed important to him.

"He wants the power of his new child for his own purposes." Aeon shook his head. "And I don't want that to happen. Give me the egg, and I'll unbind you from Chronos's pact and make another one with you instead. You will be free of his obligations without suffering death, and since I'm the more powerful time god, your magic will be tenfold."

Was Aeon the more powerful god of time? Finch doubted it. He was a *different* god of time, with different abilities and different strengths.

"You have two choices," Finch said. "One involves me kicking your Aspect ass, but none of them involve you touching the egg."

Aeon didn't reply right away. He met Finch's gaze, obviously half amused, half irritated. Then he shook his head. "Do you know who the mother of the egg is?"

"No. And even if I did, I wouldn't tell you."

"Heh. I see." Aeon stepped away, his silver horns shimmering in the otherworldly lighting of the timescape. "I had hoped to avoid unnecessary mess, but you seem determined to bleed for this. My minions are already circling, eager to resolve our little disagreement. Unfortunately for you, their method of resolution involves tearing the breath from your lungs."

"They can try," Finch stated.

Aeon tilted his head. "Try? My chosen now wears the Mark of Sagittarius—the consummate hunter. When he sets his eyes on prey, it doesn't escape. Not ever. But by all means, keep strutting with that inflated bravado. Arrogance makes the fall so much more exquisite."

Before Finch could offer a rebuttal, the black-and-white shapes of the woods melted away. He blinked, and then he was back at the party bus, the colors and the world as they once were. Enzo stood at his left, and Kull at his right.

12:04 a.m.

Enzo, human once again, exhaled. "Okay. We'll go back into the woods and kill this menace. But first..." He headed back into the bus.

Disturbed by what had just happened in the timescape,

Finch glanced at Kull. She forced a smile, and he knew in that moment that she and Enzo had seen nothing. Aeon had spoken to Finch and Finch alone.

He wanted to tell them, but he figured he could do so after they dealt with the werewolf. One problem at a time.

When Enzo returned, he held a five-inch knife wrapped in leather. With careful movements, he removed the blade from its protection. The knife was made of silver, and practically glowed in the moonlight.

"You have a silver dagger?" Kull asked, her eyes widening.

Enzo nodded. "I purchased this a few months after I became... Well, after I was cursed with lycanthropy."

The information settled over Finch like a wet blanket. He knew what it meant. Enzo had thought about taking his own life, and for whatever reason, ultimately hadn't gone through with it.

"You brought it with you?" Finch asked. "Why?"

"I usually keep it close. Just in case."

Kull frowned. "Where was it? In the cat carrier?" She chuckled at her own joke, but when Enzo said nothing, her frown only deepened. "Seriously? You had that in with Meth? That seems messed up..."

Enzo turned the silver knife around in his palm like a bad thought he couldn't quite drop. "I don't know. I feel like if it's with the cat... I'll see him before I do anything rash."

Finch completely understood that sentiment. He would've done the same. That was why he still had pictures of Carter around his apartment. Glancing at a photograph of his brother sometimes made him feel like Carter was still watching him. And Finch really didn't want to disappoint the man by doing something foolish...

"Let's stop talking about this and deal with the killer," Enzo said with a growl. "*C'mon.*"

He took off into the woods ahead of Finch and Kull, half jogging, half running.

Finch walked after, Kull following just behind. Once they entered the woods, pine needles fell onto their heads and shoulders at a steady rate. Kull strode closer to him than ever before, their hands occasionally brushing together.

"Are you still afraid?" Finch whispered.

Kull replied with a single nod, her eyes on the dirt in front of her steps. "I know this will sound silly, but... death just scares me now. It didn't as a mischief spirit, but even the thought of losing you or Enzo makes me feel like... I'll be alone again."

"That's not going to happen."

"Those red-eyed werewolves can be dangerous."

Finch shrugged. "We have the upper hand. And if it does go south, I'll get us out of the situation. I promise."

That seemed to ease her worry. Kull loosened her shoulders and genuinely smiled—the kind that made Finch a little happier whenever he saw it. "I, uh, also wanted to apologize," she whispered.

"*Hurry up, you two,*" Enzo growled from a little way ahead.

Finch waved at him. When he had all the time in the world, few things ever got him rushing.

Enzo headed to the exact spot they had met Smudge before, leaving Kull and Finch behind.

"We need to deal with this werewolf," Finch said, glancing over at Kull. "Whatever you're apologizing for, I'm sure it can wait. And also, I'm pretty certain you don't need to apologize for anything."

"No." Kull shook her head. "I do." After a short exhale, she quickly muttered, "I'm just as bad as all those other people I dated. They were all weird, or pushy, or not vibing with me at all. And here I am, doing the same thing with you... I'm sorry. You made it clear you don't want me to flirt with you. I'm just... really bad at this *finding love* thing."

Finch balled his hands into fists but kept them in his coat pockets. "You're not *that* bad. I, uh, didn't *hate* what you were doing."

Her eyes went wide with the last statement. "R-Really? *You mean it?*" Her volume increased with each syllable.

Finch motioned for her to keep her voice down. "Listen, I just don't know if I'm ready for... uh..." He hated the word, but he said it anyway. "A relationship. So, it's not you, it's me. All right? No need to apologize."

Kull hugged Finch's right arm and squeezed tight. "Really, Adair? You *liked* my flirting?" She laughed as she said, "Does that mean I can keep doing it? So long as, you know, it doesn't really go anywhere because you're not ready? Oh! Maybe you can just tell me when I do something really effective. It'll be a teachable moment!"

Before Finch could answer, they arrived in the small grove of pine trees where they had met Smudge. Finch noticed the bushes swaying, not from wind, but movement.

"We'll talk about this later," he said under his breath.

Kull nodded once, a mischievous grin plastered on her face.

"Smudge," Finch called out. "Are you there? It's me. Adair Finch."

The shrub stopped its shaking. At first, nothing else happened, but then the little pukwudgie emerged, his yellow eyes squinted. When he finally recognized Finch, he gasped.

"Friend," Smudge breathed. He took several steps forward and then stopped. "How...?"

The confusion in his broken English was evident. How did Finch know his name? How had Finch known to call for him? The rewinding of time had undone his memories.

"I rescued you from Maldonaldo's mansion," Finch said as he knelt. "I remember you."

Smudge shook his head, still bewildered. But it lasted only for a few seconds before his expression hardened. "Leave. You must. Monster is here. Will hurt Finch."

"We know. We're looking for the werewolf. Stay back—we'll handle this."

The pukwudgie blinked several times as he absorbed this information. As Finch stood, Smudge grabbed his pant leg and held firm to the fabric.

"Run," Smudge said.

"We're not going to do that."

Enzo's nostrils flared; his bones cracked as his shoulders swelled, ribs expanding as he grew taller and more intimidating. His jaw thickened, teeth lengthening into something not made for words. He dropped the silver knife, then caught it again in a paw hand before it hit the ground.

"Stay behind me," he said, his voice deeper than before. "This one's mine."

Kull nervously chuckled, her neon hoodie a glowstick in the dark. "Uh, what should I be doing about the *big bad wolf*?"

Finch pulled her back, hand closed on her wrist. "Enzo said he wants to handle it, so we'll let him." He stooped, yanking Smudge behind them as well. The little goblin squirmed, but Finch held fast. "I'll protect you. Stay behind me, got it?"

Smudge wrinkled his little gray-green nose. "Friend? Even now?"

Unsure what that meant, Finch didn't reply.

Much to everyone's surprise, the pukwudgie shouted something into the darkness. It had been in a different language—some sort of goblin—and afterward, he went silent. When Finch met his gaze, Smudge simply smiled and nodded.

He was helping?

Somehow.

Fortunately, the silence between them didn't last long. The trees went still. And then they parted.

The red-eyed wolf stepped into the grove, this time walking instead of lunging like it had last time. Eight feet of black muscle and scar tissue, fur raised across its back, its gaze two burning coals. Drool fell from its fangs, coating pine needles. The air reeked of wet copper and rot.

Enzo's fur stood on end. He spread his arms, claws catching moonlight. "There you are, fucker," he whispered, low and savage. "Come at me."

The red-eyed beast obliged.

They collided with a sound like trees splitting under storm-wind. Enzo's claws raked furrows across the monster's ribs, but the wolf slammed him back against a trunk, bark exploding around them. Enzo's answering bite tore a chunk from the wolf's shoulder, spraying black-red blood across the grove.

Kull gasped, and Finch tugged both her and Smudge backward until they were safer in the moonlit shadow of a tall pine. "Don't make any unnecessary noises," Finch whispered, every muscle coiled to spring if the fight headed their way.

The wolves tumbled through the grove, snapping and rending, a storm of fur and blood. Each impact shook the ground. Enzo fought with feral precision—every strike measured, every bite purposeful. But the red-eyed wolf fought like a feral animal, heedless of pain, driven by something deeper than instinct.

"Adair," Kull whispered, holding on to his arm.

"Everything will be fine," he said.

"I know. You'll make sure of it. I just... don't like seeing Enzo get hurt."

Enzo took a claw to the ribs, flesh tearing. He howled but didn't fall. Instead, he rolled with the blow, came up under the wolf's guard, and drove his shoulder into its chest. For a heartbeat they locked, jaws snapping inches apart, hot spittle flying between them.

Then Enzo's hand darted down. The silver knife gleamed before he plunged it into the wolf's heart.

The scream that followed wasn't an animal sound. It was human—raw, ragged, breaking. The wolf convulsed, fell, and then clawed gouges into the earth. Its red eyes flared bright before dimming.

Enzo twisted the blade once, hard. The wolf jerked, then stopped all at once. The body of the monster lay in the pine needles, blood pooling outward and soaking into the dark earth.

Enzo stood, heaving, blood dripping from his muzzle, while his chest was striped with wounds. He pulled the knife from the corpse. "You're not going to infect anyone else, *monster.*"

CHAPTER
TEN

Smudge clung to Finch's leg, whispering something in his broken English. "Bad moon... dead moon..."

Finch gestured to the area. "Enzo, you should sniff around. See if there's anything important here." Then he turned to Kull. "And you can smell magic really well, right? You should also give the area a sweep. Tell me if you notice anything unusual."

"Are we looking for something specific?" Enzo asked, huffing and puffing. "Why search around now?"

"I have a bad feeling about this," Finch muttered. "A missing kid? Rabid werewolves on the loose? We haven't even gotten into the city proper, and already we're plagued with problems. We should at least try to solve some of them before adding more."

Kull laughed and shrugged. "That's only two problems. We've handled way more than before."

"Yeah, well... When I rewound time, Aeon also found me."

"Who is *Aeon?*"

"Another god of time," Finch stated. "The one Chronos warned me about. A god out to smash his egg. And Aeon sent his hunter after me. Someone carrying the Mark of Sagittarius. And knowing my luck, it's Holt."

Enzo walked over, his hulking wolf form frightening in the dim moonlit forest. His fur was splattered with blood, and he loomed over the group, panting, his breathing rushing out in hot streams.

"So we're already swimming in problems?" Enzo exhaled and then offered a wolfish smirk. "Working with you is never dull, is it, Adair?"

After a short nod, Finch shrugged. "We just need to stay one step ahead of them. So, again, if you don't mind, we should search around. Then we should get into Tahoe City as fast as possible."

Kull gave him a sarcastic salute. "Aye, aye!"

Enzo simply nodded.

Enzo strode off first, his nose low, silver knife still clenched awkwardly in one paw hand. Kull went the opposite direction, her neon hoodie a bullseye in the gloom. Finch almost went after her. Instead, he balled his hands into fists and shoved them into his coat pockets.

She will be fine.

That was what he told himself several times until the spike of anxiety left him.

Smudge clung tighter to Finch's leg. "Bad moon... dead moon," he whispered again, like a prayer or a curse.

"You'll be okay," Finch said, easing the goblin off him.

The two waited in the grove of trees. The wind slowly combed the needles. Somewhere far off, water splashed against rocks.

About fifty feet away, Kull stopped at a ring of scuffed earth and then bent over it, her nose wrinkling. "There's a lot of magic here, Adair. This whole forest is, like, *thick*. If that makes sense? There's a lot of spirits here. And witches, I think. Maybe some mystical creatures."

"Anything dangerous?" Finch asked.

Kull laughed and waved a hand. "*So many* dangerous things! I couldn't even begin to list them all."

Joy.

Finch rolled his eyes and sighed. It was just going to be one of those days. "Anything near us or that I should be worried about?"

"Probably not. Most of it seems old. Ancient, even."

Deep within the trees, Enzo rumbled. "Over here." His voice in that half-wolf throat came out low and feral, but it carried.

Finch and Kull hurried over, Smudge skittering at their heels. Enzo stood at the base of a pine, rib cage heaving, muzzle stained. He had pushed back to something closer to human—still too tall, still too furred—but his eyes were more human than beast now. In his free hand, he held something small, limp, and wrong.

A child's sneaker.

It had blue canvas, a white rubber toe, and little rockets up the side. It was shredded along the ankle, the laces snapped. Something dark brown had dried into the fabric on one side.

Enzo stared at it, his gaze distant.

Kull half gasped. "Is that?"

"Kid-sized." Enzo turned it in his palm. The torn edge trembled a little because his hand was. "It's fresh."

Finch felt a tightness pull his chest inward. He stepped closer, took in the scuff marks around the tree—small prints, bare toes dug into dirt, then a smear where something had fallen, then... bigger prints overlaying them, pads and claws, impossibly heavy.

Lycanthropy was a terrible curse. It transformed whoever had it into a mindless werewolf monster. Even children.

Enzo swallowed. His ears had flattened to his skull at

some point; his tail hung limp. "Tell me I didn't just kill a kid."

"We don't know that," Finch said, keeping his voice steady for both their sakes.

"Have you... marked the time since I fought the... beast?"

"No. I haven't."

If Finch rewound time now, the wolf would spring back to life as though nothing had ever happened. If the werewolf really was the missing child, they had some difficult decisions to make.

Smudge tiptoed closer, his yellow eyes wide. He pointed at the shoe and frowned, but offered no words.

Kull edged in. She reached out like she might touch Enzo's arm, thought better of it, and tucked her hand back into her sleeve. "Let's not jump to sad conclusions," she said, too brightly. "Let's do a smell check. Maybe this is the missing kid's shoe, and the big bad we bagged earlier was something else."

Enzo dragged air through his teeth and bent to the ground. He sniffed long and slow, working the dirt like a bloodhound, then shifted right, then left. The fur along his spine rose again, not in anger this time.

"Two trails," he finally said. "Small human feet. A boy, I think. He ran. Then... it swerves, hits here." He tapped the scuffed patch with a claw tip. "After that, it's all paws. Same direction. Same cadence. Same scent, but... changed." He lifted the shoe, voice thinning. "He changed."

Kull's mouth opened. Closed. Her bravado evaporated like breath. "Oh," she said in a tiny voice.

Smudge tugged Finch's coat. "Bad moon." He tapped his own chest, then circled his fingers in the air, as if turning a dial. "More wolves."

"More?" Finch asked.

With a nod, Smudge pointed back toward the road. "More."

A small bit of hope welled in Finch. "Listen, maybe the red-eyed wolf isn't the same wolf as the kid. Maybe the kid was one of its victims."

"You really think that?" Enzo whispered.

"That's what red-eyed wolves do. Their curse drives them mad, and they're driven to infect others, just like vampires are driven to drink blood."

Enzo set the knife's tip into the soil and took three slow breaths. His silhouette shrank another inch toward human. When he spoke again, it was steadier. "We're going to find out. We're not guessing. That's not how I operate."

"Agreed," Finch said. He pointed at the ground. "Can we find any other clues?"

Enzo moved. When he worked a scene, he got methodical, cop-like. His circle of searching widened from the first clue. In a matter of minutes, he found a second shoe dug into a root crook twenty feet to the west—the sole gnawed through. Then a third shoe. And a fourth. As he went, he also pulled threads of a torn sock snagged on a shrub. Finally, he spotted a pair of denim jeans—ones far too large for a boy.

"Unless our kid is in his late teens and has four legs, we're dealing with several people who have transformed here," Enzo said. He returned with the evidence, and Finch nodded.

The wolf was turning people. Perhaps their missing kid was one.

Finch motioned back toward the bus. "Okay, let's head into Tahoe City and see exactly how many people are missing."

"Good idea," Kull said.

Enzo left his silver knife in the ground as he turned toward the road. "Don't re-mark the time, Adair. If the kid really is the one... cursing people... maybe we'll need another solution than the one I was offering."

The way he said it reminded Finch that Enzo was a father. He had a small daughter—one he had left so he would never hurt her with his werewolf form. Perhaps this whole case was hitting a little too close to home.

They rode the rest of the way into Tahoe City without saying much. Kull didn't even turn on the music; she just sat next to Finch, enjoying a smoothie in silence. For the remainder of the trip, Enzo held Meth in his lap, petting the elderly cat in a slow and absent-minded way.

Smudge was also with them. He sat on one of the cushioned seats, sipping on a green smoothie Kull had called *The Master Chief*. The little goblin made contented slurping noises the entire way.

At 12:45 a.m. and they finally arrived at their destination.

The bus's headlights swept over the empty streets, glinting off flakes of old snow in the gutters and the reflective eyes of a raccoon that looked like it had seen too much. The lake lay to the west, huge, black, and smooth. The docks poked out into the water like thin ribs. The mountains beyond were only shapes, a jagged promise that daylight would make good on.

There were dozens of storefronts, all housed in buildings constructed in the 1970s and never renovated. Finch spotted outfitters with mannequins dressed for business, a bakery with chairs stacked on tables, and a boutique that sold sweaters expensive enough to make a person reconsider their need for *warmth*.

"I know it's late, but I imagined Tahoe to be livelier," Kull muttered.

The traffic lights took turns blessing empty intersections with red and green.

"It closes up early around here," Enzo said. "The night doesn't belong to the mortals in these parts."

Kull tapped her lower lip with a finger. "That's odd because Harper said there were *off the hook* parties that happened in Tahoe all the time. Most parties happen at night, at least in my experience."

"Your friend is probably talking about the casinos."

They came to the roundabout by the lake, and the statue there wore snow in its creases like dandruff. Beyond, the water picked up a slow breeze and set it down again.

"Where are we going?" Enzo said, glancing out the window with a glower.

"I got us a hotel, obviously," Kull replied.

"Is it as conspicuous as this party bus?"

Kull huffed out a dismissive laugh. "No. Of course not. This place caters to high-end clients. And you know it's true because the description of the hotel on their website leaned pretty hard on words like *rustic* and *bespoke*."

"What, did the wood they used for construction go to college?" Enzo quipped.

Kull shrugged. "I dunno. But it was expensive. And expensive things are usually good, right?"

"What does the word *bespoke* even mean?"

"Oh, I had to look that up. It means *specially made to order* or like *custom made* or something like that."

Finch sometimes forgot Kull had a super popular social media alter ego named Fox-Pistol. She made millions in sponsorships and ad revenue. He wasn't really aware of the details, just that she was plenty well off.

They took a right where the road rose between shadowed

trees and expensive driveways, then another, cresting a low ridge. The hotel was made of timber and glass, nested among pines, with all peaked roofs and bronze accents. River-stone chimneys dominated the hotel's silhouette.

Kull sat up straighter. "Ooooh, look at how fun this place is!"

A brass bear squatted beside the entrance. Over the doors, a dark wooden plaque showed the hotel's name burned into it: *The Alder Crown.*

"How many rooms did you book us?" Enzo asked.

"I didn't book us rooms." Kull stood in the middle of the bus and offered him a wink. "I booked us four *suites*. They're even better."

Enzo snorted. "Going for bougie, I see."

"Is this place run by mortals?" Finch rubbed at his side. "Or is it maintained by people in the know? Elves or someone else supernatural?"

Kull shook her head. "It's just a normal, run-of-the-mill, super expensive retreat hotel. I told you—my production crew is going to come join us in the morning. They said they'd be here around nine or ten, so I figured it was better to get some normal accommodations."

In all ways sardonic, Finch slowly panned his gaze over to Smudge. "Okay, so what're we going to do about our mascot?"

Smudge waved his left hand while holding on to his smoothie with his right. Once he had finished taking a sip, he smiled, showing off his sharp teeth. "Smudge," he said as he pointed to his chest. Then he pointed to the smoothie. "Smudge like."

With a laugh, Kull swished her red hair over her shoulder. "Don't worry. We have a cat carrier, don't we? This hotel allows all sorts of animals. We'll be fine."

CHAPTER
ELEVEN

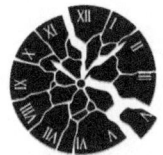

E veryone clambered out of the bus, the evening cold slapping their cheeks and turning their breath to mist. Enzo hauled the cat carrier up to the front door, Meth hissing the entire way. The cat wasn't hissing at any of the humans—just the goblin squished up against him. When Enzo put the carrier under his arm, however, it was difficult to see what all was inside.

Enzo also wore a hoodie as neon pink as Kull's. His tank top underneath was stained with so much blood he might as well be a murder scene, and even though the hoodie was a size or two too small, it was better than nothing.

Not the best disguise Finch had ever seen, but it would do.

They entered the Alder Crown as a group.

The entry rugs were thick enough to bury ankles. Somewhere inside, a piano played soft and welcoming music.

The lobby had that curated wilderness smell: cedar, lemon oil, and the ghost of cigar smoke. It also had a single piece of interesting taxidermy—an elk head, antlers curved together to resemble a crown.

The hotel was blatant with its luxury. There was heated slate underfoot, a chandelier the size of a small boat overhead, and the reception desk itself was milled alder inlaid with a darker burl, the grain curling like smoke. Behind it, shelves of small, leather-spined ledgers sat in perfect order.

The clerk—AVA, her name tag announced—lifted her gaze and smiled brightly, despite the hour. Her braid was corded neatly, her suit a shade of forest that only looked black until the light shone across it. She gave everyone the once over and made no comment.

"Welcome to the Alder Crown," she said. "Checking in?"

Kull stepped in front of Finch and held out her ID. "Yup! I have a reservation under Samantha Garson."

"Who the fuck is Samantha Garson?" Enzo whispered, his eyes narrowed.

Finch shot him a glare and replied in an equally quiet tone. "It's her human name."

"Oh. Right. I keep forgetting."

Which Finch found amusing because *Kull* wasn't in any way a human name. How could Enzo forget she had something more normal she used for government paperwork?

Ava's perfectly polite smile never faltered, but Finch saw the calculation behind her eyes: three people, one without shoes and wearing a tiny hoodie, a suspiciously lumpy carrier hissing like steam from a cursed kettle, and a redheaded woman too bubbly for the middle of the night.

But nothing said professionalism like the way she ignored that all. "Of course." Ava gestured them forward. "We've prepared your suites on the third floor. Lake view. Complimentary champagne and truffles will be waiting."

Kull clapped her hands together. "See? This is what

happens when you go classy." She shot Enzo a look over her shoulder. "Rustic. Bespoke."

The man snorted. "Those are just words that mean *a waste of money*."

Finch noticed Ava's gaze slide briefly toward the cat carrier. "Pets are welcome," she said. "Though… we do ask that exotic animals remain inside their suite at all times."

The carrier rattled. A sharp goblin cackle leaked through. Finch coughed into his fist. "He's, uh, very well-trained."

Ava handed over four keycard sleeves, each embossed with a golden pinecone. "Our evening bellhop will escort you to your rooms."

A young man practically materialized from nowhere, dressed in a uniform so crisp it could have cut paper.

"If you require anything else, simply dial zero." Ava tilted her head as she smiled even wider. "We pride ourselves on discretion."

The young bellhop took them straight to the elevators, where they were whisked up in silence. Then the doors opened, revealing a short hallway lit with decorative lanterns, and the carpet patterned with pinecones and crowns.

There were only four suites on this floor, which meant they had it all to themselves. The bellhop motioned to the first, and Kull handed over the key. Then she pointed Enzo toward it.

After a long exhale, Enzo entered his room, the carrier jostling around now. "I'll see you two in the morning." Then he stopped halfway inside. "What time?"

"Let's meet at seven," Finch replied. "We'll talk to our client then and get all the details."

"Sounds like a plan."

Enzo shut the door, and the bellhop continued to the next.

With dramatic flair, Kull held up her keycard. "Okay, thank you, Mr. Bellhop, we don't need any more assistance. Well, except for maybe when it's breakfast time."

"Each suite comes with complimentary room service," the man said.

"Oh, good." With a giggle, Kull unlocked the door. "We're probably going to abuse it."

The bellhop nervously chuckled and nodded once. Then the young man waited for half a second longer before turning on his heel and hurrying away.

Finch held out his hand. "Where's my key?"

Holding the door open, Kull motioned him inside. "The other two suites are for my crew."

"We're not sharing a suite," Finch immediately said.

"Each of these suites has three bedrooms. You can have your own, I'll have my own, and the third one will be for all the pancakes and waffles I'll be ordering in the morning." Kull let out another giggle as she flew inside.

Finch sighed, but he wasn't entirely certain what else to do. Kull was definitely *mischievous*. She had waited all the way until they were entering the suites to even bring this issue up.

Resigned to his fate, Finch entered.

The suite was sprawling, a cross between a mountain lodge and ski retreat. The main sitting area had vaulted ceilings with exposed beams carved into curling vine motifs. A river-stone fireplace dominated one wall, flames already flickering like they had been waiting for them to arrive. The furniture was all leather and fur throws, but the kind of fur that looked guilt-free and fantastically expensive.

"I love this place," Kull said, spinning in a circle. "Told you this place was fun!" Then she stopped mid-spin and stared at the minibar. "Ooooh, there's the complimentary champagne!

And a tray of truffles!" She grabbed one and popped it into her mouth with all the energy of an ADHD squirrel.

Finch took in the details: a wet bar stocked with local spirits, a glass chess set on a low table, plush chairs arranged for fireside conspiracies. A wall of windows opened onto a private balcony with a view of the lake, black and endless beneath the pale glimmer of the moon. Outside, two steaming hot tubs waited, ringed by fairy lights.

"Those tubs are calling my name," Kull said once she swallowed. "Maybe we could take a dip later? I bet flirting is a lot easier in a hot tub."

"Hard pass."

No matter how many times Kull somehow orchestrated there to be hot tubs around them, Finch adamantly refused to get in one. Although, he was impressed with how often she managed to pull it off.

"That's my room," Kull said, pointing.

The bedrooms branched off from the main area, each with its own theme.

Kull's room was all champagne-gold linens and floor-to-ceiling windows. A freestanding copper tub gleamed like treasure in the adjoining bathroom.

Finch picked the room on the opposite side of the suite. It was done in stormy grays and deep forest greens. The bed was a fortress of blankets and oversized pillows, sturdy enough to survive the craziest of evenings.

"We should get some sleep," he said.

Kull nodded once. "Oh, yeah, probably. And then we'll tackle all our problems in the morning." She gulped down a second truffle. "Sleep well, Adair!"

For some reason, Finch's face heated upon hearing that. He refused to glance in Kull's direction and instead offered her a half-hearted wave before retreating to his room.

Finch awoke to the smell of waffles, his eyelids heavy.

It wasn't the faint, fake smell of hotel breakfast batter, either. This smell was decadent. Rich vanilla, toasted sugar, and butter melting into perfect golden squares. His stomach growled.

At first, he thought he had dreamed everything. The room was too soft and perfect to be real. But the scent only grew stronger, accompanied by the muffled clatter of plates and… chortling.

Finch shoved himself upright, rubbing grit from his eyes. He immediately checked the time. An old habit he couldn't break.

6:45 a.m.

His coat lay draped over a velvet chair, Starfall and Agony holstered and within reach. That was also an old habit from when he used to carry a side piece everywhere. They always had to be within arm's reach.

He threw on his shirt, his pants, and his coat before walking barefoot out of his room and into the center of the suite.

Kull sat cross-legged on the couch like a queen of chaos. A tray of room-service breakfast was sprawled before her: waffles, pancakes, a mountain of bacon, a fruit platter arranged like an abstract painting, and a pitcher of orange juice sweating in the firelight.

She wore a pair of shorts that were short enough that Finch immediately took note and then averted his gaze. She had a long button-up shirt as a pajama top, for some reason he couldn't quite understand.

"Why are you wearing that?" he asked.

"What? This?" Kull tugged on the collar. The shirt hung

loose on her slender frame, pale fabric draping over curves that were difficult to deny. "Well, in all the cute and happy romance movies, the girl always wears the boy's clothes to bed. I wanted to get some practice in before it happened to me, so I purchased several men's shirts to sleep in."

Finch dragged a hand down his face and groaned. "You're *practicing* wearing men's shirts to bed?"

"I'm getting pretty dang good at it, too! Look at this."

Kull popped the top two buttons with deliberate slowness, the soft *click-click* of fabric releasing far too loud in the quiet room. Finch's gaze was drawn to the deep V that exposed skin almost down to her bellybutton without actually revealing any of the main events.

"Sexy, right?" she asked with a coy smile.

Finch, frozen in place, was silent for a full three seconds, which was three seconds too long. He finally shook his head and forced himself to stare at the fruit platter.

"Yes. Sexy. Good job." He gritted his teeth and took a careful step toward the table, doing his best to ignore the sight of her perched there like a temptress in a breakfast-themed porno. "But it's wildly inappropriate breakfast attire. For new couples, I mean."

She leaned forward on her elbows, which only made matters worse. "Oh? And what's the appropriate attire? Flannel onesies?"

"Yes. Exactly." He snatched a plate and loaded it with waffles, pretending this was a normal conversation and not an escalating assault on his self-control. "Preferably ones that come with several blankets. To cover yourself even more."

"Do you really want me to cover my ravishing shoulders?" She gasped theatrically, pulling the shirt slightly wider.

Finch's ears went hot. He poured syrup over his plate. He knew, at some level, this was his fault. He had given her permission to flirt with him, after all. A part of him felt bad, because he wasn't reciprocating, but another part of him had to admit, it was... fun.

It had been a long time since Finch felt anything like he had this morning. But he still couldn't seem to bring himself to flirt back.

"Kull, if you don't stop messing around, I'm going to eat all the waffles. Without you."

"*What?*" Kull grabbed her plate protectively and then pulled her shirt back up into a more suitable position. "You wouldn't really do that, would you?"

"Do you really want to find out?"

"Rude." But then she smiled. "But a little mischievous. I like that."

Finch sat down across from her, stabbing a piece of waffle with unnecessary force. "You know what's the worst kind of mischievous? You dragging me into this ridiculous romantic comedy subplot while there's a kid out there who needs our help."

Kull swirled a strawberry through a dollop of whipped cream. "Hmm, you're right. This is very serious business. A missing kid. Werewolves. Mysterious time gods. Absolutely no room for fun or breakfast shenanigans." Then she shot him a frown. "Except... Oh, wait! I'm with a man who *literally rewinds time so that we have infinite amounts of it.*"

"Don't sass me," he said, but he had to work not to smile. It was the kind of sarcastic humor he appreciated.

Perhaps a romance subplot wasn't so bad.

Just for now. Just for pretend.

"I'm just spittin' facts." Kull popped the strawberry into her mouth, winking at him over the rim of her coffee cup.

Several bangs on the main suite door echoed throughout the vast room.

"It's almost time to go," Enzo called from the other side. "C'mon. Grab your things and let's get a move on!"

CHAPTER
TWELVE

Finch and Kull exited the suite one after the other. Still wearing the same clothes he had on yesterday, Finch felt a little foolish, but at least he hadn't coated himself in blood. Kull, on the other hand, looked like a whole new person.

Her outfit was the kind of thing that made entire rooms pause mid-breath. Her black turtleneck clung to her like a sassier second skin, while her red skirt was so short it would've gotten her suspended from college. Sheer black tights stretched over her long legs, and her black heels clicked against the hardwood with a sound that screamed, *confidence or chaos—dealer's choice.*

Enzo had a new pair of Crocs. He had also traded his bloodstained tank for a dark Henley shirt and jacket, but he still wore the same gray sweatpants.

He raised an eyebrow at Kull and frowned. "Are you going to a nightclub at seven in the morning?"

Kull spun in a circle, her red skirt flaring slightly. "Oh, this little thing? I didn't think anyone would notice." She fluttered her eyelashes in faux innocence. "I just threw together some random things I packed."

"Uh-huh. You look like a femme fatale in a spy movie. Just don't get us arrested for indecent exposure. Or international espionage."

Kull sashayed past him, smiling. "Thank you, Enzo. I *was* going for the vibe of a spy movie. I'm going to be the wild card who finds a crucial clue that helps us find that missing child. Just you wait and see."

Finch motioned to the hallway. The two followed him, but halfway to the front, Finch couldn't help but glance over his shoulder several times. Was someone following him? Someone other than Enzo and Kull?

If so, he saw nothing.

The morning light over Tahoe City was grayish white, like watery milk. As a group of three, they rolled out of the Alder Crown and went straight to the party bus.

7:06 a.m.

Once everyone climbed inside, and the driver motioned he was ready, they headed off into the city. According to Finch's notes, their client lived on the outskirts of town, and it wouldn't take them long to arrive.

Apparently, the bus also came equipped with a coffee machine, and Finch took a moment to abuse that feature. Kull also had a cup, but Enzo refused, grumping something about how he hated anything that came from *beans*.

And then, much to Finch's surprise, Smudge appeared near the machine, making grabby hands at a cup as Kull poured herself some.

"Oh, hello," she said, cheery in all regards, despite the early hour. "You want some?"

Smudge nodded.

"Where did he come from?" Finch demanded.

Enzo snorted and then shrugged. "I don't know. I left him in the room with Meth."

"Pukwudgies can alter the perceptions of humans," Kull said matter-of-factly. "Maybe he seemed invisible and just followed us into the bus. That's what little goblins do most of the time, ya know. Hide around, waiting to swipe something."

Finch didn't like this. They still didn't fully understand Smudge's relationship to the werewolves. It seemed obvious to him that Smudge and the red-eyed wolf had been in cahoots, but what did that entail? And why?

"I don't know if we can trust Smudge," Finch muttered. "We don't know any of his motives and since he barely speaks English, we can't really rely on him for any sort of complex plans."

"Oh? You want to speak to him in his native goblin language?" Kull tilted her head and then turned her gaze down on Smudge.

She said something in a garbled tongue that sounded as though her mouth was full of food and she was attempting to chew through every syllable.

Widening his eyes, Smudge replied in the same strange language, his tone now gruffer and confident. He, too, sounded as though he had shoved toffee into his mouth and couldn't stop chewing through his words.

Once their weird conversation was over, Kull smiled at Finch. "Well, Smudge here said his motives are to make sure he's never captured by anyone again. He came to Tahoe to align himself with some witches or vampires, but when he was rejected, ended up working for werewolves."

"So he *was* luring people in the forest," Enzo said through gritted teeth.

Kull nodded. "Yes, but he just told me he'd much rather be with Adair. He's ready to pledge loyalty."

"Wait, wait." Finch held up hand. "You can speak *goblin*? And you didn't tell us?"

Kull threw back some of her red hair. "Uh, I'm still part mischief spirit, and *all* spirits can speak any language. That's, like, part of our charm."

"Really?" Enzo asked.

"Of course." She snorted out a laugh. "Did you think I went to elementary school to learn English?"

"I… well… Never thought about it, actually."

Finch shook his head. "Okay. Fine. That's wonderful. Ask Smudge where all the werewolves are hiding."

With a smile, Kull resumed her goblin conversation with Smudge. The pukwudgie quickly replied. Then Kull turned back to Finch. "He said you have to accept his pledge of loyalty first. Then he'll betray the werewolves."

"Feh." Finch rolled his eyes. "All right. I accept."

Another garbled round, and Kull said, "Apparently, the werewolves mostly hide in a place called Desolation Wilderness."

"What?" Finch sighed. "What is that?"

"It's a federally protected wilderness area," Enzo injected. "About sixty-three thousand acres. It used to be known as *Devil's Valley,* but now it's a backpacking location with little trails and some shit. People go fishing there."

"And they live in a federal park?" Finch asked, narrowing his eyes.

"A lot of wolves choose to live away from people after they turn." Enzo's voice grew softer with each word, his gaze becoming distant. "It's easier to avoid hurting anyone else, and your new lycanthropy senses help with survival. Hunting. Fishing. I almost went feral myself, but I had the boys back in Oakland. They got me a job at the bar. That was all that stopped me from going to a place like Desolation Wilderness."

"I see…"

"It's much too large a reservation to just walk around searching willy-nilly. I know we have all the time in the world, but that would be ridiculous."

"If we get even one tiny lead, it might make the search infinitely easier."

Kull held up a finger. "Smudge said there's two red-eyed werewolves, and they're just in the woods, but the people they turn go to the nature preserve."

Finch pinched the bridge of his nose. "And Smudge can talk to the contagious wolves? They aren't just… mindless monsters?"

One more round of chewing language, and Kull nodded. "He says he uses his pukwudgie magic to project images in their heads, and they can talk to him that way, but they aren't fully mentally stable. He convinced them to wait in the woods so they didn't destroy the city. However, in order to get their protection, he had to bring them food…"

Enzo crossed his arms and growled. He hated the thought of werewolves spreading their curse, that was for certain, but Finch was proud he didn't transform due to the information. It was obvious to Finch that Enzo was getting better at controlling the rage.

"Let's move past that for now," Finch said. "If he knows where the red-eyed wolves' victims are, we can at least go speak to them later. Maybe one of them is our missing kid."

Right as he said that, the bus came to a halt, the brakes screeching a bit in protest. They were in a residential district, parked in front of a blue-trimmed duplex. The bus door opened, and Finch stepped out first.

The entire neighborhood was plastered in flyers, each displaying the school picture of a ten-year-old boy with stubborn hair and a missing front tooth. The poster read:

Jason Stonewell
Age 10

Last seen wearing a white hoodie and cargo shorts

If you have information, please call the number below

Finch took one of the flyers and studied the picture. Then he walked over to the duplex, examined the address, and went straight to the one he had on file. Enzo and Kull joined him a moment later, each of them focused on the neighborhood.

Finch knocked on the front door. A neighbor's dog barked, and a wind chime trembled. The door opened on a woman wearing a T-shirt that read: LAKE DAY. Her brown hair was in a bun losing the battle. Purple bags hung beneath her eyes.

She looked to be in her thirties, but her face, haggard from exhaustion, had aged twenty years past that. The woman wasn't in good shape.

"Ms. Stonewell?" Finch asked.

"Y-Yes?"

"I'm Adair Finch. Private detective. You called my office, 24-Hour Investigations."

Her eyes instantly brightened as she nodded and took a step back. "Come in! Please, come in. I had no idea you were on your way, but I'm so thankful you're here."

Finch walked into the house, Kull at his side and Enzo taking his time to glance around. The front room and kitchen were just one giant rectangular room.

The place was warm, small, and clearly lived-in. Crayon art hung on the fridge, and there was a Lego fort mid-siege on the living room rug.

The whole house smelled of coffee and laundry soap, but Finch didn't mind. The pictures on the wall were what really caught his attention. There was one of Jason in a dinosaur hoodie, and one of Jason playing at the lake with a couple of friends.

"You can call me Grace," the woman said as she grabbed herself a cup of coffee and walked back to Finch.

Then she motioned to her couch and coffee table. Finch and Kull sat, but Enzo stood by the front door, as though someone might come through at any moment. Grace sat at the very edge of a cushion and faced Finch as much as possible.

"First," Finch said, "I'm sorry you're going through this. We'll move fast. Can you walk me through the last day you saw Jason? From start to finish, as precisely as you can?"

Grace wrapped both hands around a chipped mug. When she spoke, it was almost rehearsed. She had said this a hundred times before.

"It was Saturday. Two weeks ago. I had the morning shift at the bakery. He stayed with our neighbor, Eva. I came home around noon. Jason and his friends, Tommy and Ben, wanted to ride scooters. They always go to the path by the lake. Jason grabbed his white hoodie, and then took a granola bar from the kitchen. He asked me if he could take his drone. I said no, because the last time it got stuck in a tree."

Grace's mouth twitched, like a crack forming in a dam that held back all emotion. "Jason gets… big feelings. He got so sad when the drone was stuck. It was all he could think about until we got it down."

"Do you remember the approximate time he left the house?" Finch asked.

A small piece of Finch wished he had the ability to rewind time more than just a simple twenty-four hours… But that wasn't possible. This terrible event had happened long before, and he was unable to solve it with a quick use of his abilities.

Grace gathered herself. "Two fifteen. He promised to be

back by five. At five twenty I called around. None of the parents had seen him. Tommy and Ben said Jason wanted to keep going along the trail, but they ended up going home early for dinner." Her voice thinned. "The other boys made it back to their families. Jason didn't."

Kull slid a tissue box across the coffee table without making it a production. Grace took one and half smiled in thanks.

"Does Jason carry a phone?" Finch asked.

"He has a smartwatch. I would send him texts." She flicked a glance at the empty dock on the counter. "But it has to be charged every night. I doubt it's still functioning."

"Did the police search for him?" Enzo asked. His gruff voice sounded like a gunshot in the otherwise quiet room. Everyone on the couch glanced up.

Grace took a moment before nodding. "Yes. They searched that whole trail, and the city, and some of the highways. All they found was one of Jason's shoes."

One of his shoes? Finch and Enzo exchanged knowing glances. Werewolves had a keen sense of smell. Perhaps, if they had something Jason had been wearing that day—and they knew where the cops had found it—they would follow the trail straight to Jason.

Enzo walked over to the couch. "Grace, do you mind telling us where the shoe was found? And… can we borrow it for a bit?"

CHAPTER
THIRTEEN

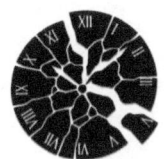

"You can have whatever you need," Grace said, no hesitation in her tone. She pointed to a shoe rack by the stairs. "The police found the shoe on the Truckee River Bike Trail. It was near the city, near a bend between trees."

Kull perked up. "You don't mind giving us this piece of evidence?"

With a simple nod, Grace continued. "You might think I'm insane… or just a mother who is drowning in too much grief, but… I went to our local fortune teller after the police failed to find Jason."

"*Fortune teller?*" Enzo sneered. "Heh."

Grace dabbed the corners of her eyes with the tissue. "Her name is Maddie the Psychic. I asked her what I could do to find Jason, and she said we'd be reunited, but that I had to contact the best PI in California. She couldn't give me the name, just that I needed *the best*. So I contacted everyone I could find. Most wouldn't make the trip to Tahoe. I'm surprised you're here, actually. Maybe you're the one she was talking about."

Finch rubbed the back of his neck. Most of the time, fortune tellers were frauds—but not all the time. Some of them were witches who used their abilities to predict things. Were they accurate? Sometimes, but it was extremely rare.

Was Maddie the Psychic the real deal? Or was she as fake as a three-dollar bill?

Kull leapt off the couch. "Adair *is* the one Maddie was talking about," she proudly proclaimed. "You can count on us to find your son, Grace. Don't worry. 24-Hour Investigations has yet to fail a client."

Her pure enthusiasm seemed to have an effect on Grace. The grieving mother's chin quavered, and obviously because her throat was tight, she just nodded and continued to wipe at her eyes.

"How much do I owe you?" Grace asked. "To take the case?"

"Nothing," Finch quickly replied.

"N-Nothing?"

"I'll find your missing kid. One way or another."

Finch wasn't about to take money from a mother who just wanted to make sure her child was safe. It went against everything he was.

Enzo grabbed the shoe. There was no rocket on the side, which meant it wasn't a match to the one they had found in the woods. Enzo carried it to the front door, his expression neutral. He subtly sniffed it, and if Finch hadn't known he was a werewolf, it would've looked like a fetish had somehow invaded this sad and personal moment.

"We should head out." Enzo opened the door. "C'mon."

After thanking the woman for her time—and after Kull gave Grace a hug—they left the small duplex and headed out.

The Truckee River Bike Trail snaked alongside the water, which was dull gray in the early light. The river shouldered past boulders with a steady flow. Frost coated the grass. Jason's smile bleached to ghost-white was all over flyers stapled to nearby trees.

7:42 a.m.

Enzo led with his head down and the sneaker in his hand, working the air in long pulls. "Damn Saturday crowd," he muttered without glancing back. "Dogs, strollers, and spilled lattes. It's difficult to pick up anything."

Kull walked beside Finch, eyes bright, cataloging joggers as they went past. "There are a *lot* of people here today."

Sure enough, when Finch panned his eyes over the area, he noticed at least half a dozen people. However, as the sun rose, most were hurrying back to parking lots. He assumed they would want to get to the lake, or perhaps now was the time for a proper breakfast.

Could they wait until the coast was clear? It would take a while.

Kull snapped her fingers. "Okay. I have a plan. Once we get to the spot Grace described, I'll distract anyone who comes our way. Then Enzo can wolf out and sniff the area properly."

"Risky," Finch said. "But let's try it. If this doesn't work, we can always try again."

They reached the spot Grace had described: a pinch in the path where the roots of nearby trees had heaved the asphalt upward. It made it difficult to see the river, and they were somewhat shielded from any unwanted gazes.

Enzo crouched and sniffed along the walkway, then the grass, and then pivoted toward the trees.

Two joggers rounded the curve—with matching headbands and martial stride. They ran a never-ending conversation as they approached, oblivious to the world around them.

"Now is my chance to shine," Kull said as she offered Finch a coy smile.

He motioned her to go.

"I need to shift," Enzo growled, low.

He peeled away into the pines. Then his bones cracked, and black fur rippled out along his spine. His fingers lengthened, nails blackening, bones snapped. Within a few short seconds, he was an eight-foot-tall werewolf, his new shirt struggling to contain him, his jacket actually ripping at the seams in the shoulders due to his increased muscle mass.

"I need just a minute," he said, and dropped to all fours, nose hovering over the dirt.

Kull leapt onto the path and offered the joggers a flat palm. "I'm sorry, the trail's closed ahead," she said. "There's a busted water pipe, and some of it turned into black ice. Keep your kneecaps intact and loop back."

"I don't see a sign or anything," the lady jogger said as she slowed a bit, her suspicion plain on her face.

Wanting to help Kull, Finch stepped forward with an authoritative frown. "Sign guy's late," he sardonically said. "Union thing."

Kull could barely contain a smile. "Yeah, turn around now unless you're eager to meet the county's liability lawyer. She's a biter."

The husband-and-wife duo stopped, but they were clearly confused. After giving Kull an odd glance—she wasn't dressed for any official business, that was certain—they obviously decided whatever was happening wasn't worth their time and turned around.

"We make the best team," Kull playfully whispered to Finch.

He snorted and rolled his eyes but otherwise didn't offer any commentary.

"Were you and your brother a great team when you were working together?" Kull asked.

Finch tensed the moment his brother was mentioned. He tried to strangle any hint of emotion, but it was too much. He took a second to calm himself before he replied, "Yes. We were a good team."

"What was he like?"

Finch crossed his arms. If someone had asked him this question a few years ago, he wouldn't have been able to answer. He would've shut down, demanded they leave, and probably never spoken to them again.

But things were different now...

He closed his eyes, took a deep breath, and exhaled. "Well... Actually, Carter was a lot like you. More charismatic than me, that's for damn sure. Better with people. He always knew what to say to get people to open up. It made questioning people easy whenever we were out and about."

Finch thought back to when they had found Chronos. It had been Carter who had convinced the titan to make the pact in the first place. If Finch had been by himself, he was certain he never could've convinced the mighty time god.

Opening his eyes, Finch sighed. "Carter was too trusting, though. The times I pulled him out of trouble are too numerous to count. He would fall for any sob story, help any cause, no matter how suspicious it seemed."

If Finch hadn't been there to keep the man grounded, Carter would've been betrayed countless times over.

It was the way they had made such a great team... They had covered a lot of each other's weaknesses.

But Finch gritted his teeth when he remembered the night Carter died. If Finch's job had been to save his brother, then it really was his fault Carter was no longer with them.

Finch hadn't been there... He hadn't been quick enough. Good enough. Talented enough.

"Obviously no one can replace your brother," Kull said, drawing Finch back to the present. "*But*, you can rely on me, okay? I'll bring so much charisma to this case that *everyone* is going to spill their secrets."

Finch snorted back a laugh. "All right. We'll see."

"Adair," Enzo hissed from the trees.

Finch stretched like a man easing a hamstring and angled his head toward the pines.

Enzo pointed with a clawed finger to some ground-in dirt between pine trees. Then he pointed to some dead grass and motioned off into the distance. "I found him. It's really faint, but he was here. So was a wolf. Then the scent just goes off in that direction."

"Can you follow it?" Finch whispered.

"Yeah. But I'll have to change back."

Enzo rotated his head as *cracks* from his bones echoed between the trees. His fur shrank back into his flesh, and his bones rearranged themselves until he was once again a bald, muscled human man with a dark complexion.

Then a hiss came from behind one of the trees. Before Finch could whip out one of his pistols, Smudge hurried out onto the trail, pines needles in his wispy hair. The little goblin held a crumpled flyer in both hands.

The cat-scratch voice didn't carry, but his urgency did. "Friend. Look." He tugged Finch's coat with bird-bone fingers, already crab-scurrying toward the trailhead billboard.

Enzo growled and then huffed. "This sneaky pukwudgie is getting under my skin."

"He's helping us, though," Kull said, holding up a finger.

"Does that make up for all the terrible things he's done? I don't think so."

They followed the pukwudgie to a bulletin board blistered by staples and sun. Jason's face looked out from a dozen spots, but Smudge slapped his palm lower, where older, curling flyers had slid behind the new. He pawed them free and fanned them on the map ledge.

LILY HERNÁNDEZ, 7 — last seen near the marina, wearing a yellow

swimsuit

BENJI LOOMIS, 14 — missing after leaving band practice

TRAVIS MARRERO, 19 — sophomore, UNR, home for the weekend

KAYLA DURANT, 16 — trail runner, North Shore Cross-Country

So many missing kids. Finch stared at the pictures for a long time. How long had the red-eyed werewolf been running rampant in Tahoe?

Kull's brightness dimmed. "Oh… All those clothes we saw in the woods…"

After a grunt of irritation, Enzo walked over. He grabbed a fistful of the flyers and then looked at each one closely. "Listen, I think I have Jason's scent, even now, as a human. If we start walking, we might be able to find where he went."

"Is the direction the same as Desolation Wilderness?" Finch asked.

Enzo nodded once, his eyes remaining on the children. Especially the seven-year-old, Lily. He gently touched her picture once before replying. "Yeah. Looks like we found the small lead we were looking for."

"Yeah. Let's just hope the kids are okay."

Enzo stuffed the flyers into his sweatpants pockets. "They better be."

CHAPTER
FOURTEEN

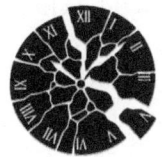

They ditched the party bus in a turnout off Highway 89 and hiked in under a sky of gold and blue. Finch took deep breaths, the cold air hurting his lungs. The granite of Desolation Wilderness shouldered up into white-scabbed ridges, and the main trail into the park was a boot-worn thread between boulders and wind-stunted pines.

8:26 a.m.

Enzo set the pace, tenser than ever. Kull kept a step behind Finch, her bright red skirt fluttering in the wind. Smudge walked behind them, mostly staying invisible, but occasionally appearing to pick up shiny bits of trash left on the trail. He seemed fascinated by coins the most.

"If these kids all have lycanthropy, do you think they'll wolf out once we find them?" Finch asked in a hushed tone.

Since the curse was tethered to the heart and soul cores, any powerful emotion could cause them to transform. Would finding their hiding place trigger their anxiety?

Enzo grunted. "We'll see."

The trail broke open onto a weathered granite slab, but on the left and right were high ridges—sheer rock faces that rose at least forty feet. This was a natural choke point. It irritated Finch. Beyond the choke point was a meadow with a ribbon of meltwater cutting it in two.

Enzo's nostrils flared.

"The boy came through here," he said, voice low. "A day or two old. I think we might actually find this kid pretty quickly."

"Don't say that." Finch crossed his arms. "You'll jinx us."

The crack of a rifle split the world.

Finch didn't think; his mind slid into combat instincts within an instant. He turned on his heel—hot lightning pain suddenly flaring through his leg—but he still managed to grab Kull and push her toward one of the boulders.

Kull gasped. Enzo roared.

A second shot was coming, Finch felt it. He dragged his willpower up from the cold well at his center, and then visualized any and all metal being deflected from his body.

"Not today," he said through clenched teeth.

A shot *cracked* from a rifle, and the bullet ricocheted off Finch's arm and struck the nearby granite, creating a brief spark. A third bullet whistled past his ear and gnawed bark from a nearby cedar.

Finch motioned to Kull. "Stay in cover." Then he palmed Starfall, but instead drew Agony.

Enzo, already in full werewolf form, spittle dripping from his maw, ran in the direction of the gunfire. A man stood at the top of a nearby ridge—forty feet above them—his broad-shouldered silhouette stiff. Finch already knew who it was.

Holt.

How had that old bastard found them?

The man stepped forward, allowing some of the morning light to reveal his features. He wore a long trench coat, and his knee was braced, but it squeaked when he shifted. His rifle sat in his hands like it belonged there.

A white tattoo marked his knuckles, one as angular and elegant as a constellation schematic. An archer-drawn bow. *The Mark of Sagittarius.*

"Oh, goddammit," Finch muttered.

Finch's leg burned as he stumbled backward. He grabbed the side of his upper thigh. The sticky heat of blood on his fingers told him the graze wasn't a small wound.

Enzo flew at the rocky ridge, but the stone was too smooth for climbing. Driven by rage, Enzo ran on all fours out of the choke point, no doubt searching for a way around. How long would it take him to reach Holt? Probably too long, but there was no reasoning with werewolves once they had lost control.

Holt ground his teeth and then called down, "*Adair Finch!* Surrender the egg, and we can do this the easy way."

"I'm not going to do that," Finch stated. "How about you throw down your weapon, and we'll talk this over like civilized men?"

"There's no need for talk. You're carrying a dangerous object. Something that could harm or kill millions."

Finch shook his head. "I'm not going to use it. I'm protecting the egg until it hatches, ya donut."

"Even worse!" Holt hefted his rifle and stared down the sights. "Humanity doesn't need any *new gods*. This is our age, our era. This egg needs to be gotten rid of before it can do any damage."

"Have it your way," Finch muttered.

And then he lifted Agony and fired. The shot sounded like a crackle of lightning, and a bright red *burst* of magical energy emanated from the barrel. Holt, completely caught off guard, was struck in the shoulder. He stumbled backward, his leg brace squeaking, all while grunting.

Then he spasmed.

Agony was a gun that caused a drastic amount of pain

whenever it injured anyone. It was magically debilitating, more so than any normal injury.

Finch hoped Holt would just collapse, but the man clearly wasn't a quitter. Holt brought the hand with the mark up to his mouth, bit down on one of his fingers, and then concentrated. A second or two later, color drained from his shoulder and body, leaving him slightly black and white.

"Adair?" Kull asked. She had her head poked halfway around the boulder. "What's going on?"

Holt's injury reversed itself. His trench coat was no longer torn or bloody, and his shoulder was in one piece. The bullet flew backward through the air until it was halfway to Finch, and then it stopped and dropped down to the granite.

The Mark of Sagittarius, obviously imbued with a piece of Aeon's magic, allowed Holt to reverse small bits of time. What else did it allow him to do?

A pit formed in Finch's stomach. Did the mark somehow allow Holt to track him? Did it somehow give Holt the ability to sense other temporal magic? That was the only explanation that made sense.

Aeon was helping the man track Finch down—no matter where he went.

With a smirk, Holt brought his rifle back up and aimed. "I'm not the only one who knows that egg is dangerous. I've got friends in high places who want to make sure it never harms a soul."

"Aeon just wants the egg for his own purposes," Finch called up to him. "He's not some righteous do-gooder. You're just a tool."

"Feh. Our goals align for the time being. That's good enough for me."

Finch fired again.

The bullet of condensed red magic screamed through the

air, only to be stopped dead cold a foot or two from Holt. The air around it was devoid of color, and the bullet eventually just fell straight down, never striking anything.

Holt didn't even flinch. "I'm not playing around anymore, Adair."

Then Holt shot his rifle. It would've struck Finch straight in the gut, but it veered off at the last second, deflected by a ripple of Finch's dwarven magic. The bullet flew off and struck the ridge.

Holt cursed under his breath.

"Looks like we have a stalemate," Finch sardonically stated. "Can we talk *now*?"

"I've fought more monsters than you've lived days. *You think I only have one weapon?*"

With a practiced motion, Holt slung the rifle over his back and reached beneath his coat. When his hand emerged, it clutched something far more primitive: a compact crossbow with a dark wooden frame. The bolts in its quiver were entirely wood—no metal tips, no steel shafts. Just smooth, sharpened stakes, their grain polished to a sinister shine.

Finch caught his breath.

Clearly, Holt kept a weapon like that for dealing with vampires or other undead susceptible to certain types of wood. But it would also work here. Finch only had the ability to control *metal*.

Holt grinned like a wolf baring its teeth. "I've got a feelin' you can't protect yourself from these."

He raised the crossbow and fired.

Finch dove sideways. The bolt hissed past his ear, striking a boulder not too far behind him.

"*Adair!*" Kull shouted from her hiding spot. Then she made an angry noise and shouted, "That does it!"

Much to Finch's surprise, a flock of birds tore through

the pine tree canopy and burst into the choke point. They weren't crows, or ravens, or owls, or any sort of bird that would naturally take up residence in the forest.

No, these were gray and blue pigeons. Hundreds of them. They swooped and moved as one, shooting through the sky as though flying for their lives.

Holt gasped and stumbled, his eyes wide. He lifted his weapon, but his hands shook, as though he knew it would do absolutely nothing against a mega flock of birds. And then, the birds turned, seemingly led by one vengeful pigeon out for Holt's blood.

The horde of pigeons rushed at Holt, slamming into him, pecking him, landing on him, tearing at his clothes with their little pigeon talons.

And mostly pooping on him. The whole ridge was a smear of white and black as the birds bombarded him with feces.

"What the fuck?" he yelled, his voice echoing throughout the whole nature preserve.

Kull giggled from behind her boulder. And while Finch's heart still beat fast, he couldn't help but chuckle to himself. Kull was still a mischief spirit. Her mischief magic did all sorts of weird and amusing things—like control pigeons.

A snarl erupted from the tree line on the ridge.

The pigeons broke apart, scattering in an instant, their wings beating frantically as they went in all directions. Holt just stood there, hair disheveled, half coated in pigeon poo, his body covered in a million tiny cuts and slashes, and all the buttons of his coat missing. The birds had probably also made off with his wallet and all his dignity.

Enzo launched himself out from between the trees, his werewolf form a black blur of claws and fury. He arced upward in a perfect leap, aiming to bring Holt down in a storm of teeth.

But Holt wasn't completely disoriented. He quickly lifted his left hand, the one branded with the Mark of Sagittarius, and the color drained from Enzo.

"No!" Holt said, glaring. "Beasts like *you* will never defeat me."

Finch already knew one of the limitations of Holt's mark. It couldn't do multiple targets. If Holt could freeze and rewind *many* objects, he would've stopped the flood of pigeons, but instead, he had been completely helpless to their swarm tactics.

But Enzo was just one man. And now Holt had him snared.

CHAPTER
FIFTEEN

Enzo was frozen inches from Holt, muscles rigid, jaws open wide in a silent roar. Even the spray of dirt kicked up by his claws hung motionless in the air.

Holt pivoted, his crossbow already loading another wooden bolt. "No more of this *nonsense*." He took aim. "Adair, surrender the egg, or else I'm gonna have to kill every last one of you."

Done with this, Finch activated his magic.

Everything froze. Holt, Kull, the swaying of the pine trees —everything. And then the colors drained from the world until it was nothing more than black and white. But just as Finch was preparing himself for the final step of the transition back in time, he realized he was once again stuck in the timescape.

"Well, well, well," a familiar voice said.

Finch turned on his heel, his leg still in pain from the bullet wound. There, standing in the middle of the stone slab between two tall ridges, was Aeon. But he was different this time...

He wore a long, high-collared coat over fitted trousers, the fabric matte as eclipse-shadow until he moved, when faint constellations skated across it like fish under black ice. His ink-black hair was swept back in a style that felt both museum-piece and runway-fresh. His eyes were the same—one human brown, and the other a magical blue.

Something about him felt otherworldly familiar. Not like remembering someone's name or a birthday, but in the same way one experienced déjà vu.

As Aeon stepped closer, silver gills unfurled along the lines of his neck. He never grew the goat horns, like he had last time... No. He just had sleek gill slits that flexed and shimmered, catching light like mercury. They rippled once, tasting the air, and then settled flat, as elegant and ominous as the rest of him.

"Aeon," Finch said, breathless. "You're going to find me every time I rewind time, aren't you?"

He chuckled as he nodded. "Oh, yes. Until the egg is in my possession, I'll be searching for your whereabouts."

"And you gave *Jack Holt* the ability to manipulate time just so he could hunt me down?" Finch exhaled. "Didn't you say you were the father of the Zodiac? Why are you teaming up with a human bounty hunter, huh? You can't get the actual Sagittarius to hunt me down?"

At some level, Finch didn't want Holt involved. Not because he was afraid of Holt, but because he was afraid of killing Holt. The man *was* a bounty hunter who clearly thought he was doing good. It left a bad taste in Finch's mouth to gun him down just for being in the way.

Aeon ran a hand through his inky hair. "It seems you don't understand what happened to my children... But they aren't here anymore. They've sacrificed themselves to become something more. Now I deal with mortals, tasking them with my minor business."

"You think he's disposable," Finch accused.

"He *is* disposable, my little warlock. His life is almost at an end. It was short, anyway. And if he falls, I'll give the Mark of Sagittarius to someone new. Forever. Until you're dead and I have the egg."

Aeon strode forward until he was within a few inches of Finch. "Unless you relent, of course. I'm more than happy to strike a deal." His smile was smug and condescending, as though he thought Finch would eventually break.

Obviously, Aeon wasn't very familiar with Finch.

"How many times do I have to tell you to fuck off before you get the hint?" Finch asked. "If there was a divine HR department, you'd be fired for harassment."

Aeon lifted an eyebrow. "Last time, I offered to break your pact with Chronos and replace it with my own. But I have other talents. Surely there's a mistake you made in the past—one you regret to this day. I could help you undo that mistake. All it would cost is… the egg."

Finch couldn't breathe. His thoughts darkened at the edges as all the implications of Aeon's offer flooded him. There was one mistake he regretted more than anything. One mistake that still followed him like a shadow.

Then Aeon stepped away, chortling. "Give it some thought. Next time you rewind time to escape my hunter." He glanced up at Holt on the ridge, and then returned his attention to Finch. "I'll be here, waiting to hear about that mistake you want undone."

And with that, Aeon vanished.

The world followed shortly afterward, melting away until Finch was left in a white void of nothing. When he blinked, he was back outside the party bus.

12:04 a.m.

Enzo stood at his left, and Kull at his right. They both

exchanged quick glances before eyeing the sky. The stars twinkled overhead.

"You rewound time?" Kull asked. "I think we could've handled that guy. Why not use your fire on him or something?"

Finch ran a shaky hand down his face. He didn't feel as though he could speak…

Enzo shook out his arms and then rotated his shoulders. "Holt doesn't know the world of hurt he's asking for."

"He froze you in time." Kull pointed at him, and then her eyes went wide. "Wait. How can Holt do stuff with *time*? I thought he was a normie. No magic, just arthritis and a bum leg."

Both Enzo and Kull turned to Finch. He still needed a moment, though, so he closed his eyes and took a deep breath. Once his composure was regained, Finch answered, "Holt carries the Mark of Sagittarius. That's why he has some minor time manipulation powers."

"Sagittarius?" Enzo snorted. "So he's Aeon's minion or something? Figures."

"I guess Aeon caught up to us." Kull frowned.

Finch took another deep breath. "Yeah. Every time I rewind time, Aeon comes to speak with me."

"Since when?" Enzo asked.

"Since we arrived in Tahoe."

Enzo mulled over the comment before asking, "So you saw him before I killed the werewolf?"

Finch nodded. "Aeon wants the egg, and asked me to surrender it, but I refused."

"Why didn't you say anything? Dammit, Adair, we should know about these kinds of developments! This changes a lot."

And while Enzo had a point, Finch still didn't want to discuss the conversation. What would he tell him? He was considering giving up the egg to change the past? To save his brother?

But Finch already knew what would happen. This was a monkey's paw situation. Aeon wasn't going to save Carter and then everything would be okay. No, whatever happened, it would have rippling consequences, some of which Finch hadn't even considered. He needed to think this scenario over carefully before he made any decisions.

"I'm sorry," Finch eventually muttered. "I wanted to focus my attention on one problem at a time. But now you both know. Aeon has sent Holt after me, and Holt has some minor time magic. It's nothing we can't handle, though."

Kull clapped her hands together once. "Well, we know Holt's location, right? He's already in the Desolation Wilderness... For some reason." She narrowed her eyes. "Wait, how *did* he know we were going to go there? Does his mark also give him the ability to see into the future or something?"

"I don't know," Finch said. "But his control over time is much less than mine. I doubt he knows I've rewound everything, which means we can get the jump on him."

"Why not alert the authorities?" Enzo asked with a tilt of his head. "I'm sure the Tahoe City PD has a supernatural division. We should call them up, tell them Holt has a rifle out in the nature preserve, and let them handle the madman. Then, once he's in cuffs, we'll go in and continue searching for Jason."

This was a great idea—at least to Finch. He didn't want to have to kill Holt, and he knew Holt wouldn't attack some cops who came out to investigate him. All they needed was for the man to get out of the way and stop following them for a bit. Perhaps he would get arrested for eight to twenty-four hours, and they wouldn't have to worry about him for quite some time...

"Good plan," Finch said.

Kull held up a hand. "Wait. Why don't we head straight to the Desolation Wilderness right now? Holt can't be there before us, right? We can get in, find the kid, and get out before Holt even arrives."

Finch liked this plan better, though he wasn't entirely certain where Holt was. Technically, after seeing him in Dave Wong's, Finch had waited in Stockton and then taken a bus to Tahoe, which wasn't the fastest transportation. If Holt knew where they were going to be in the future, there was a chance he was already there, even at this bizarre hour.

"It's worth a try," Finch said. "Let's get in the bus. Maybe we can beat him there."

They made the nature preserve in under an hour, running on coffee that, for some reason, had edible glitter in it. Finch stared out the window the whole trek, his mind on his brother and the egg.

Ahead, Desolation Wilderness was spooky at night—granite rocks jutting into the sky looked like bones, and the points of the pine trees made everything appear sharp and unforgiving. The moon had dragged itself higher into the sky, its crescent shape somehow ominous.

Once out of the vehicle, and away from the driver, Enzo transformed. The crack of his bones echoed off the rocks, but it was over in a matter of seconds. Then Enzo searched and sniffed, the hair on his forearms bristling like angry grass. "You two smell this? Oil. Old leather. Wintergreen chew. Holt wears his aftershave like a confession." Enzo's nose twitched. "He's here."

Kull fell in at his shoulder, her neon pink hoodie

practically glowing in the dark. Finch had almost forgotten he had rewound time, and thus, reset Kull back to her original outfit. He wouldn't admit he missed her audacious red skirt, but he had approved of the fact that her last outfit was mostly black. Her pink was like a target for all to see.

"Okay, team," Kull whispered. "I think I might've made a bad call. If Holt is already here… that means he beat us to the punch. What's our play?"

"We could hunt him in the dark." Enzo tapped the side of his canine snout. "But I suspect he has traps."

Finch crossed his arms. "And he has a limited ability to freeze people in time."

Both Kull and Enzo turned to him, silent. They wanted instructions. What was the best course of action?

"We shouldn't fight him at night," Finch said. "He's set up somewhere with angles and elevation. A patient man with a rifle beats a brave idiot with a heartbeat."

"That's good," Kull said as she pretended to wipe sweat from her brow. "Because I left my *brave idiot* in my other pants."

Enzo groaned in response, which only got Kull giggling. Sometimes it seemed Kull just said things to get reactions. More of her mischief spirit side, Finch supposed.

But he shook the thought away and tried to focus on the immediate. He *could* make himself immune to bullets, but Finch knew Holt had his crossbow. One wrong shot and everything would be all over—if Finch died, he couldn't rewind time.

And he wanted to play things a little more cautiously. There was no need to risk death. At least, not yet. They had other options.

"Let's go with Enzo's idea," Finch said.

Enzo's left ear twitched at the sound of his name. He smiled, showing off his fangs. "Call the cops? I like this plan."

"We'll go in tomorrow morning after we've rested. Maybe we can speak to the supernatural division about the red-eyed werewolves and the missing kids."

"I like it."

"Until then, let's get some rest so we're prepared for everything tomorrow."

CHAPTER
SIXTEEN

The party bus pulled up to the Alder Crown, and everyone exited the vehicle as soon as they could. Finch was exhausted, but mostly from the mental workout. Could Aeon save his brother? And how did Holt know they were going to Desolation Wilderness before even *they* knew they were going there? Finch's mind refused to rest.

With as little interaction as possible, they entered the fancy hotel, got their keys, and then went straight to their suites. Enzo took Meth to his suite, and Finch went with Kull to their suite. Hoping to avoid any shenanigans about dating and love, Finch retired straight to his room. Once the door was closed, he allowed himself to relax, but it was brief. He glanced at his phone.

1:56 a.m.

First, he needed rest. Finch got into bed, and set his alarm for close to seven in the morning.

When Finch awoke, the sky had gone from coal to slate. Dawn had arrived, and frost smoked all the windows as though Earth was trying, but failing, to quit cigarettes.

Finch rolled out of bed, every joint signing a petition against mornings, and shrugged into his coat out of instinct more than modesty. Starfall and Agony were right where he'd left them on the chair. He holstered them both and then checked the time.

8:15 a.m.

He cursed under his breath. His alarm hadn't woken him.

After a long exhale, Finch went barefoot across the expensive carpet, which was a fantastic choice he wished he could make more often.

He walked into the main room of the suite but only got three steps before he was ambushed.

"Option one," Kull announced from the couch, lying across it on her back, her arms up around her head, "—the cozy domestic."

She wore a black silk outfit that didn't qualify as clothing. A robe, technically, but in practice, it was a suggestion. It was semi-sheer, but dark enough to hide details. It was enough to catch Finch off guard. He didn't know where to rest his gaze, so he stared intently at Kull's forehead.

"Good morning, darling," Kull said, her voice deeper than normal. She threw back some of her fiery red hair. "Did you sleep well?"

Finch blinked. "*What?*"

"Did you sleep well?"

"N-No."

Kull's smile flickered, then brightened. "Honest. I respect that. Okay." She held up a finger. "Option two: *the noir classic.*"

She sat up on the couch and then grabbed things off the side table. When she faced him again, she wore a pair of glasses and held a long cigarette between her lips. "Well, well," she drawled. "Look what the night dragged in."

"What the night dragged in?" Finch repeated, still baffled. "What are you doing?"

"Wait, just give me a second. Option three: *the wholesome neighbor.*"

She ditched the props in a flicker of mischief—one heartbeat they were there, the next they were apparently ashamed of themselves and had turned invisible. She clasped her hands, sat straight on the couch, at the edge of the cushion, and summoned a bright smile. "Howdy! I made pancakes."

Finch slowly scanned the coffee table. "No, you didn't."

"Well, I had the idea of pancakes," she said. "Very trendy. Calorie-free."

After rubbing his eyes, Finch took a seat in an empty chair that faced the couch. "Kull, what's going on? Have you slept? Are you... drunk?"

She tapped her temple. "I'm testing wake-up greetings to find the most attractive one. For future use. Data-led romance."

"Oh, Jesus Christ," Finch muttered under his breath. He pinched the bridge of his nose. "Are you serious? Can you at least put on some pants?"

"Pants are anti-data," Kull playfully replied.

A tiny piece of Finch wanted to laugh. It was such a random comment, but he refused to let her win this game. He fixed his face in the shape of *disapproval* and then glowered at her. "Why would you need a wake-up greeting?"

"Because when someone likes someone, you have to say good morning to them in a super cute and attractive way. Every human does it. I need to find *the best way* to say hello to my lover."

"I'm not your…" Finch exhaled and stopped himself from arguing. "We're late. We should've left an hour ago."

"Well, I tried knocking on your door, but you didn't answer. Then I tried knocking on Enzo's door, and he didn't answer, either. I figured you both needed your beauty rest."

That was unfortunate, but Finch understood. After everything they had been dealing with, sometimes mental stress caused more fatigue than physical stress. He had to admit, he felt better now. He just needed some breakfast.

"So, while we wait for Enzo…" Kull held up a hand. "Option four: *the dangerous stranger*." She leaned against the couch's armrest and let the robe slip off her shoulders, but not fall into scandalous territory. "Sleep well, Detective?" she asked, her tone barely above a whisper. "Or did your demons hog the pillow?"

Finch's face heated. He didn't even know how to respond.

Kull sat up, her eyes wider. "Oh! Did you like that one? I'm getting closer, aren't I?"

"I'm getting closer to leaving this damn suite."

"Wait, wait! I have one more. Just one, I promise." Before he could respond, Kull said, "Option five: *the honest me*." She stared into his eyes and grinned her usual grin. "Morning, Adair. I hope you slept well."

Finch found his hands had knotted together. He unknotted them. "K-Kull… Listen. I don't think anyone has ever tried as hard as you to—"

"I'm making up for lost time," Kull interjected. She scooted to the edge of the couch, her bare knees almost touching his. "Apparently, I'm going to die in just *seventy years*. That's such a short time, Adair! I have to master this morning greeting while I can. That way I can find my true love. Every day I'm not with them is a day wasted."

"You literally know a warlock who can control time,"

Finch sardonically replied. "If you need a few hundred mornings to master something, I can help you. But that's not what I was going to say."

"Oh. Well, thank you for the offer." She pointed at him. "I'm going to hold you to it. Just like how you still owe me a dessert date. However, I'm sorry for interrupting. Say what you meant to say."

Finch sighed. "No one has ever tried as hard as you to get my attention. It's... *weird*. I'm not even entirely certain how to respond."

"So you're saying you can't help me improve my flirting?" Kull lifted an eyebrow. "Because if that's what you're trying to say, you don't have to worry, Adair. I just want your honest reactions. I thought it was cute when I finally got you to blush."

Again, Finch was at a loss for words. How did she always manage to say things that disarmed him so quickly? He had been prepared to rebuff her flirting, but her quirky honesty had a charm to it the likes of which he had never experienced before.

Even if she was rather aggressive with her advances.

Kull's grin eased into something gentler. "All right. New option. Number six." She tucked one bare foot under the other calf and leaned forward, elbows on knees, staring up at him through her lashes. "Good morning, Adair. I'm really glad we can have this moment together."

His throat went tight. He leaned away a bit, hoping to maintain a poker face. "That one's... fine."

"*Fine?*" Kull laughed as she sat up straight. "Sir, that was an A-tier greeting. An artisanal greeting. It was bespoke."

He groaned. "If you say *rustic*, I'm leaving."

"Rustic," she whispered, offering him a coy smile.

A banging sounded from the main door. Flinching, both

Kull and Finch stood from their seats. Enzo's voice quickly rang out through the wood.

"Are you two awake yet? Get some breakfast, and let's meet in the lobby. We've already way overslept."

"We'll be there," Finch called back.

He was happy to get some food and leave the suite before he said or did anything he regretted.

After eating a couple omelets brought to their suite by the hotel's staff, Kull vanished into her room, making a racket. Drawers slid. A hanger clinked. A *thump* suggested she had won a wrestling match with some of the furniture.

When she reappeared, she wore a purple beanie, a cropped violet sweater that left a soft crescent window open for the midriff, and a high-waisted black pair of jeans so tight they might as well have been paint simply poured over her.

Her whole ensemble was completed with a thick black belt, and sleek ankle boots.

She glanced down at herself, pinched the hem of one sleeve, and did a little shimmy that made the sweater's edge ripple.

"Do I look super cute?" Kull asked. "I want to turn heads."

Finch took a breath he pretended was about oxygen. "It's... good."

"Good is good." Kull laughed as she went over to the kitchen. She poked a few buttons on their fancy coffee machine, and it produced a hot drink. When she handed it to Finch, she winked. "Here. Hot chocolate. It's like coffee that believes in a softer world."

"Hot chocolate is for children."

"This is *fancy* hot chocolate meant for adults. Trust me. You have to try it."

"Fine."

Finch took a sip. It tasted like childhood, back when choices came in small sizes. He almost didn't want to admit he liked it, but he couldn't stop himself from half smiling.

Kull motioned to the door. "All right. Let's face the day."

9:04 a.m.

It was so late, Finch almost couldn't believe how long they had messed around. Perhaps, if they waited long enough, Holt would get tired and just leave the Desolation Wilderness himself. The thought caused Finch to chuckle under his breath as he sipped his liquid sugar.

Then they exited their suite and rode the elevator down to the ground floor. Enzo was already waiting in the lobby by the time the doors opened—bald, broad, and wearing a dark Henley that said *bar bouncer* while his new Crocs said *dad who's given up on society's rules.*

"About time," Enzo grunted, then paused, eyes flicking to Kull's beanie, then to her boots, and then to her exposed midriff. "Are you a vampire?"

Kull dismissively waved her hand. "No. At least, not last I checked."

"So, you saw your reflection in the mirror and still decided to show up wearing that?"

"*What?* I look super cute!"

"You look like a slutty ski bunny. If you were my daughter, I wouldn't let you leave the hotel wearing that."

Kull placed her hands on her hips. "Adair said I looked good, thank you very much."

"Yeah, I bet he did," Enzo muttered under his breath, shooting Finch a sideways glance.

"I would've said that no matter what she wore," Finch said

before taking another sip of his hot chocolate. "And leave me out of this. I'm not telling any other grown-ass adult what they can or cannot wear."

"Fox-Pistol!" someone shouted. "There you are! We've been waiting here for almost thirty minutes. The receptionist said you had our keys to the suites."

CHAPTER
SEVENTEEN

Finch froze mid-sip, nearly choking on his hot chocolate. He recognized that voice—smooth, with a French accent, and dripping with theatrical irritation.

Standing at the center of the Alder Crown's lobby were four individuals, but the one yelling was none other than Louis Dion, Kull's social media manager. Even dressed for a mountain town, he somehow managed to look like he had walked off a glossy magazine cover. His slim-fit, cream-colored puffer jacket practically sparkled, perfectly tailored to his lanky frame. Designer ski pants hugged his legs, and his fur-lined boots belonged in a runway show more than on a trail.

Louis whipped off a pair of mirrored ski goggles and let them dangle from his neck like a medal of honor.

"Fox-Pistol," Louis said with a smile. "I cannot—I repeat, *cannot*—believe you picked the most beautiful hotel in all of Tahoe to visit. We can make a few killer videos here, darling. Your instincts are improving!"

Kull lit up. "Oh, Louis! You look like a skiing marshmallow."

Louis gasped, offended but also secretly pleased. "Merci, cherie. It is haute couture, not marshmallow chic."

A woman stepped around the marshmallow prince. Finch recognized her, too. It was *Harper*, Fox-Pistol's "best friend." In reality, the woman had been the best friend of Kull's body. The real Fox-Pistol had died, though Harper didn't know that. Now, they were friends through circumstance, though Finch wasn't really a fan of the woman.

Harper wore a scarlet parka that clung to her figure, the faux-fur-lined hood framing her glossy, ink-black hair. Black leggings tucked neatly into knee-high boots, and her lipstick matched the exact shade of her coat. She wouldn't have been out of place on the cover of a winter romance novel, that was how beautiful she was.

"Samantha!" Harper danced over to Kull and then hugged her tight. "I can't believe you sometimes. Why do you always leave us at bizarre times, only to show up in weird locations?" Harper held Kull at arm's length. "Why come to Tahoe? If you wanted a ski resort, there are better options, *trust me.*"

Kull fluffed her hair. "Well, I've never been here before, so I wanted to check it out. You know how I am. *Whimsical.*"

"Uh-huh. Well, whatever. I have a surprise for you."

"R-Really? What is it?"

Harper's evil smile put Finch on edge. "You'll see soon enough."

"I don't like this," Finch whispered to Enzo.

The other man snorted. "At least she's dressed for the weather."

A third person approached Kull. She was a thin trembling woman, nearly obscured by an oversized pale-blue parka stuffed to the gills with down. If Finch squinted, she looked as though she were being consumed by her own coat. The hood's faux fur practically engulfed her frizzy blonde hair, but strands still escaped in all directions like a static-charged halo. Her snow pants were loose, almost flapping, and she carried a bright pink tablet in both hands.

The moment she spotted Finch, her watery brown eyes went wide with horror. "O-Oh. It's *you*."

Finch recognized her.

Sort of.

She was a half-spirit. Like Kull. But Finch had to think hard to remember, and it came to him as soon as she hid behind Louis.

This was *Whisptenthera the Disquiet*, a spirit of anxiety. Although, now she preferred to be called *Whisp*. Kull had hired her to help with social media—to give her a real job—because Kull wanted to lift up all her fellow half-spirits.

The final person to approach was also a half-spirit, but this time, it was a man. *Garinmirgorthan the Error*, a spirit of delusion. He went by the human name of *Garret*.

And he definitely had a personality.

Garret looked like he'd been dragged out of bed and reluctantly forced into luxury apparel. His white puffer vest hung open over a deep-blue cashmere sweater, and his designer snow pants were just slightly wrinkled, as though he hadn't cared enough to smooth them out. His heterochromatic eyes—one blue, one brown—took in the room with lazy indifference.

"Ugh," Garret muttered, scratching at his shoulder-length chestnut hair. "It's too bright in here. Can we just get our rooms so I can take a nap?"

"Garret," Harper said sweetly, though her tone contained venom, "maybe try not sounding like a cryptid in public? That would be great."

He dismissively waved away her comment. "I'm fine.

Everyone will pay so much attention to Fox-Pistol that they won't even know I went for a little break."

Harper rolled her eyes, grabbed Kull by the upper arm, and yanked her toward the elevators. "Come on, Samantha. Show us to our rooms."

"Wait," Kull said, her smile forced. "You remember Adair and Enzo, don't you?" She pointed over at the two men.

Finch held his breath. He had been hoping no one would pay attention to him. Enzo seemed to be in the same state of mind because he just crossed his arms and frowned.

"I have no idea who they are," Harper said with a sneer. She gave both Finch and Enzo a thorough once-over. "Are they bodyguards?"

Of course she didn't remember. Finch had rewound time after every meeting. *He* knew who she was, but Harper had no idea they had met outside this hotel.

The two half-spirits, on the other hand, already knew who Finch was. As a warlock bound to Chronos, most spirits were vaguely aware he was powerful, and tended to avoid him. That was no doubt why Whisp was frightened.

But she probably didn't remember meeting Finch in Oakland, either.

"This is Adair." Kull walked over and gently touched Enzo's shoulder. "And this is Enzo. They're, uh, my personal assistants while in Tahoe!"

Harper's sneer never left her face. She would've been ten times more beautiful if she didn't look as though everything smelled rotten.

"We don't need any personal assistants," Harper said. "We have everyone we need right here. Our crew. We're extremely talented and don't need to be bogged down with... *randos.*"

Finch pointed at Garret. "What's *his* talent?"

"I give one hell of a hand job," Garret said with a grin.

Louis sputtered out a laugh and then playfully smacked Garret's shoulder. "Oh, you're naughty. *I love it.*"

"I'm not even lying. Lots of practice made me an expert."

"I bet," Louis said with a purr, one blond eyebrow rising.

Pinching the bridge of his nose, Finch just sighed. He regretted asking the question.

"I need Finch and Enzo," Kull interjected. "They're my... *tour guides*. They know everything about Tahoe. All the best local food, places to see—and they're also gofers. They've gotten me all sorts of amazing things already. Right, boys?"

Enzo didn't reply with words, only a snort.

"Yeah, tour guides," Finch muttered. "Woo. That's us. *24-Hour Tour Guides*. That's our company."

His sardonic commentary got Kull smiling—which almost got *him* smiling, but Finch killed the urge before it manifested.

The Alder Crown's lobby doors slid open with a soft hiss, letting in a rush of cold Tahoe air. Heads turned as a man strolled inside like he owned the place.

He wore a sleek, black-and-silver bomber jacket with fur trim, open to reveal a fitted charcoal turtleneck. His dark jeans were tucked into high-end snow boots, their laces a striking crimson that matched the embroidery on his jacket's sleeves. A small silver chain glinted at his throat, and his black hair was styled to perfectly walk the line between effortlessly tousled and meticulously curated.

And then there were his eyes. Sharp, warm brown eyes that locked instantly on Kull.

The room seemed to collectively swoon. Even Whisp peeked out from behind Louis with a dreamy expression, temporarily forgetting about her fear of Finch.

"Oh, here's your surprise, Samantha!" Harper announced with a flourish, her evil smile in full effect. "May I introduce the hottest thing to hit YouTube since unboxing videos and mukbangs—Jace Min, the famed pop singer!"

Jace grinned, flashing white teeth that could sell a thousand toothpaste products. He gave a smooth, practiced wave that made the hotel receptionist actually fan herself.

Kull froze like someone had hit pause on her life. "Uh. Huh. What. Uh." She pointed at Jace like he was a rare Pokémon. "That's the surprise? That's… that's a very *nice* surprise."

Harper smirked. "You haven't been yourself lately, Samantha. You've been focused *way* too much on dating and not at all on your Twitch or YouTube channel." She leaned in close and lowered her voice. "I figured I'd bring you someone who is actually worth dating."

Finch sputtered on his hot chocolate. "Wait, *what?*"

"Mind your own business," Harper said, her words practically a hiss. She pulled Kull a few feet away.

Louis squealed, vibrating with excitement as Jace strode over.

"Oh my god, this is genius, Harper! A crossover! Fox-Pistol and Jace Min—two titans of social media! Your couple name could be 'Jamantha' or maybe 'Sace.' The hashtags write themselves."

The man immediately pulled out his phone and began typing notes. Then he smacked Whisp a couple times and pointed at the tablet in her hands.

"Start brainstorming," he said. "We're going to film *tonight.*"

"Y-Yes, sir," Whisp said before pointing away at the tablet. Then she clutched the edge of the device and mumbled, "Dirty, dirty hashtags…"

Jace chuckled smoothly and walked toward Kull, his stride a perfect mix of confidence and casual charm. "So you're the famous Fox-Pistol," he said, his voice low and warm. His accent had a faint lilt to it—Californian with a soft undercurrent of Seoul. "Harper's been telling me about you non-stop. I've been dying to meet you."

Kull's mouth opened, but only a strangled squeak came out. She tried again. "I, uh, yes, I'm... me. I mean, yes! Hi!" She coughed and steadied herself, but her smile threatened to split her face. "I've seen your videos. Most of them, anyway. You sing the most *beautiful* love songs."

Jace nodded once. "Love is my inspiration."

"Mine, too!"

"Really? I find that fascinating."

Kull clapped her hands together once. "I'm so happy you're here. We can talk about all your inspiration for all your amazing lyrics! I can't wait." Then she turned to face Finch. "Uh, tour guides? Would you, uh, go on without me? I'll stay back here. To work. On my Twitch and YouTube channels."

With his irritation rising, Finch took a deep breath before motioning Kull over. She pried herself from Harper's grip before dancing over to Finch's side.

"What's wrong?" she whispered. "You don't need me at the Tahoe Police Department, right?"

"You can't possibly want to date this peacock," Finch muttered under his breath.

"Why not?"

"Well, I mean..." Finch rubbed the back of his neck. "We're in the middle of something. We haven't even found the kid yet."

Kull waggled a finger. "We have an infinite amount of time, remember? You just told me that back in the suite."

"I did say that..."

"Besides, I'm *not* dating anyone. You made that perfectly clear." Kull leaned in closer to him. Almost uncomfortably close. Her eyes locked onto his. "Unless... the person I've been flirting with this whole time has changed his mind?"

Finch held his breath for a prolonged moment. He searched Kull's gaze, almost shocked she had been so serious about being with him. A part of Finch really had thought it was all a mischievous game to Kull.

It hadn't been real.

Right?

"I haven't... changed my mind," Finch said, though it pained him to do so.

"Then there's no problem! We're just really good friends, and we'll always be that no matter what." Kull patted his shoulder, smiled, and then bounded back over to Jace. "Okay! I have suites for us all. I think everyone will be quite pleased!"

Harper clasped her hands like a wicked matchmaker. "Isn't he perfect for her? They could collab on music videos, prank duets, even a romantic Q&A series."

Louis chortled. "This will break the algorithm. Break it!"

CHAPTER
EIGHTEEN

The party bus was dark inside despite the fact it was morning. The windows were tinted for privacy, and the smell of spilled champagne made it seem like a nightclub.

Enzo took one of the rear seats, shoulders filling half the row, while Finch claimed a window seat. Pines marched past in tidy ranks, the lake shone between buildings in the distance, and everyone seemed to prefer to stay indoors to beat the incoming chill.

9:22 a.m.

"We can both agree we hate that singer, right?" Enzo asked, breaking the silence.

"What singer?" Finch asked.

"Jace Min."

Finch snorted back a dark chuckle. "Yeah, we can definitely agree on that."

The bus rumbled along the lakefront and meandered into town. After a few turns down narrow streets flanked by tall pine trees, the vehicle came to park in front of the Placer County Sheriff's Tahoe Substation.

Enzo got up from his seat, stormed to the front, and banged on the driver's privacy window. When it opened, the driver called out, "Is something wrong?"

"We wanted to go to the Tahoe City PD, not the sheriff's office," Enzo said.

"Look, there's no such place. Tahoe City doesn't have a PD office. The sheriffs service this area. The nearest PD is South Lake Tahoe, and that's over an hour away."

Interesting. Finch quickly pulled up his phone to check the accuracy of the statements. To his surprise, the driver was correct. The Placer County Sheriffs covered the largest portion of Lake Tahoe, servicing nineteen different communities.

Tahoe City was unincorporated. Finch hadn't known that, but it was starting to make sense why so many supernaturals called this area home.

There were fewer people. Less law enforcement. Less trouble for them.

"I guess we'll speak with the sheriff," Finch said, sighing as he stood.

Enzo nodded once, and they both exited the party bus into the parking lot.

The sheriff substation was a small and unimpressive building mostly painted beige. Someone had set a planter of dead petunias by the front door, and they, too, were beige. A patrol SUV idled at the curb, surrounded by road salt.

Once inside, Finch wrinkled his nose. The place smelled of coffee and printer ink. A corkboard bragged about a charity 5K and an officer-of-the-month. At the front counter, a woman in her fifties—hair like steel wool polished to a shine, name tag that read *R. KENDRICK*—looked up from a stack of forms. She wore reading glasses, a dark gray blouse, and pants.

"Morning," she said. "If you're here to pay a parking ticket, you'll need to come back after noon."

Finch slid his PI license across the counter, followed by a laminated card that—if you knew what you were looking at —held a watermark sigil nested inside the state seal. To the uninitiated, it read like bureaucracy had gotten creative.

"I'm Adair Finch. We're looking to speak with your Special Circumstances liaison regarding a Category Seven wildlife concern with... nonstandard bite morphology. It touches juvenile welfare and backcountry safety. We'll also need to log a courtesy heads-up per CalGov 402.31(b), interagency courtesy clause."

He had said it all in the hopes of getting the Supernatural Division. Some of the sheriffs had to be in the know about magic. Usually, they would appear from the woodwork whenever certain phrases were used. The watermark in the sigil was a dead giveaway that Finch was a registered warlock with the state.

Kendrick blinked once. Twice. Bureaucrat soul met bureaucrat phrase and decided it didn't want the paperwork. "Special... circumstances." Her tone didn't change, but something behind her eyes took inventory. "And you mentioned a specific clause."

Enzo leaned an elbow on the counter. "We're trying not to spook hikers or start rumors. A quiet chat with whoever handles your... outliers... would help us keep this tidy."

Kendrick's gaze flicked to the card again, then to Finch, then over the top of the counter at Enzo. "You boys wait right here." She picked up a phone and pressed a button with the confidence of a woman who'd pressed a lot of buttons. "Tate? Front desk. I've got a consult for you. They've got... a card. I think you need to handle this."

Someone spoke on the other end, but it was too muffled to make out any words.

"Uh-huh. Uh-huh. Yep. Big." Kendrick subtly glanced at Enzo and then lowered her voice. "Bigger than the chair in conference B."

Enzo snorted.

For some reason, Kendrick blushed and turned away, mumbling something else into the phone. After a long sigh, Enzo stood straight and folded his arms across his chest. As Kendrick continued her hushed conversation, Enzo met Finch's gaze.

"So, you and Kull *aren't* a thing?" he asked.

Finch shook his head. "No. I already told you that."

"Uh-huh. Well, I'm just surprised."

"Why?"

"I dunno. How many women throw themselves at you like that? Even my wife—ex-wife, I suppose—didn't come at me that hard. As a matter of fact..." Enzo chuckled. He rubbed his chin as his gaze fell to the floor. "... she hated me for the first few weeks we knew each other. I had to prove to her I was worthy before I could even take her on a date."

Finch shrugged. "I told you, I just... don't think I could handle losing someone close. What if... What if she dies the same way Carter did? What if someone targets her to get to me?"

"That's a lot of *what if.* In my experience, if you switch that phrase with *why not*, your life gets a whole lot better."

Irritated, Finch glowered at the man. "You *want* me to date Kull?"

"I want you to let go of whatever guilt you're clinging to," Enzo said, all confidence. "If you don't like Kull because she's *too intense*, that's one thing. If you're avoiding her because you're afraid, that's another."

"I don't think we should have this conversation in the middle of the sheriff's lobby," Finch snapped under his breath.

But at some level, he understood. Enzo was calling him out. Forcing him to face reality.

It stung. Only a true friend would even attempt to broach the subject.

Kendrick hung up her phone and slid Finch his IDs back. "Detective Tate will be with you in a minute. You can have a seat."

They took the bench. A poster behind them read:

SEE SOMETHING, SAY SOMETHING, then in smaller print: *BUT MAYBE SAY IT TO THE RIGHT PERSON*.

Finch massaged the knot in his thigh where last timeline's graze still haunted his muscle memory. Enzo watched the entrance, quieter now.

The door beside Records opened, drawing Finch's attention. The man who came through it was *big* with a capital *B*. He was broad through the chest and shoulders, tall enough that the ceiling tiles thought about their life choices. His beard was trimmed close and mountain-gray at the edges.

He wore the standard Placer County Sheriff uniform, all grey-green with a few bright yellow stars on the chest and shoulders. The man also had a black baseball cap and a thick vest with various pouches.

"Finch?" His voice was gravelly. "I'm Detective Tate."

Finch and Enzo stood. Tate offered a hand the size of a shovel. Finch shook it and felt strength held politely in reserve. Enzo's shake got a fractional smile, like Tate appreciated a solid wall when he met another one.

Standing side by side, Enzo might've been an inch taller, but that was about it.

"This way, gentlemen." Tate tipped his head toward the back. "Lobby's for tourism."

They passed a corkboard with trail closures, and a framed topo map spiderwebbed with pencil lines, but never any flyers for the missing children. Finch briefly wondered why. Tate keyed them into a corner office. The window in the room looked out to a grouping of pine trees and half a slice of the lake.

The room contained a number of unusual objects. One was a shadow box with a battered deputy's pin and a photo of a younger Tate in a raincoat. Another was a dried cedar leaf preserved in golden amber, hung too high to just be decoration. On the bookcase sat cop literature—procedure manuals, a field guide to scat, plus a coffee mug with a chip—and also a smooth fist-sized stone with a hole worn clean through it, hanging on a red cord.

Tate shut the door and hit a white-noise machine that said **TIDEPOOL** in blue LEDs. Then he dropped into the chair behind his desk and gestured to the two that faced him. The chairs appeared to be twenty years old.

Finch sat, but Enzo had to carefully lower himself so as not to break the elderly furniture.

"All right," Tate said, lowering his voice. "Ms. Kendrick isn't in the know, but I am. As part of the Supernatural Division, I handle most of the cases involving witches and warlocks." He sniffed and then narrowed his eyes. "And it's been a long time since a werewolf stepped foot into this facility. You must have something real important to say."

Enzo immediately stiffened. He had once been a cop in Oakland, and he probably knew law enforcement was suspicious by nature, but it obviously hurt him at some deeper level whenever someone assumed he was a criminal because of his curse.

Finch set his card on the desk, the watermark sigil catching the light. "Enzo is with me. We're here looking for a missing kid. We're pretty certain there's a werewolf infestation to blame, but I can't find the child because there's an even bigger problem."

"Bigger than a *werewolf infestation?*" Tate asked, raising an eyebrow.

"There's an armed adult male trying to kill me," Finch stated. "His name is Jack Holt, and he's taken shots at me already, both with a gun *and* a crossbow. He thinks he's saving the world but he's actually a lunatic endangering others. I was hoping you might be able to talk some sense into the man."

"Or arrest him," Enzo cut in.

"Or that."

Detective Tate's eyebrows lifted at the name. "Jack Holt." He leaned back in his chair, folding his hands on his stomach. "The legendary bounty hunter? *That* Jack Holt?"

Enzo offered a wolfish grin. "He's old and off his rocker. Trust me. That lunatic busted into our PI office and rummaged through our desks and files. Why would any sane person do that?"

"That's what I'm wondering." Tate narrowed his eyes. "You two wanted for something I should know about? Or something you're not telling me?"

"We're clean," Finch said. "I'm a registered warlock who has worked with the Stockton PD for years. And Enzo's on my payroll. Former Oakland PD. No warrants. No bounties. Holt's chasing the wrong people."

Tate grunted. "Let's find out." He turned his monitor slightly, typed something with two thick fingers, and muttered under his breath. The screen glowed faint blue as he scrolled through pages the public would never see.

For a long moment, only the white-noise machine spoke. Enzo shifted in his seat, the tips of his fingers pointed slightly, betraying his building rage. Thankfully, after a few deep breaths, all traces of wolf vanished. He managed to calm himself.

Finch was proud.

Finally, Tate exhaled through his nose. "Well, well. You're right. Neither of you are on any active warrants, state or federal. No sealed warrants either. Only thing on file is a note that you, Finch, are licensed to handle even the most dangerous of anomalies, with 'special supervision recommended.'" His eyes flicked to Enzo. "You're marked as 'hazardous species, low threat.'"

"Hazardous?" Enzo growled. His fingers once again became claw-like.

"Relax. It's a database label, not a sentence." Tate shut the monitor off with a click. "Point is, Holt doesn't have a contract on you. At least, not a legal one."

"Then can you arrest him?" Finch asked.

"That's the million-dollar question." Tate steepled his fingers. "But before we go any further, you should understand something about the local area. The Desolation Wilderness isn't just a federal park."

Enzo relaxed a bit. "We figured as much."

"The sheriffs don't enter without permission. Not the rangers, not Fish and Game, not even the state troopers. You think we're lazy? No. We've lost people out there. Good people. You know why?"

Finch lifted an eyebrow. "Why?"

"Because a *spirit of death* rules that place."

A spirit of death?

Finch's throat tightened. While most spirits were quite weak and harmless, some were a terrible mistake to deal with. A mischief spirit like Kull once was, would do things just to be mischievous. It was their nature.

But *mischief* and *anxiety* and *delusion* were all simple and non-life-threatening emotions or problems.

A spirit of death, on the other hand, would sometimes cause untold devastation as part of their nature. They thrived on death. Dealt death. Reveled in death. They were still weak compared to other creatures who used *death* in their title, but it wasn't something to take lightly. Just because a spirit of death couldn't kill a town with a snap of its fingers didn't mean it couldn't kill a single person with barely any thought.

Detective Tate continued. "It's as old as the granite, that damn spirit. It decides who comes in and who goes out of the Desolation Wilderness. It decides who stays." Tate's voice had dropped low enough to rattle. "If we step in, it's because the spirit gave us a nod to handle a non-magical problem— search and rescue, a lost hiker, a rogue black bear. Anything else? It's the spirit's business. Even federal agencies know better than to press."

Finch sighed. "Damn."

Tate gestured at the cedar leaf above his desk. "That's my permission slip if I ever want to get into the park, but if I try to assert my authority over anything magical, the spirit will still come for me. Cost me a year of my life earning that stupid leaf, I'll have you know. Still worth it. But unless that spirit wants Holt gone, my badge means nothing in there. Holt either got permission or he's already doomed."

The leaf…

Finch took special note of its location.

Enzo's nostrils flared. "So, you can't stop Holt? And if we want into the Desolation Wilderness, we're going to have to appease a spirit of death until it gives us a goddamn hall pass to traipse around the park? Is that it?"

"That's about the size of it." Tate shrugged. "The spirit isn't fond of surprise guests, so unless you want to end up dead on a trail somewhere, I suggest you think long and hard about what you're gonna do."

CHAPTER
NINETEEN

Finch and Enzo stood from their chairs. As Finch shook Tate's hand, he asked, "When do you take your lunch today, Detective? I'd love to ask you a few more questions about the area. Privately, of course."

"I always take my lunch at eleven sharp," Tate replied, harshness in his voice that betrayed the truth of what he was saying.

Finch loved people who followed strict schedules. They were always so much easier to deal with than others. He smiled, nodded, and then headed for the door. After Enzo shook the detective's hand, he followed as well.

Once the door closed behind them, Enzo shot Finch a glare. "You want to come back?" he asked under his breath.

"No, I think we might need to—" he used air quotes for the next word, "—*borrow* a certain leaf, and I just want to know the right time to do that."

A smile spread across Enzo's face. "Heh. Right. I see."

As Finch and Enzo walked through the lobby, Kendrick peered over her reading glasses as they passed the counter. "Everything squared away, gentlemen?"

"Squared-ish," Enzo said.

"Good," she replied, tone suggesting she preferred circles anyway.

Once outside, the cold washed over them, even though it was sunny, not a cloud in the sky. Finch paused at the patrol SUV, his mind constantly replaying Tate's words. A spirit of death ran the Desolation Wilderness. Permission slips were made of leaves and amber. If they couldn't ask the sheriff's office to help them, what other magical beings in town could?

"What's the plan?" Enzo asked. Although his breath was visible, he didn't shiver or shake. He looked perfectly content.

"We're going to visit *Maddie the Psychic*," Finch said.

Enzo side-eyed him. "The woman who told Grace to find the best PI in California without naming names?"

"That's the one."

"And you think, since you're here, that maybe she's got some actual future sight abilities?"

Finch shrugged. "It's worth a shot. I think she might be able to point us in a direction we hadn't even considered yet."

10:07 a.m.

The bus rumbled along the lake, the glitter confetti embedded in the carpet sparkling like the night sky. Pines flicked past in regimented ranks. Sunlight shone off the water in shards.

Enzo sprawled out in a rear seat, one Croc dangling from a toe. "You know the *hazardous species, low threat* thing Tate said?"

"Yeah," Finch said, sitting in the middle of the bus.

"I should put that on a shirt. Or a mug."

The image of Enzo wearing a shirt, while in werewolf form, that classified him as a low threat got Finch chuckling. Then Enzo joined him, and for a short moment, that was all they did.

"I've always thought it would be funny if you put *Petting Zoo Escapee* on a shirt, to be honest," Finch said.

Enzo laughed again. "Fuck you."

He had said it playfully, and it elicited another round of chuckles from Finch.

But then Finch's thoughts went back to the missing kid, Jason. If he was a werewolf, what would they do? They couldn't return him to his mother in that state. Most werewolves never learned how to control their wolf forms properly. They would get upset, transform, and then hurt or kill everyone around them, including their loved ones.

"Is there a cure to the lycanthropy curse?" Finch asked, his voice low.

All mirth disappeared from Enzo. He sighed as he said, "There are a couple."

"Do you know what they are?"

"You bet your ass I know." Enzo sat forward, his expression icy serious. "But you have to get cured *soon* after you're infected. And the requirements aren't easy or cheap, mind you."

"What's one of them?"

Whenever Finch ran across dangerous werewolves, his solution had always been to kill them. Then again, he had never run across children who were cursed like this. Knowing an alternative route would be useful.

"The first one I know for certain works, is getting Khonsu, the moon god, to break the curse," Enzo stated, though he didn't sound happy about it. "Unfortunately, this lazy bastard hasn't been seen for hundreds of years, so if he's even still around is a mystery."

"Hmm." Finch rubbed his chin. "What's another way?"

"A Sliver of the Moon." Enzo held up his hands, trying to show the shape of an odd flower. "If you take the petals, and grind them up, and make a kind of witch's brew out of it, it'll cure lycanthropy. But only if you drink within thirty days of getting cursed. If you drink after that, you die."

That sounded hazardous. And Finch immediately thought of Enzo, and how he had been cursed for years now.

"Anything else?" Finch asked.

Enzo half shrugged. "Apparently, there are some fae who worship the moon, and somehow get *moon magic* or some other hippie-dippie nonsense. Supposedly, they can cure lycanthropy, but it *also* has to be within the first thirty days of being cursed. Otherwise, you're fresh out of luck."

But this information gave Finch some hope. "Jason has only been missing for two weeks…"

"You want to cure him?" Enzo asked, narrowing his eyes. "Is that it?"

"It hasn't been thirty days yet. Perhaps we can."

"Yeah, but we don't have a Sliver of the Moon or any fae friends. All we've got is *Jack* and *shit*."

That also got Finch chuckling, mostly because a man named Jack Holt was hunting them. A clever play on words.

"We should keep it in mind," Finch said. "If we can save the ten-year-old boy, I'd want to."

"It might cost us. Big."

"I know."

The quiet that settled between them wasn't uncomfortable. Finch knew Enzo felt the same way. If they could save the kid, even if it meant a large sacrifice on their part, they would do it.

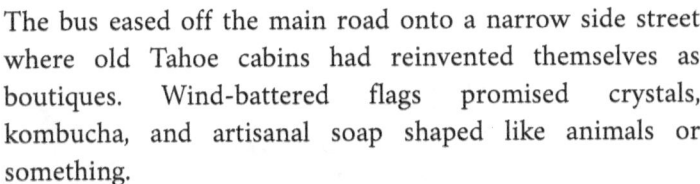

The bus eased off the main road onto a narrow side street where old Tahoe cabins had reinvented themselves as boutiques. Wind-battered flags promised crystals, kombucha, and artisanal soap shaped like animals or something.

Maddie the Psychic had colonized a squat A-frame cottage wedged between a bike-repair shop and a place that sold nothing but beanies. A neon hand blinked in the window—PALM READINGS—with nails painted gold. The hand alternated with a crescent moon that flickered brightly, even in the daylight.

The party bus parked in the lot across the way. Finch and Enzo strode out, their attention on their destination. A chalkboard on the front steps of the shop read:

YES, I KNEW YOU'D COME
WALK-INS WELCOME, SKEPTICS COST
EXTRA

Wind chimes made of mismatched spoons clinked together as Finch and Enzo headed to the front door.

"I hate this place," Enzo said, eyeing the whimsical decorations.

"I've seen worse." Finch opened the door.

The inside smelled like library books and oranges. Warmth rolled at them from a heater that wheezed in the corner of the main room.

The far back room had chosen a theme, and that theme was *confetti cannon*. Bead curtains hung not with beads but with hundreds of keys, all shapes sizes, and colors imaginable. On one wall, a pegboard held tarot decks in tidy rows. On the opposite side of the room was a shelf of crystals that glittered brightly. Each of them was labeled in blocky handwriting:

THIS ONE IS HONEST
THIS ONE IS PRETTY
THIS ONE JUST LIKES YOU

A sand-colored rug painted with a zodiac wheel sprawled under a round table. Finch took special note of it, wondering if Aeon somehow had anything to do with this. After telling himself that was illogical, Finch pushed the thought from his head.

The table wore a lace cloth and was covered in a mismatched tea set. The teapot was shaped like a sleeping fox, and Finch was already tired of this place. It was too whimsical and nonsensical for him. In that moment, he regretted not bringing Kull. She would've appreciated all the bizarre and unique features.

The thought of her with Jace, the singer, made him irrationally angry, and for a short moment, he just glowered at the floor, wondering what he should even do with these thoughts.

"Adair," Enzo whispered, a smile in his tone. "Look."

A fat gray cat in a sweater that read, "I bite authority," napped in a sunbeam, tail flicking like a metronome. The creature had clearly never skipped a meal, and its fur glistened with health.

"You think he'd like Meth?" Finch asked.

"Are you trying to give my cat *meth*?" came a shout from behind the key-bead curtain.

Then a woman emerged in a flash of outrage.

It had to be Maddie.

She was in her fifties, maybe sixties. Her hair was a streaked tumble of silver and plum, piled up with a pencil stabbed through a messy bun. She wore a cardigan with tiny embroidered moons, over a black dress that flowed when she walked. Bangles adorned one wrist, while on the other she wore a chunky digital watch with a cracked face.

Her eyes were bright brown, lively and somehow youthful, despite her apparent age.

"My precious Poopsiekins doesn't even get catnip— there's no way I'd allow him any sort of illegal substances!" Maddie hefted the large gray cat into her arms. Then she stroked his short fur, nuzzling him close. Poopsiekins radiated slight annoyance, but he didn't move or struggle in any way.

"I didn't mean actual meth," Finch said with a groan. "I meant... another cat named Meth."

This took Maddie a moment to process. Once she was finished, she nodded, placed her cat back into his sunbeam, and then chuckled.

"Oh. What an interesting name for a kitty. I'm sure there's a story!"

"We found him in a meth lab," Enzo said matter-of-fact, no hint of sarcasm or subterfuge.

This also got Maddie chuckling. "Fascinating, truly. You must be police officers or something adjacent. Come in! Have a seat. Let me get you a reading." Then she motioned to a sign by the door. "But first, please follow instructions."

The wooden sign read:

PLEASE REMOVE YOUR SHOES, HATRED, AND SKEPTICISM

Enzo toed off his Crocs with a dramatic sigh. Finch

stepped out of his shoes and set them on a tray, next to a basket of loaner socks knitted in colors that refused to coordinate.

Then they took a seat at the tiny table. Maddie joined them, her smile as bright as her eyes.

"I see you're a warlock, and you're... cursed." She narrowed her eyes at Enzo. "But you weren't cursed by anything dwelling around Tahoe."

Enzo shook his head. "No, I was—"

Maddie dramatically held up a hand, silencing him. "No. Don't tell me. Let me divine it." She reached into a pocket of her black dress and withdrew a deck of cards.

It was a small deck, made up of long tarot cards, but there were only twenty-two of them. Most full tarot decks came with seventy-eight cards.

Without any explanation, Maddie pulled the top card and laid it on the table for Finch and Enzo to see. It was *Justice*, with a picture of a king holding a sword in one hand and a set of scales in the other.

Then Maddie placed a second card. *The Hermit*. It depicted an old man holding a lantern.

When Maddie placed the last card, she widened her eyes. *The Tower*. The picture showed an old stone tower being struck by lightning and crumbling on one side.

"Oh, I was right," Maddie said, more to herself than to anyone else. She tapped the Justice card. "You are a police officer. Or perhaps you *were* one." Then she grazed the edge of The Hermit. "But your curse took a toll..." Finally, she sighed at The Tower. "And now your life has taken a dramatic turn. You're becoming a new man. Striving for something better."

"You can tell all that from the damn cards?" Enzo asked, lifting an eyebrow. "Are you a witch? Or maybe—"

Maddie laughed and nodded. "Of course! I'm a waning

crescent witch, though don't let that get out to the locals. I prefer they think of me as a psychic." She tapped the side of her head. "My divination comes from my father's side of the family, though. He's a descendant of one of the Norns."

The Norns were a trio of women named Urd, Verdandi, and Skuld. Supposedly, they could control people's fates, or so Finch had read, though they weren't gods or anything exceptionally powerful. No one knew where they had gotten their fate-bending magic from, and many considered them a small coven of witches who lived far longer than any witches should have.

However, Finch had never heard of them having any children, and their deaths were recorded, though strange. How could Maddie's father possibly be descended from them? Finch doubted he was.

Then again, her tarot cards had done a fairly accurate reading on Enzo. Not precise, but generally accurate.

"Listen, Ms. Maddie," Finch said.

"Just call me Maddie." She waved a dismissive hand. "We're all friends here." Then she awkwardly chuckled. "What did you say your names were?"

"Enzo."

Finch sighed. "I'm Adair Finch."

He had expected her to recognize his name, but the woman gave no indication she did. Instead, her smile simply returned.

"Ah, yes. *Now* we are all friends."

"Uh… Sure. Maddie. I'm here because I want to find a missing child. I'm fairly certain he's in the Desolation Wilderness, but I'm being hunted by a crazy bounty hunter who is in league with Aeon, Father of the Zodiac. Can your cards help me outsmart them? Or at least tell me if I'm on the right track to finding this kid?"

CHAPTER
TWENTY

Maddie swept up the cards on the table and shuffled her strange deck. When she met Finch's gaze, her expression was aggressively neutral. Finch had no idea what she was thinking.

"It sounds like you're in a lot of trouble," Maddie whispered.

As she continued to shuffle, she stood from the table, walked around the whole front room, and closed all the blinds. Darkness swept over her cabin, and Poopsiekins snorted the moment his sunbeam was taken from him. Maddie then lit a few candles and set them around, their flickering light glinting on all the metal trinkets scattered throughout the space.

"The darkness helps me concentrate," she said as she took her seat. "It also deepens my connection with the night, and strengthens my magic."

Enzo leaned back and crossed his arms. He appeared both skeptical and somewhat impressed, like at any moment he was willing to declare her either a fraud or a genius.

Maddie fanned the twenty-two cards in a crescent before

her. Her bangles clicked against the table as she hovered her hands above the deck. The candles flickered, releasing thin tendrils of smoke that smelled faintly of clove and cedar.

Finch felt the hair rise on the back of his neck. He had seen countless charlatans do readings for sad sacks, and it always involved a bunch of needless theatrics. However, this was one of the few times he felt something in the air. Magic? Or something more.

Maddie's fingers dipped into the arc of cards and drew the first. She placed it in the center of the table.

The Lovers. The picture had two figures intertwined, each facing the other.

Enzo snorted. "Ironic. Adair has been having romance issues lately."

"I'm not—" Finch pinched the bridge of his nose. "I'm not having *romance issues.*"

"Uh-huh."

Maddie's lips twitched. "This card isn't always about romance. It's about a choice. Two paths, two halves of a self." She tapped the card. "But I drew this card upside down, which means it's causing you turmoil. Something about your choices is haunting you. Perhaps you've made the wrong one. Or, at least, you *think* you've made the wrong one."

Finch stared at the card, jaw tight. He didn't look at Enzo.

Maddie drew the second card and laid it beside the first.

Judgement. The card depicted an angel blowing a horn over a field of open graves. The bodies rising from the earth had no faces. Only mouths, all screaming.

This time, Enzo didn't crack a joke.

Maddie whispered the next part. "Adair, you said you were being chased by Aeon?"

"Yes," Finch muttered.

"In a standard American tarot deck, this is the *Judgement* card, but in the Book of Thoth, this is known as *The Aeon.* It's about earning a second chance. Having a rebirth, if you will. If I had to guess, you've been given an opportunity to make something right—to overcome a terrible wrong in your past."

Finch's heart nearly stopped. He glanced up at Maddie, meeting her gaze.

Aeon had... offered him the chance to correct a mistake. And Finch knew, in his heart of hearts, the only wrong that needed undoing was the death of his brother. Were the cards pushing him toward that outcome? Was he supposed to hand over the egg to Aeon and get Carter back, forsaking his ability to rewind time forever?

Finch knew in that moment, he would pay any price.

Was this the push he needed to make a decision? Aeon would see him again the moment he rewound time...

Finch's fingers curled against his knee.

Maddie reached for the deck a third time. She hesitated, then plucked the card with a flick of her wrist and turned it over.

Death. The picture showed a skeleton cloaked in black, riding a pale horse across a barren field. Its scythe wasn't raised but lowered, dragging furrows in the earth as if planting something instead of harvesting. The silver ink on the card caught the candlelight, shimmering like moonlight.

Enzo's breath came out as a low growl. "That's not ominous at all."

Maddie waggled a finger. "You misunderstand again, I'm afraid. The Death card doesn't represent a physical death. It's about the end of something important. Possibly a relationship or an interest, and it sometimes means an increased sense of self-awareness."

"So it's good?" Enzo asked.

After a long moment, Maddie touched *Death* and slid it closer to Finch. "I also drew this card upside down, which typically means petrification. Inertia. Or... an inability to move forward. The reluctance to end things."

Enzo leaned forward, rapt at Maddie's description.

The psychic closed her eyes. "These cards all regard choices and outcomes. Adair, based on my reading, you're having problems deciding. You are held in place by your paralysis, afraid to step forward, unwilling to go back. Yes, you're searching for a missing child, but it is a distraction to keep you from glancing inward and doing what you know must be done."

A draft flew through the bead-curtain of keys. Somewhere, Poopsiekins hissed at nothing and bolted under a chair.

Finch took a deep breath. Was she correct? Was he avoiding what truly mattered?

That was when Enzo let out a huff and a laugh. "That's *it*? We came to you, asking about where to go, and you gave us a therapy lecture?" He jutted his thumb at the door. "Let's get out of here, Adair. I've had enough of this."

"No! Don't run off!" Maddie leapt from her seat, almost knocking over some of the candles on the table. "We're on the cusp of something important. *I can feel it!*"

Enzo stood—he was good foot and a half taller—and sneered. "We didn't even pay for this, and I'm still disappointed."

"This is of *grave* importance. I felt it in the cards. They tingled. Adair has some sort of greater destiny. Something that could affect not just himself, but *all* mankind." All her words carried a hefty amount of gravitas.

Rolling his eyes, Enzo pushed his chair in. "You're not just a drama queen; you're a whole damn royal family."

Shaken, Finch didn't stand. Instead, he activated his magic. Everything froze. The flickering of the flames on the candles, the rising and falling of Poopsiekins's chest, and even the flail of Maddie's arms as she was preparing to persuade Enzo a third time.

Then the colors drained from the cabin, leaving everything a stark black and white.

Finch waited.

Sure enough, the timescape was frozen, and after a few tense seconds, he heard footfalls echo throughout the room.

Finch turned just as Aeon stepped out from between two frozen strands of keys. Again, his Aspect had changed. Instead of having horns, or gills, he now wore a long, silver mantle draped over his shoulders like moonlight woven into cloth. It was fastened with a pin in the shape of a crab, and Finch finally understood.

Aeon sometimes took on small features of the Zodiac himself. The horns had been Aries. The gills had been Pisces. And now the crab was to represent Cancer.

Aeon's high-collared shirt was the deep blue of the midnight sea, patterned faintly with shells that shifted when he moved. Water clung to him without dripping, and every breath he drew fogged like tides pulling in and out.

With precise movements, Aeon pulled out one of Maddie's dainty chairs and took a seat opposite Finch. Maddie remained frozen not but two inches away. She might as well be a lamp.

"You can't avoid me," Aeon said.

"I'm not," Finch replied, cold and confident. "I summoned you here."

Aeon lifted both eyebrows. "Is that so? I take it you've thought of something you want—some mistake you want undone."

"I want you to change time so that Carter—" Finch's voice cracked. He tried again. "So that my brother never died."

For the first time, Aeon's expression softened. It wasn't with kindness, though. It was more like a scientist examining a rare specimen. "Eleven years ago," Aeon murmured. "Carter died in Paris. The catacombs."

Finch caught his breath. The frozen room around him blurred, and for a moment Aeon's Cancer Aspect became an undertow, dragging Finch's consciousness backward.

The catacombs of Paris...

The air had been damp with chalk and rot. Bones lined the walls in endless mosaics. Femurs were stacked like cordwood, skulls fitted into hearts, and crosses by anonymous hands centuries dead. Between them seeped black water, dripping onto the floor, creating a sound akin to teeth clicking.

The ceiling was so low in places they had to crawl, their knees grinding into wet limestone dust. Carter had gotten ahead.

Finch remembered with disturbing clarity when Carter's scream echoed in the corridors all around him.

The memory snapped like a rubber band, and the timescape room steadied. Aeon still sat across from him, cloak glimmering, eyes patient and one blue, one brown.

"You do know I won't save you from your broken pact this time," Aeon said. "I made that offer before, and you refused. This is a new offer—and once you hand me the egg, you'll have betrayed Chronos."

"And I'll die," Finch finished.

He glanced down at the *Death* card, wondering if it really had meant a physical death. Perhaps Maddie didn't know what she was talking about after all.

CHAPTER
TWENTY-ONE

"So we have a deal?" Aeon asked, no rush in his tone. "You give me the egg, and I'll make this change?"

Finch hesitated. Part of him wanted nothing more than to see Carter's face again, to give him the years stolen in the dark. That hunger had never left Finch. It had carved him hollow and cold for almost a decade.

But another part of him, the man he had become since, didn't want to think about the cost.

Enzo, who had gone from client to brother-in-arms.

Jessie, Carter's widow, who still trusted him enough to call.

Bree, bright and stubborn, the apprentice who made him believe in teaching again.

Liam, who had slipped past his defenses and become a friend.

The brand-new PI office with its room to grow.

And Kull, a spirit-turned-human who loved life so fiercely Finch was somehow coming to love it as well.

All those years ago, after Carter died, Finch had had

nothing. He would have gladly burned the world to bring his brother back. But now... Now he had built something worth keeping.

As he rubbed at his ribs, he imagined what Bree would say to him betraying his pact. She would be so disappointed. Killing another being to help Carter? Finch would do it. He knew. But he was supposed to be teaching Bree about how to be a proper warlock, and a proper warlock adhered to honor and duty.

And what would Carter think? Would he want this?

Finch knew the answer.

"I... don't know," Finch muttered. "Maybe this is a mistake."

"Since I'm so generous and merciful," Aeon said with a condescending laugh. "I'll change Carter's fate and allow you to speak with him one last time. *Then* you will give me the egg. Do you understand?"

Finch glared at the time god. He wasn't being merciful. He was trying to sway Finch with emotional manipulation. Once he saw Carter, would he really be able to say no?

Aeon grabbed Finch's shoulder with a strange intensity. Finch's head spun, and it felt as though the floor had fallen out from under him. The black-and-white cabin dissolved, silver threads glittered all around them, and for a heartbeat there was only the undertow of Aeon's power, the sound of tides moving backward, bone-deep and cold.

He felt Aeon's presence like a hand digging into the fabric of his life, unspooling it.

Then something went wrong.

A sound like teeth gnashing through silk shuddered across the timescape. Aeon's silver magic shuddered.

"No," Aeon whispered. "This is..."

The distortion in time yanked Finch back into the catacombs of Paris. Not just memory this time, but something heavier—Aeon's power threaded through the environment, attempting to change things. The walls of bones groaned. Water ran backward up the stone. Carter's scream became an echo trapped in ice.

And then another sound emerged beneath it: a scraping void. It was not breath or voice but the hush of something chewing on existence itself. The mosaics of skulls warped inward as if being inhaled.

"What's happening?" Finch demanded.

Aeon kept his grip on Finch's shoulder, but his gaze was on something distant, his expression pained.

In the flicker of Aeon's working, Finch saw something he wished he hadn't—the shape of something scurrying through the corridor.

It slithered like a centipede made from nightmares; its countless legs weren't even true limbs but twisted, humanlike arms, some ending in hands, others in jagged stumps that scraped against the limestone as it moved. Its body was pale and almost translucent, veins black and branching like roots under ice. The wet sound of its motion was wrong. It was a rhythmic grinding, as if bones were scraping together.

Gixmoth the Desolate.

The magic-eating god who had killed Carter.

Its head emerged from the mountain of skulls, blind and lipless, a disk of concentric mouths opening and closing in silence, each ring of teeth working independently. In place of eyes were clusters of finger-like stalks that writhed and twitched as though tasting the air.

From Gixmoth's many mouths came a sound that wasn't English. It was a vibration in Finch's teeth and spine, but somehow, he knew the monster was speaking, and exactly what it was saying.

"No god touches me," Gixmoth whispered.

And then several of its mouths laughed. Taunting them. Mocking them.

As Finch stared, horrified, he realized the fell god wasn't merely moving through the catacombs—it was eating them. Segments of stone wall dissolved into powder and were sucked into the churning rings of its maw. Even the magic of Aeon's silver light fizzled on contact, devoured like a candle dropped into a storm drain.

And with a *snap*, the world around them shattered. Paris. The catacombs. When the pieces of reality reformed, they were back in Maddie's cabin, sitting at her small table, three cards on display.

Aeon stood and staggered back, his face pale, his silver cloak fluttering.

"I didn't realize," he breathed, voice trembling. "Your brother wasn't killed by circumstance. He was killed by a god. A god who feasts on magic and the bones of the world."

Finch's stomach twisted. "I know. I... I know."

He hadn't been close to Gixmoth. He had never truly seen the god up close. It was disturbing. Disgusting.

Everything wrong with the world and more.

Deep in Finch's gut, a hatred grew. He already despised Gixmoth, but now it was something more. Finch's self-loathing had been worse, but that was fading, leaving him with nothing but rage. Gixmoth had spoken to him through the tunnel in time that Aeon had created...

The god of anti-magic had seen them, and laughed at them.

If it was the last thing Finch ever did, he would vivisect that monster and burn every piece of its body.

"I cannot," Aeon breathed. "Carter's thread ends in the maw of Gixmoth the Desolate. A god who eats magic... even mine. Even Chronos's. Nothing woven touches it. Time breaks on its teeth."

A piece of Finch was glad he wouldn't have to leave Enzo, Kull, Jessie, Bree, everyone, for a promise Aeon couldn't keep. But another piece of him, the old wound, throbbed with fresh pain. Carter was still gone. Carter would always be gone.

Aeon stared at his cloak as though it were an injury. "I have not been denied in an age. This... creature... it should not exist. It should not be allowed to feed."

Finch's throat tightened. "I agree."

Aeon's mismatched eyes flicked to him, and for a heartbeat Finch saw not a god but something almost human. Aeon was baffled, furious, and somehow also diminished.

"I'm sorry," Aeon said. "I cannot undo what happened to your brother."

The words hung between them for a prolonged moment.

Finch sat back in his chair, hands trembling in his lap. "Then I guess the deal's off."

Aeon didn't argue. He didn't even offer a counter deal. His attention went to the cards on the table, and his expression shifted to something pensive.

"Gixmoth," Aeon whispered again, tasting the name like poison. "This changes things."

He stood, silver cloak shuddering. "For now, you may keep your egg, Adair Finch. Keep your pact. We will speak again soon... but not about your brother."

And then he was gone, leaving the timescape echoing with the faint sound of something chewing in the dark.

Finch stared at the space where Aeon had sat, his relief and devastation braided together until he couldn't tell them apart. He reached for the Death card with shaking fingers, but then everything fell away from him until he was left in a void of white.

When he blinked, he was back next to the party bus on

the side of the road. Enzo stood at his left, and Kull at his right.

12:04 a.m.

CHAPTER
TWENTY-TWO

Cold air pressed against Finch's face. The party bus idled beside the road, its windows like mirrors, reflecting moonlight.

Enzo blinked, nostrils flaring, head cocking like a dog catching an old scent on a new wind. "You rewound time," he said. Not a question, but an accusation wrapped in fatigue. "*Why?*"

Kull let out a frustrated gasp. "Wait, what? We're back here? But I was doing so good with Jace! Like, I had a whole conversation that didn't combust. Do you know how rare that is?" She threw her hands up. "And now it's gone. *Poof*. Did something happen, Adair?"

Finch swallowed. His mouth tasted like rust and old stone. "I—"

"Don't say it seemed efficient," Enzo cut in, stepping closer. "We could've used more of the day to question some people."

When Finch was quiet for a beat too long, Kull's irritation vanished. She stepped closer, her emerald eyes searching his.

"Oh, no," she whispered. "Something bad *did* happen. What is it, Adair?"

Finch only then realized his hands were shaking. He curled them into fists and shoved them into his coat pockets. "I'm sorry," he said, and the words came out thin. "I thought I could fix something. I thought—" He cut himself off.

Both of them went still.

"Fix what?" Enzo asked, voice lowered.

"Carter," Finch said. The name scraped going out. "Aeon said he could make it so... he didn't die."

The night swallowed the next few seconds. The wind rushed through the pine trees, causing a rustling, but then nothing.

Enzo's shoulders eased, just a fraction. "And?"

"And he couldn't," Finch said. "Gixmoth the Desolate prevented it." Saying it made his head hurt. "It eats magic. Even Aeon's. Even Chronos's. Carter's... life ends there. No one can change that."

Kull stepped closer, and without another word, she hugged Finch tight. For a moment, Finch didn't even know what to do about the situation. Then he gently hugged her back, trying not to think about what he had almost lost.

"I almost made a deal with Aeon," Finch whispered. "I almost gave him my life and the egg to bring Carter back. But in the last moment... I just couldn't."

It wasn't right. Finch knew.

Enzo didn't curse. Didn't pace. He just stared. "I understand," Enzo finally said. "It would be tempting for anyone. And Carter knows that, too. Everyone knows you would've done anything to save him, if you could."

Kull's fingers tightened her hug around Finch's torso. "Are you okay?" she whispered. "I mean—no, obviously not, and you feel a little lumpy, to be honest, but—are you... here?" She reached a hand around and patted his chest.

Finch let out a breath that felt like it had been trapped for eleven years. "I will be."

Kull nodded like that was an acceptable answer. "Okay. Then you know we're here to help." She finally released him and smiled. "You said you wanted to stop Gixmoth and the witches who helped him. We're going to help with that, too."

After a long exhale, Finch rubbed at his ribs. "I keep putting it off. One excuse after another. This egg was just another reason to avoid what I should've been doing this whole time."

"What should you have been doing?" Kull asked.

"Killing a god."

Enzo slowly smiled. "Fuck yeah. Now that's what I'm talkin' about."

"But I should've told you both what I was doing before seeing Aeon," Finch muttered.

"Yeah. Don't even think about pulling the plug without giving us a heads up in the future."

Kull tilted her head, eyes glossy in the dark. "Okay, well, before we kill a god, you owe me a redo with Jace Min, you time-rewinding menace." She sniffed once, then tried on a wobbly grin. "But I guess I can forgive you if you buy me *two* desserts on our dessert date. The fancy adult kind. With marshmallows."

A laugh escaped Finch, small and broken but real. "Deal."

Kull squeezed his arm, then let go, stepping back just enough to give him air. "So," she said, brisk now, slipping into mission voice, "we still have a kid to save. And a bounty hunter to outfox. And a spirit of death to sweet-talk. We're not done here just yet."

Enzo rolled his shoulders, the wolf in him stretching without showing teeth. "I've got a plan. We get some rest at the Alder Crown until around ten or so, then we steal the leaf from Tate and make our play in daylight. We don't split up; we just enter the Desolation Wilderness from an unorthodox location to avoid Holt and his traps."

"Sounds like a plan," Finch said.

Kull lifted a finger. "You also won't be a martyr. For any reason. We like you alive. It's our favorite version of you."

He nodded once. "Fine. I'll be careful. We'll do this the right way."

Enzo clapped him on the back, solid and warm. "Then it's settled."

Kull brightened, mischief sparking back to life like a pilot light. "Oh! And what if we get Smudge this time around? He seems to know the werewolves because he's working for them. I bet if we bring him to the Desolation Wilderness, he can just show us around. It'll be faster than Enzo sniffing them out, I think. What do you think?"

Although dragging a goblin around the park wasn't high on his priority list, Finch shrugged. "Fine. We'll get Smudge, too."

"Oh, excellent! I love his little goblin face."

The party bus roared down the road, neon strips along the ceiling doing their best impression of starlight. The driver stayed in his private cabin up front, oblivious to their newest passenger, Smudge.

12:18 a.m.

Finch slid into the middle row. Enzo took the rear bench, where Meth was loafed like a judgmental baguette outside his carrier. Kull plopped beside Smudge, cross-legged, already buzzing with questions.

"Can't you speak goblin?" Enzo asked.

"Yup!" Kull replied, chin up. "I'm so glad you remembered."

Smudge blinked, then unleashed a watery trill of syllables that clicked at the back of his throat. Kull perked up, answered in the same cadence, her voice going lower, throatier.

Finch watched their conversation and let it blur in his mind. The bus hummed onto the lakeside road, where the windows showed pine shadows sliding past like the pages of a book being thumbed.

Kull shifted into translator mode without missing a beat. "Okay. Smudge wants to swear loyalty to Finch again, just like last time."

"Fine," Finch said.

Smudge hopped off his seat, bowed to Finch, and then said something in goblin. Once finished, he retook his seat, his yellow eyes watery with admiration. Finch sighed as he gave him a nod.

Smudge patted his chest. "Smudge like."

"Finch like, too, I guess," he muttered.

Kull held up a finger. "Now, to business. Smudge, we're trying to avoid a weird bounty hunter. He's old, smells like oil, and carries a crossbow. Do you know him?"

Smudge's eyes widened. He slapped his palm twice against his sternum, then made a little walking motion with two fingers. A string of clacks and hisses.

Kull covered her mouth as she giggled.

"What is it?" Enzo asked.

"Smudge said he saw a bounty hunter earlier in the night. He said he looks like a toddler who ate a waterbed."

Finch snorted out a laugh. He hadn't thought of it that way, but Holt did hold himself awkwardly with his bum leg. A toddler, though? Maybe a goblin toddler.

"So he does know Holt," Enzo muttered. "Perfect."

Meth stood, walked over to Enzo, turned three disdainful circles on Enzo's thigh, and sat again. Smudge, emboldened, reached toward the cat. Meth swatted his hand, claws sheathed, an imperial *no*.

With a gentle touch, Kull guided Smudge away from the cat. "Okay, we should focus. Next question!" She sat Smudge down. "The spirit of death. The one who rules the Desolation. Smudge, do your people have a name for it?"

Smudge's posture changed. His ears flattened. Not with fear, exactly, but reverence with an edge. He whispered something in goblin.

"Sevengaias," Kull whispered to Enzo and Finch. "Her name is *Sevengaias the Antediluvian*. Smudge says she is as old as the mountain's first breath."

Finch let that sink in. "What does she want? What's this spirit's personality?"

Smudge touched his own throat, then held his palm just in front of his mouth, exhaling. He caught the breath in his hand and pushed it gently downward, as if setting something on the earth. Then he tapped his chest again, three times, each strike lighter than the last. When he spoke, it was rougher.

Kull tilted her head. "Apparently, she wants her land. She wants a cycle of life? She wants renewal and death."

The bus took a slow curve. Through the glass, the lake flashed between buildings like a coin being flipped again and again. Kull dropped her voice into goblin again. Smudge answered with quick, birdlike head tilts, claws clicking on the seat with nervous energy.

"He says Sevengaias doesn't like fire," Kull added after another round. "Not because it scares her, but because it cheats. Fire takes without asking. She wants to be in control, and will go out of her way to stop all fires within her territory, no matter how small."

Finch thought of Ke-Koh's might burning within him. "Hm. This is good to know. Thank you, Kull. You've really helped us out."

Kull blinked, like she hadn't expected the gratitude to sound so sincere. A faint flush rose in her cheeks, quick as a match strike. She smoothed her hoodie over her knees, then she slid across the seat to sit beside Finch.

"You're welcome," she said. Not flippant, not teasing. Just… genuine.

For a few beats, the bus hummed and rattled around them. Kull angled toward him, one elbow draped along the backrest, green eyes steady on his profile. "You know," she murmured, "I know sometimes you find me exhausting. And even though you sigh a lot, you're the only person who's ever made me feel… like it's okay to constantly be myself."

Finch turned his head. Her words landed heavier than he expected, sinking past the noise of his thoughts. He searched her expression, the way mischief still tugged faintly at her mouth but didn't quite reach her eyes.

"You made it pretty clear you wanted a human life," he said. "Humans are weird. They're unique. They're… complicated. And you're definitely all those things. So, congrats. You're human, Kull."

Kull's lips parted like she meant to crack a joke, but she stopped herself. Instead, she leaned in just close enough that her shoulder brushed his coat. "Careful, Adair Finch," she whispered. "If you keep saying things like that, I'll start thinking you actually like me."

The corner of his mouth lifted, involuntary. "I've always liked you. If I didn't, you wouldn't be traveling around with me, solving crimes."

For a moment, silence lived between them. Not

uncomfortable, not charged, just… present. The kind of quiet that felt like the world was at peace.

Then, with her usual spark returning, Kull tapped a finger against his knee. "I know. You like me as a person. I just… Could you imagine going on adventures *all the time*? It would be the best life ever."

Finch huffed a laugh. "That's what Carter always said."

CHAPTER
TWENTY-THREE

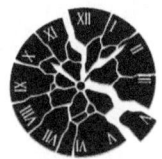

They arrived back at the Alder Crown, and while Enzo took Meth and Smudge to his suite, Finch and Kull retreated to theirs. This time, they barely spoke to one another. It was quiet, and they went to their personal rooms to get as much sleep as possible.

Finch even set his alarm.

Then he crawled into bed and enjoyed a dreamless sleep. He would never admit it to anyone, but it was rare for him to have peaceful moments at night. There were so many evenings he had awoken to nightmares, he couldn't even count them all.

But not this time.

Time passed so quickly, Finch was shocked when his phone beeped.

9:45 a.m.

For two heartbeats he didn't know where he was, but as soon as he saw the lake out the window, his mind calmed. He grabbed his jacket, his two handguns, and then pulled on his pants. After a long stretch, he went out into the central room, wondering what kind of practice flirtations Kull would try this morning.

Finch spotted her standing by the window, half-turned, adjusting the hem of a white dress that hugged her like paint. The dress had long sleeves, a little collar with a zipper that stopped just shy of trouble, and the side scrunched upward with a cinched drawstring that made the skirt tilt up into sexy territory.

Kull had styled her hair into lazy waves and, for once, wore no bright colors—just simple gold at her throat and wrists, accenting her slender frame.

Finch's brain did that thing where it pretended to be a reasonable animal and failed. He looked at the curtains. At the fireplace. At a very interesting knot in the wooden beam. Anything but the person-shaped problem eight feet away.

"Oh! Good morning," Kull said to the glass, catching Finch's reflection before she caught him. She tugged the drawstring at her side, eyed the way the fabric skimmed her hips, then tugged it again. "I'm going for *polished and devastating*. What do you think? Am I pulling it off?"

Finch cleared his throat. "It's functional." His voice betrayed him by being several shades drier than normal.

"Functional?" She spun. "Sir. This is a masterclass in aerodynamic flirtation. This is a wind-tunnel-tested dress. Look at how tight it is!"

"Yeah… I can see," he muttered, and glanced at his phone with a level of focus historically reserved for bomb defusals.

Kull studied him, mouth tilting downward. Then she pivoted to the minibar, where a silver dome waited beside the coffee setup. "Breakfast?" she asked, lifting the lid with a flourish.

Steam rose from the fresh food. There were waffles and bacon, each piled high. A bowl of strawberries sat off to the side.

"That looks like one plate," Finch said. "Where's yours? You eat it already?"

"Nope." She snapped the lid shut, as if she had caught a raccoon stealing. "None for me. I have to be slim and radiant and aerodynamic, remember? Jace likes that look."

Ugh. *Jace.*

Finch had almost forgotten about that social media lunatic.

He sighed. "You also need to be alive. Humans eat food."

She waved him off, gliding past to a mirror and slicking on something clear that made her mouth gleam. "I'll have a cloud for lunch. Maybe I'll even nibble two almonds. That'll hold me."

Finch drank coffee like he was punishing it for existing. The mug was hot enough to sting. Good. Something uncomplicated. He preferred those kinds of sensations.

After a short pause, he grabbed his plate of waffles and bacon and took a seat on the couch.

Kull snatched her phone from the counter. "Anyway! Since you're clearly too nervous to compliment me properly, I'll distract you with art." She unlocked the screen and sat down next to him, angling the phone so he couldn't escape a view of the screen. "These are the lyrics to Jace Min's most amazing love songs. I did a deep dive last night and listened to them all again."

Oh, God.

Finch honestly wished he were both blind and deaf.

Kull cleared her throat like a conductor. "Okay. This one's called *Binary Hearts (feat. DJ SweetLoaf)*." She sang some of the lyrics aloud.

"I log in,
you log in,
the Wi-Fi password is *us,*

> your smile uploads to my soul,
> buffering… buffering… love."

Finch inhaled coffee wrong and had to cough into his sleeve to keep his soul from uploading into the heavenly cloud. "Mmmm."

"I know," Kull breathed, fanning herself. "The beauty of it. So modern. So bold."

"Bold," he sardonically echoed.

"Here's another." She swiped. "This one made me cry. It's called *Lake of My Feelings*." This time, she just sang the chorus.

> "You're my lake,
> I'm your boat,
> tie me up to your heart with a rope."

Kull pressed the phone to her chest. "He's so vulnerable."

Finch stared at the balcony door, wondering how far a man would need to throw himself to induce a non-lethal coma. "Yeah. Vulnerable."

"Oh! Oh! Last one. My favorite." She inhaled and smiled bright. "*Kiss Me in the Algorithm*." When she sang, it was more emotional.

> "Swipe right on destiny,
> tap twice if you agree,
> I'm trending toward your love,
> sponsored by *you and me*."

She looked up at him, eyes glossy. "He believes in destiny *and* ad revenue. It's modern myth-making."

Finch put his mug down. "It's *something*, I'll give you that."

Kull eyed him, practically glaring. "You're not being

honest with me. What do you really feel? C'mon. You can tell me. Is Jace's music moving you?"

He forked a triangle of waffle. "You're planning to starve for a singer who rhymes *boat* with *rope*."

"I'm not starving." She stood and checked the mirror again, smoothing the dress over her waist with flat palms. For a flicker, her smile fell from her face. "I just... If he likes a certain... shape." She shrugged. "I can be that."

Finch's fork hovered. A sentence assembled itself in his mouth, stubborn and heavy. Should he be blunt and honest? Why not? He didn't owe Jace anything, and he kind of hated the man.

"Kull, I have no idea why this jackass is popular." Finch shrugged. "I assume it's because he's young and hot and his voice doesn't actively grate people's ears. But his lyrics are the song equivalent of fat-free cookies or a Ken doll's genitals."

Kull placed her hands on her hips. "How can you say that? He's singing about love, which is obviously the most beautiful thing ever."

"Anyone can make some half-baked rhymes about love." Finch cleared his throat. "Look, I'll do it right now." In the most sardonic of singing, Finch made something up on the spot.

> "Baby, you're my coffee lid,
> I thought you didn't fit, but you did.
> Our love's a candle labeled *spruce*,
> smells like hope and citrus juice."

Kull's eyes went wide, and she had to cover her mouth to hide her smile. "Adair, you made that up on the spot? That's so good!"

"You can't be serious," he said with a groan.

"Do another one! Please." She shook his arm. "Please, Adair."

He rolled his eyes and then sang something random, his tone still as dry as the Mojave Desert.

> "Oh, love, you're a spirit that I don't understand,
>   like IKEA instructions for one extra hand.
>   We'll build us a future with an Allen key,
>   and lose three screws, because that's irony."

Kull wiped at the corner of one eye, beaming. "That's really good, Adair. And you even brought in that I'm a spirit, and building a future together. You're... so amazing at writing lyrics."

"I think you're just easily impressed." Finch sighed. "Which was what I was trying to tell you. Maybe this *Jace Min* isn't as talented as you think he is."

Kull's smile grew softer. "You know what I like most about your songs?"

"How I called it an Allen *key* instead of an Allen *wrench*?"

"That you sang for me! I feel like you never would've done that a few months ago." Kull took her seat next to him again. "You were too grumpy, then."

A knock sounded. Enzo's voice rumbled through the door. "You two decent? Let's go steal a leaf."

Kull bounced to her feet, dress flashing a dangerous amount of skin in his peripheral vision. "We'll be right there!" Then she pointed at Finch's breakfast. "But first, you should have three more bites. Dr. Fox-Pistol's orders, okay? If I'm not going to eat, you have to enjoy it for the both of us."

Finch obliged, because arguing would take longer. She watched, satisfied, then pulled on a pair of leather boots that went up to her knees. Once fully dressed, she linked her arm through Finch's and headed for the door, careful not to move her dress around too much. She didn't have much leeway in any direction.

As Kull reached for the handle, Finch stopped her.

"Wait," he muttered.

She lifted an eyebrow.

"Instead of... hanging out with Jace like you did before... Why not accompany me and Enzo? I think... we could benefit from your mischief magic. And..."

"And?" Kull stared up at him, her eyes big.

"And I'd appreciate your company," Finch hastily concluded.

Kull's smile returned tenfold. "*Really*? You appreciate my company? Why didn't you say so before?"

"I—"

"Oh, never mind! That's not important." Kull threw open the door. "Let's go borrow us a magical leaf or whatever!"

CHAPTER
TWENTY-FOUR

The lobby of the Alder Crown glowed with its usual morning veneer of expensive calm—polished hardwood floors, antique chandeliers, and the scent of cedar delicately hanging in the air.

Finch, Kull, and Enzo exited the elevator together. This morning, Enzo wore a black fleece shirt and a baseball cap. Finch had his coat zipped, hands in pockets. Kull sauntered between them in her white dress, her figure striking enough to be on the cover of a fashion magazine.

The lobby was, of course, filled with Kull's entourage.

Louis paced the lobby while on his phone, his voice, and his French accent, loud enough for people to hear everything from outside. Harper perched on a velvet chair like a sexy gargoyle, Whisp was half-hidden behind a potted palm, and Garret stretched across a couch in a pose that might've been called "innocent" if not for the sunglasses and half-open shirt.

Jace was also here. Finch had been hoping they would've missed him, but that clearly wasn't in the stars.

The Korean pop singer leaned against the espresso bar with a latte in one hand. His hair had been styled into the kind of tousled waves you get from either an ocean breeze or a stylist whose fees include rent.

As soon as Kull appeared, her group lit up.

"Samantha, there you are," Harper said as she hopped off her chair. "I was wondering when you'd come to greet us." She gave Kull a big hug before offering Finch and Enzo a sneer. "Who are these meatheads? Bodyguards?"

Kull waved away the comment. "Oh, they're here to help me navigate Tahoe. Speaking of which..." She handed over a pair of suite keys. "I got us the most bougie hotel this place had to offer. Why don't you all get settled in, and I'll come to see you later?"

With a huff, Harper frowned. "What? Why? You're leaving? You haven't even heard the good news."

"Good news?"

Harper grabbed Kull's arm and turned her to face Jace. "Look who I brought to hang with us for the whole weekend." When Harper's smile reappeared, it was far more wicked. "Come on. I know you've been looking for a guy."

"Uh..." Kull nervously laughed as she pulled herself from Harper's grip. "That's so nice of you to invite him! Why don't you keep Jace warm while I go out on the town, and I'll chat with him later, okay? Kisses!"

Kull hurried away before Harper could even process what had been said.

"Hey there, Fox-Pistol," Garret said, raising a hand. "Breakfast date with us? Come on. We've been brainstorming content, and I want to share it with you."

Whisp peeked out, eyes darting toward Finch and Enzo like a rabbit spotting a pair of hawks.

Kull smiled, tucking a strand of hair behind her ear. "Oh, I'd love to, but I'm booked this morning. I'll be back, though!"

Louis abruptly hung up his phone and turned. "You're *leaving?*"

"Yeah. I need to do something in town. Uh... Guided meditation with, uh..." Kull gestured vaguely. "Rocks. Very old rocks. Very spiritual."

Enzo grunted, deadpan. "Us non-hippies call it *geology.*"

"Right, that." Kull gave a firm nod. "Geology. I need some geology to focus."

Garret chuckled. "Oh... All right. Sounds hot. Don't let us stop you."

Finch resisted the urge to roll his eyes. He adjusted his coat instead, letting Kull do her thing. These weren't *his* friends, after all. The sooner they left the hotel, the better.

Detective Tate would take his lunch break at eleven sharp.

Finch glanced at his phone.

10:18 a.m.

They still had plenty of time, but he wanted to make sure they didn't miss their window of opportunity.

However, before they could escape the lobby, Jace pushed off the counter and sauntered over. He moved like a cat, slow and deliberate, all angles. His sunglasses hung from his shirt collar, his smile the exact width of self-promotion.

"Hey, Samantha," Jace said, dropping his voice as though he were about to narrate his own TikTok. "You look incredible. That dress? Wow. You're even more stunning in person than in your videos."

Kull shrugged and half laughed. "Ah. Well, thank you so much."

"Why don't you skip the... rock thing... and hang with us? I hear Tahoe has some amazing sights. And hot tubs. We could get some stunning sunset shots, maybe some reels. You would look *insane* in that lighting."

Kull tilted her head, caught between pleased and wary.

"That's... nice of you, but no. I'll be back later. I can't just cancel my—"

"C'mon." Jace's smile sharpened. "Just a couple of hours. I came all this way to see you, after all. I'm a busy guy. I could be anywhere. With anyone. I'd *rather* be spending my day with you, but if you're too busy... Maybe I should take off."

Finch moved forward.

He didn't even think about it. He just stepped between them, calm as a door closing on a draft. He planted himself slightly sideways, not aggressive, just occupying space. The effect was simple and devastating: Jace was now looking at Finch's shoulder instead of Kull's neckline.

Finch's tone was mild, almost polite. "She's busy. You're lucky she has time for you at all this weekend."

Jace blinked, thrown off by the flatness of it. "Uh. Okay, but I was just—"

"She said no." Finch adjusted his cuff and stared Jace dead in the eyes. "No is a full sentence."

Jace tried a laugh, but it came out thin. "Dude, relax. I'm just inviting her to hang out."

"And maybe you will tonight, if she isn't occupied," Finch said. No heat, just cool certainty.

Kull stepped to Finch's side, biting the inside of her cheek to hide a smile. Enzo walked over to the front door and crossed his arms, his expression radiating impatience.

Jace shifted his weight, tried for charm. "You her bodyguard or something?"

"Something." Finch's mouth curved just a little.

For a heartbeat, the whole lobby was quiet. Harper appeared incredulous, Louis intrigued. Whisp hid further behind the plant, and the only one to break the silence was Garret, who whistled low as though this was hilariously entertaining.

Then Kull slid her arm through Finch's and smiled at Jace. "Sorry, Jace. Rain check. Magical geology waits for no one."

Enzo straightened, his voice a low rumble. "We'll be back later this evening. Maybe."

"Yeah," Kull added brightly. "I'll DM you if we're free. Byeee."

She let Finch guide her toward the door. Enzo went out with them.

As the lobby doors swung shut behind them, Kull hissed a laugh under her breath. "Adair, I think you just cock-blocked a pop star."

Finch kept walking, hands in pockets. "He had it coming."

"It reminds me of this one movie about when a famous singer was undercover as a normal person and he got totally showed up by this construction worker." Kull gave his arm a squeeze. "You could be a movie star if you wanted, ya know."

Enzo chuckled, low and wolfish. "I'd kill to see that."

"It's not going to happen," Finch said with an exhale. But he did fantasize about it for a short moment. Kull would also make for an excellent actress.

The party bus rocked as it went down Tahoe's narrow roads. Neon strips glowed over Finch's head. The driver kept to his private cab. Tahoe slid by the smoked windows in pine-green bands, the lake flickering silver whenever the buildings cracked apart.

The sight never got old.

At the back of the bus, a symphony of strange noises seemingly came from nowhere.

Slllluuuurp. Pause. *Slllllllurp.* Then a satisfied little, "Ahh."

"Kull," Finch said without looking over, "tell Smudge if he's going to be invisible, he has to be quiet as well."

Kull squinted at the air beside her. "Smudge, honey? Silent mode."

The invisible smoothie-drinking goblin answered: *sllllluuuuurp.*

Without warning, Enzo leaned forward, gripping the edges of his seat. When he growled, everyone in the bus felt it. Smudge choked, and his smoothie fell to the floor, becoming visible the instant it left his tiny gray-green hands.

"There," Enzo said with a satisfied smile. He leaned back in his chair. "We're done with that."

Finch checked his phone.

10:33 a.m.

Plenty of time to make their play. They would scope Tate's office, confirm access, and be ready to "borrow" the leaf the moment the detective took lunch at eleven sharp.

The bus rolled into the sheriff's substation lot and let out a pneumatic sigh like it was going through seasonal depression. The beige box of a building sat under a bright sky. Salt-streaked patrol SUVs idled in a row. The planter of dead petunias by the door definitely gave the place some unique charm.

Charm wasn't the right word, but Finch was feeling generous.

When they exited the vehicle, they didn't go in through the front.

Enzo led the way along the side of the building with an attitude of *I belong anywhere I want.* Kull followed behind, white dress and knee-high boots a tad conspicuous, but since there weren't many people out and about, Finch wasn't worried. Finch brought up the rear, hands in his coat pockets, gaze unremarkable.

"Third window from the corner," Finch said. "Office with a pine view."

They found it: narrow pane, wire glass, sticker sun-faded around the edges. Through the slats of the blinds, Finch could make out a desk, shelves, the faint glint of something framed high on the wall.

Detective Tate was inside, his silhouette moving back and forth.

Having arrived early, Finch, Kull, and Enzo just waited among the trees. Exactly at eleven, Tate left his room, his door shutting with a *snap* that pierced through the window.

Then Enzo hurried over to the sill. He grabbed the glass as best he could and shoved upward. The window rattled on a lock, and threatened to shatter under Enzo's strength. Finch leapt forward and motioned him away.

Finch glared at the window. The latch was an old slide type, brushed steel, clamped shut on the inside. Someone had been diligent with the paint.

Kull bounced on her toes, eager. "Want me to mischief it?"

"You're up," Finch said, gesturing her over. Her mischief magic would allow her to undo any lock or security measure. It was the height of trickster magic.

She planted her palms to either side of the frame and took a breath. "Okay, little lock," she murmured. "Time to be a naughty boy and let us all in."

Nothing happened.

Kull frowned, shook out her hands, and tried again. The air fizzed with the tiniest bit of magic, a static prickle across Finch's knuckles. One blind slat twitched.

The latch remained latched.

Enzo leaned in, voice low. "What's the holdup, Houdini?"

Kull put both thumbs against the glass, as if she could massage the concept of "open" through osmosis. "Shh. I'm seducing the hardware."

She exhaled, concentrated harder. A single flake of dried paint gave up and flittered down to the sill. The latch... didn't care. Finally, she stepped back, cheeks flushed with effort and annoyance.

"Okay. So. Tiny update."

Enzo cocked a brow. "Update like you need more runway for your magic to work? Or update like we need a crowbar?"

Kull chewed her lower lip, then glanced between them, the humor easing out of her voice. "It's fading."

"What's fading?" Finch asked.

"My magic." Kull's gaze dropped to the ground. "Ever since I inhabited this human body, I've been losing it. Bit by bit."

Finch shook his head. "You haven't lost it. I saw you summon a whole flock of birds when Holt attacked us. That was clearly your mischief spirit magic."

"Yes. It was." Kull hugged herself. "But that was because I was worried about you. My heart core is tied to control mischievous animals. When you were in danger, what little magic I had left surged. But you saw what happened. The pigeons were scared away so easily... Even my most powerful of magic was weak."

Enzo slid a hand along the painted frame, testing. "How long do you have before you lose all of it?"

"It's not like a countdown." Kull shrugged. "It's more like... waking up and realizing you can't remember a word you used every day. Then a week later you forget another one. I'm becoming more human, and that eats away at my spirit-self. If that makes sense."

An invisible shape bumped Kull's hip. Kull reached down and patted something.

Smudge.

Was he trying to comfort her?

Finch studied Kull's profile for a beat. She wasn't being

dramatic—no performance. Just honest. It tugged at something in him.

"Don't worry about it," he said. "We can find other mischief spirits. We'll adapt. This doesn't make you any less of a person."

Kull blinked and then flashed him a grateful smile that hit like sunlight. "Okay. But we can't give up here. I hate quitting on a lock. It feels personal. How can we break in?"

"Plan B is punching in the glass while you two distract the sheriffs," Enzo said. Was he joking? Finch couldn't tell.

"I'll handle this," Finch muttered. He pressed his fingertips to the glass directly over the latch, feeling for the metal through the pane. He'd used his dwarven magic mostly defensively—against bullets, blades—but metal was metal.

He focused, thin line of will tightening. Unstick. Loosen. Since the magic was attached to his eyes core, he just needed to visualize it working.

A faint creak answered inside the frame. Paint whispered. The latch didn't pop, but it sighed in the spiritual key of "this might go somewhere."

Another slow creak. Then the metal bubbled and folded outward.

Click.

The latch peeled away, releasing the window and allowing it to be pushed upward.

"There," Finch said with an exhale. "Done."

Kull golf clapped. "Wow! You're more mischief spirit than me, it seems."

Enzo gave her shoulder a bump with the back of his hand. "Don't say that. You're the only mischief spirit we need around here."

Footsteps scuffed from inside the building—in the hallway, not Tate's room. Finch stepped back automatically, casual as could be. Kull smoothed her dress. Enzo pretended to be very interested in a pinecone.

The footsteps passed.

Finch returned to the glass, eyes scanning the office again. The cedar leaf glowed faintly in its amber prison, high on the wall, smug. He checked his phone.

11:06 a.m.

CHAPTER
TWENTY-FIVE

"Let's get this and go," Finch murmured.

Enzo didn't waste a breath. He opened the window, lifted the blinds just enough, and flowed through the gap like a very large, very confident cat. For a man built like a fridge, he moved with surprising grace. His Crocs kissed carpet, and thankfully nothing creaked.

Kull and Finch flattened in the sliver of shade beside the wall. From inside came the ghost-sounds of an office: the hum of a tired monitor, the sigh of an AC vent.

Enzo effortlessly reached up and grabbed the amber-covered leaf and pulled it from the string that held it in place.

"Easy," Finch whispered.

As quiet as could be, Enzo slid out under the blinds and then shut the window behind him. With a smirk, Enzo handed over the leaf. Finch slid it into the inside pocket of his coat, over his heart.

They hurried back around the building, across the gravel, past the planter of deceased petunias, and into the bright, indifferent morning. The party bus was waiting; the driver didn't look back.

As soon as they were inside, the patter of Smudge's footfalls echoed around Finch. The goblin headed straight for his seat in the back.

"Atta goblin," Enzo said, dropping into the rear bench.

Finch and Kull took seats close to one another.

"To the Desolation Wilderness," she shouted to the driver.

The drive curled along the lake, past cabins and wildly popular paths. Then the traffic thinned. Pines thickened. The bus left the highway for a smaller road, then a smaller one still, until they reached a paved lot that thought highly of itself: map kiosk, bear-proof trash cans, a wooden rail fence worthy of a catalog.

11:44 a.m.

"Official entrance is that way," Enzo said, chin-tilting at the broad, obvious trail that led away from the lot.

"And Holt is waiting for us there, remember?" Finch asked. "We need to be unorthodox. We're hopping a fence."

Kull eyed her boots, then a chain-link fence in the far distance, then the hem of her white dress. "I can do this in a dignified manner. I think."

Enzo hopped the fence, one planted palm and a flex, and landed silently, way more graceful than a man his size should be. When Finch arrived at the fence, he hesitated. Leaping over it wouldn't be a problem, but he didn't want Kull to mess up her outfit or have a difficult time. So instead of just hoisting himself over, he placed a hand on the chain-link and visualized it moving apart.

Sure enough, the fence bent to his will. The links became putty, melting through one another until they were able to stretch open and create an opening large enough for an adult.

Finch stepped through with ease and then motioned Kull to follow.

"Oh, thank you, Adair," Kull said with an awkward chuckle as she hurried through. Her smile was genuine, though, which confused Finch.

He thought she would've been happier with this solution...

"Showoff," Enzo said with a snort.

Finch placed his hand back on the fence and visualized it stitching itself back together. "You're just jealous."

"I can manhandle that whole fence if I want to," Enzo stated. "Your metal party trick doesn't impress me."

Then the fence rattled, and Finch whirled around. At first, he thought they were under attack, but then he heard the little goblin grunts of Smudge and realized too late that he had shut the fence before the pukwudgie had a chance to go through his makeshift opening.

"I'm sorry about that," Finch muttered as Smudge landed on the ground next to him.

"Smudge okay," the goblin replied, cheery.

Once all together, Enzo led them to what appeared to be a trail. Well, it wasn't really a trail. It was a seam between wind-stunted pines and boulders glazed with lichen. The air smelled like sun-warmed sap.

And underneath it all was a scent of ancient magic.

The scent slicked Finch's tongue, sour around the edges. The kind of taste a penny left on the gums. He slowed, nostrils flaring.

"You all smell that?" he asked, low.

The hair on Enzo's forearms bristled. "Yeah."

"You two aren't going to like this." Kull hugged her

elbows. "But I think there might be fae wolves nearby. And also *water babies*. Maybe something undead?"

"What are water babies?" Enzo asked, one eyebrow raised.

"They're little demons resembling infants. They cry to lure humans near water, and then they cause madness through their shrieking, and the humans usually drown themselves. They used to kill *so many* people, but I think they've mostly been driven away… I haven't smelled them in years."

Finch sighed. Magical wolves and murderous infants? Just his luck.

They continued down the makeshift trail, the sun high in the sky, but the pine tree canopy was growing thicker the further they went into the park. And Finch could've sworn that the deeper they went, the more the wilderness rearranged itself around them.

A granite slab ahead pinched into a natural hallway between two rises, not unlike the choke point where Holt had tried to ambush them yesterday-in-another-timeline.

As they walked toward it, Kull held out a hand. Both Enzo and Finch stopped.

With a nervous chuckle, and her eyes on the ground, Kull whispered, "Do you two think less of me? F-For having less magic, I mean."

Finch and Enzo answered at the same time, talking over one another in their haste to reply.

"Of course not."

"Hell no."

Kull lifted her gaze and half smiled. "Even though a simple chain-link fence would stop me now? I mean, when I was a mischief spirit, I could change into a pigeon and fly over. Or even a ferret and squish through the links. Now I can't even undo simple locks…"

Finch shrugged. "You can develop magic in other ways. And you still have plenty of useful abilities."

"Like what?"

"Speaking goblin."

Kull perked up and stood a little straighter. "Oh, right. Yeah, that hasn't faded much at all. I still *can* do that." Then she bounded over to Finch, her bright smile returning. "Thank you, Adair. You always know exactly what to say!"

They continued through the narrow choke point, the tall white stones on either side of them. Kull, cheerier than before, glanced around without a visible care in the world. Enzo stayed up front, and when the boulders narrowed further, he crept forward, sniffing deep as he went.

Before he escaped the narrow pathway of rock, he stopped.

"Something wrong?" Finch whispered.

"Yeah." Enzo inched backward, never turning around. "Something dead. Maybe even moving."

"I did say I smelled some undead," Kull quietly chimed in.

"Bad things," Smudge said from invisibility, causing everyone to flinch.

For some reason, Finch found it difficult to remember the little goblin was still with them.

Then a thing stepped around one of the boulders, entering their narrow passage.

It was an elk once. Now it wore an elk like a memory. Ribs showed even though there were no bones—only arching lengths of white fungus ribbing an empty chest cavity. Its hide was a collection of moss and torn bark braided with old fishing line. Antlers looked like driftwood, tines sprouting new tines, almost with no rhyme or reason.

What stared at them from the skull wasn't eyes. It was moths.

A swarm of them, pale and dusty, crowding the sockets, restless. When the creature breathed, they fluttered about.

Did it need to breathe? Most undead didn't, but some did so to better blend with the environment. Finch suspected, due to the plants on its body, the creature was some sort of hybrid undead.

Kull's hand found Finch's sleeve and stayed there. Enzo growled, and black fur sprouted across him as his lycanthropy curse took hold.

The elk-thing didn't lower its head to threaten. It tilted its head, curious.

Smudge appeared in front of Finch, his arms out wide. "No. No harm." Then he turned and said something in goblin.

Kull shook her head. "Apparently, this elk wants us to leave, and if we don't, it'll try to force us. Smudge said he thinks it's too dangerous."

"What is it?" Finch asked.

Smudge answered in goblin. Kull translated.

"He says it's a *Hollow*," she said. "But that's silly because Hollows are typically made by spirits, and I've never known *any* spirit strong enough to make a Hollow as large as this one." With a frown, she added, "Spirits usually make tiny Hollows, like things the size of a mouse."

This undead creature wasn't about to stop him. Finch stepped forward, confident. "We're here to save some lost children. If you know where they are, we'd appreciate the escort."

The Hollow didn't lunge. It didn't move. It just listened. The moths stirred, then settled again, and the air grew colder.

Finch stepped forward a second time. "If you don't know where they are, just get out of the way. We'll find them ourselves."

The Hollow rasped, and the moths of its eyes shivered. Then the undead beast did something Finch didn't expect.

It stepped sideways, hooves placing themselves with orchestra precision, and revealed the path behind it: a narrow deer track that hadn't been there a blink ago, threaded between tall pines so thick, the light had trouble piercing the needle canopy.

Enzo crossed his arms. "Oh, hell no."

"What's wrong?" Finch asked.

"Have you ever seen a horror movie? This thing is going to try to kill us."

"It's letting us pass."

"Into a dark and spooky trail that wasn't there a moment before. No. It's not a friendly corpse deer. This is *Bambi 2: The Revenge of Bambi's Mom*."

Finch exhaled, fearing Enzo might be right, but also not wanting to wait around. He had a terrible feeling Holt knew they were in the park, and he wanted to find the missing boy as soon as possible. As soon as he knew *where* in the park that Jason was hiding, he could devise a quicker way to get there after rewinding time.

"I'll go first," Finch said. "And if it's safe, I'll motion you through."

Smudge whirled around on his heel, his brow furrowed. "Not safe. *Not safe*."

Enzo pointed at the pukwudgie. "See? The goblin knows what's up."

"Aren't you a big bad werewolf?" Kull asked, tilting her head to the side. "Are you telling me you're afraid of a corpse elk? It doesn't seem like you."

Enzo huffed for a moment before striding forward. "I'm not afraid. I'm just not a damn fool. But if we *have* to go this way, I'll gladly do it."

"Then we'll go together," Finch stated.

"Fine."

Finch walked around Smudge and headed for the dark trail. When Kull and Smudge caught up to him, he glanced over his shoulder and frowned.

"You two can wait here," he said.

"Why don't you just give me one of your handguns?" Kull asked, her tone sweet. "And I'll help you?"

"Do you know how to shoot?"

"Yes?"

Her half question reply wasn't reassuring. However, since his two handguns were magical, they were much easier to use than standard firearms. Finch reached into his coat and drew Agony. Then he handed it to Kull.

"Don't shoot either of us." Finch motioned to himself and Enzo.

"Got it," Kull replied with a sarcastic salute.

Then, as a team, they walked toward the dark trail. The Hollow leapt ahead, diving into the darkness.

CHAPTER
TWENTY-SIX

Enzo went first, already half-shifted—nails blackening, teeth forming into fangs—and Kull kept a hand hooked in Finch's sleeve as if she could turn him with the smallest tug. Smudge scuttled behind, imperceptible except for the occasional crunch of pine needles and his nervous little huffs.

The trail was wrong in the same way AI gets things wrong—angles that shouldn't meet, distances that lasted longer than they looked. Pine trunks crowded close, oozing amber that glistened in the tiny amount of light streaming down.

"Anyone else feel like we just walked into somebody's mouth?" Kull whispered.

"We're fine," Finch said. "Let's just get through here quickly."

Then something strange happened. Stranger than even the undead elk.

Moths fell like snow. Not a drift, but a deluge of them. They poured from the canopy, soft bodies thudding against everyone's clothes and skin, and even pattering on stone. The air went dusty-cold. Finch got a mouthful of powder and spit it out, tasting mausoleum.

Then the underbrush stood up.

A wolf, or what a wolf would look like if a child made one out of nettles and ribs, slid into the path and showed a jaw full of acorn caps. Behind it, a bobcat stitched together from birch bark and tendon. To the right, a fox wearing a pelt of moss and sinew. Overhead, owls dropped from the branches, each with skulls for faces, wing bones webbed with spider silk. A bear shouldered through the trees, its hide a patchwork of rotten bark and sodden hair, one eye a knothole full of peering moths.

Hollows. Dozens of them. Maybe more.

"I motherfuckin' called it," Enzo said through gritted teeth, his tone a growl.

The first wolf lunged.

Finch drew his pistol as if his hand had always been holding it. When he fired Starfall, blue light blazed through the darkness. The wolf came apart in a mist of spores and mulch, but the mulch wriggled, gathering itself back into the shape of a wolf in a matter of moments.

Enzo's shoulders exploded outward with muscle, the last of the human in him slipping behind the eyes as fur ripped across his back. He sank his claws into the bear and dragged it down, black on black, teeth punching through rot and root. The bear's ribs flexed like wicker. The two of them rolled, smashing saplings flat.

Owls came for Finch. Six of them, silent and hateful, winging at his face with beaks like sewing needles. He threw his forearm up and felt a dozen pinpricks through his coat. He fired point-blank, eyes stinging from moth dust, and Starfall's sapphire rounds blew chalk out of their owl skulls. New ones swooped down. They kept clawing and tearing at Finch's jacket.

"Damn birds," he growled.

A fox-leech monster went for Kull's throat.

She didn't back up. She stepped in. A flare of weak magic surged from her, manifesting as a slight green sparkle. The fox's front legs tangled in roots that had not been there a heartbeat before. It face-planted into a rock with a noise like a book slammed shut.

"Too slow," Kull said as she lifted Agony and fired.

The red shot cracked, and the fox twitched before it stopped moving. An undead bobcat flew from the branches of a nearby tree, and Kull whipped her gun up just in time to fire again. The bobcat spasmed and hit the ground, creating a furrow.

"Ha!" Kull barked, eyes bright. "Take that, you compost gremlin!"

Smudge materialized near Finch's boot, just long enough to tug at Finch's coat hem and jab a gray finger toward the bear fight. "Not teeth," the goblin rasped. "The little flutter in the heads. Kill flutters."

Moths. Smudge wanted him to deal with the moths.

"Enzo!" Finch shouted, pointing. "The moths—" Then he shot four more owls, their corpses piling up near his feet.

Enzo didn't answer. His jaws were full of bear. He tore free something that had once been a shoulder and used it to hammer the rest of the Hollow into pieces, spraying wet fungus in arcs. The moths in the knothole eye boiled up, angry and stupid. Enzo lunged, and his mouth became a cloud of white.

He ate the moths. He ate them. The bear went slack under him, suddenly only a dead stump again.

"Oh," Kull said, a little strangled. "That's a choice."

Enzo spit a mouthful of wings.

More came.

A herd of undead deer clattered from between the trunks

—antlers grown so large they were curling into themselves. Their legs were too long, joints bent wrong. A raccoon with glass bottle bottoms for eyes hissed and scuttled sideways, hands clacking like knitting needles.

Finch moved forward.

He holstered Starfall and threw a hand up. A blaze of fire erupted from the creases in his palms; his connection with Ke-Koh was strong, but not as strong as usual. Since this magic was tied to his heart, it was empowered by emotion, and currently, he felt mostly annoyance, followed closely by delight.

Destroying a horde of undead goons always made him feel good.

The inferno rushed over the undead deer and then over the raccoon. Embers rained through the dark forest, some catching on the pine needles. The fire licked upward, singeing the moths and destroying their wings by the dozens.

Kull whooped and then gagged on moth dust and smoke. Smudge disappeared again, his invisibility nearly perfect.

"Left!" Kull shouted through a wheeze.

Finch turned and saw the cat—no, a mountain lion—slip out from the darkness, its hide a suit of bark stitched with sinew, its tail a frayed rope ending in a clump of burs. It came without sound, the way real cats do when they mean it.

He whirled and unleashed another round of flames. The mountain lion twisted in midair, but it couldn't get out of the way. Fire rushed over its disgusting body, and then it hit Finch anyway.

They went down together. Finch's shoulder met stone and politely exploded. The lion's teeth closed on his forearm, and he felt pressure, not pain. He pulled his handgun and then shoved Starfall up into the lion's chest and fired three times. The bullets found whatever passed for a heart. The cat sagged. Moths spilled from its mouth in a pale waterfall.

Kull was there, hauling the cat's skull back with its rope tail. She jammed Agony into its eye socket and shot. The skull made a noise like glass shattering.

"You okay?" she asked, panting.

"Fine." Finch tried to push himself up with the forearm that had just been bitten in half by a tree-cat. His arm almost gave out, but he pushed away the pain, unwilling to let this slow him down.

Enzo thundered past them. The Hollows broke against him. Enzo clawed at anything in his way. He ducked under a charging elk and came up inside the rack, then tore the rack off like a man ripping a door from a car to get at the driver. He used it as a plow, smashing it against three deer that came for him, battering them until their bodies shattered.

The ground shook. Finch thought it was Enzo, then realized this had a pattern to it. A heavy, steady thump. The pines ahead parted like curtains being dragged aside by an annoyed stagehand.

A moose.

Its legs were long white bones wound with river weeds, hooves shod in stones. Its skull sprouted a cathedral of antlers. Every tine was crowned with a wasp's nest that hummed with moths instead. Its breath steamed out and came back, like a fog that didn't want to leave.

"How many of these things are there?" Finch asked with a sigh.

"I don't think spirits are ever meant to get this strong," Kull whispered.

Finch took aim and then fired Starfall into the nests—blue lights stuttering through the air like falling stars—and the nests burst, moths blooming out in pale swarms. Kull fired, Agony's pain bursting among them like invisible nails. The moths jerked and tumbled, spiraling into the snow of their kin.

The moose charged forward.

Enzo braced, met the moose head-on with a noise that was half roar, half howl. He grabbed the skull around the sockets and pushed.

For half a breath, the moose and the werewolf were a statue: death crowned in winter and rage wrapped in fur. Then Enzo twisted. The antlers groaned. The skull split down the middle like a rotten log. Moths poured out, and Enzo crunched his fangs down on them, killing more than three dozen in a single bite.

The other Hollows faltered. The flock of owls tried to climb straight up through branches they couldn't fit between. The smaller things went still, listening. It seemed the fewer moths there were, the less they were coordinated, and now they simply could not fight.

"Is it... over?" Kull whispered.

Enzo dropped the moose and huffed, his black fur standing on end.

Small fires burned around them. Smoke wafted up past the tree branches, heading into the afternoon sunlight far above. Embers twirled through the air, threatening to light the entire pine forest ablaze.

Something clapped. Not hands. Not hooves. A sound, made by no mouth. The air steadied. The moths drew together. A large shape—something bigger than a house—moved through the darkness nearby.

"Sevengaias," Kull whispered. Not fear, only awe.

Finch held up the amber-covered leaf. He didn't want to face a spirit of death. Would their hall pass work? Would this be enough to convince the gigantic spirit to leave them alone?

To his shock, the amber around the leaf glowed a soft golden color that effortlessly cut through the darkness. But even with the shine, Finch never caught a glimpse of the death spirit. She backed away from the golden glow, her massive body almost liquid in her movements.

One by one, the fires were snuffed all around them. *Whoosh. Whoosh. Whoosh.* An icy chill surged between the trees. Although Finch didn't really see the spirit, he knew she was here. Was she going to attack them for harming the Hollows?

But nothing happened. Once the fires were out, the cold slowly faded.

Then the amber stopped glowing, and the massive presence of the spirit was no more.

It had worked. The leaf had protected them.

The Hollow elk reappeared on the path ahead. It had no business being whole again, but there it was, moth eyes solemn and bright. It stepped once, slow, and lowered its head.

Not a threat. A direction.

Finch glanced at Enzo. Enzo spit out a moth leg and rolled his sore shoulder, fur rippling. He had a few gouges across his arms, but his injuries weren't threatening. He was already healing, thanks to his werewolf form.

"*We done?*" Enzo shouted at the darkness.

Nothing replied.

The Hollows parted in a ragged corridor. The path the elk had shown them before yawned open again, narrower than ever and somehow straighter. Finch shoved the leaf into his pocket.

Kull wiped moth dust off her lips with the back of her wrist and nodded, eyes too bright. "Okay, let's get out of here. Jason is waiting for us."

They went. The Hollow animals watched, heads tilted, moths murmuring in their skulls. Enzo kept one eye on the moose ruin in case it decided to reassemble itself into a bad idea. Smudge reappeared just long enough to steal a button off Finch's coat.

"For luck," the goblin said, which was not reassuring. Then he vanished again.

They walked until the trees thinned and the sunlight reached them. A vast field stretched out before Finch, and that was when he turned to where Smudge had been.

"All right, show us how to get to the werewolves," he commanded.

CHAPTER
TWENTY-SEVEN

After a few seconds, Smudge appeared. He was frozen in place, halfway through gnawing on his newly acquired button. His yellow eyes went wide, round as coins. Then, he nodded and tucked the button away in his little cargo shorts.

"Need piece," the goblin said. "Piece of wolf."

Enzo lifted a brow. "You can see I'm right here, yeah?"

"Magic piece." Smudge pointed a gray finger at Enzo's chest. "Hair, claw, blood. Little bit."

Kull perked up. "Pukwudgies have, like, mind magic. Remember? They can make you see things, or not see them? Well, they can call to other magical beings through their mind if they've got a sympathetic thread. Like having werewolf fur would allow them telepathy with werewolves. It's kind of adorable. Gross, but adorable."

Finch narrowed his eyes, suspicious. "You're telling me he can call werewolves with a furball?"

"Well, yeah. It's like… pukwudgie Bluetooth."

"That's not a thing," Enzo muttered.

"It's sort of a thing," Kull replied with a smile. "It's magic that connects creatures through recognition. Telepathy, even a limited form, is super useful, so I think you shouldn't knock it."

"Is he going to speak to every werewolf in a mile radius of us?" Finch asked.

Smudge shook his head.

"I think he can target it," Kull muttered. "But I'm not sure."

Smudge trotted over to Enzo, hand out expectantly.

Enzo crossed his arms, his wolf tail swishing back and forth. "You want me to just start shedding for you?"

With a small, impatient nod, Smudge said, "Small piece."

Enzo sighed through his fangs, then reached up and ripped out a tuft of fur from his shoulder. "There. Happy?"

Cradling the black fur like a holy relic, Smudge grinned. The goblin then held his cupped hands to his mouth, blew once, and began to hum a strange song.

It wasn't a sound meant for human ears. The air quivered. The pine needles trembled on their stems. It wasn't an unpleasant song; it was just strange. Finch took the moment to rip off some of his coat sleeve and wrap it around his injured arm.

The adrenaline of combat was fading, and his arm flared with pain whenever he moved it. Blood dripped onto the old pine needles on the ground, and Finch had to keep his teeth gritted as he pulled the coat tight.

With concern in her eyes, Kull stepped forward and wordlessly assisted. She grabbed some of the coat and helped tie it off.

Enzo's wolf ears twitched, but he said nothing.

The humming increased in volume, higher and higher, until it turned to clicks and then to a warbling keening sound. After a minute of that, Smudge stopped and tucked the fur into one of his cargo shorts pockets.

Then silence.

Finch waited. "Well?"

"Wait," Smudge said. "They hear. They come." He puffed out his chest, his expression rather proud.

"They'd better," Enzo said with a snort.

After a few minutes, the silence changed. It went thicker somehow, like breath being held by an entire forest. Then a sound broke through it—faint at first, a ripple of motion far off in the trees. Branches cracking. A rhythm of many feet.

Finch raised Starfall instinctively, the familiar weight steady in his hand. "If any of them have red eyes, I'm putting a bullet in their muzzle."

Enzo's nostrils flared. "No," he murmured. "There aren't any contagious wolves nearby."

Trusting his werewolf associate, Finch holstered his weapon.

The forest stirred. Shapes emerged between the pines. Small ones. Thin ones. All human.

They came out one by one.

The first was a girl, maybe seven. She was barefoot, and her legs were striped with pine scratches. A grimy yellow swimsuit clung to her shoulders, faded almost to beige, and one strap had snapped and been tied back together with what looked like fishing line.

Her hair was a thicket of dark curls matted with sap and needles, and someone had woven a ring of dandelions through the mess in the shape of a crown. Her brown eyes were enormous, luminous, catching every flicker of light.

Enzo and Kull froze, their breath held, but Finch knew who this was. Ever since he saw the many flyers about the missing children, he hadn't forgotten their names, pictures, or descriptions.

"Lily?" he asked.

Kull's instant recognition caused her to gasp. "Oh! Lily Hernández! The missing girl…"

Lily didn't flinch at her name. She tilted her chin up instead, wary but unafraid, her small nostrils flaring as though she was scenting them.

The lycanthropy curse wafted from her…

She was, in fact, a werewolf now.

Behind her came a boy of fourteen, all elbows and knees, his frame thin to the point of transparency. He wore what used to be a band T-shirt, now torn into a sleeveless rag, the logo stretched beyond recognition. His jeans had been cut off at the knee with something serrated, and one of the pant legs was tied around his hand like a makeshift bandage.

Finch recognized him, too.

Benji Loomis. The band kid who never made it home from practice.

His brown hair stood on end, the kind of haircut you get when you stop trying. Mud streaked his cheeks like camouflage paint. His eyes—gray-green and too bright— moved restlessly between Finch, Enzo's claws, and the tree line.

The next figure was older. He was a young man built with a college athlete's shoulders, but hollowed by hunger and sleepless nights. Nineteen. His hoodie had been shredded by brambles, the blue fabric stiff with dirt and old rain.

His jaw was dark with weeks of stubble, and his expression belonged to someone who had been responsible for too long. There were scratches along his collarbone, some healed, others fresh. His lips were cracked, but his posture was solid, protective. He stepped in front of the others, especially Lily.

"You're Travis," Finch said. "Travis Marrero."

The young man's eyes widened. "You... know me?" he asked, his voice rusty.

"Is it okay to come out?" a girl asked as she emerged from the darkness of the trees.

She was lean and long-limbed, moving with a quiet, grounded grace that looked half-feral, half-trained. Sixteen. She wore a runner's tank top faded to gray and shorts shredded up the sides. Mud painted her shins in deliberate stripes, and there was a pink scrunchie around her wrist, frayed but intact.

Her blonde hair was tangled, yet her eyes—sharp blue—missed nothing.

Kayla Durant.

"Stay behind me for now," Travis said, holding out his arm.

"I'm here, too..." one more voice said from the trees.

The last was a boy no older than ten. He stepped out of the shadows slower than the rest. His white hoodie was torn across the stomach, the fabric stiff with pine sap, and his cargo shorts hung in rags. He was dirty to the elbows, his small hands scraped raw.

This was the boy.

Jason Stonewell.

The reason they were here.

Jason's hair stuck up in a wild, uneven halo, and under the grime, his skin was pale as moonlight. The five missing kids stood in a half-circle at the edge of the trees, a makeshift pack blinking in the bright daylight. Thin. Wild. But at least they were all alive.

"Are you all okay?" Kull walked forward, but Enzo jerked her back by the shoulder. She shot him a glare. "What's wrong? They're just kids..."

"Not *just*," he growled. "Not anymore. Now they're part wolf, and that makes them dangerous."

Acting as the de facto leader, Travis stood straighter. He moved so he was square in the middle of both groups. When he spoke, he turned his attention to the eight-foot-tall Enzo. "Are you another one who got infected by the werewolves running around the wilds?"

Enzo shook his canine head. "No. I've been this way for nearly eight years, kid. I'm a private investigator now along with these two."

"Well, actually, I'm an influencer," Kull whispered.

"*That's not a real job,*" Enzo snapped under his breath before continuing his conversation with Travis. "We're here to find Jason and bring him home to his family."

"But also help everyone," Kull interjected.

Finch nodded to that. "Yeah. We'll get you all back to your families."

Jason walked up behind Travis, his nostrils flared. "You all smell like... metal and fire."

"That's accurate," Finch replied dryly.

Lily's stomach growled loud enough for everyone to hear. She clutched it, obviously embarrassed, but when she moved backward, she grimaced. Pine needles and sap clung to the bottom of her bare feet. She took a moment to dislodge everything.

Kull crouched slowly, pulling one of her knee-high boots off and setting it in the dirt. "Trade you," she whispered. "You wear these. I'll go barefoot."

Lily stared at the boot, eyes round. "Uh... But... You're gonna hurt your feet."

"I've been through worse. Besides, they'll look better on you!"

Lily hesitated, giving Travis a glance. He nodded to her, and then Lily shuffled forward.

The girl's tiny toes disappeared into the boot, which nearly swallowed her leg whole. Kayla helped zip it halfway up, her fingers gentle. Travis's jaw tightened as he watched. Annoyance, maybe. Or relief.

Benji cleared his throat. "So you all are… taking us home? Even though we're werewolves now?"

"Trying to," Finch said. "But first, we need to make sure you're safe to move."

"Safe?" Travis echoed. His voice carried more growl than it should have for a human throat. "We were told we'd never be safe. Sevengaias told us everything. She said we're cursed, and that we'll hurt anyone nearby if we accidentally transform."

Enzo took a deep breath as he approached the children. "And she was right."

"So we aren't *safe to move*. Ever. This is our new home now."

The other four kids exchanged sad glances.

Travis continued. "Sevengaias gave us, like, an old radio tower and ranger station to live in, and it's been tough, but okay. We haven't hurt anyone. We have food. Well, we *get* food."

"I'm still hungry," Lily whispered.

"*It'll be fine*," Travis growled. "Besides, Sevengaias also said if we leave the nature preserve, the authorities would come and put us down like rabid dogs. Th-The cops and stuff don't come here. They're not allowed. It's the only place where we won't be killed, or kill anyone else."

Finch couldn't disagree with any of this logic. They were a danger to anyone around them. The authorities *would* come if they transformed and hurt anyone. The forest, protected by a spirit of death, was likely the safest place for them, even though it wasn't comfortable or pleasant.

"How long ago were each of you infected with lycanthropy?" Finch asked.

Perhaps, if they could figure out a way to cure them, all the kids could go home without any worries…

"We haven't been infected long," Travis muttered. "A couple weeks? Maybe three?"

A short distance away, branches snapped like knuckles.

Finch tensed. "*Get down*," he shouted, but it was too late. A crossbow bolt struck him just under the ribs.

CHAPTER
TWENTY-EIGHT

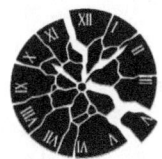

A flash of white-hot pain blinded Finch for a moment. He stumbled forward, the bolt half in his body, half protruding from his front. He heard Kull make a noise like someone had yanked a violin string too hard.

Holt. That old-man-aftershave of wintergreen and gun oil slid in on a new wind, and everything in Finch went cold. Holt was using crossbow bolts *first*? And not his gun? Did his Mark of Sagittarius give him connections to Aeon that allowed him to remember what would be most effective in a hunt, even though a time rewind?

"Coward!" Enzo leapt to his side, all his fur standing on end, his fangs bared.

Holt stepped from the woods, thirty yards off, elevated on a run of granite like a hunter posing for a calendar. Trench coat fluttering behind him, leg brace squeaking, hair slicked back into the idea of tidy. The compact crossbow sat easy in his hands. His left hand was bare to the knuckles. The white Mark of Sagittarius caught the light, sparkling with intense power.

"Hello again," Holt called, conversational, as if they'd met at a farmer's market. "You can't escape me."

Kull went for Finch. Enzo moved toward the kids, trying to shield them.

"*Stay back*," Finch barked at both of them, and then had to breathe around the bolt because his lungs didn't love that idea.

Pain came in like static. He clamped a hand around the smooth shaft to keep it from jostling and tasted copper. He could pull it—no, that was a mistake. The bolt would prevent him from bleeding out. If he ripped it from his body, he would risk passing out in a matter of minutes.

Despite the agony in both his arm and torso, Finch yanked Kull down as another bolt hissed over them and nicked a pine behind his head. Sap splattered the ground.

The kids reacted in a panic. Lily tried to press into Travis's leg, but Benji yanked her farther into the shadows. Travis squared his shoulders at Holt like the nineteen-year-old could stop bullets. Kayla didn't duck. Her eyes went pale-amber in the sun, and fur rippled across her body.

"*Don't*," Enzo warned, voice half-growl.

Holt switched weapons with the kind of efficiency that betrayed his skill as a hunter. The crossbow snapped onto a sling; a stubby revolver slid into his palm. Polished, ugly. Holt loaded it with shiny silver bullets that caught what little light shone through the trees.

"*Run*," Enzo commanded, but his voice went unheard.

Jason's hoodie ripped at the seams with a sound like paper being torn underwater. His spine arched into the shape it had been wanting, and his hands hit the dirt as paws in the same breath. Bones popped, tendons sang, a small body remembered a larger blueprint. The change took him like a wave—fast, mean, inevitable.

He charged Holt, completely consumed by blind rage.

Travis tried to pull him back, but he was too late. "Jason! Come back!"

Kayla followed Jason. She went quieter. Leaner. Hair lifting, muscles cording, teeth lengthening. Her shorts split along a stitch, and she didn't notice. She was a runner built for hills, and her wolf form just improved her skills.

"Shit," Enzo growled as he chased after.

Holt shot Jason the moment he got within twenty feet.

The silver round hit the ten-year-old's shoulder and spun him, fur blooming dark with blood that steamed in the cold. Jason yelped—a sound that was too much boy and not enough animal—and careened into the pine needles, legs scrabbling.

"Stop!" Finch shouted, pushing to a knee.

The bolt in his side reminded him he was made of meat after all. That wasn't going to stop him, though. He held his hand up and visualized the metal pistol bending to his commands. The revolver jammed.

Holt smiled like he'd been expecting it, and much of Finch's theory was confirmed. Somehow, this man had information on Finch. From Aeon? From remembering what happened in a time rewind? He wasn't certain, but there was no denying something was happening.

Finch's left hand twitched. Color drained out of the gun, the magazine, Finch's hold, and the revolver twitched back into place as if the last heartbeat hadn't happened. Single-object time rewind. Finch's magic slipped off like water.

"Neat tricks," Holt said, and fired again.

Kayla was wickedly fast and attempted to dodge. The silver tore a furrow along her ribs and left a smoke-leaking wound that refused to bleed right. She snarled, and hit Holt at the knees. They went down hard. Holt rolled with it, braced, and jammed the pistol into her flank.

Finch hadn't even seen when Enzo moved, but a second

later, Enzo was in the middle of the fight. He hit both Holt and Kayla as he charged.

Black fur, blacker intent. He took Holt from the side, claws raking the coat, teeth flashing inches from the man's throat. Holt's magic covered him, and Enzo stuttered, the world around him paling. For a heartbeat, the wolf became a statue mid-lunge, every hair a bristle of glass.

Kayla took that heartbeat and ripped Holt's pistol from his grip with her teeth. It skittered away through the undergrowth. Holt pulled a knife from within his duster and slashed Kayla's face down her muzzle. She howled as she stumbled backward, grabbing at the injury.

Silver. It had to be. Holt was prepared to fight a whole legion of cursed individuals.

Benji and Lily were screaming now. Travis had his body angled between them and the fight and kept saying, "It's okay, it's okay," like saying it would manufacture the truth.

While Enzo was frozen in time, Holt stabbed him in the back. Blood didn't gush from the injury—it, too, was held in time and incapable of moving.

"You motherfucker." Finch pulled Starfall one-handed and went to put a magic bullet into Holt's crossbow hand, but Starfall didn't move.

It wasn't jammed. It was frozen. Color leached from the gun, from Finch's fingers, from the idea of firing, and then time snapped back so hard his wrist ached. Holt had tagged the pistol itself. Enzo dropped from the air, unfrozen, his back now actively gushing blood.

"Eyes up, warlock," Holt taunted. He had the crossbow again.

"I don't have the egg on me," Finch shouted. "Killing me won't do you any good!"

Holt glared. "Don't lie! I know you have it. *I can smell it.* That egg is here! And who said I was going to kill you? At some point the pain will become too much. Then you're going to give me the egg because—"

An injured Kayla lunged for Holt's face.

Holt pivoted and hammered the crossbow into Kayla's jaw. Bone thumped. She reeled. Holt used the opening to wedge the crossbow under Enzo's shoulder and shoved. The wolf slid backward, claws digging furrows. But then Enzo gave out, his back spasming. He collapsed into the pine needles, a growl escaping his clenched fangs.

Holt turned on his heel and loosed a bolt. He didn't even aim. The Mark of Sagittarius lit up briefly, and the bolt went straight for its target.

Finch.

"*Adair!*" Kull moved.

He didn't have time to tell her no. He didn't have time to do anything but watch her act on the bad idea. She launched herself with both feet, white dress flashing, hair a comet.

The bolt hit Kull in the side just below the zipper line, punched through fabric, and buried itself a handspan deep. Her breath left her in a sound he never wanted to hear again.

Momentum carried her into him. They crashed to the dirt together, rolled once. When they finally stopped, Finch pulled Kull close. His hand ran over her side, finding the smooth shaft protruding from her flesh. Her blood was so hot and sticky.

"*Kull,*" he said, and the name was a raw edge.

Somehow, despite everything, she smiled up at him. It was the smallest, messiest smile. "Adair," she whispered, voice thin. "If you die, I'm going to be so mad at you."

It was difficult to concentrate when he had a torn-up arm and a crossbow bolt sticking out of his gut, but in that moment, Finch found the focus. He activated his magic, and the whole world froze.

Travis was in the middle of transforming.

Enzo was somehow pushing himself to his feet.

Holt already had another crossbow bolt in hand and ready to reload.

But none of them moved. They were all statues in the forest, suspended in time. Then the colors drained. No green pine trees. No afternoon sunshine. It became a world of black and white.

At first, Finch thought Aeon would come to taunt him, but the Father of Zodiac didn't appear this time. Had he really given up on the egg? Was he too worried about Gixmoth to care now?

All the shapes of the world fell away, including Kull, leaving Finch in a void of white.

When he blinked, he stood on the road that led into Tahoe City. Enzo was at his left, and Kull at his right.

12:04 a.m.

It took them all a full thirty seconds to really grasp what had happened. Kull immediately touched every inch of her body. She was back in her neon pink hoodie, and she even lifted it a bit to gaze at her stomach.

"Wow," she said, genuine awe in her voice. "That was... *crazy*."

Enzo ran a hand down his face. "What is with that damn bounty hunter, huh?" He whirled on his heel and faced Finch. "How does he have so much magic? *He's no warlock*. He's not cursed."

"The Mark of Sagittarius," Finch muttered. "It seems to give him access to some of Aeon's abilities. He's making good use of it."

"Don't praise him. Fuck that guy," Enzo yelled so loud, Finch was a little afraid he would wolf-out on them right here and now.

Fortunately, Enzo huffed and began to pace instead. He redirected his anger fast enough that his curse couldn't take him. Finch was impressed, but it was brief. It was obvious that Holt didn't know *everything*. He never came searching Finch out. He waited in the Desolation Wilderness. It was as if he got only some information and acted on what he could. That still gave Finch the advantage.

"How did he find us?" Kull asked.

Finch shrugged. "I assume with the mark somehow. But I don't know. All I do know is we'll have to subdue him in some way if we're going to do anything in the Desolation Wilderness and save those kids."

"We definitely have to help them." Kull's tone shifted to something determined and beyond optimistic. "We can't let them just stay there in the woods! We're the best private investigators around. Right?"

Finch wanted to tell her that private investigators didn't normally rush into dangerous scenarios to rescue missing persons, but he decided against it. Her optimism reminded him of Bree, and he knew his young apprentice would *also* want him to save everyone and everything within his power.

"We'll help them," Finch finally said. "And I think it'll be a little easier, too. Aeon didn't speak to me when I rewound time. I think he might've... given up. Or gone elsewhere."

Enzo stopped pacing. "Why?"

"After he saw Gixmoth, he didn't seem as interested in Chronos's egg."

"So why is Holt still chasing us? Wasn't he hired by Aeon?"

"It's a righteous mission for him, remember?" Finch exhaled. "He thinks he's saving humanity by taking the egg from me. I doubt he'd ever give up so long as he thinks I have it."

Enzo growled some sort of obscenity under his breath, but otherwise didn't reply.

"What're we going to do now?" Kull asked. She rubbed her arms and glanced at the night sky.

The stress of combat and nearly dying weighed on Finch's mind. He also didn't have a solution for the kids. Either they had to break the curse, or they would have to live in the Desolation Wilderness forever.

"We should rest," Finch said. "And once we wake up in the morning, we'll devise a new plan. Something to fix this mess once and for all."

CHAPTER
TWENTY-NINE

he Alder Crown had become a cozy comfort. The
lobby's fire pit crackled, and the scent of cedar
smoke curled through the air as Finch, Kull, and
Enzo gathered the keys to their suites. The quiet ride on the
elevator only added to the weight on Finch's eyelids.

Enzo peeled off toward his own suite with a grunt that
was both good night and warning. "Don't do anything
stupid."

"Define *stupid*," Kull playfully said.

He said nothing, and shut the door with a harsh *click* that
betrayed his annoyance.

Kull frowned. "We didn't agree on a time to wake up." She
unlocked the next suite over and went inside.

"As long as we get up semi early, everything will be fine,"
Finch muttered as he followed.

Once inside, he went straight for his room. It felt as
though he hadn't rested in weeks. What he needed was time
to think everything over. What was the best course of action
to take down Holt, save a group of werewolf-cursed children,
and defend a god egg?

Had such a question ever been asked?

Finch let himself fall backward onto the bed, shoes still on, coat half-buttoned. The ceiling looked like the inside of a jewelry box—mirrors, carved molding, too much effort. He stared at it until his heartbeat slowed.

A soft tapping at his door confused him.

"Come in," he said.

Kull opened the door and slid into his room, a bright smile on her face. She walked over to the side of Finch's bed and fluffed her red hair. Her bright neon pink hoodie clashed with the stormy grays and deep forest greens of Finch's room, but he didn't care.

Finally, Kull stared down at him. There was a faint tremor in her hands, but her grin covered it.

"So," she said, "how do heroes usually get thanked for saving the day?"

"Are you saying you want to reward me for rewinding time?"

"No, I was talking about when I saved your life. I took that crossbow bolt for you." She stepped closer, bare feet whispering on the carpet. "I think that earns me something nice. Maybe."

Finch pushed up onto his elbows. "Like a bonus? I can buy you *three* desserts whenever we go out. They'll be so *bespoke* they'll blow your goddamn mind."

Kull leapt knees-first onto his bed and hopped twice before settling next to him. "No. Three desserts are too many. Plus, I almost died for you. I'm thinking I deserve something better."

Finch sat up all the way. "Fine. Name it. What do you want?"

Her eyes flicked to his, bright and playful, but there was a heartbeat of real uncertainty before she spoke. "A kiss."

The words hung between them, curdling into an awkward silence.

Finch thought about the crossbow bolt that had pierced her, and about Holt still out there somewhere winding time backward and forward like thread. Then he thought about Carter—about how the loss rocked him. What if Holt kept targeting Kull? What if Gixmoth got her?

And they would target her. Of course they would. As soon as they knew she was his weakness, there would be no end to the villains who would use that against him.

The silence had gone on too long.

"You don't have to," Kull finally said, leaning away from him. "I just thought—after all that—it might be nice. To experience something special. You get what I mean, right?"

Finch wanted to say a lot of things. First, he hadn't been in an actual romantic relationship in over a decade. Second, he hadn't kissed anyone sober for years, and even then, all he could remember were the sloppy encounters. It wasn't like he had a secret technique that would blow someone's mind.

But he wasn't about to say any of that.

Because he just had to make a decision. Kull was actively pursuing him. Or perhaps *chasing him until he ran out of stamina and eventually collapsed* was a better way to phrase it. Her dedication was more than just a normal compliment, and he had to admit, he was getting tired of running.

He still didn't want to endanger her, though.

"Listen, Kull…" Finch ran a hand through his hair. "I don't want to be in a relationship with anyone because what if people like Holt target my significant other? Even if I can rewind time, sometimes it isn't enough. Carter proves that. And I just can't… I can't lose someone so close to me ever again."

He had said everything as earnestly as he could. It wasn't Kull's fault, but he didn't know what else to do.

Finch had expected her to deflate and become sullen, but to his surprise, a flicker of mischief glinted in her eyes.

"That makes a lot of sense," she said.

"I'm… shocked… and pleased that you understand."

"Well, hear me out first." Kull leaned in close and lowered her voice to a whisper. "What if we kept it a secret?"

"Kept what a secret?" he asked in an equally quiet tone.

"The kiss. And maybe anything else we do. No one has to know." She lifted both her eyebrows. "It's more fun that way, anyway."

"How would you know that?" Finch dryly asked.

Kull laughed and then dismissively waved away the question. "I'm still part mischief spirit, Adair. Anything tricksy is automatically hotter in my book, thank you very much."

Enzo was right. She was *determined*.

Did Finch even have a counterargument? He wished he hadn't drawn a Mark of Chronos on her before he marked the time… If she didn't have the mark, he could just test out how dating her would be and undo things if he regretted it. But as it stood, whatever he decided now, Kull would remember.

The weird psychic witch and her tarot cards flashed in his head. He needed to make a decision.

So… Why not? Finch had to admit, the thought of being near Kull more often did fill his thoughts with happier times. Maybe… it would work out…

Maybe.

"Fine," Finch said with a sigh, resigned to this path. "We can try it your way."

Kull leapt off the bed, her expression giddy. "Oh! Really?"

"Don't get too excited." Finch's face heated as he stood from the bed. "*It's just a single kiss*. And it's going to stay between us."

Kull mimed zipping her mouth shut. Then she threw away the invisible key.

He motioned her over. Unfortunately, Kull had different plans. She hurried over to the nearest wall that didn't have any paintings or decorations.

"Okay, we'll do it right here," she said.

Confused, Finch narrowed his eyes. "Why? What's so special about *over there?*"

"I have a whole scene in my head for how this should go. You see, I should have my back pressed up against a wall, and you should be, like, looming over me. We'll be so close that I'll feel your breath on my collarbone."

Kull grabbed the bottom of her hoodie and then yanked it over her head. She threw the piece of clothing unceremoniously onto the bed and then leaned back against the wall.

She wore only a pink tank top and skin-tight black leggings. That was it. Nothing else, Finch was certain.

His chest tightened as he stared for a moment. When he walked over, it was hesitant. He wasn't sure what else Kull was going to spring on him.

Doing as she wanted, Finch stepped close to her, until there was only an inch between them. He did *loom*. He had to be a foot taller than her.

Kull stared up at him through her eyelashes. Her smile was half teasing, half excited. "Okay, next you should use your left hand to hold up one of my legs. Like, really grab my upper leg and just pull me into you."

How thoroughly had she imagined this? Finch kept his gaze on hers as he reached down. Kull lifted her right leg, and stood tippytoe on her left foot, making it easy to grab her under the knee and hold it high. They were pressed against each other now, Finch's breathing heavier than before.

Kull felt... firmer... than he had thought. Athletic. Smooth.

"Okay, now you should grab both my wrists and pin them over my head."

"Did you see this in a movie or something?" Finch asked, still surprised at how detailed this fantasy of hers was becoming.

Kull chuckled and then bit her lower lip. "I've seen it in so many movies, you wouldn't even believe it. And it's always the best scene ever. It's so passionate and amazing." Her eyes fluttered as she sighed. "Okay, here are my wrists."

Complying with her demands, Finch gathered her slender wrists in one hand and pinned them against the wall above her head. The pulse beneath his thumb was quick.

They were body-to-body so firmly Finch could feel her every inhale.

"Now you can kiss me," Kull whispered.

Finch's voice came out rough. "You're sure?"

She nodded once. "I've prepared my body for this moment."

He almost laughed, which helped ease the rising tension.

The world shrank to her face, the faint sparkle in her eyes, the scent of perfume clinging to her hair. He leaned down slowly, deliberately, closing the gap until their breaths mingled, hot and anticipatory. His lips brushed the corner of hers, a feather-light graze that sent a shiver racing through her, her fingers twitching against the top of his hand as if begging him not to be a tease. So, Finch complied with that, too.

His lips captured hers in a kiss that started soft, exploratory, their tongues barely touching. But the longer they went, the more the heat between them grew. Finch angled his head, deepening the connection. She moaned into his mouth, raw and needy, her body melting against his.

The world blurred. Finch hadn't expected to enjoy the connection as much as he was.

Their kiss turned more passionate than he had anticipated. It almost felt desperate. He groaned, losing himself in her taste, her scent, the way she fit against him like she was the missing piece he had been denying himself.

But then the piece of him that could never be happy gave him a reality check. The dangers, the way this could end in blood. With a Herculean effort, Finch broke away, his chest heaving. He released Kull's leg and her wrists and took several steps back.

"I—" Finch began. But he didn't have the words to finish his sentence.

Kull blinked up at him, cheeks flushed. "Wow," she said, breathless. "That was... better than all the mischief in the world."

Finch rubbed the back of his neck as he glanced away. "Uh, well, I'm glad you enjoyed it. But I think we should get some sleep. In our own separate rooms. With the doors locked."

"Did *you* enjoy it?" Kull cleared her throat and spoke a bit louder. "I mean, was *I* a good kisser? I didn't screw it up?"

"No. It was great. You did amazing." Finch walked over and opened the door to the main room of the suite. "But it's late. We've been through a lot. Getting some rest is the best course of action."

Kull practically floated over to the door. With her cheeks still a bright pink, she turned to him. "I've kissed a few people since becoming human, and none of them made me feel like that, Adair."

He didn't know what to say. His chest tightened, and he almost asked her to stay, but he held back.

"I knew you'd be amazing," she said with a wistful sigh.

"My stomach feels like it's infested with so many butterflies I might die."

"That's one way to put it," he sardonically replied.

"Good night, Adair." She left the room, her tone singsong. "I hope you have pleasant dreams."

"You, too."

Finch shut the door and took several deep breaths.

What kind of trouble had he gotten himself into now?

CHAPTER
THIRTY

Finch woke to sunlight doing its best impression of a police interrogation lamp. It burned through the hotel curtains like it had a warrant.

He grabbed his phone.

11:33 a.m.

Finch swore into his pillow.

It had taken him hours to fall asleep last night. Kull had left her hoodie on his bed, and he had stared at it longer than he cared to admit. The ghost-touch of the kiss had lingered on his mind for far too long, and then there was the ever-growing dread that perhaps he had made a mistake. How often had he allowed lust to get him into a bad situation?

Well, when he was younger... too often. But he was thirty-nine now for fuck's sake. Now wasn't the time to think with anything other than the head above his shoulders.

Finch swung his legs off the bed and sat there for a long minute. Once mentally prepared to greet Kull, he stood. He grabbed his coat and pants, but before putting them on, he hesitated. Instead, he took a quick shower. Why? He knew why. Everyone who had seen last night would know why.

Once finished, he dressed and exited his bedroom.

He had expected to see Kull—not random company.

"Morning, Sunshine," a voice drawled from the couch.

Garret the half-spirit lounged there in one of the hotel robes, legs spread wide, remote in one hand, half-eaten pastry in the other. The TV was on low, playing a daytime cooking show where someone was aggressively whisking eggs.

Finch stopped dead. "What the hell are you doing in my suite?"

Garret gestured lazily with his croissant. "Technically, it's Fox-Pistol's suite. I came over because the other room's Wi-Fi was haunted."

"The Wi-Fi."

"Yeah. It kept asking me to *accept cookies*. I don't trust that kind of optimism."

Finch glared at the man. "That's not how that works."

Garret shrugged. "I'm a spirit of delusion, not IT support."

Glancing around the suite, Finch was disappointed to see he was alone with the bum of a spirit. "Where's Kull?"

He could use her real name with Garret because the man was half-spirit himself. He knew who Kull *really* was, even if the humans in her entourage didn't.

"With the rest of the circus," Garret said, mouth full as he chewed a particularly large bite. "Harper, Whisp, Jace, and Louis dragged her off to make videos. I think something about a *Tahoe Gamer Party*, or something like that. There were ring lights. And pancakes."

"Wonderful." Finch ran a hand down his face. "And you're just… staying here? Eating my food?"

Garret sucked down the last of the croissant. "Correction: her food. But yes. Room service is comforting. The lady on the phone called me 'sir' and believed everything I said. It was almost romantic."

Finch eyed the crumbs, the half-drunk orange juice, and the fact that Garret had apparently drawn smiley faces on the napkins with jam. "Aren't you a part of Kull's team? Why aren't you helping her make TikToks or whatever the hell you all do?"

"I help with video editing and sound effects," Garret countered. "Once they're done filming, I'm going to make it look hip to the jive. Sometimes I even use my delusion magic to help get everything right."

Finch exhaled through his nose. He wanted to be angry, but the man's lethargic charm made it impossible. He stared at Garret for a long moment, though, thinking about spirits in general. Then something clicked in his head. Garret was a half-spirit of delusion.

He turned away from the mess, pacing once across the suite. "Garret," he said, tone shifting from exasperation to something sharper. "You've been inhabiting a human body longer than Kull, right?"

Garret nodded. "Yeah. Several years longer."

"And your magic is still strong? It hasn't faded away?"

"No, sir. I made sure not to lose it."

Finch stopped walking. "How?"

The man waved his hand through the air. "Well, spirits come into existence whenever their favored element, emotion, or *thing* is in abundance. I, for one, came into existence inside an insane asylum."

"Uh-huh," Finch said with a frown.

"Delusion gave me life, and it also fuels my magic. So, I can recharge myself by siphoning from people, or making deals with mystical creatures who share the same kind of magic. Kind of like a warlock, but less complicated."

Something else clicked for Finch. "Pukwudgies are goblins who specialize in driving people insane."

Garret snapped his fingers and pointed at Finch. "Yes.

Exactly. I love pukwudgies. If you know where any are, you need to tell me, all right, bro? If I make a little bond with one of those punks, my magic is all better. Sometimes even stronger."

"I see..."

All this information was enlightening, and Finch couldn't wait to share with Kull, but he was bothered by one strange detail.

"Why haven't you told Kull about any of this?" Finch asked.

Garret shrugged. "Why would I? Does she need help with her magic or something?"

"She hasn't told you it's fading?"

"No. She never mentioned it to me." Garret wiggled into the couch, somehow descending deeper into the cushions. "We don't talk about *heavy stuff*. That's not my jam."

Wanting to use every angle he had available to him, Finch asked, "And your magic can make humans see things?"

Garret lifted an eyebrow. "Technically, I can make them believe things that aren't true. Seeing's optional. Sometimes the mind fills in the art direction."

"Could you do it to someone specific?"

"Depends. Mortal? Spirit?"

"Mortal. A bounty hunter." Finch walked around to the front of the couch. "One who thinks he's on a holy mission to save the world. Name's Jack Holt."

Garret tilted his head. "Oh, the silver-bullet grandpa. Fox-Pistol mentioned him." He flicked the remote, muting the TV. "Why?"

"Because he's dangerous. Because he's using a mark from a god to track us. And because I can't keep fighting him forever. If we can get him to believe something false—something that makes him stop hunting us—maybe we can buy time."

Garret considered that, tapping the remote against his knee. "Sounds fun. You have something in mind?"

"I'm going to make a plan today. I'll tell you about it later."

On the TV, the chef triumphantly flipped an omelet that landed perfectly on the plate. Garret watched for a moment before stretching and then getting up from the couch. During that whole process, his robes spilled open.

He wore nothing underneath.

Finch exhaled. "You and Kull are going to be the death of me."

Garret grinned. "Maybe. But at least it'll be interesting."

Finch didn't disagree. He just reached for the coffeepot and tried not to think about how the day was already off the rails before it had properly started.

Finch exited his suite and then went two doors down the hall until he found a door with music leaking out underneath it. Someone inside was singing—badly—and someone else was laughing even worse.

He knocked once.

Whisp opened the door, wearing a headset mic and an oversized T-shirt that read: **CONTENT NEVER SLEEPS.** Her hair was damp and her eyeliner smudged. "Oh! U-Uh, Adair Finch. I'm sorry. Kull's in the middle of a shoot, but you can t-totally come in. She said to let you in when you got here."

Finch said nothing as he stepped around her. Inside, the suite had been rearranged into a miniature studio: ring lights, tripods, a wall of fake ivy, and one inflatable pink flamingo that looked like it regretted everything.

The sliding doors to the balcony stood open. Beyond

them, steam rose from a hot tub situated on the balcony. Kull sat in the bubbling water with Jace Min, both of them wearing sunglasses and ridiculous matching towels around their heads like spa queens.

A smartphone mounted on a tripod recorded as Kull leaned toward Jace, voice sugar-smooth. "And I was so lucky to run into Jace Min! I've admired his songs for *forever,* and he's so talented." She hit a button, and the tub frothed faster. "Now we're going to relax, come up with some new song lyrics, and maybe even play some video games."

Jace held up two bottles of sparkling wine, both labeled in marker: **LYRIC FUEL.**

"Remember to hit like and *smash* that subscribe button," Kull said with a giggle. "If you want more hot tub interviews, leave a comment down below about what color bathing suit I should wear next."

She tugged on the spaghetti strap of her two-piece suit, showing off how bright red it was.

Finch watched from the middle of the living room, unable to walk any closer. He crossed his arms, keeping his expression neutral. He never watched Kull's videos—not because he avoided Kull's content, but because he just didn't watch videos on social media. Period.

Did she *always* do things in hot tubs? With other men?

Would it really be a problem? Finch thought about it rationally. Actresses constantly worked closely with other actors, even when they had families at home. This was almost the same thing. Wasn't it?

"And don't worry, we'll be showing you all the fun sights in Tahoe," Kull continued, striking a pose that nearly made her towel slip. "We might even pull off a skiing prank I've been meaning to try!"

She giggled afterward, and Louis, her manager, gave her a thumbs up behind the camera.

Jace nodded, mock serious. "Okay, let's start with the lyrics. I've already got some. *Moonlight drips through broken Wi-Fi.*"

Kull gasped. "That's so emotionally unavailable. I love it."

Finch stayed at the threshold, gritting his teeth. It was stupid, harmless fun—and it still knotted something in his chest. The morning light caught the water, painting Kull in soft gold. Every time she laughed, it landed somewhere between adorable and weaponized.

He told himself it was fine. They were coworkers. They were friends. Finch and Kull had kissed. Once. Secretly. Totally fine.

Whisp noticed him watching and nervously walked over. She whispered, "Do you want t-to take a seat?"

"No," he stated.

"Uh, o-okay."

Out on the balcony, Kull tossed her sunglasses aside and said, "Okay, final bit! Jace, look serious. Like, philosopher serious."

He tried. He looked constipated instead.

She giggled so hard she snorted, then sank lower into the bubbles, muttering, "Perfect for the outtake reel."

When the shoot wrapped a minute later, Louis clapped his hands. "This is good! Perfect. Absolute gold. I love the softer direction you've been going as Fox-Pistol." He blew little chef's kisses.

Then he and Whisp grabbed all the film equipment. Jace leapt out of the water. He wore a speedo and nothing else. Finch rolled his eyes.

Kull stayed behind, towel crown slightly crooked, cheeks flushed from laughter and heat. When she saw Finch, her grin brightened. "Adair! You're awake!"

"Apparently," he said, stepping closer. "You didn't wake me."

She blinked. "You didn't wake when I knocked on your door. And you kept it locked, remember? If it makes you feel better, Enzo didn't wake, either."

Finch narrowed his eyes. "We're supposed to be planning how to handle Holt and save five cursed children, not... doing hot tub musicals."

"Well, I was bored, and I need to make content," Kull said. "My fans expect updates! Plus, it was good team bonding. Multitasking is how you win as a content creator, Adair."

She stepped out of the hot tub, water rushing over her sleek body. Her bright red bathing suit was exactly the kind of skimpy that would attract followers on social media. Finch wasn't about to complain, but he also didn't want to stare. He glanced at the scenery over Kull's shoulder.

"We should go because Jace wants you to drink more of his *lyric juice*," he muttered.

Kull tilted her head. "Ooooh. You're jealous."

"*I'm not*. I'm... just ready to concoct some plans. I spoke to Garret, and I have some new ideas."

With a coy smile, Kull whispered, "Adair, *you're* the one who said you wanted everything to be secret. Isn't this the perfect cover? I thought you'd be pleased. But... if you're not... *you* could always get in the hot tub with me."

He opened his mouth to shoot back with something sarcastic, but he held back. Kull was right. He had asked that everything between them remain a secret. Her filming videos with someone like *Jace Min* was the perfect cover.

Damn. That was good.

He didn't have a logical reply to that.

"Maybe we'll be in a hot tub later," he murmured. "For now, finish drying off. We've got work to do."

She giggled as she wrapped herself in a towel. "Aye, aye!"

CHAPTER
THIRTY-ONE

Once Kull had dried herself, she went to one of the suite's bedrooms and changed. She emerged swaddled in influencer glam.

She wore black shorts with silver zippers, sheer black tights patterned with tiny stars, and a cropped cream sweater that hung off one shoulder. Her chunky combat boots clomped softly against the carpet as she stepped over to Finch.

"Well?" she asked. "How do I look?" Her hair was loose, wind-tousled in that suspiciously deliberate way.

Finch gave her the once-over. "You always look good."

"Pfft." Kull dismissively waved away the comment. "No one looks good *all* the time."

"You do."

His compliment seemed to quiet her for a moment. Her cheeks flushed, and when she smiled, it was cuter than normal. "You're a good guy, Adair."

It was true. There was no outfit she wore that wasn't better with her in it.

As they were heading out, Louis leapt in their way. His perfectly styled blond hair didn't move an inch, even when he stood below the suite's powerful AC unit.

"Oh, darling, where are you going?" he asked. "We still need to film the sponsorship portion of the video. Kay-Cons wants you to pimp their little wireless earphones."

Kull nodded once and patted him on the shoulder. "I'll be back soon. Don't worry. I'm just going to get something to eat with my, uh, new bodyguard here."

Louis looked Finch up and down. "Why not take Jace? He's showering, but I know he wants to spend more time with you this weekend. Maybe wait a moment?"

"Nah. Just make an excuse for me so Jace's feelings aren't hurt, okay?" Kull gave Louis two fake kisses before stepping around him. "I'll be back soon!"

"W-Well, but—"

Finch also casually went around the man, ignoring his protests. Once in the hallway, they shut the door and continued forward.

Enzo waited in the hall, arms folded, the picture of silent judgment. The sleeve of his Henley was rolled up just enough to show off his muscles in impressive ways. His bald head was smooth enough to reflect some of the hall lights.

"Morning," Finch said, as if it were possible to greet a storm cloud politely.

"Afternoon," Enzo corrected.

"Hey, don't look at me like that. Kull said you were sleeping this morning and wouldn't get up, either."

Enzo snorted. "You two could've knocked louder. Or gotten the front desk to call me."

Kull tugged on Finch's coat sleeve and motioned him to lean down. Finch did, and then Kull whispered into his ear, "Can we tell Enzo about what we've done? Or does it have to be a secret-secret from everyone?"

"Don't tell Enzo," Finch snapped.

But their whispering had garnered them trouble. Enzo narrowed his eyes and shot glances between them. "Wait a minute… You two did something stupid last night, didn't you?"

Finch frowned and shook his head. "No. Why would you think that?"

"You took a shower this morning. I smell the shampoo on you. That's not your normal MO."

"That's because…" Finch grappled with several different excuses, but in the end, he realized it was futile. He rolled his eyes. "All right, Kull. You can tell Enzo everything."

She shook her hands with glee. "Oh! Thank you." In a cheery tone, she announced, "Adair and I kissed, and it was magical."

"Uh-huh." Enzo exhaled and gave Finch a knowing stare. "Really?"

Kull placed her hands on her hips. "Hey. You're ruining the vibes here. You should be happy."

"I don't ruin vibes," Enzo muttered. "They just die naturally around me."

"Still! I was hoping you'd be happy and celebrate with us. As a matter of fact, we should go to a cute café to celebrate *and* discuss our next course of action. Because this is nothing but good news."

Enzo met Finch's gaze and had an entirely silent conversation with the other man. Finch basically confirmed everything with his stare, and then half shrugged. A part of him wanted to remind Enzo that he had recommended this route, but Finch held back.

"Well, just don't let this interfere with anything," Enzo said, a scolding tone to his words.

"Never." Kull giggled and then pointed to the elevator. "Now, c'mon! Let's hurry. I'm hungry."

The Sugar Peak Café sat at the corner of Tahoe's main road, all pinewood and mismatched metal chairs. A handful of tourists sat in puffy jackets with lattes that steamed with fresh brew. The sun was pale, filtered through a thin frost haze. Finch chose the farthest table, one that gave him a view of the street and both exits.

Kull sat extra close, and Enzo on the opposite side of the round table.

12:05 p.m.

A waitress came by, too perky for Finch's liking. She took their order—black coffee for Finch, espresso drowned in honey for Kull, and an entire stack of pancakes for Enzo. When she left, the table settled into the kind of silence that only long-running problems deserved.

Kull propped her chin on her hands. "So. We have five werewolf kids living in a death-spirit nature preserve. One bounty hunter with a time-god cheat code. And us. What's the plan, boss?"

The waitress dropped off Finch's coffee a moment afterward and hurried back to her other tables. Finch didn't wait for his drink to cool. He drank once, grimaced, and then set it down.

"First thing we should do is come up with a solution to Holt. He's tracking us with his mark. He *will* find us if we go into the nature preserve. Since we want to save the kids, entering the preserve is unavoidable."

"We can't hide," Enzo said. "We can't outrun him. And we can't kill him, because you don't want that, right?"

"No. I don't want to kill the man. Even if he's wrong, and old, and maybe delusional, I don't think lethal force is necessary."

"You know he's tried to kill us several times, right? He wouldn't hesitate. If we mess up, and you die, we won't even be able to rewind time anymore."

Finch sighed. That was true. But still. He didn't want Holt's death on his soul. "There are other ways. We just need him to believe something false long enough to give us room."

Enzo lifted both eyebrows. Kull stared at him with admiration in her eyes.

"I'm thinking we could enlist the help of Kull's team." Finch nodded to her. "Garret is a half-spirit of delusion, and apparently he knows how to keep his magic stable."

"*He does?*" she asked with half a gasp.

"Garret siphons or bonds with other creatures who specialize in delusion. Since Smudge is theoretically on our team, and doesn't seem to have the ability to really mess with people's minds outside of his telepathy and invisibility, I figure we can get Garret to mess with Holt. Maybe make him think I've left town, or make a rock look like Chronos's egg so we can hand it over and he'll leave."

The waitress dropped off Kull's drink and Enzo's pancakes. Without a word, Enzo poked one of his cakes, put it on a small plate, and then slid it over to Kull. She happily took it, and then pulled it apart into tiny bits. Carefully, and somewhat bizarrely, she dunked the pancake pieces into her espresso and ate them one at a time.

Enzo stabbed a fork into his remaining pancakes hard enough to make the plate crackle. "You really trust that half-spirit idiot?"

"No," Finch said. "But I trust that he owes Kull, and that he'll follow her instructions."

Kull's smile went slow and sharp. "So, step one: delusions for Holt. Step two: save cursed children. Step three: break the curse." She frowned after the last statement. "I think step three is going to be the most difficult..."

Finch drummed his fingers on his coffee mug. "Perhaps we should return to Maddie and ask her if she knows anything. Since the kids are newly cursed, we still have time. Maybe some of those flowers, or..." He caught his breath when an idea struck him.

It was risky.

But maybe...

Enzo eyed him. "Think of something?"

"Yeah," Finch muttered. "We need to visit Maddie. I have a few questions for her."

"I can't wait to meet her." Kull flashed him a glitter-bright look that made Enzo groan and mutter something about "new couples" under his breath.

Once finished with their food and drinks at the café, they took their favorite party bus over to Maddie's. The wind chimes made of spoons clinked as the door opened, and the neon palm in the window blinked several times when the door shut.

Inside smelled like oranges and old library. The heater still wheezed in the corner like a retired dragon. The same bead curtain of mismatched keys hung in the archway. The fat gray cat, Poopsiekins, in a sweater that read I BITE AUTHORITY, dozed in a sunbeam. His tail flicked once as his eyes followed them.

"Hello?" Finch called out.

In dramatic fashion, Maddie swept out from behind the keys with her plum-and-silver hair up in a pencil-stabbed bun. Her eyes were bright and kind as she glanced between them.

"New faces! Welcome!" She clapped once. "I'm Maddie. Part-time waning crescent witch, full-time psychic. Shoes, hatred, and skepticism in the basket, please." She pointed at the wooden sign by the door.

PLEASE REMOVE YOUR SHOES, HATRED, AND SKEPTICISM

Kull squeed and toed off her combat boots, tights starlit against the rug. "Hi, Maddie! I love everything here. Just... everything."

Maddie preened. "Oh, stop, you'll swell my ego, and that's never good."

"I mean it!"

"I know, love. You have the look of an honest person. Too pure for this world." She leaned past Kull, peering at Finch and Enzo. "And you two... look like problems wearing clothes."

Enzo grunted, noncommittal, and drifted to a wall of jars. Finch slid his hands into his pockets and offered a thin smile. Maddie didn't recognize them—of course she didn't. Rewinding time wiped the slate. This day only existed so long as Finch permitted it to.

"I want a reading," Kull said, bouncing once. "Like... the good kind. The dramatic kind. With warnings and romance. Oh! I just started a new relationship. Kind of." She eyed Finch before continuing. "And I want to know how that goes."

Finch didn't like where this was going. "We came here for other reasons," he growled.

"It'll only take a second!"

Maddie smiled. "I have plenty of time!" She nervously chuckled. The emptiness of the front room became quite apparent in that moment. Then Maddie cleared her throat. "Come."

She swept over to the round lace-dressed table and patted a chair.

"Sit, dear heart. We'll see what the cards want to gossip about today."

Kull glanced at Finch—he reluctantly nodded—and then she sank into the chair, hair falling in deliberate waves.

While she settled into her seat, Finch took the opportunity to drift. He moved along the pegboard of tinctures and tins, reading labels that alternated between earnest and unhinged. He wanted to find a *healing brew*. The stronger the better. Would Maddie have something like that? Finch could only hope.

Some of her jars and cans read:

KNITBONE CORDIAL (for bruises & "oopsies")
SILVERBURN SALVE (for the very specific problem you're imagining)
MOTH-DUST TEA (do not inhale during preparation)
NIGHT-QUIET TINCTURE (for anxious hearts, not legal advice)

His fingers paused over the SILVERBURN SALVE. The tin was stamped with a crescent. The ingredient list promised comfrey, honey, a pinch of cold-iron water. Not what he was looking for, but he considered it interesting. Would it harm werewolves?

They had two red-eyed beasts they had to deal with, after all.

Could they cure them, too? Or would they need to be put down? Finch wasn't entirely certain yet.

He scanned higher, hoping to find something useful. There was a narrow wooden box with a brass catch, neatly labeled in tidy block letters:

SLIVER OF THE MOON.

He thumbed it open anyway. Lined with velvet. No flower. No luck.

Behind Finch, cards rushed across the table. Maddie's voice went soft.

"All right. Breathe. I'll now read your fortune."

Kull inhaled and exhaled.

Maddie fanned the long cards in a crescent. Candlelight made the gilt edges shimmer like fish scales. She drew three without looking and turned the first.

"*The Moon.*"

Kull's eyebrows leapt. "Whoa! Like the wolves!"

"The Moon isn't fear," Maddie murmured. "It's the part of the road that only shows up at night. Instinct, tide, the howl you pretend not to hear." She tapped at the card's picture, which contained twin towers, a path, a dog and a wolf. "You're walking with both halves—a wild one and a clever one. Don't let anyone shame the other."

"I won't," Kull whispered.

Maddie turned the second card.

"*Strength.*"

Kull leaned closer. "Is that me petting a lion?"

The picture on the card depicted a beautiful woman opening a lion's mouth.

Maddie pointed. "It's you opening its mouth with gentleness. Not force—trust. Strength is another word for patience and persistence. You can do the impossible with enough time and willpower."

"I see."

The third card flicked out and landed with a tiny hiss.

"*The Devil*. And I drew it upside down…"

Kull half frowned. "Is that… good?"

The picture was of a demon standing over a man and woman, both shackled.

"These chains are slipping off," Maddie said. "This card represents compulsion broken. A contract losing its teeth." She glanced up, eyes catching on Finch across the room like she'd felt a draft. "Someone near you has made interesting decisions that will affect your life."

Kull went very still, then smiled a careful smile. "Hmm. I wonder."

Maddie's gaze slid back to the spread. "The Moon, Strength, Devil reversed. In plain speech? You can lead a beast out of its cage without a key. But you'll need to do it kindly, on a night that belongs to nobody."

"Can I ask a for follow-up fortune? Hypothetically speaking, what if I'm in love with a man who's allergic to happiness?"

Enzo snorted back a laugh. Finch shot the man a glare.

Maddie's mouth curved. "Then Strength again. Open the jaw. Put your hand in. Try not to get bitten. But remember that you cannot control what the lion does. It is its own beast."

"I would never." Kull gazed at the card with a growing grin.

Finch pretended the shelf label for WITCH VITAMINS (mostly sugar) had him rapt. Enzo huffed another laugh into his sleeve.

"Do you do brews?" Finch finally asked, his voice louder than usual. "Maybe a cure for lycanthropy?"

Maddie turned her attention to him fully, cards forgotten. "Oh, no. I had one Sliver of the Moon years ago, but I sold it to an individual who had been cursed, and I've never found a second."

Finch sighed. "All right. Do you have a restorative brew? For wounds. Lethal wounds."

"A healing brew… People come asking for that a lot."

"I assume that's a no, then?"

"Not necessarily…" Maddie stood, crossed to a high shelf, reached without looking, and came down with a beeswax-sealed jar. Inside: pale petals suspended in something that caught light like milk. She set it on the counter and didn't take her hand off it. "When people come to me, they want a cure for cancer or some scar that healed naturally, only ages ago. My brew is for an immediate injury. If you're currently bleeding, or if your bone is broken, this will mend you in a matter of moments."

"That's perfect," Finch said. "Exactly what I need."

Maddie tapped the jar. "This isn't cheap."

Finch was about to answer, but Kull sprang from her seat. She grabbed her wallet from her shorts pocket and held it up. "I'll pay! How much is it?"

After a deep breath, Maddie whispered, "Five hundred dollars."

There was a moment of silence. Finch waited for the *just kidding*, but it never came. That was absurdly cheap.

Kull laughed and waved her hand. "That's it? Are you sure? I mean, it sounds pretty amazing."

"That's what I usually charge," Maddie nervously replied.

"I charge about fifty thousand per sponsorship on one of my videos," Kull said, tilting her head. "But I guess if you want to sell me this for five hundred… I'll just have to tip you extra well."

"Fifty *thousand*?" Enzo whispered. "Damn. I'm in the wrong line of work."

Finch gave him a sideways glance. "You think you have the temperament for social media?"

"I can't get through watching the news without wanting to tear someone's throat out," Enzo earnestly replied. "So, no. You're probably right. Let's just forget this and move on."

CHAPTER
THIRTY-TWO

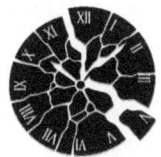

inch, Kull, and Enzo left Maddie's shop, stepping back into the cold of Tahoe. Wind off the lake carried the smell of pine and wet asphalt. Somewhere far down the street, a car groaned as it turned onto a narrow dirt road.

Kull held the jar of healing brew to her chest like it was a cat she had just adopted. She sniffed the top. "This is amazing. It smells like marshmallows." Then Kull frowned. "But why do we need a healing brew? This won't cure lycanthropy, will it?"

"No," Finch said. "It won't. I need it for myself... But I'll need it later. Don't worry." He held out his hand.

With a skeptical glance, Kull handed it over.

Enzo squinted. "You paid five hundred bucks for glorified flower milk."

"Worth it." Kull pointed. "It sparkles."

Finch shoved the brew into his coat pocket. "Playtime's over. Now that we have this, I want to test my theory."

"With Garret?" Enzo asked.

"Yeah. We need him, and we need Smudge."

Finch never thought he would ever say that, but it was true. The pukwudgie was key to his plans... in more ways than one.

"Kull, you'll get Garret. Enzo and I will head out of town and search for Smudge. Enzo, you could track him, right?"

Enzo nodded once. "Yeah. The little guy has a distinct *stink*."

The trees outside Tahoe City grew straight and tall, most of them without branches for the bottom half of their trunks. Late afternoon light broke through the needles, flashing across the cold, dark dirt. Finch's shoes sank into the wet earth with each step, and every now and then Enzo would stop, sniff the air, and scowl.

"Nothing yet?" Finch adjusted his coat collar against the chill.

"Nothing but pine and wet dog," Enzo muttered. "Smudge has a smell like burnt sugar and rust. I'll catch it eventually."

"Comforting."

They walked another stretch in silence. The forest around them was alive with tiny noises—branches cracking somewhere distant, a jay calling, the creak of thawing bark. Every sound made Finch's shoulders tighten. For some reason, he envisioned Holt around every corner. To help with his paranoia, Finch always kept his metal repelling magic active around his body.

When Enzo finally spoke again, his voice was quieter. "You know... if we can't fix those kids, I think I'm going to stay here."

Finch turned to him. "Stay here?"

"Yeah." Enzo's gaze remained on the ground in front of

him. "They're too young to figure this curse out alone. I've seen what happens when new wolves don't have anyone teaching them control. They'll tear each other apart. Or maybe one of them will endanger some hikers. You never know."

Finch said nothing.

After a short round of silence, Enzo continued. "I know what it's like to wake up in an unfamiliar place with blood on your hands and no memory of how it got there. Someone helped me through it once. Seems right I return the favor."

This made sense to Finch. He understood wanting to repay a debt of karma. And the kids had no one.

Enzo crouched, pressed two fingers into the mud, lifted them to his nose. "When we met the kids, they all reeked of fear and confusion. I can still… faintly detect it… whenever I think about them."

"So, what's your plan? Build a commune out here?" Finch was trying to lighten the mood, but his statement came off more sarcastic.

"Call it a sanctuary. I'll teach them how to really hunt. Maybe bring them to Oakland someday, once they're stable. I know a few wolves who could take them in."

"You've given this a lot of thought."

Enzo stood and rotated his shoulders. "Well, while you were making out last night, all I had was the darkness and my thoughts."

"We kissed once," Finch snapped. Then he crossed his arms. "And you constantly tell everyone you're married, even though your wife thinks you're dead. You could move on. You could have someone else with you."

Enzo continued forward, his nose wrinkled. "Feh. We'll see. I'm not in the mood to deal with that at the moment."

He didn't say anything for a long while. The wind hissed through the trees, shaking loose pine needles. Enzo walked a short way, stopped, sniffed, and then went in another direction. Finch kept pace.

Finally, Finch said, "Well, I understand if you have to go, but everyone at the office will miss you. *I'll* miss you."

Enzo gave a dry laugh. "You could replace me in a week. Hire some other asshole who growls and does all the heavy lifting."

"Doubt it. How am I going to find an ex-cop who also gets along with Bree, doesn't get too irritated with her father, and actually knows how to speak to my reclusive ex-sister-in-law? And let's not mention someone who can hold their own in a fight."

"That a compliment?"

"It's whatever you want it to be."

Enzo kicked a branch out of the way. "Look, I'm not saying I'm leaving for sure. Just... if we can't find any cure for the kids, I can't walk away from them." He held up a hand. "And I know you already paid me for a year of work. I'll either find a way to get the money back to you, or I'll return to work out the rest of my contract after the kids are okay."

"Stop it," Finch muttered. "We'll find a cure. I don't care if I have to break into the gods' pantry and steal it myself. We're not leaving those kids cursed, and you're not going to rot in the woods playing den mother."

Enzo's mouth twitched. "That's one hell of an image."

"Yeah, well. Consider it motivation."

They reached a small creek, one that had been much larger months ago. Finch crouched to study a set of tiny footprints in the mud.

"Smudge," he said.

Enzo nodded. "Told you I'd find him."

"I never doubted it." Finch straightened, brushing off his hands. "Then let's get our goblin before he scurries off again."

They followed the creek until it narrowed into a rocky trickle between mossy stones. A cold wind snaked down from the higher slopes, carrying with it the scent of iron, wet bark... and something else.

Burnt sugar and rust.

Enzo snapped his attention toward the smell before Finch could even open his mouth. The werewolf's nostrils flared, and a slow grin split his face. "Got him."

A small, gray shape darted behind a fallen log twenty yards away. Just a blur at first, but Finch caught the twitch of pointed ears and the glint of two yellow eyes. A pinecone rolled from the top of the log and hit the ground with a dull *thunk*.

"Smudge," Finch called out. "We're not here to hurt you."

There was a long pause. Then a squeak. Then a head popped up—a mess of white hair, little nose, and sharper teeth than Finch remembered. Smudge froze, one hand gripping the log like he might pull it up as a shield.

"Who you?" the goblin demanded. His voice cracked in the middle, like an ungreased hinge.

Since Finch had never drawn the Mark of Chronos on the pukwudgie, Smudge would always forget their meeting after every time rewind.

"It's me, Adair Finch."

Smudge blinked and then stared for a long time. Finally, a smile bloomed across his little face. He hopped over the log and hurried over, his yellow eyes wide with excitement. "Finch... Finch friend!"

Finch nodded. "Exactly."

Once close, Smudge stopped dead in his tracks and stared upward. After a deep breath, he puffed out his chest. "Finch. Friend. Me, Smudge. I want..." Then he said something in goblin, his words garbled, as though they were chewed before being spoken.

But Finch knew what he wanted.

"You want to pledge loyalty to me," he said.

Smudge's eyes widened further. "Y-Yes."

"I accept."

Finch didn't want to go through this song and dance every time, but he also didn't want to give Smudge any piece of his magic. He'd instead just speed things along. He held out his hand, and Smudge took it, awe in his gaze.

Once Smudge touched Finch's knuckles to his forehead, Finch pulled away.

"Congrats." Finch shoved his hands into his pockets. "But we came here because we need your help with someone named Holt. He's dangerous and an ally of Aeon. We're working with another spirit, Garret. Well, a *half*-spirit of delusion."

Smudge cocked his head, long ears drooping. "Delusion? Trick-magic? Like Smudge?"

"Exactly. Garret can make people see things that aren't real. And you—you can whisper to minds, can't you? Nudge thoughts?"

"Little bit," Smudge admitted, scuffing the ground with one foot. "I whisper. Smudge not good. Sometimes."

Finch motioned to the path they had come along. "Doesn't matter. I just need you two to work together to help with Holt."

"O-Oh…"

Enzo crossed his arms, looming behind Finch like a shadow made of muscle. "Holt won't be trouble, if that's what's bothering you. That man is owed several ass whuppins."

"Smudge like." The goblin grabbed Finch's pant leg. "Good."

Finch exhaled through his nose. "All right. Let's go."

"Shortcut." Smudge pointed. Then he tugged Finch's pant leg and tried to take him there. "Shorter."

"Fine. Lead on."

They followed Smudge deeper into the trees, the goblin tugging Finch forward, humming something that sounded suspiciously like a murder ballad. The light filtered green and gold through the branches above them, and though the air was cold, Finch's coat kept him plenty warm. It wasn't yet the season for snow in Tahoe, but around the lake always felt chilly to him.

But then he realized they were going deeper into the woods.

"Wait." Finch stopped. "We need to get back to the road."

Smudge tilted his head. "Not Holt?"

"You're taking us to *Holt*?" Enzo growled. "Not yet. We need Garret first." He gestured back to the creek. "C'mon, ya donut. This way. We'll face Holt once we're ready."

Smudge nodded along with Enzo's words.

Then, as a group, they made their way back to the road.

CHAPTER
THIRTY-THREE

Finch, Enzo, and Smudge waited on the side of the road until Kull's massive party bus swung by to pick them up. They piled inside, thankful for the temperature controls.

1:30 p.m.

The party bus rumbled down the cracked highway toward the Desolation Wilderness. The neon strip lights lining the ceiling blinked between pink and teal, giving the ride the strange energy of an afterparty no one had agreed to attend. Despite that, Finch was starting to enjoy it.

He wouldn't admit that, of course.

Garret sat cross-legged on one of the seats, wearing ripped jeans and a T-shirt, his hair a disaster of static and not-giving-a-damn. Across from him, Smudge perched on the armrest, swinging his short legs and humming a song Finch had never heard before.

In the weird chewing language of goblin, Garret occasionally said something to Smudge. The goblin always replied in cheery tones.

"I need to learn goblin," Enzo muttered.

Finch shrugged. "I trust Kull will keep us informed."

At the end of the bus, pouring herself a smoothie, Kull perked up. Her drink was bright yellow, and she held it up with a smile. "Look! I'm drinking a *Samus*. And of course I'll translate. Nothing interesting yet. Just small talk."

Garret shot her a grin. "I'm buttering him up so he'll let me use some of his magic."

The goblin snorted and frowned.

"Oh, can he fully understand English?" Garret placed both hands behind his head. "My bad. But yeah, I'd like some of your magic, little guy. Daddy needs a recharge."

The mere mention of the word *daddy* had Enzo growling curse words under his breath. Finch chuckled. He had forgotten how much the man hated that term.

"You recharge your magic with other creatures?" Kull sat next to Garret. "Finch briefly mentioned that, and I wanted to know more specifics."

Garret shrugged. "You just need to find a powerful creature with trickster magic. I mean, if you find one strong enough, you could even, maybe, get stronger than you ever were before. I've done it. I think."

"Stronger than before?" Kull sipped her bright yellow smoothie. Then her eyes widened. "Oh... Like Sevengaias. I wondered why she was so strong. I thought spirits couldn't get as powerful as her... So she must know a creature of death. A super powerful one."

Wanting to discuss tactics, Finch scooted forward in his seat. "Listen, I need your help, Garret. I was hoping you'd bond with Smudge, or whatever you need, and then you'll trick Holt. We need to make it look good. I'm thinking we'll approach, he'll attempt to intimidate me, and then I'll hand over a fake egg, pretending to be afraid."

"That's never going to work," Enzo drawled.

"Why not?"

"You're too much of a sardonic smartass. No one is going to believe you're scared or intimidated."

Kull raised her hand. Once everyone in the party bus turned her way, she smiled and sat a bit straighter. "How about I let Holt take me hostage, and *then* Adair gives up the fake egg? I'm a pretty good actress, if I do say so myself."

"No," Finch said.

"Why not?"

"There's no reason to put you in danger."

Kull threw back some of her fiery hair. "I won't be in any danger. We have this plan, remember? You'll hand over the egg, and I'll be fine. Plus, if he doesn't give me back, you can always rewind time!"

Garret's eyebrows shot for his hairline. Smudge also perked up, his goblin ears shaking.

"Did you just say he would *rewind time?*" Garret asked. "Can Adair Finch rewind time? For real? That's extremely powerful."

"Smudge like," the goblin said, nodding his head several dozen times.

Finch dragged a hand down his face.

"I'm sorry," Kull whispered. Her posture slumped, and her shoulders drooped. "I forgot they didn't know. The party bus is our safe space in my mind."

"It's fine," Finch drawled. "This problem will take care of itself."

Enzo shrugged. "Kull has a point, though. I can see you giving up the egg to protect her, so you'll probably easily trick Holt with that plan. Assuming he doesn't have some way to detect the real egg or something."

"I'm worried about that," Finch said. "But that's why we're going to do this test run. If this plan works, we'll know we have a solution. If it doesn't... We'll go back to the drawing board."

As the bus turned off the main road onto a dirt path, Finch stood, gripping the rail overhead.

Garret leaned further back in his seat. "The egg you keep talking about… It can't be a normal egg, right? What's it look like?"

"About the size of a baseball." Finch rubbed at his ribs. "Spherical. It glows a bright white. It's obviously magical."

"Okay. I got a good mental picture."

The bus jolted to a stop, brakes hissing. Out the window stretched the chain-link fence and the dark sprawl of the forest beyond. The door to the bus hissed open, and Finch walked out. The afternoon had gone gray, clouds building in layers thick as stone. The air tasted of ice.

Enzo, Kull, Smudge, and Garret exited shortly after.

Finch turned back to everyone. "All right, once we're inside, stay close. Holt will probably track us down immediately. As soon as someone suspects he's nearby, I want Kull to wander away from the group. Say something about spotting a flower, and then go."

She offered a salute. "I will put all my acting into this one moment."

"Just… make sure it feels real."

"Aye, aye."

"Garret and Smudge, what do you need for this delusion?" Finch narrowed his eyes at them. "Anything?"

Garret knelt and picked up a pinecone. "This will do." He handed it to Finch. "Put that bad boy in your pocket."

"That's it?" Finch asked.

"Yup. I think I can do the rest." He cracked his knuckles. "At least, I'm pretty sure."

Enzo rolled his eyes. "What do you want me to do? Growl threateningly?"

"Whenever I hand over the egg, I want you to try to

convince me otherwise. I think Holt will really believe us if you're trying to stop me from handing over the egg."

"Really?" Enzo groaned. "I'm not the best at *acting*."

"Just a few sentences. It shouldn't be a big deal."

"Hmm…"

Garret's grin widened. "Well, time to earn my keep." He snapped his fingers at the nature preserve. "Let's go, people! And prepare to be impressed."

Once past the fence, Enzo led the way into the Desolation Wilderness. Finch, Kull, Garret, and Smudge walked a good ten feet behind him, keeping their distance and also staying extra vigilant. The darker clouds meant less light. Everything was gloomier now. Haunting.

The pines loomed so high that their tops dissolved into fog. Damp moss clung to the trunks, and the ground smelled of wet roots.

They hadn't gone far before Enzo slowed his pace. He held up a hand, and everyone came to a halt. "Do you hear that?"

Finch shook his head. "What?"

"Someone's coming."

Finch's shoulders stiffened. "Already?" He glanced at his clock.

1:43 p.m.

Was it because they were here so late? Had Holt been on the verge of leaving himself? It seemed he was much closer to the fence than last time. Or could he somehow predict their patterns? Did Aeon's time magic give him some sort of advantage even though Finch was rewinding time? Or perhaps Holt could remember some things from one loop to the next?

Finch didn't know any of the answers, but given all the odd things Holt was doing, he suspected time magic was giving the man a slight edge. That made him worry more about the plan.

"Wait, I feel him," Garret whispered. "Damn, this guy doesn't even play hard to get."

Finch snapped his fingers once. "Positions. Remember the plan."

Kull straightened, cracked her neck, and whispered, "This is my moment." She dramatically gasped and pointed. "Oh, my gods!" Her volume was five times louder than it ever needed to be. "*A flower!* A rare alpine bluebell in this climate? Impossible! I must see it up close!"

She leapt away from the group and wandered into the darkness between the trees, walking like an old-school Disney princess.

Garret laughed and then turned it into a cough when Finch shot him a glare. The man then bit his hand to keep from snickering further.

Enzo came back to the group, his frown prominent. "She's about as believable as a YouTuber apology video."

Kull stomped through the brush in exaggerated steps, her voice pitching up in mock wonder. "Such delicate petals! Nature is a miracle!"

It occurred to Finch then that Kull's social media videos probably didn't need a lot of acting. They were videos of her playing in a hot tub, playing video games, or pulling pranks. Why would she ever think she was an expert at acting?

But to Finch's surprise, Holt did emerge from the gloom, not far from Kull. His duster flapped behind him, and his crossbow was flung over his shoulder. His leg brace squeaked when he lunged, and Kull—noticing him long before he moved—remained frozen in place and shrieked.

"Oh no! It's the terrible man!"

Holt grabbed her by the wrist and twisted it behind her back, eliciting an actual shout from her that sounded more like she was cursing him out.

"*Watch it*," she snapped. Then her voice and tone returned to something more dramatic. "Unhand me, you brute! Your touch is as cold as your empty heart!"

Garret wheezed.

Ignoring Kull's hammy acting, Finch stepped forward. "Kull!"

Obviously a tad confused, Holt backed away, keeping Kull between him and Finch. He reached into his trench coat and withdrew a silver Desert Eagle. He pushed it against the side of Kull's head.

"Adair Finch," he said through clenched teeth. "No more games. I have your woman."

Kull couldn't stop herself from smiling. "D'aww. He said I was *your woman*."

"She's not my woman," Finch called back, irritated.

Holt scoffed. "I saw you two at the Chinese restaurant. I know what you are."

Holding back the urge to roll his eyes so hard he would die from the torsion, Finch took a deep breath. "Fine. Just leave her alone, Holt! She's got nothing to do with this."

"Give me the egg," Holt shouted back.

"You'd really kill an innocent girl to get the egg? That's not the Jack Holt I know. He's a good man—one who saved a lot of people once. If you want the egg, that's between me and you. Let her go."

Holt went silent. He held Kull close, but his eyes were dark with doubt. Then, to everyone's shock, he pushed Kull away, releasing her fully. "You know me too well, it seems," he said in a gruff but determined tone. "If you won't surrender the egg, I'll have to take it from you by force. Anyone who gets in the way will pay the price… but I won't hurt no innocent women."

Finch opened his mouth to say something, and then just closed it.

Damn.

He had just wanted to act the part. How had he fucked up his own plan?

"*What the hell?*" Enzo whispered to him. "You were supposed to just hand him the egg. What the fuck was that?"

"It all happened so fast," Finch snapped back.

This was comedy gold to Garret. He doubled over, laughing harder now, but trying to stifle it. Even Holt gave the man an odd stare, bewildered.

Kull, standing only a few feet from Holt, narrowed her eyes. "Oh, you'll only hold me hostage if I'm a threat? I'm totally a threat! Don't count me out!" She leapt at the man with feral energy and collided with his side.

He grunted, staggered back a few steps, and then immediately grabbed her wrist again. She struggled, and it was painful to watch, but Holt eventually twisted it back around until the back of her hand was flat against her spine.

"Ow, ow, ow," she said. Then Kull turned to Finch. "Save yourselves! This monster has me!"

"I was letting you go," Holt growled. "You came back and attacked me. What's wrong with you?"

Not wanting to mess this up twice, Finch reached into his coat pocket and withdrew the pinecone. But it didn't look like a pinecone. No, Garret's magic worked well. It was a sphere of glowing white light, almost identical to the real egg. That gave Finch hope for this plan. He wouldn't have to kill Holt, and he could get the man off his back.

The egg dazzled everyone as Finch held it aloft.

"Don't hurt her!" Finch then held out the egg. "You can have it."

Enzo cleared his throat. "Don't... don't do it, Adair. He's... uh, evil."

Finch glared at him over his shoulder. *"Seriously?"* he mouthed.

Holt blinked again, his grip on Kull faltering. "What is wrong with all you people?"

But before Finch could continue with his charade, wind blasted through the woods like a hammer. Branches bent, pine needles went everywhere, and the air seemed to howl in anger. In the darkness, something massive moved. It shifted from tree to tree, quickly closing in.

Finch caught his breath.

Sevengaias.

And in this time loop, they had forgotten to steal the leaf from Detective Tate's office.

CHAPTER
THIRTY-FOUR

Holt froze, handgun lowering on instinct. Garret's laughter died in his throat. Kull held her breath. The shadowy presence was massive, and the gloom thickened around them.

Ice shot through Finch's veins.

He felt Sevengaias's magic creeping under his skin, cold as groundwater, curling around his ribs like fingers. He wasn't sure where Sevengaias was siphoning her magic from, but it was from something powerful. A lord of death.

The forest inhaled.

And not *air*, but *age*. Pine trees bowed as though remembering a storm from a century ago. Lichen curled. Sap turned the color of tea and hardened in an instant.

Sevengaias was practically the size of a cathedral, and she slid between the trunks without ever resolving into a shape. Her presence pressed the forest into a negative: light went thin, and life drained from everything at the edges.

The first touch of her magic was polite, but *fast*.

Every needle on every branch crisped into ash at once. A

gray hush fell from the canopy like snow. The moss browned and fell away in sheets. Ants spilled from a split log, raced two inches, and simply... gave up. Their legs tucked. Their tiny bodies sank into the dirt as if gravity had been upgraded.

"Adair!" Kull shouted. "Be careful!"

The wind went still. Then the forest screamed.

The sound didn't come from Sevengaias. It came from everything else. The trees groaned, the birds fell silent, and the ground sank inward like lungs collapsing. Frost spread outward from where the spirit stood. It raced across roots and stones and the bones of fallen branches, turning everything it touched brittle and hollow.

Enzo wasn't even fast enough to speak before the death magic reached him.

His skin blanched. The light in his eyes dulled. His veins turned black, then gray, then empty. He staggered backward, clutching at his throat as the color drained from his face. Flesh fell from his scalp in clumps, his skin tightening against his bones like parchment pulled too thin. The breath left him in a choking rasp. His lips withered to dust.

He tried to snarl when his body *folded in on itself*, collapsing into a silhouette made of ash.

"*Enzo!*" Kull screamed.

Garret stumbled backward. "No, no, no..." He thrust his hands outward, summoning the shimmer of delusion—phantom shapes flickering, hallucinations peeling into being like smoke. They flickered once, twice... and then cracked apart.

Sevengaias's death magic rolled through him like a tide. His skin aged by centuries in an instant. Wrinkles carved into his face. His teeth blackened. Fingertips split. Color drained from his arms. His laughter—half-hysterical, half-defiant—cut off mid-breath as his chest collapsed inward.

Garret's body dried up.

His bones bowed, skin caving, until he looked less like a man and more like something the sun had forgotten to finish. His final exhale left his throat in a dry whisper—then the wind took him, scattering him like a burnt page.

Smudge shrieked. His tiny hands clutched the earth, nails clawing the dirt as if to hold it together. The ground crumbled between his fingers.

Sevengaias took another step forward.

Her outline wavered—an unholy radiance, the color of unlight. The trees around her split down their trunks, leaking black sap that steamed and hissed. Frost rolled in waves, coating bark, grass, and even the very air. The world withered wherever she looked.

But Finch didn't allow her time enough to look at him.

He activated his magic, and the world snapped. Sevengaias was halted in place, as was Holt, Kull, and Smudge.

Finch hadn't wanted to rewind time just yet. He hadn't tried out his healing potion, and he wasn't yet certain if Holt would be completely fooled by the delusion, but he also wasn't going to sit around and fight a spirit of death on its home turf.

All colors drained from the area. Then the shapes fell away, leaving Finch in a void of white. When he blinked his eyes, he was back on the road outside Tahoe City, the chill of a cold evening washing over him in a *whoosh*.

12:04 a.m.

Enzo stood to his left, and Kull to his right.

"Enzo, are you okay?" Kull immediately asked.

The man turned to her, his hands unsteady as he wiped his face. "Yeah. Yeah... I'm fine."

Kull leapt to his side and touched his arms, shoulders, and sides. "Was it painful? I... I got really scared there for a moment..."

"You and me both." He exhaled. "But it wasn't painful. It just *happened*."

"Don't ever do that again." Kull whirled on her heel to face Finch. "We forgot the leaf!"

He half shrugged. "I had been focused on fighting Holt, not traveling through the Desolation Wilderness. It hadn't occurred to me—but that's not a mistake I'll repeat."

After Enzo got his shaking hands under control, he inhaled and rotated his shoulders. "All right. What's the plan now?"

"We gather all the pieces to this puzzle right now," Finch stated. "First. Smudge in the woods. Then Maddie's shop for the potion. Then the leaf inside Detective Tate's. We do it all before two in the morning, and then we check in to the Alder Crown. Got it?"

The others nodded.

Finch hoped beyond reason nothing would go wrong this time.

Finch went into the trees himself and called for Smudge, announcing his name before he got too far from the road. Smudge came to him effortlessly, and Finch thanked Chronos that he didn't have to encounter the red-eyed werewolf to recruit the little pukwudgie.

Once on the party bus, they drove straight into Tahoe City.

A thin fog dragged itself up from the lake and across the streets like silk, muting the world into shades of blue and white. The streetlamps flickered within the mist, each one haloed and half-asleep.

The bus parked a block away from Maddie's shop. The

front sign was off, but the neon tubes still held a faint afterglow.

"She's closed," Kull as she stepped out of the vehicle. "Are we breaking in?"

Finch pulled his coat tight against his body. "We're going to buy her healing brew and leave. We already know she doesn't mind selling it, and we know the price. This should be an easy in-and-out operation where we harm nothing of hers."

Enzo snorted from inside the bus. He called out, "I'll watch the goblin."

"You're grumpy when you're tired, you know that?" Finch called back.

"Yeah, yeah, smartass. Just get the damn brew and get back here."

"Fine."

In the cold of night, Finch and Kull walked over to the front door of the psychic's shop. It was locked. Of course it was. He laid his hand against the knob and visualized the metal molding. The handle responded like an obedient hound. It rippled under his palm and softened, the brass rearranging itself until the lock *clicked* open.

"In and out," Finch muttered.

They slipped inside. The shop smelled exactly the same as before, though the room was far colder. The jars on the shelves glinted in the dark, reflecting slices of moonlight that fell through the blinds.

Finch went straight for the high shelf. The jar of healing brew sat behind a row of mismatched bottles labeled things like *Heartsease* and *Dream-Salt for Lovers*. He knew it was the right jar when he spotted the beeswax seal.

"Got it," he said.

Kull golf clapped. "Okay. Let's get out of here."

Finch pulled out six hundred dollars and set it all on

Maddie's little table. He took a pen from the counter, hesitated, and scrawled a note:

I made an emergency purchase. You probably saw it coming.
A.F.

Then he set the note on top of the money and exited the shop alongside Kull. Finch used his magic to relock the door before they left, though the handle didn't look quite right afterward. He frowned at the messy dents in the brass, but then he shook his head and left. Now wasn't the time for perfection.

They took their bus back into the city, driving without much conversation between them. Tahoe City's main strip was empty this late, only the hum of power lines and the slow pulse of traffic lights cycling through colors for no one.

When they pulled into the small parking lot beside the sheriff's office, the building looked sterile and faintly blue under the security lamps. Its windows were half-covered by vertical blinds, and there were a couple police vehicles parked behind a fenced-in lot, but otherwise, it looked rather deserted.

Finch, Enzo, Smudge, and Kull exited the bus. They headed for the corner of the building, but thanks to the darkness, Finch noticed something he hadn't before. A small red blinking light near the gutter. Cameras.

"Damn," he muttered. "They're recording the perimeter."

"Why is that a problem?" Kull asked.

"No matter what, we'll need Tate's leaf. Which means we need to find a way to get it without any evidence of our theft."

Kull crossed her arms. "If my mischief magic were

normal, it would protect me from cameras. I could slip right past them. Then I could unlock the window, grab the leaf, and no one would ever know."

That was true. Finch remembered using her magic in the past to avoid police cameras. "Hmm…"

Kull furrowed her brow as she thought aloud. "If I could just siphon mischief magic from something… Or bond with a creature that was mischievous…"

Smudge perked up. "Mischief?"

Everyone turned toward him.

The goblin pointed at himself, chest puffed with pride. "Smudge, mischief. Trick magic. Delusion."

And it made a mild amount of sense to Finch. Pukwudgies used their magic to steal from humans, after all. It wasn't just making delusions. Was it mischievous? Could it be both?

"Can creatures have multiple magical sources?" Finch asked.

Enzo nodded. "Lycanthropy is moon magic, and also a curse. And *Smudge* sounds like a name you'd give a mischievous creature."

"Can Smudge bond with both Garret and Kull? Is that possible?"

Smudge tapped his chest. "Smudge share."

Kull crouched in front of Smudge, eyes widening. "*Really*? You'd let me take some of your magic?"

Grinning with rows of sharp teeth, Smudge nodded. Then he said something in goblin, and Kull replied in a happy tone. She held out her hand, and the goblin took it. After a few moments of silence, Kull stood.

"I feel… so much better," she whispered. When she turned to Finch, it was with a smile, her complexion somehow smoother and brighter than ever before. "I think I can get the leaf without anyone noticing."

She was, of course, back in her neon pink hoodie. Finch wondered if that would be a problem, but he didn't voice his concern. He motioned to the area behind the sheriff's building. "You know where it is."

"I'll be right back!"

CHAPTER
THIRTY-FIVE

Finch leaned against the side of the party bus, eyes fixed on the sheriff's building across the parking lot. The red lights of the cameras still blinked in their lazy rhythm, as if mocking him. The fog had thickened, swallowing most of the surrounding area.

Enzo paced beside him, his Crocs making slow, irritated crunches against the frost.

"How long's she been gone?" Enzo asked.

After glancing at his phone, Finch replied, "Two minutes."

"Isn't that a bit long for this simple theft?"

"Hmm. I'm sure she's fine."

That was what Finch kept repeating to himself in his head. *She's fine. This is fine. Everything's fine.*

Smudge occasionally glanced out the bus's window, since he couldn't stay outside. Finch didn't want to risk a sheriff coming up to question them. Smudge *could* be invisible, but it would still be awkward if someone caught a glimpse of the goblin.

Finch exhaled, watching his breath fog. "Maybe I should go look for her."

"Don't be ridiculous," Enzo replied.

"She could be in trouble."

"She also could be perfectly fine."

"Perfect, she's Schrödinger's influencer," Finch quipped. "Just what I've always wanted."

Enzo made a sound halfway between a laugh and a growl.

Before Finch could say something else to fill the waiting, Kull rounded the corner of the building. She jogged over to the party bus, all smiles and sunshine, despite the late hour.

"Miss me?" Kull asked as she approached.

"What took you so long?" Finch asked.

She reached into her hoodie pocket and produced the amber-covered leaf. "Well, first, I had to get this. And it was kinda high up, so I had to get a chair. While I was pushing it around, I noticed a ton of files in a filing cabinet. They were all neatly labeled with things like *evidence* and *suspects*, so I quickly used the computer to print off new labels like *embarrassing photos* and *spank bank*."

Attempting to hide a laugh, Enzo coughed loudly and headed into the bus. Finch held back all criticism. Kull had just been given a boost of mischief magic. Of course she would take the time to pull a random prank in the middle of a simple heist. Of course.

"Well, thank you for getting the leaf." Finch motioned to the bus. "But now we should get out of here as quickly as possible."

Kull practically danced onto the bus. "Yup! We just need Garret, and we'll be all set to go!"

Tahoe City's streets were just long ribbons of asphalt glossed with fog. By the time they reached the Alder Crown, even the neon signs had gone to sleep.

2:03 a.m.

Once inside, Kull got their suite keys, and then they were off to the elevator. Kull's crew would arrive at the hotel around 8:30 a.m. That was the earliest they could recruit Garret for his help, and this time around, Finch didn't want to wait any longer than necessary.

They headed up the elevator, and then went straight to their rooms. Smudge attempted to follow Kull and Finch, but Enzo pulled him back and led him to his.

Kull entered the suite first. She skipped over to the minibar and placed the leaf down. Then she frowned and turned to Finch. "I've been trying to wear a new outfit per time loop, but I think I might run out of them soon."

"You haven't run out of them already?" Finch balked.

"Well, no. I brought several changes because I figured I'd be filming."

"Right..."

After an exhale, Finch headed for his bedroom. Kull glided her way in front of him, blocking his path right before he reached the door. "Wait a second. I have a question."

He stared down at her, his eyes narrowing. "Okay. What is it?"

"So... when no one's looking, how often do we get to kiss?"

"*What?*" he asked.

"You know. You and me. You want to keep everything hidden—even though Holt already knows about us, I guess— but since we're alone *now*, doesn't that mean we could be kissing?"

Finch gently moved her to the side and then entered his bedroom. "Aren't you tired? We should be getting as much rest as possible."

Kull casually followed after. As Finch took off his coat and unholstered his guns, she flopped down onto the bed, arms out, hair spilling around her like flame. "But our kiss was so magical and amazing. Don't you want to do it *all the time*? I mean, how can humans who are in love resist kissing their partners? I've been fantasizing about it all day."

His face growing warm, Finch turned to face her. "You've been daydreaming about kissing me the whole day?"

Kull earnestly nodded. "That's what I just said."

"People don't usually admit things like that."

"I don't mind admitting it to you. I figured you'd be the same way, right?" Kull rolled onto her side and smiled. "So? Can we kiss right now? I think we still have thirty minutes before we absolutely need to get some sleep. *We could be making out that whole time.*"

Finch sat at the edge of the bed, half of him eager to give in to her demands, but the other half of him wanted to do everything right by Kull. Since this was one of her first relationships ever, Finch didn't want her to confuse lust with love.

"Kull," he began. "There's a big difference between a fleeting fire that warms you at night, but is gone by morning, and a steady sun."

"What do you mean?" she asked, her brow furrowed.

"It's a metaphor." He sighed. "Never mind. Why don't we date a bit more before we start having nonstop make-out sessions whenever we're alone?"

Kull sat up straight. "I've been wanting to finish our date and have a million ice cream dates with you ever since we arrived at Tahoe! You're the one who dislikes dates. But it sure did seem like you enjoyed the kiss."

Finch didn't respond to that. He turned away, his jaw tight. "Look, we don't know much about each other. Like, what's my favorite color?"

"Blue," Kull immediately replied.

Shocked, Finch met her gaze. "How did you know that?"

She shrugged. "One time, when you were helping Bree with something, she tried to get you a gift. She wanted to know your favorite color, and you replied with *blue*."

"And you committed that to memory?"

"Of course," Kull said, rolling her eyes. "You said it was your *favorite color*. There are over ten million colors! Out of *all the millions of colors*, blue is your favorite? I definitely had to remember that."

Finch had never thought of anything like that before. Sometimes, he forgot how alien Kull's mind was when it came to human preferences.

"Okay, what's my favorite movie?" Finch asked.

"Star Wars: Episode IV—A New Hope."

This stunned him. How did she know his favorite movie? He had never spoken to her about it, nor anyone else in years.

Kull giggled as a sly smile spread across her face. "I'm a mischief spirit, remember? I can bypass passwords and all sorts of fun things. Back when I was a full spirit, and hanging out in your apartment, I fiddled on your computer while you were asleep. Most of your passwords related to the movie. R2-D2istherealhero, anewhope1977, ihatepasswordsasmuchastheempire, and so on."

Damn. Finch didn't know what to do with this information.

Kull patted his shoulder. "Okay, this is fun. Now tell me my favorite movie and color."

He was about to tell her that he didn't know, and that was why they needed to date more, but then the answers came to him.

"Bullets and Butterflies," he muttered.

Kull clapped her hands together a few times. "That's

right! I love that one so much! I'm so happy you remembered."

"And your favorite color is purple," Finch said with an exhale. "Because it's a mischievous color that can't decide whether it's blue or red." She had said that to him one time, and it never left his mind. It had been just an oddball statement to make.

"Right again!" Kull leaned onto him. "Is this what awesome humans do on their dates? Make sure they know everything about each other? Because I like it."

Finch rubbed the back of his neck. "I was trying to say we need to know more about each other before we go straight to the physical…"

"We know each other pretty well. I think a second kissing session isn't off the table."

"Movies and colors are superficial things," Finch said, shaking his head. "What about our life goals? Our long-term plans? Deeply held beliefs and desires?"

Kull dismissively waved away the questions. "Pfft. We know that, too. You want to avenge your brother, fulfill all your pacts, and regain your mojo so you feel like your old self again." She placed her hand on her chest and smiled. "And I want to find true love, and experience the depth of humanity, both emotionally and in the greater sense of life. Right? We're both on the same page?"

Finch couldn't argue. Those were his goals.

And he knew Kull's goals rather well…

How was she out-arguing him on this? What kind of bizarre world had they stumbled into where Kull knew more about their relationship status than he did? Maybe they knew each other *too* well.

She had seen him at his lowest, broken and barely able to leave his apartment, and he had watched her go from just a spirit to a woman who wanted to unravel the human world with wide-eyed wonder. Denying her now felt like denying the pull of gravity.

But still, a flicker of hesitation burned in his chest. This wasn't just lust; it was something deeper, fiercer, and he didn't want to rush it, to let the fire consume them before they could build something lasting.

"Kull," he murmured, his voice rough, "I'm not saying no. Just… we should take it slow."

Her smile softened. She touched his shoulder and then slid her hand to his chest, fingers splaying over his heart. "Slow is fine. As long as it's *us*."

She leaned in, her breath warm against his skin, the scent of her—wildflowers and something electric—wrapping around him.

He closed the distance, his lips meeting hers in a tentative brush. Kull froze for a heartbeat, as if surprised by his gentleness, then she melted against him with a sigh.

But Kull wasn't one for *tentative*. No, not her.

She pressed forward, grabbing his shirt and twisting her fingers into the fabric, pulling him closer until there was no space left between them. Her kiss deepened, hungry and unyielding, her lips parting to claim his with a passion that ignited every nerve in his body. It was like she had poured all her daydreams into this one moment—fierce, unrelenting, a wildfire that refused to be contained.

Her free hand went to his head, her fingers threading through his hair, tugging just enough to send sparks down his spine. He responded by angling his head, deepening the kiss until the world narrowed to the heat of her mouth, the press of her body.

He wanted more, but he never lost himself fully.

When they finally broke apart, gasping, foreheads pressed together, Finch's heart thundered like a war drum. Kull's eyes were dazed, a satisfied grin blooming across her face.

"Okay, I think we need to stop," Kull whispered.

Finch huffed out a chuckle. "Weren't you the one talking about how we should do this for thirty minutes straight?"

"Yeah, well, I need time to... process all these feelings." Kull gestured to her head, but then to her chest, and finally to her stomach. "It's like my whole body is reacting to our intimacy, and I want to savor everything."

"I did say we should take it slow."

"You also said we have to keep this a secret, but I don't want any of the other ladies to think they have a chance with you," Kull whispered, playfully narrowing her eyes. "Maybe I should leave a hickey on your neck so everyone knows you're taken. Like they did in that one movie about kissing booths or something."

Finch half smiled. "Hickeys are for high schoolers."

"You're right... I should give you a black eye so all the other women know I'm *really* serious."

Again, Finch found himself laughing. But knowing Kull, she might do it. Finch shook his head and pressed one last, lingering kiss to her forehead. "You should go to your own room. It's late. We should get some rest."

Kull reluctantly got off his lap and sighed. "Well, fine. I guess." She walked over to the door, but stopped once she touched the handle. "And I don't want to be a fleeting fire, Adair. I want to be your steady sun. Just so we're on the same page."

Finch's throat tightened.

Then Kull waved to him, whispered a *good night*, and left.

CHAPTER
THIRTY-SIX

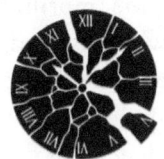

F inch woke at 8:00 on the dot.

The phone alarm chirped once—polite, businesslike—and he was already halfway upright as his hand tapped the screen to turn it off. No heaviness glued his eyelids shut. No dream-gunk clung to his thoughts. He felt clear, keyed-up in that razor way that meant the world would be forced to cooperate for *him* this time.

Finch washed, dressed, holstered his guns, and stepped into the suite's main room to the sound of a blender winding down. Kull stood at the kitchenette in a cropped sweater and star-dotted tights, hair pulled back with a purple scrunchie, pouring out something the color of sunlit lemons.

"Morning!" She gestured with her elbow at the counter. "Coffee's ready. Eggs, toast, and... some juice I made. Don't ask what's in it."

Finch eyed the drink. "What's in it?"

"Ha! Fine. I'll tell you. Banana, mango, yogurt, a whisper of mischief." She wiggled her eyebrows. "The usual."

He took the coffee, then demolished the eggs while Kull went methodically through her half slice of toast and bacon.

"You slept?" she asked.

"Like a normal person for once. Which is a first."

Kull smiled. "Today's the day, Adair. I can feel it. We're going to nail this."

He believed her. The leaf they had stolen lay on the table in its amber, catching the morning light and turning it honey. The healing brew was tucked in his coat, a soft clink of glass when he moved. Smudge had juiced her mischief back up. Garret would be easy to recruit at 8:30. The plan had edges, seams, redundancies. It would hold.

They finished in companionable silence, rinsed plates, left them to drip dry. Then they exited their suite and found Enzo already waiting for them in the hallway. He wore his Crocs, a Henley, his trusty sweatpants, and a pleased smile.

"Morning," Finch said.

"I'm glad we're all on time," Enzo replied.

Behind them, Enzo's suite door cracked open. Smudge shuffled out with both arms full of Meth, the cat sprawled across him like a judgmental fur cape. Meth's pupils were the size of coins. His tail swishing back and forth.

"Smudge bring lucky charm," the goblin announced. "For victory."

Enzo didn't even blink. "Put the cat back."

"But—"

"*Back*," Enzo repeated, pointing with two fingers like a traffic cop who had bitten a man before and would again.

Smudge sighed and slunk inside. The door thumped shut. A second later it cracked open just enough for nothing to exit—air rippled, and Smudge's footsteps padded past them invisibly.

Kull gave the empty space a thumbs up. "Great stealth, buddy."

The elevator dinged. They rode down together, a triangle of focus. In the lobby, Finch lifted his phone.

8:27 a.m.

They only had to wait a few minutes before Kull's social media crew came waltzing through the front door.

Louis led the charge, as usual. His hair was styled into golden perfection, the faint smell of expensive hair spray following him like a force field. Behind him came Whisp and Harper, carrying bags and ring lights. Garret trailed last, half awake, wearing the same clothing as always. Designer snow pants, white puffer vest, and a deep-blue cashmere sweater.

"Fox-Pistol," Louis said with a smile. "I cannot—I repeat, *cannot*—believe you picked the most beautiful hotel in all of Tahoe to visit. We can make a few killer videos here, darling. Your instincts are improving!"

Kull gave the man a quick hug. "I'm trying!"

"Did you check in yet? If we have our accommodations, we can start filming."

"Your suites are on the third floor." Kull handed over the keys. "I'm going to go out to get some breakfast, and I'll be back in a couple of hours, okay? Get everything set up while I'm gone."

Louis frowned and then gave her the once-over. After a long moment, he finally nodded. "Very well. You get some fuel. It's much needed."

Harper walked over, hugged Kull, and then shook her head. "I brought you a present, Samantha. You sure you don't want to wait just a little bit?"

"I'll be back soon," Kull said, slipping away from her. Then she grabbed Garret's arm. "Actually, I need Garret to accompany me. Super-urgent sponsorship thing. Business call vibes. The rest of you go ahead and start unpacking."

Garret, halfway through yawning, looked up. "Wait —*what?*"

She grabbed his sleeve before he could finish the word,

tugging him toward the front doors. "No time to explain. You love chaos. Let's go."

Louis opened his mouth. "Garret's our sound guy—"

"He'll meet you in the suite," Kull said, already pushing her way outside. "Promise! Just, uh, make sure the ring light's not facing the window this time. Last shoot made me look like a haunted tangerine."

Whisp trembled a bit. "C-Copy that."

Kull slipped outside with Garret. Finch and Enzo followed, Enzo managing a curt nod that went entirely unnoticed by the crew. Once outside, they all headed toward the party bus. Kull was already texting the driver that they wanted to leave.

Garret glanced at Finch and Enzo, and then blinked at her. "Who are these two weirdos? Fans? Gooners?"

"Bodyguards," Finch said. "Try to keep up."

"I'll explain everything in the bus," Kull said, pulling Garret faster. "But hurry! We have lots to get done, and nothing is going to stop us this time!"

The party bus rumbled through the misty morning, its neon ceiling lights cycling lazily between pink and teal. The lake was a long sheet of glass at their flank, and beyond it, the pine ridges crouched in a haze that looked almost metallic.

Finch explained everything to Garret. The man bonded with Smudge again, and just like before, was empowered.

Still confident, Finch stood at the front of the bus, one hand steadying him on the rail. Enzo sat opposite Garret, who was half-reclined in a booth seat, humming under his breath. Kull had her phone in her hands, lips pursed in a mix of determination and glee. Smudge, invisible as always, occasionally tapped at Finch's shoes.

The bus continued along, tires crackling over old asphalt.

Kull glanced up, all brightness. "Okay, everyone. Remember the plan: Holt gets the fake egg, believes he's won, and leaves. We stay alive. We save some werewolf children. The end. Happily ever after."

"You make it sound like an order through a drive-thru," Garret said with a chuckle.

"Well, I just want to make sure we're on the same page."

"Don't worry. I'm a professional. I got this."

Finch hadn't been worried before, but now he was.

The bus hissed to a stop in front of the chain-link fence guarding the Desolation Wilderness. The trees loomed like green pillars, their tips blurred by fog. The group filed out.

Finch glanced between everyone. "All right, this time we stick to the script, but I want it ten times subtler. Everyone understand? We do this clean."

"*Clean* is my middle name." Garret gave him finger guns.

"Pretty sure it's *Regret*," Enzo quipped.

Finch ignored them and stepped forward. Using his metal-bending magic, he opened the fence and allowed everyone through. Once in, the forest swallowed them in silence that felt alive, every branch holding its breath.

And much to his surprise, Kull didn't dramatically announce her departure. She simply hurried off a way and started searching through the gloom between trees, whistling to herself as though distracted.

Finch kept one eye on her as he walked forward with Enzo, Garret, and an invisible Smudge, his nerves eating away at his confidence. Why did he have so much anxiety over the plan now?

However, Holt didn't appear as quickly as before. Finch had to slow his pace, or else he would leave Kull completely behind. He walked around some trees, circling three times before meandering back.

"Maybe we're too early," Enzo muttered.

"No, he's here," Finch replied. "He's just taking his sweet-ass time getting to us."

"Hmm."

Then the wind shifted. A hush rippled through the pines, so deep it felt subterranean. The temperature dropped. Frost snaked out across fallen needles. Even the fog went still.

Finch's spine straightened. "Everyone hold," he whispered.

Between the trees, a massive shadow moved. It swept across the ground without leaving tracks, its form somewhat liquid but also solid. Sevengaias. She was here before Holt.

Her presence stretched over the clearing, vast and suffocating. The world bent around her, rot leaking out of bark. This time, Finch was ready.

The amber leaf in his coat flared gold, the glow spilling like molten sunlight. The frost stopped spreading. The dead air sighed and reversed, pulling color back into the trees. Finch grabbed the leaf and held it aloft.

Sevengaias paused, her formless shape rippling, her ancient head turning toward the light. Gold reflected in the emptiness of her gaze.

For a heartbeat, everything stilled.

Then the spirit of death stepped backward. Her shadow unspooled, dissolving into mist. The forest exhaled. After a few prolonged moments, the world returned to normal. Even the birds began their morning songs once again.

Garret let out a nervous laugh. "Wow... That was one powerful spirit."

Finch kept the leaf in his hand, even though it had stopped glowing gold. He stared at where Sevengaias had been, then slowly tucked the amber-covered leaf away.

But then the crunch of boots drew Finch's attention. He caught sight of Holt exiting the darkness near Kull. She wasn't paying attention, however. Her gaze lingered on the spot where Sevengaias had been. Finch *could* have called out to her, but he held his tongue.

Holt grabbed her wrist and twisted Kull's arm behind her back. "Got you!"

"Ah! *Adair!*"

Kull's cry actually sounded genuine. It sent ice through Finch's veins, but he held back.

"Holt! Let her go!"

"You can't hide from me, Adair Finch!" Holt held Kull close. "Give me the egg, and we can end this!"

Finch nodded once. "All right. Fine. You win. *Just don't hurt her.*"

Behind him, Enzo took a step forward, growling just enough for the scene. "Adair, don't! That man is dangerous!"

Everyone's acting was much smoother this time around. Finch almost believed Enzo was concerned.

Kull gasped dramatically, playing her part. "Don't give up the egg! It's too precious."

Garret, half hidden behind a cluster of trees, wasn't laughing this time. He watched as though this were a blockbuster. The pinecone in Finch's pocket shimmered, and he pulled it out. The thing looked like a spherical glowing egg. The perfect delusion.

Holt's eyes widened, and his breath caught. "You... You're giving it over?"

Finch didn't hesitate. He stepped forward, arm outstretched. "You wanted it, now take it."

The bounty hunter stepped forward, keeping Kull as a shield. Once close, he reached out and took the glowing sphere. The illusion didn't waver. It had weight, texture, the faint hum of divine static. Holt's jaw flexed.

"I knew you'd see reason," he said.

Then he let Kull go. She stumbled forward and landed in Finch's arms. Finch said nothing. He helped Kull get her footing and tried his best to scowl.

Holt tucked the false egg into his trench coat, glancing between Finch and the others. For the first time, suspicion didn't cloud his face. He looked... relieved.

"Now all crises will be averted," he said. "You made the right choice."

CHAPTER
THIRTY-SEVEN

"And what exactly are you going to do with the egg?" Enzo asked with a sneer. "It'd be just as easy for you to commit some sort of atrocity now that the egg is in your hands."

Holt shook his head as he took a few steps toward the trees, never turning his back to the group. "I'm not a monster like you, *wolf*. I'm going to make sure this egg is disposed of. It can't get into the wrong hands."

Finch wished he would just leave. He held back the urge to tell him to scram. "I was never going to use it for anything nefarious. You're a lunatic for jumping to conclusions, breaking into my office, opening fire on me while on a date, and chasing me all the way to Tahoe. Dress it up however you like, but you handled this all wrong, Holt."

The man's face brightened to a shade of scarlet as he pursed his lips. "Aeon told me all about your and Chronos's plans." He spoke every word through clenched teeth. "How you're going to destroy any other gods with power over time."

That was an interesting theory. Was that Aeon's fear?

That Chronos and his new child would try to come after him?

"Well, you have the egg now, so do whatever you want, but the only god I intend to kill is Gixmoth." Finch huffed. "Next time, don't let a manipulative time god override your common sense. You could've just spoken to me before acting like a maniac."

Kull straightened herself and nodded once. "Yeah, seriously. Humans are supposed to be great communicators capable of discussion and debate. That's one of your strengths!"

Holt narrowed his eyes at her. "Are you... not human?"

"W-Well, I'm half human, half spirit."

"And one hundred percent heart," Garret interjected. "Don't let this guy judge you."

Obviously irritated, Holt continued backing up until he shifted into the darkness. "Don't even think about chasing me, Adair. The Mark of Sagittarius helps me in more ways than one."

Finch didn't reply. He actually had to hold back a chuckle. He had absolutely no plans to chase the older man, but he wasn't about to say that.

Then Holt turned and ran off into the woods. Everyone waited a few moments before collectively exhaling. Kull then clapped her hands and wheeled on Finch. "We did so good!"

He nodded. "This was much better than last time, I will admit."

Enzo ran a hand over his bald head. "I may have practiced my lines a few times last night. I think I nailed them."

"Last time?" Garret whispered.

But Finch ignored the man. He wasn't about to explain anything. Snapping his fingers, Finch pointed to a path. "C'mon. The kids said that Sevengaias gave them an abandoned ranger station, right? We should follow the trails until we get there. It can't be far. Last time when we summoned the children, they got to us pretty quick."

They traveled along a trail covered in pine needles. Several old signs were scattered around the nature preserve, some with facts about the wildlife, some with maps. Finch located a radio tower and ranger station on the maps, and both were marked as *inoperable*. He had no doubt in his mind that the kids were staying there.

Ten minutes into the hike, Garret clearly couldn't handle the silence.

"Ya know," he said, addressing no one in particular, "your average banana bunch grows on trees in groups of twenty or thirty, but they're often split and sold in smaller groups at the stores. Meaning a single bunch rarely stays together after harvest, which also means every time you buy a few bananas, somewhere someone else might have the rest of that same bunch. Meaning you can share a single fruit cluster with a stranger from hundreds of miles away, and I think that's really beautiful."

"How much sleep are you getting at night?" Enzo sarcastically asked.

"Not enough, my guy."

Finch sighed. "Let's keep all our thoughts inside our own heads, shall we?"

They continued walking for another ten minutes. The forest thickened around them until they came to a clearing where the ghost of civilization lingered. There was a rust-bitten ranger station nestled beneath a leaning radio tower. The tower's red paint had long since faded to brown, and its metal ribs groaned in the breeze like an old lung.

There were no lights, and all the shades were drawn.

Kull tucked some of her hair behind an ear. "This place looks haunted."

"It probably is." Enzo walked forward first. "This far out, the only visitors are bears, ghosts, and idiots like us."

Smudge appeared at Finch's side in a shimmer of half-light, his yellow eyes wide. "There," the goblin said, pointing a gnarled finger toward the far end of the radio tower. "Little wolves. Watching."

Finch followed the gesture. Shapes flickered between the trees—small, pale, wary. The missing children. He held up a hand, wordless, motioning for the others to stay. Then he stepped into the open.

"Hello, there! My name is Adair Finch. I'm a private investigator. We're not here to hurt you. We know what happened—we know about the lycanthropy. You can come out."

A pause.

Then the shadows moved.

Travis emerged first. His was spine stiff, eyes scanning for betrayal. Kayla slipped from behind him, muscles tense. Lily, Benji, and Jason, the younger ones, appeared one by one, their clothes torn, their faces older than they should've been.

Enzo halted halfway to them. He sniffed the air. "You can tell what I am, can't you?"

The kids smelled him in return. Their eyes widened slightly, some of the fear draining from their expressions.

"My name is Enzo. You don't have to be afraid."

Travis, the oldest, tried to smooth his ripped-up hoodie. Then he crossed his arms. "You shouldn't be here."

"We're here to help."

"You can't *help*. There's nothing to do. The-The spirit who protects this place said this curse is forever."

Enzo waggled his hand back and forth. "That's not

entirely true. We know ways to cure it... But you need to take the cure quickly. Within thirty days of being cursed."

"Really?" Jason asked.

Lily, the youngest, grabbed Travis's pants and held them tight. "I want to go home."

"Why don't we talk inside the ranger station?" Enzo motioned to it. "We'll explain everything."

The five kids hurried to the station and then gestured for everyone else to follow. The door stuck halfway, swollen from old weather. Travis had to put his shoulder to it before the thing would budge open.

The inside was a casserole of scents. Wet wool, kid-shampoo, canned beans, and the musk of copper all swirled in the air. Finch wrinkled his nose as he stepped inside. Dust motes hung in the strip of light like tired fireflies.

The main room had been a square once, utilitarian and bare. The kids had attempted to carve it into a house.

Finch casually walked around, taking everything in.

"This is where you live?" Kull whispered.

Travis nodded. "We're safe here. No one gets hurt if we transform."

"I miss my bed," Lily muttered.

But no one answered her.

On the left, a "kitchen" had been assembled from a folding table and a rescued cabinet door balanced on rocks. Two camp stoves sat on top, their fuel canisters lined up nearby. Someone had taped labels over chipped mugs —JASON, LILY, KAYLA, BENJI, TRAVIS—in blocky Sharpie. A sixth mug read GUEST and had a smiley face with vampire teeth.

A saucepan dried upside down on a rag that had once been a T-shirt. Next to it, a little dish held three pinecones brushed with glitter glue. Centerpieces. Because homes had centerpieces.

To the right, the kids had made a living room. Blankets were slung between filing cabinets and a toppled bookcase, a soft fort of scrap quilts and emergency space blankets that sparkled like fish scales. A ranger's corkboard, long freed of memos, had been turned into an art wall. Crayon thunderheads. A wolf that was actually five wolves if you looked long enough. A shaky drawing of a cul-de-sac with every window colored yellow.

A couch sat in the middle of the room, but it was sunken, ugly, and sad to glance upon. Its cushions were patched with duct tape and two mismatched pillowcases. A stuffed-animal raccoon, pale gray from love, perched on the arm like a sentinel. It had button eyes and a stitched-on tag: *IF LOST RETURN TO LILY.*

Lily, noticing Finch's stare, brushed past him and adjusted the plushie, as though trying to make sure it was presentable for guests.

Near the doorjamb, pencil marks climbed in a ladder:

KAYLA 5'2" (HUMAN).

Then lower:

KAYLA 6'1" (NOT HUMAN).

Under that, a wobble at ankle height:

LILY 4'0" 🤍 !!!

In the far corner of the room, a chore wheel made from a pizza box spun lazily in the draft. Next to it was a list of house rules, each one written by a different child, as evidenced by the varying handwriting.

1) *If angry, take deep breaths and go outside*

2) *No yelling*

3) *If you have a bad dream, wake someone up*

4) *Shoes go by the door, so the floor doesn't get mad*

5) *We're not monsters*

"I like your rules," Enzo said.

Travis tapped his balled fist against his hip. "We agreed we should have them. It, uh, kinda feels like elementary school, but Lily has done a lot better since we have them. She wrote rule four."

Jason hovered by the radio desk, a museum of rescued wires and dead switches. He had organized them, it seemed. Each coil of cable had a bread clip tag: MAYBE WORKS, NO SPARKS, HOT BAD.

"This is my area," Jason said when Finch stared a little too long.

"I spoke to your mother," Finch muttered. "She's worried about you."

Jason stood a little straighter, his eyes growing wide and glassy in equal amounts. "Wh-What did she say?"

"She hired us to look for you. That's why I'm here in the first place. She wants you home as soon as possible."

Jason's watery gaze fell to the floor. "I can't." His throat was tight and his words almost cracking. "I don't want to... hurt her... if I transform."

"I understand, but that's why we're here." Finch nodded to him. "We'll find a way to lift the curse. Just you wait and see."

Kull gestured to a bunch of curtains on the floor. Well, it was more than curtains. There were also ripped-up shirts, old school banners, and even a tarp.

"Did you all make this?" she asked, her head tilted.

Travis's chin lifted a fraction. "We had to." He gestured in an awkward, proud, and simultaneously apologetic way. "There weren't beds, so we made... sleeping places. We tried to keep it clean. The spirit said we should try to do that."

"Sevengaias?"

"Y-Yeah. Do you know her?"

Kull nervously chuckled. "Kind of."

Smudge crept in at Finch's calf, peering up at the chore wheel with scholarly interest. "House," he whispered. "Safe."

Enzo inhaled and then let the breath out slow. He set his hands on his hips and nodded once, like he was saluting a well-run precinct.

"You've done good," he said.

Garret shoved both hands into his pockets and half shrugged. "Reminds me of when I was homeless in Oakland. We had the sickest tent with the warmest of barrel fires. This gives me the same vibes."

He was trying to be sincere. Finch could tell. But his commentary wasn't helping. It just made the situation sadder somehow.

"So you all sleep in this pile?" Kull asked, still staring at the odd human nest.

Benji pointed. "I get this end, by the map because I like to study it before going to sleep." He motioned to the other end. "Lily gets the corner near the space blanket because she likes how it sparkles. Kayla's on the couch because her back hurts when she's on the floor."

Kayla's face went pink. "It's just, that, my muscles feel wrong after... you know."

Being the only teenage girl living in the woods was probably a bother, but Finch refused to comment on it. The situation clearly embarrassed her.

Benji continued. "Jason sleeps in the middle, and Travis usually sleeps at the station desk."

"Do you eat enough?" Finch asked, keeping his voice even. "Real question, not a lecture."

"The spirit brings us food," Travis muttered. "Sevengaias takes care of us."

"And what about the two red-eyed wolves?" Enzo asked.

His tone was much icier than before. Everyone in the ranger station turned to face him.

When he glowered, the kids took several steps away.

"I want to know about them, too." Finch turned his gaze on Travis. "Do you know who they are? Or where they are? If they infected you all with the lycanthropy curse, they have a lot to answer for."

CHAPTER
THIRTY-EIGHT

Travis didn't answer the question right away. He waited a long moment, his eyes on the window. Finally, he exhaled.

"They stalk around the ranger station at dusk," he said. "Every day. They don't really talk to us, because I don't think they can speak anymore. I just think they know we're wolves, like them, so they... come to check up on us."

Everyone remained quiet. Lily grabbed her raccoon plushie and held it close. Benji's fingers worried the frayed edge of the pizza-box spinner until it squeaked.

"You don't know their identities?" Enzo asked. "Are they children, like you?"

Travis shook his head. "No. Not children. But I don't know who they are, and I don't think they remember, either. They watch us. Sevengaias doesn't kill them, even though they keep making new werewolves. I don't know why she doesn't... She won't ever say."

Kull pursed her lips. "I think this is a safe haven for them, too, in her mind. Or maybe she likes the death they bring. Also plausible."

Kayla's eyes had gone dark. "I think they like knowing we're afraid. I hate those two red-eyed wolves. They took everything from us… But killing them won't break our curse, apparently."

Jason sat at the radio desk and fidgeted with the wires. "We can fight back."

"No," Travis said. Not harsh, just automatic. "If we transform, we'll rage out of control."

"But they might keep cursing people…"

"Yeah, well… I don't know what to do about that."

Enzo snorted out a laugh. "What are we? Chopped liver? You kids don't need to worry about anything now. When those two wolves come tonight, *we'll* handle them. And after that, we'll break your curse. Right, Adair?"

Finch nodded along with his words. "Exactly."

Jason leapt off his chair and stepped forward. "I can help."

Enzo put a hand up, palm out. "Kid—" He adjusted, softer. "Jason. Your job is to breathe when you think you don't have air. That's the hardest thing in a fight like this. Let us handle everything dangerous. Besides, Lily needs you all with her."

Jason looked like he wanted to argue. Then he caught Lily watching him with big eyes and shut his mouth.

Kayla wrapped her arms around herself. "What if Sevengaias comes? She hates when the magical creatures she's protecting get harmed. She might hate that you're killing the red-eyed ones."

Finch touched the inside pocket where the amber leaf sat. He felt the faint cool of it even through his coat and shirt. "If she arrives, I can hold up my hall pass. If it doesn't work, we'll deal with everything in a different way."

Perhaps with fire.

The mood in the ranger station shifted. The kids exchanged nervous glances, their brows furrowed. Their uncertainty was thick in the air, and they clearly didn't understand how powerful Finch and his crew were.

They would see when the time came, but until then, the plan obviously filled them with dread.

"Okay," Enzo said, clapping his hands once. It sounded like a small thunderclap in the old room. He pointed as he spoke. "Since we have some time to kill, I say we grab a pack of cards and play a couple games. What do you all say?"

"Really?" Kayla asked. "Games? At a time like this?"

"Trust me. What we need right now is to stop worrying."

Garret gave Enzo finger guns. "Yes! My man! That's what I'm saying. Chill time."

The kids, who a moment ago had been sinking into depression, lit up as they ran to various corners of the large room to grabs decks of cards.

The games were simple. Go Fish, War, and a few rounds of blackjack. Kull and Garret played every single one, but Finch and Enzo sat a few out to look around.

Enzo paced the station like he was measuring it with his bones. He tested the couch's weight, the filing cabinets' drag, the friction on the floor whenever he slid the bookcase.

Finch set his healing brew on the desk and then went outside to walk the perimeter.

The radio tower's service gate was ruined, and there was no lock, but that wasn't a problem for Finch. He pulled three large bolts from the tower's lower lattice and walked them over to the fence. Thanks to his magic, the metal flowed, rearranged, thickened into the shape of a chain. He secured the gate closed and locked it, feeling more confident with his metal-working.

The more he practiced with magic, the more control and confidence he had.

Feeling inspired, he grabbed two more bolts and shoved them into his pockets. He could use them later.

Now that the gate was locked, the base under the radio tower was cordoned off. Would it hinder the red-eyed wolves? They were basically mindless at this point, and having the gate closed might confuse them. Finch wasn't certain, but he wanted to limit the size of the battlefield. It was better for him if they remained close.

Fire would kill a wolf if enough was applied.

Silver was best, of course, but Enzo was the only one with a silver weapon, currently.

When Finch and Enzo returned to the group, they ate what passed for lunch: a can of peaches split five ways between the kids and spoonfuls of peanut butter passed around like communion. Garret found a sleeve of stale crackers and performed a ceremony of breaking them over the sink while telling a story about a coyote who fell in love with a stop sign. It had bad morals, but at least it had a great ending. Even Kayla snorted.

And it kept the kids entertained.

Halfway through the day, Enzo cursed under his breath.

"What's wrong?" Finch asked.

"I left Meth in the suite."

Travis snapped into an upright position. "Did you just say you do meth?"

Enzo rolled his eyes. "My cat, Meth, is all alone in my suite back in town. I'm worried about him."

"You named him *Meth*?"

Jason and Benji both snickered at that.

"I told him he should just use *Paws*," Finch muttered. "But the man won't listen to me."

Lily nodded once. "Paws is much better."

The conversation died down after that. Enzo wasn't in the mood to debate the name of his cat.

Time thinned the way it does before a storm. The light went cold. The shadows along the ceiling corners stretched and grew darker. The tower outside groaned once, moving slightly with the wind.

It was almost time.

"Enzo," Finch said. "We should probably head out and wait for our new friends."

The man nodded. "Everyone else—you wait here, all right? Move the bookcase in front of the door once we're out and keep the blinds drawn. Adair and I shouldn't take long."

Travis hesitantly nodded. "Okay."

The air outside was already leaning toward night, all lavender edges and long, blue shadows. The trees rustled as they swayed in the wind.

Finch stepped out first, shoes crunching down on pine needles, the weight of his two pistols a familiar comfort at his ribs. Enzo followed, rolling his shoulders until they popped. He pulled his silver knife, and it gleamed in his hand under the last of the sunlight.

"I'm not going to transform," he whispered.

"Why?" Finch asked. "We might need the advantage."

"Just in case the children are watching. I want them to know… it's possible to control the beast."

"All right. If that's what you want."

Finch scanned the clearing. The chain-link gate at the tower base caught a little light from the dying sun. His handiwork glinted, and it steadied him. One more boundary. No one would sneak up from under the tower, not without rattling the fence or gate in some way.

They took positions. Finch crouched ten paces out from the door, half behind the stump of a fallen pine. Enzo knelt by the tower stairs, knife drawn, steady. Neither spoke. The forest had that pre-night stillness.

Finch checked the slide on Agony, then Starfall. They were ready. He flexed his fingers, reminding himself to not get close to the red-eyed monsters. The curse lived in blood, in spit, in the smallest graze of claw. He could fight anything except infection. It would follow him even through a time rewind.

The first sound came soft—a pinecone tumbling down the slope. Then a breath.

"They're here," Enzo whispered. His pupils had gone wide, dark swallowing the brown. "Get ready."

Finch felt the monsters before he saw them: the pressure of eyes, the hot pulse of something wrong behind the trees. Then they stepped out of the gloom.

Men once. Now only wolf beasts—patchy fur, muscles corded, red eyes glowing from their sockets like hot coals. Their breathing rasped through fanged maws. Each step was predatory in nature, and they kept their claws extended at all times, perhaps unable to retract them.

They wore no clothes. Finch only just registered that. Thankfully, their fur grew in long clumps, preserving some form of modesty.

"Let's do this," Enzo said, knife steady in his hands.

He stood and revealed himself. The red-eyed werewolves turned, sniffed hard, and then dashed forward, running with their arms and legs. Finch moved out from cover, drawing the attention of the monsters. One veered toward Finch, the other toward Enzo.

Finch didn't hesitate. He opened fire. Starfall's muzzle flashed blue, cutting through the shadows. His shots struck the attacking werewolf in the shoulder. The creature spun and then hit the ground, only to get back up with a snarl, empowered by cursed magic. It crashed through the underbrush, jaws snapping.

Finch rolled sideways, right through mud. The wolf slammed into the fallen pine, splinters bursting upward. Finch fired once more, at close-range. The bullet hit ribs. The werewolf half howled and half screamed, the noise disturbing.

Enzo's fight grew louder with the clash of body against body. He bashed into the enemy wolf with a tackle, knife flashing silver in the gloom. The blade cut across the black fur of the werewolf, and steam rose from the monster's torso. The beast shrieked and kicked; claws tore Enzo's shirt and skin. Blood splashed across the needle-covered ground.

"*Enzo!*"

"I'm fine!" he barked back. He wasn't, though.

His eyes flashed for a heartbeat, the wolf under his skin begging to come out. He clenched his jaw so hard Finch could hear the teeth grind.

The rabid werewolf fighting Finch lunged again.

Finch ducked and brought Agony up under the wolf's throat. He fired, and the burst of white pain-magic hit like a hammer, hurling the creature backward. The monster rolled twice and then landed on its feet, staggering. Its breath steamed in furious bursts.

Enzo and the other monster were locked in a grapple. Enzo managed to slash his knife down the creature's arm. When the wolf tried to pull away, Enzo slashed at the beast's neck. Blood sprayed outward, and the werewolf shuddered, practically hissing. Enzo leapt away, breathing like a furnace.

Fur sprouted over Enzo's shoulders.

"Keep it together!" Finch yelled.

Enzo took several deep breaths, and his transformation halted. He wasn't going to change; Finch was sure of it.

But Finch's foe came again, this time faster than ever

before. Finch dove sideways, firing both guns at once. One bullet grazed the creature's muzzle; the other hit a leg. It stumbled, turned, and came anyway. Finch smelled its breath —rotted copper, wild rot—and for one panicked second, he thought of lycanthropy infection.

When the werewolf slammed Finch back-first on the ground, Finch kicked upward, his shoe connecting with the beast's jaw. Teeth snapped inches from Finch's thigh. As the wolf reeled, Finch snatched the metal bolts from his pocket.

He visualized them shifting into a bear-trap-like object. The metal conformed to his will, and when the werewolf came for Finch's face, he slammed the trap up into the beast's snout. The metal folded around his muzzle, and steel spikes dug into the wolf's flesh. It howled again.

"Down!" Enzo shouted.

Finch went flat without thinking. Enzo threw his knife. The silver streaked through the dim light and sank deep into the wolf's throat. It jerked as it stood, gagged on its own growl, and then ripped the blade from its body. With frantic movements the beast clawed at its own neck. After a few bloody moments, it hit the ground hard. Smoke curled from the wound.

Enzo's wolf wasn't dead, though.

It charged.

The remaining wolf howled a furious broken sound, and charged. Enzo ran forward and plucked his knife off the ground. Then he whirled on his heel and met the monster head-on. He went to one knee, driving the blade upward into its belly, twisting. The wolf clamped its jaws around his shoulder and bit.

Finch fired, once, twice, three times. The bullets tore through the werewolf's side, the last punching through its skull. The creature fell off Enzo, dead weight thudding into the dirt.

For a prolonged second, Finch was worried his wolf wasn't actually dead, either. He wheeled on the beast and unleashed a torrent of flames all over the werewolf, burning it to ash in a matter of minutes. Once he was certain it was incinerated, Finch stomped out the remaining flames.

Enzo staggered back, knife still in hand, panting. His eyes were canine-like, but not fully transformed, the wolf pressing hard. His pulse was a visible thing under his jaw.

"Don't," Finch said, stepping closer, guns down. "You're still here. Stay here."

Enzo's teeth lengthened for a second—small, sharp—and then receded. He wiped the blood from his arm, smearing more than cleaning. "I'm… here," he managed. "I'm good."

CHAPTER
THIRTY-NINE

Finch stared at the non-charred werewolf. It was already shrinking, the monstrous form giving way to the human again. A pale, ruined face, empty eyes. It was sad, really. Finch wondered if there was a cure for red-eyed wolves, but from what he knew, there wasn't.

He holstered Agony and Starfall, heart still jackhammering. Finch eyed his friend. "You're bleeding."

"I've been worse." Enzo glanced at the corpses. "Plus, I feel pretty damn good. We won."

"True."

He wiped his knife on a patch of moss. "They won't hurt any more kids."

Finch exhaled slowly, the adrenaline leaving in one painful sweep. "Let's get back inside before Sevengaias decides this qualifies as a disturbance."

Enzo nodded, limping toward the ranger station, knife at his side. The forest took back its silence, one cold breath at a time.

They shouldered through the door of the ranger station.

The kids moved the bookshelf and once everyone was inside, the room detonated into noise.

Lily squealed, ran straight at Enzo, and then stopped short as soon as she saw the blood splattered across his body. She settled for hugging his leg below the wounds. Benji whooped loud enough to rattle the old blinds. Kayla's shoulders dropped a full inch, and then she clapped as though at a concert. Jason did a small, tight-fisted jump and then immediately tried to make it look like he hadn't.

Travis didn't whoop. He stood there, jaw clenched, eyes glossy. "You... actually did it," he whispered, voice rough. "They're gone?"

"They won't be back," Enzo answered. It wasn't a boast. Just fact. He placed his knife on the desk and didn't look at the gash in his shoulder.

Kull arrowed in, hands fluttering. "Your arm! Sit, sit." She ripped some of Enzo's shirt to use as a bandage. "Werewolves super heal fast, right?"

"Yeah," Enzo muttered.

"Okay. I'm going to do a little triage, and you just take it easy until your body puts itself back together."

"Feh."

"We should celebrate," Benji blurted, as if worried the moment would evaporate if no one named it. He skidded across the room, dug under the folding table, and came up with a dented can. "These are pears. We were saving them, but now seems like a great time."

Kayla huffed a laugh. "For what, still being werewolves?"

"For not dying," Benji said, dead serious.

They ate victory pears right out of the can with the one clean spoon, rotating it like communion again, and Lily gave the raccoon plush a sticky kiss on its stitched nose. Even the centerpieces on the counter—pinecones with googly eyes— seemed to sit a little taller.

Once the food was gone, Travis exhaled. "Thank you," he said, and there was a weight to it that filled the room. "All of you."

Finch checked the window. Night had slid in, the trees turning to a paper cutout of black. He glanced at his phone.

7:17 p.m.

"Okay," he said, and the word shifted the room again, celebration surrendering to attention. "Coats. Shoes. Outside. We're not done."

Kayla's smile faltered. "There's... more?"

"There's the part where we fix this," Finch said. He rubbed at his side and then grabbed his healing brew off the desk. "Everyone, come on. Enzo, grab a clean knife, not your silver one. It's covered in cursed blood. We're going to need something to cut flesh."

Stars dotted the sky, and the moon—fat and milk-pale—hung low and large. The radio tower groaned once as wind swept over the area, then held its peace.

Finch positioned them without making it sound like an order. The kids stood in a loose half circle. Kull flanked them, eyes bright, chin up. Garret leaned on a fence post, interested but obviously distant. Enzo stood to Finch's right, bandage already spotted through.

"What are we doing?" Travis asked, not defiant, just baffled.

Finch half shrugged. "We're going to cure you."

"How?"

"We're going to ask the moon for a favor."

Kayla swallowed. "Ask... what?"

"Khonsu," Finch said. "A god of the moon. One of them, at

least. Keeper of months, measurer of hearts, traveler." He glanced at Enzo. "According to some reliable sources, Khonsu hates curses. He's the one who made silver so damaging to werewolves and vampires."

Travis nervously chuckled. "Yeah, don't flash your silver around Sevengaias. She protects a vampire who sleeps here in the forest. Or, well, under the forest."

Finch lifted an eyebrow.

Was *that* where Sevengaias got all her power? She was siphoning death magic from a slumbering vampire? Interesting. But Finch shook away the thought. Now wasn't the time to dwell on that.

Enzo snorted and frowned. "And how exactly are we calling up a moon god, Adair? You got a hotline I don't know about?"

"I have a goblin." Finch pointed to Smudge.

The pukwudgie had been doing his best impression of a shrub near Kull's boot. He perked, delighted to be called upon. "Me?"

Finch nodded. "Smudge connected to the werewolves before, using a thread of sympathy—a bit of fur, something to link minds."

"I remember when he took my fur, yeah," Enzo said.

But Smudge didn't remember. Nor did the kids. That had been in a different time loop, and they all exchanged questioning glances.

"We don't have Khonsu's fur," Enzo sardonically said. "So how are we going to speak with him, huh?"

"We don't have god fur. We have a *god egg*."

The mere mention of the real egg caused Enzo to tense. And while Finch didn't have it on him... He did have it *inside* him.

Long before he took Kull on their fake date, he had figured the only place to hide the egg so it wouldn't be stolen was within his body. He had cut open his side, painfully fitted the egg within, and then used one of his healing brews to immediately correct the damage.

The egg wasn't *comfortable*. He always felt it, jabbing at his side, just below his ribcage. But it was there.

Now, with the clean knife in hand, he had a way to retrieve it. Well, with that and the second healing brew.

Finch removed his coat, sighed, and then pulled up his shirt.

"Wait," Kull said as she hurried forward. "You mean… the reason you smell extra Chronos-y is because you have the egg right now?" She pointed to his exposed side. "And the reason you felt lumpy during our hugs is because the egg was *in your body* this whole time?"

"Yeah," Finch muttered. "Exactly."

"That's hilarious." Kull smiled brighter than ever. "I can't believe I didn't guess that! I should've known."

"Please don't make this a thing."

"Oh, it's already a thing! You're about to give birth to a god egg. There's no way I'm not making that a thing."

Garret whistled. "Man's about to C-section himself for the moon. I've seen weirder, but not by much."

"Everyone, back up," Finch ordered. "I don't need commentary."

Enzo stayed close, though, eyes steady. "You sure you can do this out here? No sterile tools, no mirror—"

"I'm not digging for a bullet. I know where it is."

Finch tapped the place under his ribs where the faint, cold weight of divinity pressed against muscle and bone. It was like touching a second heartbeat that didn't belong to him.

He exhaled, gritted his teeth, and placed the tip of the knife against his skin. The metal was cold.

Kull winced. "You're—oh my mischief, you're actually—"

The knife slid into his flesh in one easy go. The white-hot pain flared through his body, almost blinding him. He held back any urge to scream or shout, and instead clenched his jaw to weather the agony.

There was a harsh, wet sound, and then the glow. A pale white light welled from under his skin as he opened himself up. The air smelled like ozone and time-worn dust, the scent of clocks bleeding. The cut shimmered.

Blood poured down his side, soaking into his pants.

Finch worked fast, jaw locked, hand steady. He reached in two fingers deep, found the smooth curve, and pulled.

The god egg came free with a sound like glass leaving water. The light swelled, spilling over his fingers, shining over his whole body. For a heartbeat, everyone held their breath.

Then it was done. Finch held the baseball-sized sphere in his palm, slick with his blood, gleaming like a captured star.

Kull blinked. "That's... honestly the coolest and most disgusting thing I've ever seen."

"We should've filmed it," Garret called out.

"You're right... We should've." Kull playfully snapped her fingers. "Okay, do your thing to time. We can take this from the top, people."

Finch didn't answer. He dropped the knife, grabbed the healing vial from his pocket, popped the cork with his teeth, and swallowed. The liquid burned its way down like fire, but it tasted like honey. In a matter of moments, the cut sealed in slow motion, light knitting into skin until all that remained was a faint scar and a dull ache.

Color came back to his face. Finch wiped sweat from his brow and then turned to Smudge.

"Ready?" he asked.

Smudge had gone still, eyes wide at the miracle of

extraction. He nodded fast, both awe and greed in the gesture. "Smudge ready."

Finch crouched, held out the sphere. Its glow painted the goblin's gray face in soft ivory. "Careful," he muttered. "If you harm the egg, it'll be the last thing you do."

Smudge's long fingers curled around it. The glow softened, as if recognizing someone new and not entirely liking them. The goblin shivered, ears twitching. "It speaks," he whispered. "Whispers. Loud. Loud."

"Just... use it to speak to Khonsu. Then hand it back."

Finch rose, rolled his shoulders, and glanced at the others. The children clung to each other, faces lit by the shifting light. Enzo's expression was tight with worry, but he nodded once, ready to follow Finch's lead no matter how mad it looked.

Finch glanced up at the moon, its pale face huge above the tips of the pine trees. "Any day now, Smudge."

They only had a handful of hours left in this loop before Finch *had* to rewind time or be stuck with this outcome forever. He wanted to make sure Khonsu would help before he settled on a final route, however.

Smudge straightened, egg cupped to his chest like a lantern. His small body trembled. "Smudge try." Then he shut his eyes.

The egg pulsed once, twice, and a ripple went through the clearing. The wind stilled. The stars sharpened.

Finch felt the air change. He grabbed his coat and wrapped it around his bloody shirt.

Smudge's eyes snapped open. "Oh! The moon! It heard. *It's coming.*"

CHAPTER
FORTY

The moonlight thickened.

It was no longer a slight wash of white. Rays from the moon now had substance. They had weight and geometry. The stars above the clearing flickered out, leaving just the moon and its intense shine on this one specific location in the Desolation Wilderness. Frost lifted off the pines in a sigh and hung in midair, glitter caught in an invisible tide.

Smudge went stiff, Chronos's egg clutched to his chest. The sphere pulsed again, syncing the entire forest to a heartbeat that wasn't the forest's.

The solid moon rays merged, creating a bridge. Silver bled from them, running down the sky and becoming a door. The silver door opened wider and wider, revealing a realm of the night the likes of which Finch had never seen.

Probably no human had seen...

Then a humanoid figure exited the silver doorway on a path made of hieroglyphs. Each step drew itself in shining script and faded behind the man: a crescent, a crook, a hawk's eye, a sickle of time. When his foot met the ground, the dirt under it smoothed and polished like river stone.

This was Khonsu, a God of the Moon.

And while he was shaped like a man, he wasn't entirely.

Khonsu wore a crown. It was a full moon, bright and shining. He was mummified at the torso, linen strips tight as vows, but the fabric moved like water. A broad collar gleamed at his throat—gold with little blue suns. His arms were bare and young and old at once, his muscles prominent.

His head was that of a blue falcon. His eyes were night itself—obsidian wet with stars—watchful and amused.

"Do we bow or curtsy for gods?" Kull whispered.

Garret tried to bow and invented a new way to misuse his spine. The kids pressed together out of fear and awe. Lily clutched her raccoon plushie so hard its button eyes bulged.

Finch shook his head and half held up his hand. "I'll handle this."

Khonsu turned his starry eyes to each individual, his gaze lingering for a few moments before he moved on to the next. He tilted his head.

"My sky, my people," Khonsu said. His voice wasn't heard with ears and instead went straight to Finch's mind. A form of telepathy. It made sense, since falcons didn't have lips to aid in speech. "I have been gone too long."

Finch stepped forward. "O Great Khonsu. My name is Adair Finch, and I'm the warlock who asked this pukwudgie to summon you."

"I am aware." Khonsu held up his arms as he turned his gaze to their surroundings. "When the moon has domain of the sky, I see all." He lowered his arms and then met Finch's gaze. "I saw you rid the world of those who spread curses."

"Yes."

"I saw your cursed associate do the same."

Enzo straightened. He had been standing in the back, not

moving, barely breathing, as though trying to disappear at the edge of the intense moonlight. However, once the god had acknowledged him, Enzo stepped forward until he was side by side with Finch.

"My name is Elijah Harris." Enzo bowed his head. "It's an honor."

"I have not touched Earth in some while. It has been some time since I've seen members of your kind act with such control and restraint. You have almost mastered the curse."

"Thank you…" Enzo's voice became quieter, as though he didn't appreciate the compliment.

When Khonsu returned his attention to Finch, his falcon eyes were narrowed.

"You called, and I arrived. State your business."

"It's about the curses…"

Khonsu's gaze went past him then, sweeping the clearing. It snagged on the scorched patch where one red-eyed wolf had been reduced to a bad memory. It slid to the other corpse, shrinking back toward human shame. His face didn't change, but the air did.

When he spoke through telepathy again, the words felt like anger. "Hunger without tether. Blood taught to lie. I despise these things. Curses are the unraveling of the world. The first herald of the end. They must be stopped."

Then the god relaxed, his exhale coming out a silvery mist.

"You destroyed two curse-carriers, and I will reward you for that demonstration."

Hopeful, Finch motioned to the five children. "If you mean that, mighty Khonsu, then I implore you to break the curse on everyone here. Surely your moonlight and silver are up to the task."

Khonsu inhaled. The night got crisp around the edges.

Travis flinched but then quickly straightened his spine.

Kayla remained at his side and even placed a hand on his shoulder. Jason tried to hide his trembling by fidgeting with a non-existent radio switch, while Benji's eyes were as big and bright as road reflectors. Lily tucked her raccoon under her chin and held it there.

Khonsu's eyes softened. The moon on his head dimmed by a breath.

Then Khonsu's crown answered, a pale flare whispering around its rim. He stepped closer to Finch. Not threatening. Or perhaps exactly that, Finch wasn't entirely sure. The smell of his linen was clean and old. The light at his brow flickered like laughter.

"You ask me a favor, and that favor is exactly the sort of action I would've taken regardless." Khonsu tilted his head like only a bird could. "I will take note of this."

Khonsu held out an arm. The air rippled. Moonlight dripped from his fingers in slow silver threads that tangled in midair, weaving themselves into a net of light.

The god walked over to the children, the web of magic dangling from his hand.

They shrank together like shadows pulled by dawn, but when Khonsu threw his net over them, the fear left. The threads sank into their skin seemingly without pain. They all relaxed, their eyes wide.

For an instant their shadows doubled, one human, one beast, and then the beast-shapes tore free, thin black silhouettes of wolves that lifted from their backs like smoke. Khonsu raised his palm. The five phantoms arched into the air, twisting, snarling silently—then burst into motes of light that spiraled up and vanished into the waiting moon.

When it was over, the clearing smelled of rain that hadn't fallen.

"Curses begin with hunger," Khonsu said, his voice soft but enormous. "I feed that hunger something truer."

Travis patted his body. "I think... it worked."

"Really?" Kayla also patted her body. "I can't transform anymore? I can go home?"

Jason's hands flew to his face. "My mom is going to freak out when I get home."

Benji laughed—high, wild, scared—and Lily nervously joined him, her raccoon still held close.

Khonsu inclined his falcon head. "The night is meant for rest, not ruin. You may dream again."

"Thank you," Finch said. His chest loosened, the knots of worry gone.

Khonsu's eyes turned to him then, and then past him—to Enzo. The god's crown dimmed. The silver net still hung between his fingers, but when he threw it over Enzo's body, the light faltered.

Khonsu studied him for a long, silent moment. "You have been cursed too long, it seems. The infection is in your marrow. To break it now would unmake what remains of the man."

Enzo didn't flinch. He just stared at his own hands, flexed them once, and gave a small, tired smile. "Figures. I guess I'm grandfathered in."

Kull frowned. "That's not fair... Enzo fought so hard to get it under control..."

Khonsu tilted his head again, feathers catching light. "Fairness is a human invention. Nature is older than fairness." He returned his attention to Enzo, and something almost kind moved through that obsidian gaze. "But you fought without calling to the wolf. You bled as man and refused the beast. Few ever try. Fewer still succeed."

Enzo gave a shrug that was half pride, half pain. "Had to set a good example."

"That choice... has weight."

He turned his hand. The silver net disintegrated into dust.

"If I cannot free you, I can temper you. A god cannot erase an old word, but he can write beside it."

The crown on Khonsu's head brightened until every pine needle in the forest glowed like glass. He pointed at Enzo.

"I offer to bind some of my magic to you," Khonsu announced, his telepathic voice brilliant. "To bind a thread of my essence to your crown core, the place where your will sits. My light will braid with your darkness. You will carry a piece of me as counterweight. It will grant you my calm, my sight, and when you call, a fraction of my power."

Enzo stared, caught between awe and confusion. "You mean... like a pact? Like warlocks make with gods?"

"It is the same. Only, my pact will have no condition. You have already proven yourself worthy, and I wish nothing you have to offer."

Enzo hesitantly stepped forward. "There's no catch?"

"Mortals are not always skeptical of divine gifts. You insult me by suggesting I would speak false?"

"N-No. That's not what I meant... I'm just not used to things going my way, is all."

"Ah." Khonsu nodded. "The curse has taken a toll in more ways than one. I understand. But fear not, for I am here now."

Enzo looked down at his bandaged arm, then at the kids celebrating under the moonlight. "Well, I'd be a fool to refuse you, I suppose. So... Sure. Please grant me a piece of your magic."

"Then kneel."

He did. The moonlight gathered above them, a whirl of silver dust forming a luminous thread. Khonsu reached out and touched the crown of Enzo's shaved head with one finger. His magical thread sank beneath Enzo's flesh. For a heartbeat, Finch saw a symbol bloom across Enzo's skin—a crescent nested within a sunburst—and then it vanished, absorbed.

Enzo inhaled sharply. His pupils thinned to gold slits, then widened back. The glow faded, leaving him steady, eyes clear.

Then his skin rippled. Fur erupted from his arms like silver flame. Not the matted black of the curse, but clean, luminous strands, shining where the moon touched them. His spine curved, bones reshaping with muted cracks that sounded more like relief than pain. The transformation wasn't violent. It was graceful.

Kull's mouth fell open. "Oh my mischief," she whispered. "You're... *beautiful.*"

He was. The old wolf-form had been a monster: rage and shadow, teeth that wanted blood. This was a myth reborn. Enzo's fur shimmered with an inner silver gleam. The markings on his muzzle traced faint crescent patterns, as though Khonsu himself had painted them there.

When Enzo rose to his full height, taller and broader now, the light played across him in splashes. His claws sparkled silver; his eyes, radiant gold, burned with steady, human intelligence.

Khonsu stepped back. "It is done. You will not be free of the curse, wolf-man, but it will never again own you."

Enzo nodded once. "Thank you," he said, his werewolf voice steadier than before.

"Use my magic well."

Finch couldn't stop himself from smiling. The children were safe, Enzo stood taller, and for the first time in weeks, the world didn't feel like it was ending... It was just spinning, beautifully, under a patient moon.

Khonsu turned back toward the silver path in the sky. "My work here ends. But the night still watches."

The hieroglyphs unfurled again, step by step, leading

upward. The god of the moon started to ascend, his glow pulling the frost and mist after him like a tide returning home.

And then he was gone. The silver light collapsed back into ordinary moonshine, and the world returned to normal.

For a while, no one spoke. The children stared at Enzo with awe and the kind of relief that lives close to worship. Smudge softly clapped once, then twice.

"Dang, I should hang out with you all more," Garret said, startling Finch.

He had forgotten the half-spirit was even with them.

After steadying himself, Finch stepped beside the newly anointed werewolf. The silver fur shimmered, then began to recede as Enzo shifted back, the change smooth and soundless. He stood again in human form, shirt torn, but no injuries on his body. They had healed, likely due to Khonsu's power.

Finch placed a hand on his shoulder. "Silver suits you."

Enzo half smiled. "Yeah... For the first time in a long time, I finally feel like myself again."

CHAPTER
FORTY-ONE

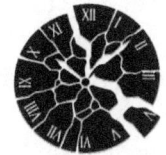

The quiet after Khonsu's departure didn't last long.

For a few blessed seconds the world was nothing but moonlight and peace. The children broke first—Lily with a squeak, then Benji, then all of them in a rush of limbs and laughter. They barreled across the clearing, a human avalanche, and collided with Finch, Kull, and Enzo.

Finch almost staggered under the weight. Tiny arms wrapped around his ribs. Kayla's sleeve caught his holster. Someone's hair smelled like peanut butter. He didn't care. They were alive. The curse was broken. He understood why they were delighted.

"There, there." Finch awkwardly patted their backs.

Kull laughed and spun Lily once before hugging her tight. "No more sleeping in a cabin! You get to go home!"

The girl beamed and nodded so hard the raccoon plush flopped.

Enzo, still wiping the last glimmer of silver from his forearms, took the collision like a champion. Jason latched on around his middle and refused to let go. Enzo gave a huff that was half-growl, half-laugh. "All right, easy. I'm not Santa Claus."

Garret stood off to the side, hands in pockets, smiling like a man watching a particularly wholesome TV show. "Look at us. We're practically an after-school special. Quick, one of you talk about how it's not cool to do drugs, and this scene will be complete."

Smudge waddled into view, both hands wrapped solemnly around Chronos's egg. It pulsed gently, light breathing under its shell. "And Smudge helped," he announced. "Smudge good."

"You're the best," Kull said as she patted his head.

Smudge's grey-green cheeks darkened to an emerald color.

Then a gust tore through the clearing—cold, sharp, smelling familiar.

Holt strode out of the woods, Mark of Sagittarius glowing like a brand made of starlight. His coat whipped around him. One hand shot out, faster than Finch's eye could track, and the next instant Smudge was in a hunter's net, squeaking. He was dragged halfway across the clearing in a matter of seconds, and once at Holt's feet, the man snatched the egg from his hands, tearing it out of the net.

The egg gleamed in Holt's fist.

"No!" Finch shouted, already moving. "Drop it!"

"Step back!" Holt's voice was ragged. "Step back, or I'll crush this godspawn where it glows."

Enzo bared his teeth. "Try it."

Holt's eyes flicked between them, fever-bright, half mad. "You thought I wouldn't sense all the crazy you were up to in the woods? The god you summoned? *I knew you were up to no good with this egg.* Aeon was right. You're using it as a tool for your own power."

He raised the egg higher, moonlight bending toward it. Power shivered through the clearing.

Kull grabbed the children and pulled them behind her. "Stay back, everyone. That man's delulu."

Tired of Holt's lunacy, Finch lunged. Embers laced his breath with each exhale as his rage fueled Ke-Koh's fire. But Holt's mark flared first.

Finch froze in midair—literally—his body caught halfway to the strike, coat hanging suspended in time. The sound of his breath stopped in his throat. Even the dust motes around him hung motionless.

"You're an idiot for coming back." Enzo charged.

In two heartbeats he was on Holt, eyes blazing as he effortlessly shifted again. Instead of rending Holt with his claws, Enzo punched down onto the man's face, hitting him like a jackhammer. Holt reeled but didn't drop the egg. The mark on his arm burned brighter.

"Stay back!" Holt snarled, swinging his gun up and then firing. Enzo tilted his head. The bullet whined past, ripping bark off a tree.

"*Your weapons don't scare me,*" Enzo growled as he slashed his claws down one of Holt's arms.

Blood splattered onto Enzo's silver fur, marring it. Holt almost dropped the egg, but instead transferred his time-freezing magic to Enzo, releasing Finch. Unable to move, Enzo was trapped in a downward posture, at the end of his attacking arc.

Finch stumbled forward, and instead of relying on his fire, he pulled Starfall from its holster and shot, grazing Holt's arm. The man sucked in air through his teeth and took a step back.

"I will, if I have to. I swear to every god still listening—one more step, and I'll break the egg!" The glowing sphere in Holt's palm flared brighter.

Finch contemplated rewinding time, but he didn't act on it. Not yet. If he could retrieve the egg, and subdue Holt once and for all, then this would all be solved.

Finch didn't give himself time to think. He angled Starfall, sighted on a tendon, and fired. The sapphire round cracked the night, and punched clean through Holt's forearm just above the wrist.

Holt screamed. His fingers opened in reflex.

The egg fell to the ground, bounced once and then rolled through pine needles. Holt turned his attention to it, but Kull moved with intention and speed. She flew over to the egg, crouching low to scoop it up as she ran, and then held it to her chest as she angled back around, grabbed Smudge, and then went straight for the ranger station.

"Everyone, inside," she shouted to the children.

They all followed her lead.

Holt staggered, clutching his bleeding arm. Then he reached into his coat with his good arm, no doubt going for a weapon. But Finch wasn't about to play that game.

He ran at the man and tackled him, sending them both to the dirt. Holt's gun skittered off into pine needles. Finch drove a fist into Holt's ribs. Once. Twice. Again. He didn't aim for elegant; he aimed for punishing. Bones thudded under his knuckles. Holt snarled, and his Mark of Sagittarius grew bright.

Finch felt the tug as the world tried to stall—but Holt was bleeding, focus split, and the lock didn't catch right. The freezing on Enzo broke first. The werewolf sucked air in like a drowning man remembering how lungs worked.

Enzo rose. His eyes went bright-gold and calm. Then he crossed the distance in an instant, grabbed Holt by the back of the coat, and hauled him up like he weighed nothing.

"*Enough*," Enzo growled, voice deep and steady.

Holt tried to throw a punch, but Enzo grabbed his fist

mid-swing, one huge clawed hand closing around Holt's. Moonlight shimmered across Enzo's fur, and then it washed over Holt's body like a mist.

At first, Finch wasn't entirely sure what was happening. He sat up, his eyes wide, but as soon as the scent of lilies hit his nose, he knew this was some sort of magic. And powerful, at that.

Holt's body twitched, every muscle shouting at once, then unclenched. His eyes rolled white for a heartbeat, then closed. His mark petered out, all glow leaving him. Then the man was asleep, snoring in Enzo's grasp.

If Chronos had given Finch the ability to rewind time, Khonsu had clearly given Enzo the ability to induce slumber. Probably a deep and powerful slumber, by the looks of things.

The clearing was quiet until Garret poked his head out from behind a stump. He honestly clapped and smiled. "Nice. That was so ASMR, I almost took a nap, too."

"Why didn't you go inside the ranger station with everyone else?" Finch barked.

Garret shrugged as he walked out of his hiding place. "I don't know. I trusted you all could handle it. And I wanted to see." He held up his phone. "Plus, I got some good footage."

After a long sigh, Finch held out his hand. "Let me see."

Garret sauntered over and then held out his phone. "I mean, I know you probably don't want this on the internet, but if we added a blur filter, and maybe cut the sound, I'm sure we could sell it as a bigfoot vid or something."

Fire erupted from Finch's palm and engulfed the phone. Within seconds, the screen cracked and the shell melted, destroying all evidence. "Oops," Finch sarcastically muttered.

Garret quickly glared and frowned, but he didn't actually say anything. It was obvious from his expression that he had figured something like this might happen, but he had hoped it wouldn't.

Once the phone was fully charred, Finch threw it to the ground. He would buy Garret a new phone; he just wasn't going to trust a spirit of delusion to carry around evidence of highly magical occurrences, like god-touched werewolves, and Chronos's egg.

Then Enzo walked over, holding the sleeping Holt in both his arms. "I don't think he's going to wake for quite some time."

"Sounds good to me." Finch pointed at the woods. "I say we put him in his car, cover him in booze, and then call the sheriff and say we saw him driving sporadically. That'll keep him busy for a few days, and maybe he'll even think everything that happened out here was a strange bourbon-induced nightmare."

"You're not going to kill him?" Garret tilted his head. "I mean, you exploded my phone because that was easier than asking me to delete the videos. I figured you'd just bury this guy and be done with it."

Finch shook his head. "Your phone is a piece of junk. Jack Holt is a man who *has* done a lot of good. He deserves better than a forgotten death in the middle of nowhere."

Enzo placed the unconscious man over his shoulder. "I don't mind your DUI plan, but we should probably get out of here. I'd hate if we *also* had to deal with Sevengaias a second time."

Kull reappeared at the station door, the egg tucked against her sternum. She panted, cheeks bright. "Baby secured," she said as she jogged over. "We are not throwing it in the air again. Zero out of ten, do not recommend."

"Thank you for keeping it safe," Finch said. "I'll go get the kids, and then we're all leaving. Right now. Tonight. Okay? Let's put an end to all the crazy happening here in Tahoe."

CHAPTER
FORTY-TWO

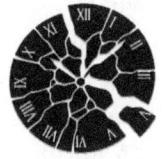

They left the Desolation Wilderness like a small parade.

Finch took point, Kull a step behind with the god egg held tightly in her hands. Enzo dressed Holt's wounds as best as possible and then followed behind everyone, carrying Holt over his shoulder in a gentle fireman's lift. The bounty hunter snored, moon-sleep preventing him from waking, even when a couple pine branches accidentally smacked him in the face.

The kids moved in a loose cluster, jittery with new freedom. Smudge hurried alongside them, sometimes visible, sometimes only footprints, humming a goblin song that sounded like someone sharpening a spoon.

The forest had that rinsed-clean feeling of after a storm. No wind. No moth dust. No random Hollows attempting to stop them. Only the brittle stutter of old needles underfoot.

No one spoke until the fence appeared, chain links silver with frost. Then Lily gave a tiny gasp. "Are you sure it's okay we leave?"

"Yeah," Kayla whispered, voice raw. "Everything is fine now."

Finch opened a hole in the fence with a lazy twist of his fingers. Metal softened for him now the way old dogs sometimes did: grudgingly, but with love. They slipped out of the nature preserve, where the party bus waited like a neon whale beached on asphalt. Its underglow was cycling between pink and teal, soft as a heartbeat.

The driver hopped down, took one look at their crowd—a blood-splattered man, an unconscious grandpa, five feral children, a woman cradling a glowing baseball—and went professionally blank.

"Uh," he said, "back to Tahoe City?"

"As fast as you can take us," Finch said.

"You got it."

They loaded in. Enzo heaved Holt to the last row and buckled him in like the world's worst toddler. Kull found a fluffy blanket under a seat and draped it over the bounty hunter, then clandestinely tucked a mini bottle of whiskey in his coat as a prop.

"Sleep tight, Jack," she murmured. "Dream of therapy."

Then she handed the egg to Finch, who tucked it into his coat pocket. He didn't have any more healing brews to tuck it into his body a second time, so he'd have to protect it the good ol' fashioned way.

The kids saw the inside of the bus and forgot the rest of the world existed.

"*Whoa*," Jason said, eyes gone plate-wide at the strip lights and the small dance floor and the chrome poles that pretended not to be chrome poles. "*This* is what you guys are riding around in? I thought, like, you were cops or something."

"I'm a private investigator," Finch said.

Kull shook her head. "I'm an influencer."

"Guess which one picked out our ride?" Enzo quipped.

Garret took a seat and exhaled. "Man, is it great to have friends in high places."

Benji poked a button. Colored stars appeared across the ceiling. Lily clutched her raccoon and spun until she got dizzy. Kayla found the window switch and tested it twice, then sat with her chin on her knees, grinning at nothing. Travis stood in the aisle, fists at his hips, unable to hide his delight.

Kull clapped once. Business mode. Sparkles in her eyes.

"Okay, ex-wolf-cubs and wolf-adjacent people," she announced, hopping up onto the little karaoke stage like it had been waiting for her all its life. "Welcome to the Fox-Pistol Recovery Party. Rule one: you're safe. Rule two: you're allowed to be happy. Rule three: smoothies."

She pointed at Garret. "You're the DJ and the smoothie bartender!"

At first, he didn't react, but after a moment of contemplation, the man shifted personalities completely. He bobbed his head to unheard music and squinted his eyes like he was an all-too-serious rapper in a music video.

With a flourish, Garret moved over to the smoothie machine. "What's your poison, gremlins?" he asked the people in the party bus. "We have a *ton* of video-game-inspired drinks. We've got the *Blue Shell*, a blueberry and coconut flavor that doesn't also ruin friends, unlike real blue shells. We also have a *Phoenix Down*, a strawberry and yogurt concoction that literally resurrects your mood."

The party bus slowly exited the parking lot, and all the kids gathered close around Garret.

He continued, "Want a *Hadouken Mango?* That's just a knuckle sandwich, don't order it." He laughed at his own joke. "Or maybe you want a *Health Potion?* It's all spinach."

"Eww," Jason said, his nose wrinkled.

"And last but not least, we have the *Mega Man Special!* Banana, peanut butter, and blueberries. This one is fun."

Smudge pushed his way between the kids and somehow made himself first in line. "Phoenix! Phoenix!"

"All right. One Phoenix Down, coming right up."

All the kids ordered a drink.

The blender roared. Neon lights slowly shifted. Finch leaned back and allowed himself to breathe.

Enzo drifted past him. His clothes were a mess after transforming and fighting several times in one evening, yet he still held himself like a professional. He reached up, tapped the ceiling once, and gave Finch a look that said both thank you and don't bring it up. Finch didn't.

"Okay!" Kull sang, flipping the karaoke screen down from the ceiling. "We are doing this properly."

"Please no," Finch said in reflex.

"Please *yes*," Kull replied with a giggle, and all the kids on the bus cheered, because of course they did.

She queued an upbeat track with a four-note intro that could raise the dead. Lyrics marched across the screen. Kull didn't sing so much as throw herself at the song. She handed the backup mic to Lily, who squeaked a syllable and then another and before long was yelling joyfully into the mic.

Kayla clapped along. Benji banged a rhythm on his empty smoothie cup. Jason discovered the fog machine button, and under Finch's death glower, did not press it. Smudge bobbed his head like a guy at a rave.

Garret slid smoothies down the bar with ridiculous panache.

"Health Potion for our reluctant dad," he said, handing Finch a green thing that smelled like a garden.

Finch took the cup and sipped. Spinach was probably good for him. He glanced at his phone.

9:33 p.m.

The bus slid onto the highway. Lake Tahoe flashed between the trees. The kids rotated seats every ninety seconds the way kids do when they're trying to absorb a place by osmosis: window, middle, aisle, window again. Kull filmed a thirty-second no-context clip of Lily and her raccoon harmonizing with Benji's drumming and Kayla's off-key whistle, then put her phone down and just kept singing.

They were loud. They were chaotic. For the first time in weeks, the noise in Finch's head was quieter than the room he was in. He let the thought be true without interrogating it.

At the first stop sign near the trailhead, Finch asked the driver to find the nearby parking lot. A single vehicle was there—and Finch had to assume it was Holt's. They stopped the bus, and Enzo hefted Holt back onto his shoulder.

Finch grabbed some booze and then led Enzo outside. They went straight for the mud-caked SUV sitting all by its lonesome. Enzo dug through Holt's pockets until he found a key ring and then unlocked the bizarre vehicle. With little grace, Enzo arranged Holt in the driver's seat.

Finch cracked the top on a bottle and splashed it artfully around the interior. The smell of liquor bloomed.

"You really going to call it in?" Enzo asked.

"Anonymously," Finch said. "They pick him up, he sleeps it off under fluorescent lights, we get three days."

Enzo shoved the key into the ignition and then slammed the door shut. "Sleep tight, Holt."

They jogged back. The bus doors sighed open. Warmth hit them like applause. Once back on the road, it wasn't long before they reached the city.

The first storefront appeared, then a string of motels, then the big sign with its sun-faded skier. People existed again. Stoplights cycled for someone. It felt as though they had left a fantasy world and were now back on Earth.

Four of the kids pressed faces to glass. Lily left a halo of breath the size of her head. Benji narrated everything. Jason pointed to some locations he loved and missed. Kayla arranged her hair in the reflection like the person there was one she recognized. Only Travis sat back and watched them more than he did the city.

While they were distracted, he turned his attention to Finch and lowered his voice. "You said you are a private investigator?"

"That's right," Finch replied.

"And you handle supernatural cases?"

Finch nodded.

"Are you gonna wipe our memory or anything? I mean, what're we supposed to tell everyone when we get back? That we were werewolves for a bit, but we're all better now?"

Finch had already thought about their cover story, but it wasn't the best story he had ever woven. "We're going to tell your family that we found you in the Desolation Wilderness trapped in a rusty old ranger station. The doors were jammed and the windows boarded up and blocked. You survived on the food in the cabin until I managed to locate you."

"Will people believe that?" Travis asked, his brow furrowed.

"What choice will they have? There's no magical evidence left on any of you. There's no one to apprehend to turn over to the police. And if you try to tell them the truth, they'll likely think you were having hallucinations brought about by dehydration."

"And what do we do? Just forget anything ever happened to us?"

Finch nodded once. "Probably your best bet. I'd recommend not wandering off into the forest by yourself.

There are worse things in this world than werewolves, vampires, and death spirits."

Travis chuckled at the last bit. Then he sighed. "Uh… Well, once I'm back home…" He hesitated, as though speaking the last part aloud was too much.

"What is it?" Finch demanded.

"Are you hiring at all?" Travis awkwardly looked away. "I mean, I've been looking for a job ever since I graduated high school, and then *this* happened, and I figured my life was over, but after seeing you handle everything… I don't think I can ever forget what happened, ya know?"

Finch sipped the last of his Health Potion. He didn't really need anyone else at the office, currently. Technically, they were overstaffed. Bree was his apprentice. Liam was their accountant and researcher. Enzo was a second PI. They even had Jessie as part of their crew, though Finch hadn't come up with a title for her. Part of him suspected she would only accept *third PI*.

What would Travis be?

Second apprentice?

But Finch could already hear everyone else's opinions in his head. Even Carter's. They would want Finch to help the kid.

"If you want a job working at my office, you'll need to move to Stockton," Finch muttered. "Which is a big change from Tahoe."

Travis lit up. He whipped his attention over to Finch, meeting his gaze. "R-Really? You have room for me?"

"My office is huge. We have room for a few more people."

Just not the work.

Finch didn't say that last part aloud, though. Sometime soon, it'd pick up. Hopefully. Otherwise, everyone's paychecks would be coming out of his savings.

"I'm so excited." Travis grabbed Finch's hand and shook it

with much enthusiasm. "You won't regret this. I'm going to become the best there is at supernatural *everything*. After all I went through, I really don't want to be helpless again. I want to *do* something. Solve problems. Save people."

Travis had been the leader of the little group out in the Desolation Wilderness... And he had taken care of the others as best as a nineteen-year-old could.

"You might want to consider going to school for a year or two," Finch said. "To study criminal justice. It'll help you, both in my office, and in any other career."

"Are there other supernatural agencies and stuff? Other PI people?"

Finch nodded. "You could join the FBOI, or become an agent in SHADOW. Maybe join a police force as a person in-the-know. Maybe even become a warlock... But I would definitely recommend you get a solid grasp of *law* before you move forward."

"Oh, yeah. I get it. I can't wait to learn. Honestly." He smiled wide. "Thank you so much."

CHAPTER
FORTY-THREE

While it was close to ten at night, Finch, Kull, and Enzo dropped the kids off one by one. They explained the situation to the families, and even alerted the sheriffs.

They started with Lily, then Benji, then Kayla, and then Travis.

Jason was last, as he was the reason they were in Tahoe in the first place. When the party bus pulled up to Jason's home, he jumped up and down on his seat, all smiles.

"That's it!" he shouted. "That's my house! I thought I'd never see it again."

Finch stood and readied himself to deliver the kid. Jason was already halfway down the steps before the brakes sighed.

The porch light snapped on. A woman stepped into view, hand over her mouth. Grace Stonewell looked like someone who hadn't slept in days—pale skin, red eyes, sweater frayed at the sleeves. When she saw Jason running toward her, she made a sound between a sob and a laugh, and stumbled forward to meet him halfway, her energy visibly returning in a matter of seconds.

"Jason?" she whispered. Then Grace's voice turned into a shout. "Jason!"

He collided with her like gravity had switched directions for just a moment. She dropped to her knees and held him, fingers gripping the back of his hoodie, murmuring his name over and over as if saying it might anchor him to the world.

Finch stopped on the sidewalk and waited. Kull and Enzo both kept to the shadows of the bus door. The reunion would've made for a perfect social media post, but Kull never once reached for her phone.

Grace finally looked up, eyes rimmed with tears. "You found him," she said, voice cracking.

Finch walked over and gave a small nod. "We did. He's all right, and I've already spoken to the sheriff about what happened. He got trapped in the nature preserve, but I managed to save him just in time."

With one arm around her son, Grace stood. "I—I don't know how to thank you."

"You don't have to," Finch said, but she was already turning back toward the house. Grace disappeared inside for a moment and returned with a thick white envelope. Her hands trembled as she held it out. "Please. It's not enough, I know, but—"

Finch took it automatically, feeling the weight of it. Cash. A lot. He opened the flap just far enough to see the stacks of bills. They were all neatly folded, rubber-banded.

Roughly twenty thousand dollars. Hope, in paper form. No doubt she had offered to pay it to the PI who found her son first.

He closed the envelope and handed it back. "No."

Grace blinked. "What? But, Mr. Finch—"

"I don't need it," he said. "Jason's been through enough already. So have you. Keep it. Use it to help him. Maybe find a good therapist, or go on a vacation that doesn't involve hiking."

Her chin trembled. "But you—"

"Everything will be okay. And even if it isn't, this isn't the kind of case I take for the reward."

In truth, Finch had a considerable amount of money in savings and stocks. He and Carter had taken plenty of high-paying jobs in the past, and for the last decade, Finch had done little with it besides exist. He could go awhile just dipping into that before he needed to make sure every assignment taken was making him money.

Grace stared down at the envelope, fingers tightening around it like she wasn't sure it was real. Then she gave a shaky nod and clutched Jason closer. "Thank you. Thank you so much. You have no idea what this means."

Red in the face, but still composed, Jason stared up at Finch. He then stepped forward and hugged him without warning. It was a small, fierce squeeze. *"Thank you,"* he said into Finch's coat, and then darted back to his mother before either of them could get embarrassed about it.

Grace gave one last nod of gratitude, ushered Jason inside, and shut the door behind them. Warm light glowed in the windows.

Finch exhaled. "That's the last of them."

Kull brushed a sleeve across her eyes. "I love happy endings. All the best movies have them."

Finch climbed back into the bus. The engine rumbled, the lights of the neighborhood fading behind them as they rolled toward the Alder Crown.

The hotel glowed within a mountain fog. Warm light spilled through the glass doors, and a valet in a tailored coat straightened when the group approached. Finch made sure Smudge came with them, but invisible.

It was 11:50 p.m. Only a few minutes before Finch couldn't reset time.

Inside, the lobby was alive with Kull's social media crew.

Louis stood at the center of the lobby, expression sharp enough to cut fabric, cologne sprayed on thick enough to hide his angry smell. Whisp and Harper flanked him while Jace lounged nearby, sunglasses on indoors, chewing gum.

The moment Kull stepped through the doors, Louis's eyes widened. "You vanished for the whole day. *The whole day*. I had sponsors texting me crying emojis."

Kull raised both hands like a suspect. "I'm sorry, I'm sorry. I lost track of time. It won't happen again."

"Sorry won't bring back several hours of my life." Louis crossed his arms, stomped his foot, and huffed. After a moment, he relaxed a bit and smoothed his perfectly coiffed blond hair. "Well, I suspect I can forgive you, darling. So long as we wake at seven in the morning *sharp* and bang out a few high-quality videos."

"Sounds good." Kull gave him a thumbs up. "I'll be so ready."

Louis clapped his hands together twice. "Excellent. We shoot the earbud campaign first thing in the morning. No disappearing, no breaks, all A game, understood?"

"Aye, aye! I guess I'll see you all in the morning, then."

Harper stepped forward, practically pushing Louis out of the way. "*That's it*? You're not going to tell us where you were or what you were doing? Or come hang with us in the suite? Samantha, what's gotten into you?"

"Oh, well..." Kull fidgeted with a lock of her red hair.

"You know. Doing all the Twitch streams, and videos, and being worried about drama... There's a lot of, uh..."

"Burnout?" Louis chimed in. "It's burnout, isn't it? I knew it. That's why we're here."

Kull nodded along with his words and even pointed at him. "Yes. Exactly. That's it. I was burnt out, but now I feel a lot better." She walked over to Harper and gave her a hug. "Thank you for being so worried about me. You're such a good friend."

Harper's expression softened as she hugged Kull back. "That's what besties are for, obviously." Then she held Kull out at arm's length. "But if you were suffering from burnout, you should've said something to me. Nothing fixes that like a good party. Right, Jace?"

Jace Min stood from the couch and sauntered over. "Oh, I agree. Tahoe City has a lot of *crazy* places for people like us, and I was hoping you'd accompany me to a few. I totally understand burnout. Writing all my lyrics myself can really take its toll."

"Oh, yeah, that sounds good." Kull smiled. "But let's see how I feel tomorrow after all that filming, okay?"

While Louis, Harper, Jace, and Kull were discussing their plans, Whisp caught sight of Enzo's bloodstained clothes and decided not to ask questions. She simply handed him a bottled water and then hurried over to Garret's side.

Louis rubbed his temples. "Okay. Fine. We pivot to make sure Fox-Pistol isn't overwhelmed. Whisp, open our schedule a bit. Harper, we need a new wardrobe." Louis narrowed his eyes as he realized Enzo and Finch were also in the lobby. "Who are you two?"

"We're just background characters," Finch dryly replied. Then he brushed past the man and headed toward the elevators.

Kull laughed under her breath and jogged to catch up with him. "These are my bodyguards for Tahoe! Don't worry, I paid extra for their sense of humor." She waved at her crew. "I'll see you all in the morning, all bright eyed and bushy tailed! Fox-Pistol out!"

Finch frowned, almost unable to believe she actually had a sign-out line.

Once in the elevator, Kull wiped imaginary sweat from her brow. "Well, it looks like I have a lot of work to do tomorrow."

"Is being an influencer even *work*?" Enzo asked.

"Uh, duh. Of course it is. I have to make a lot of videos, and come up with new content, and maintain viewer retention. Plus, most sponsors want super-specific things in the videos they're featured in, and I have to memorize scripts, and make sure I look good from all angles." Kull heaved a dramatic sigh. "But at least in a few vids I get to play pranks on people! It nurtures my inner mischief spirit."

Enzo shrugged. "Well, I'll take your word for it, but it seems like a lot of nonsense to me."

The elevator dinged. The doors slid open. Enzo wandered out, looking half-asleep already, Smudge became visible briefly as he walked around the man's legs, heading for the suite with Meth.

"Wait, Smudge," Finch said. "You stay in my room tonight."

The little goblin pointed to himself and then smiled. "Really?"

"Yeah. I need your help."

"Smudge help."

Kull practically danced to her suite room. "Well, as much as I'd love to hang with you all for the whole night, I'm pretty tired. I think we should wake up super early and have the best breakfast ever."

Enzo went to his room. "All right. Just make sure to wake up."

"Hey, I *always* get up. It's you two who sometimes sleep in."

Dismissively waving away the comment, Enzo headed into his room.

Once Finch, Smudge, and Kull were in theirs, Kull narrowed her eyes. "Why do you need Smudge's help? Haven't we solved everything here in Tahoe? I was looking forward to leaving soon."

"Everything here is fine. But I have other work to do once we get back to Stockton."

"Okay. Don't stay up too late."

Finch nodded once.

But before Kull could fully hop off, she stopped and turned. "And don't think I've forgotten about all your promised dates. I know you want to keep everything a secret, but this just means I'm going to visit you a whole bunch in Stockton."

With a snort, Finch held back a laugh. "You're going back to LA after this?"

"Yeah. My studio is down there. But like I said—I'll visit *so* much. And we'll do all the dating things. Privately. Away from people." She smiled as she added, "And so much kissing."

Smudge stuck out his dark-green tongue.

Finch's face heated. "Please. When you say it like that, it sounds… childish."

But that just got Kull giggling. She hurried off to her room and quickly shut the door behind her.

There was a prolonged moment of silence. For the first time in weeks, Finch let his shoulders drop. The Alder Crown hummed with warmth, the smell of cedar and expensive detergent in the air.

Finch led Smudge into his bedroom, and then he shut the door. The little goblin hopped onto the edge of the bed and took a seat.

That was when Finch pulled Chronos's egg out of his pocket. The glow added some illumination to the room, but not much.

"I need you to use this again," Finch muttered. "I need you to speak with another god and summon them here."

Smudge held his hands out and took the egg. Then he nodded. "Which?"

"Gixmoth the Desolate."

Smudge's ears twitched at the name. His long fingers tightened around the eggshell. "Bad choice," he muttered. "Gixmoth eat magic. Maybe even pukwudgie magic."

Yeah, Finch was worried about that. Gixmoth was strong enough to halt Aeon's magic. If the beast didn't want to speak with Smudge, it could likely prevent all telepathic communication. But Finch wanted to try. He was so close. What if he could summon Gixmoth to him? And end this once and for all?

"Just do your best," Finch finally said. He sat on the edge of the bed, elbows on his knees. "If you can't contact it, I'll figure something else out."

"Yes, yes," Smudge said. "Will do. Try hardest." He set the egg on his lap and cupped his hands around it like it was a candle flame that might be blown out at any moment.

The light inside dimmed. The air in the room grew heavy, like a storm pressing its face against the glass.

Smudge closed his eyes. There was no verbal announcement, only a mental connection Finch wasn't privy to. He remembered the leaf coated in amber and wondered if he should sneak it back into the sheriff's office or just mail it to the man later.

The air temperature dropped ten degrees. Finch felt the hairs on his arms rise.

Then Smudge snapped his eyes open. "Smudge did it."

"You did?" Finch scooted closer to him. "It worked? You spoke with Gixmoth?"

"Yes."

A long silence. The lights flickered. Smudge shivered and then frowned. "It's coming."

"Coming?" Finch asked. "When?"

"Soon. But Gixmoth walk here. Not travel, like other god."

Although Smudge's words were a bit disjointed, Finch understood perfectly. Khonsu could travel through a realm of the night, clearly to anywhere the moonlight touched. Gixmoth, on the other hand, wasn't a creature of fantastical magic. It was the opposite, actually. That monstrosity would have to scurry its freakish centipede body across the land in order to answer Finch's summons.

"His flesh move slow," Smudge said. Then he held out the egg. "But it be here. Soon. Coming. Wants to speak to Finch."

Finch held his breath. The abomination wanted to speak to him? Well, it made some sense. Gixmoth had made pacts with humans in the past. Perhaps Gixmoth wanted a new warlock to carry out a task.

But Finch wasn't going to work with that beast. Not now, not ever. As soon as Gixmoth stepped foot anywhere near him, Finch was going to be ready.

"At least I have some time to prepare," Finch muttered.

He reached for the egg and froze.

The shell pulsed once, brighter than before. Then again, harder. A hairline fracture crawled up one side with a noise like cracking ice.

"Wow," Smudge whispered.

Finch's stomach dropped. "That's... not supposed to happen."

Another crack split across the surface, thin light bleeding through. The room filled with the sound of something alive trying to breathe for the first time—soft and wet.

"Smudge innocent," the goblin said quickly, scooting back on the bed.

The cracks met, a bright seam forming down the middle. Then, with a delicate click, a fragment of shell fell away. Inside, something shimmered. It looked similar to light and shadow folding together. Like oil on water.

Finch stared, pulse hammering in his throat, as another piece of shell slipped free and the glow poured into the room, painting the walls in the color of dawn.

12:07 a.m.

Three minutes too late to rewind time.

And the egg was about to hatch.

THANK YOU SO MUCH FOR READING!

Please consider leaving a review—any and all feedback is much appreciated!

Adair Finch's story continues in book five, *Anti-Magic Warlock*!

To find out more about Shami Stovall and Adair Finch, take a look at her website:
https://sastovallauthor.com/newsletter/

To help Shami Stovall (and see advanced chapters ahead of time, including Anti-Magic Warlock) take a look at her Patreon:
https://www.patreon.com/shamistovall

ABOUT THE AUTHOR

Shami Stovall is a multi-award-winning author of fantasy and science fiction. Before that, she taught history and criminal law at the college level and loved every second. When she's not reading fascinating articles and books about ancient China or the Byzantine Empire, Stovall can be found playing way too many video games, especially RPGs and tactics simulators.

Shami loves John, John IV, reading, video games, and writing about herself in the third person.

If you want to contact her, you can do so at the following locations:

Website: https://sastovallauthor.com
Email: s.adelle.s@gmail.com

 facebook.com/SAStovall
x.com/GameOverStation